Disney

DESCENDANTS

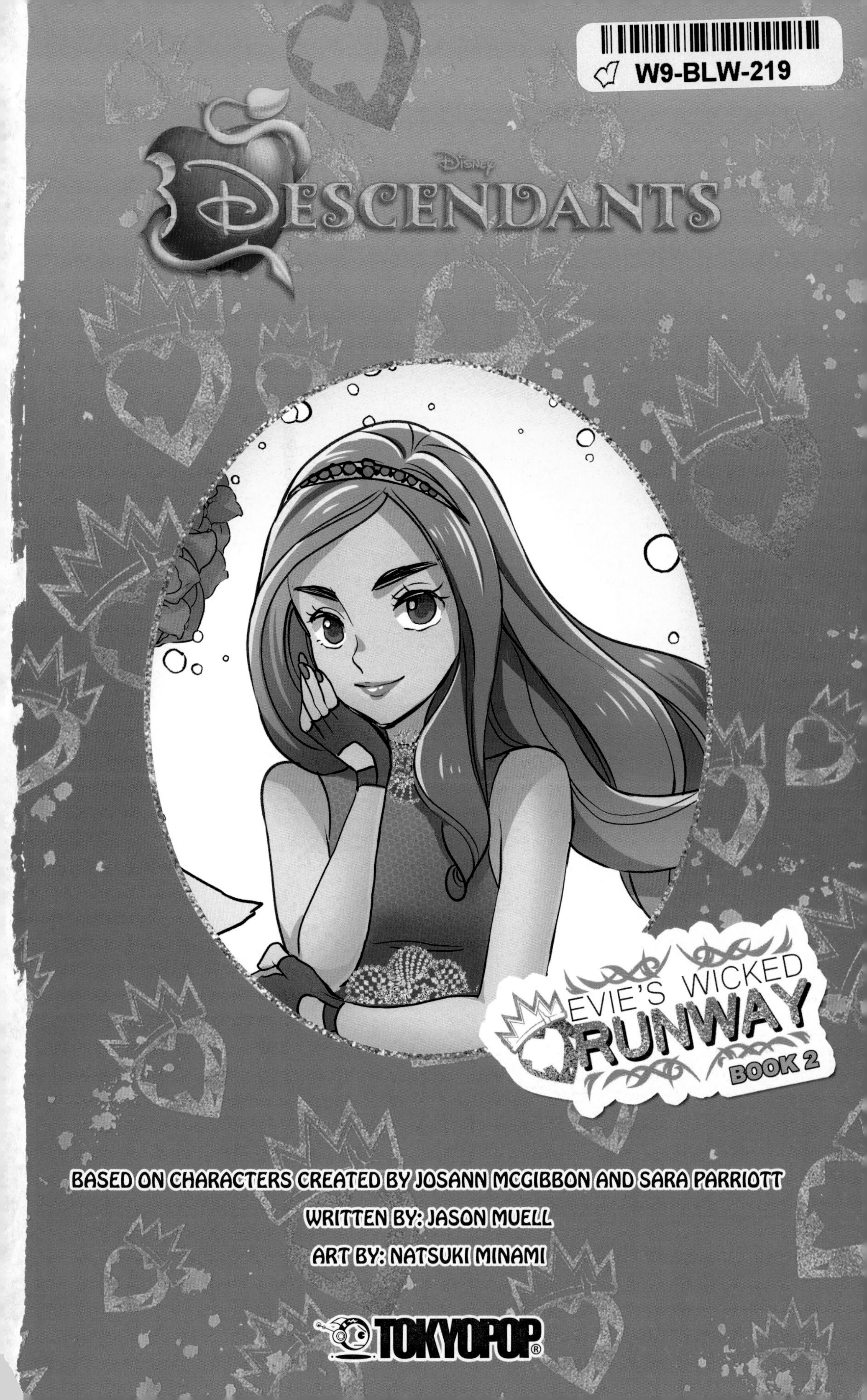

EVIE'S WICKED RUNWAY

BOOK 2

BASED ON CHARACTERS CREATED BY JOSANN MCGIBBON AND SARA PARRIOTT

WRITTEN BY: JASON MUELL

ART BY: NATSUKI MINAMI

TOKYOPOP®

Table of Contents

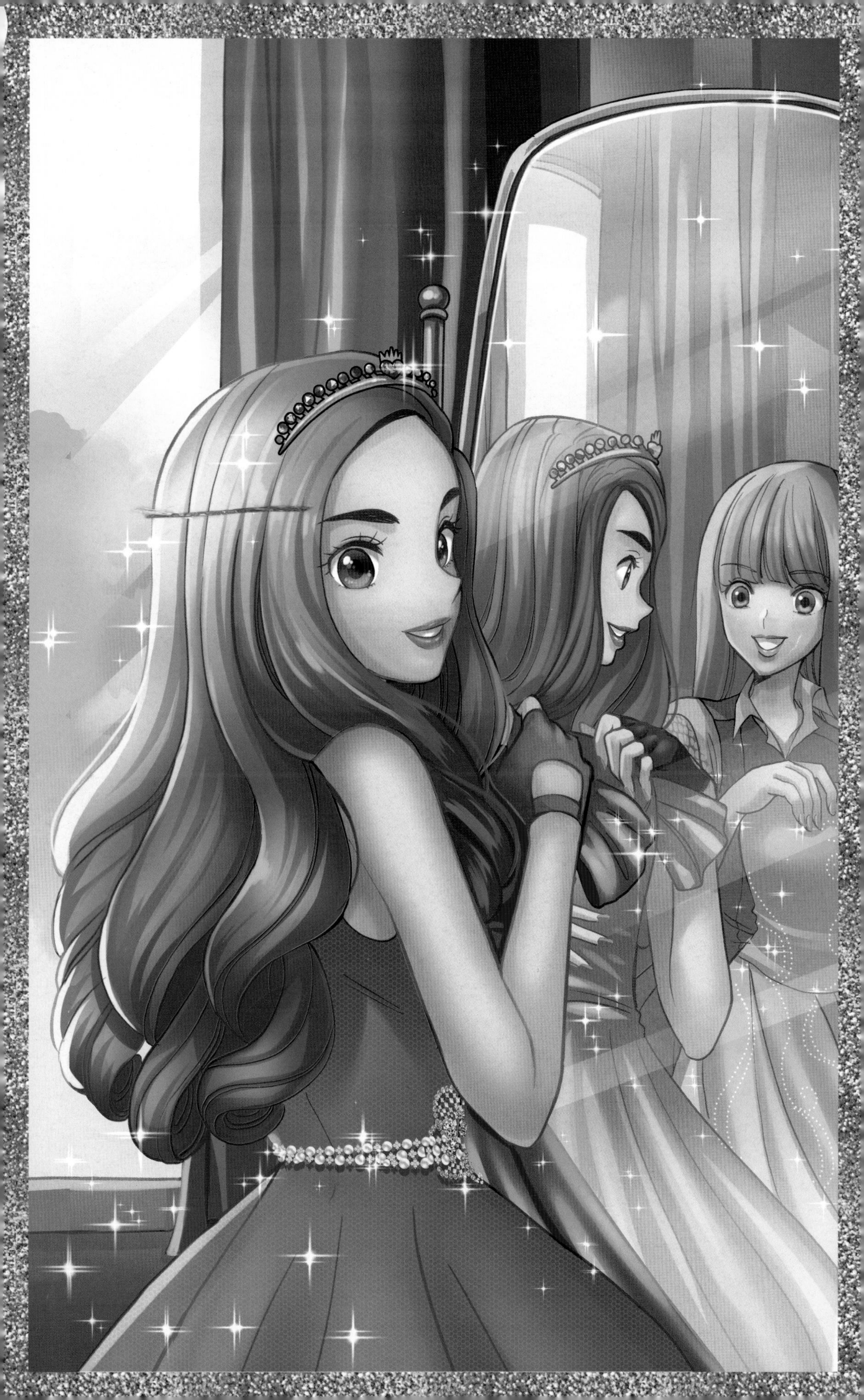

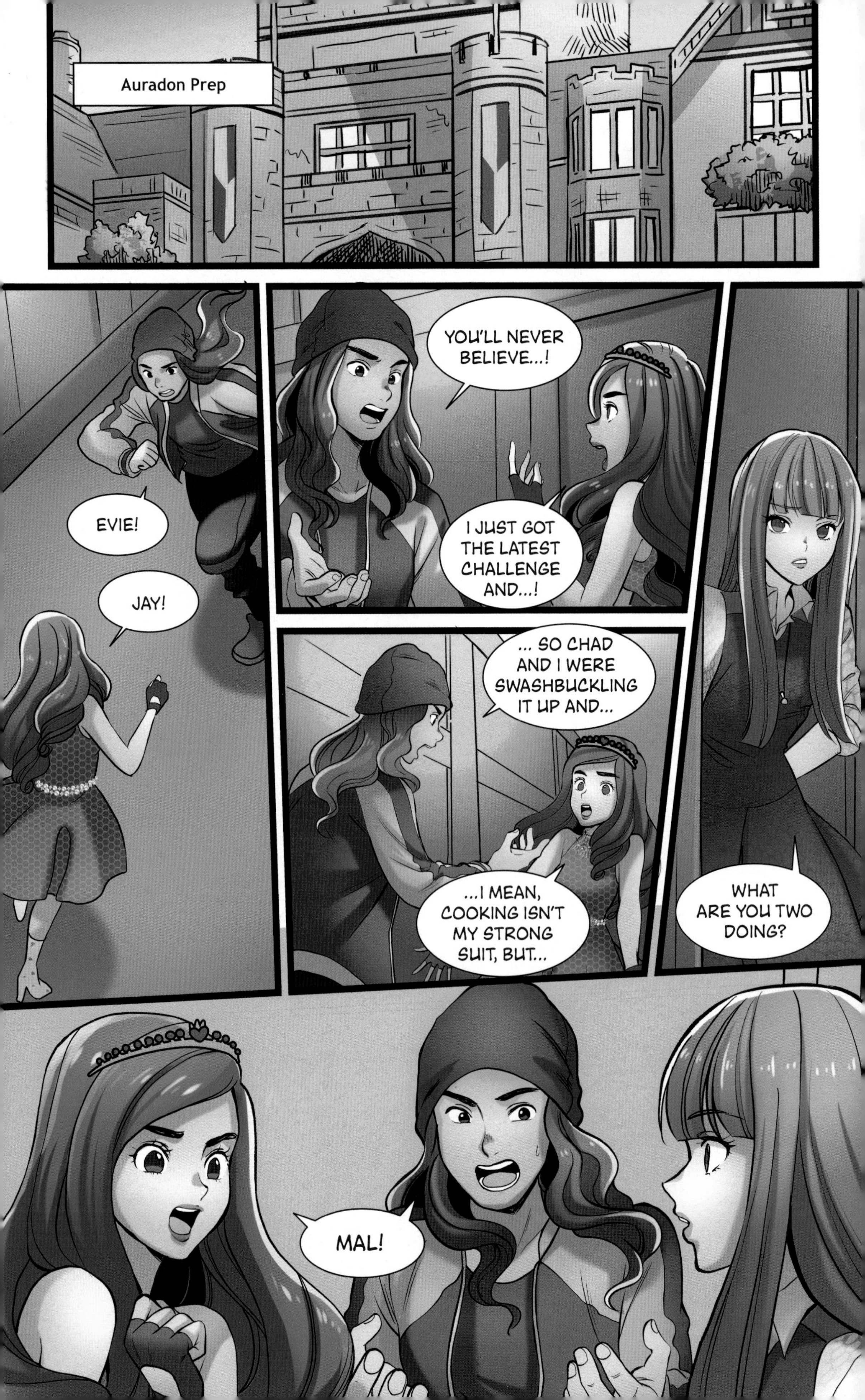
Auradon Prep
EVIE!
JAY!
YOU'LL NEVER BELIEVE...!
I JUST GOT THE LATEST CHALLENGE AND...!
... SO CHAD AND I WERE SWASHBUCKLING IT UP AND...
...I MEAN, COOKING ISN'T MY STRONG SUIT, BUT...
WHAT ARE YOU TWO DOING?
MAL!

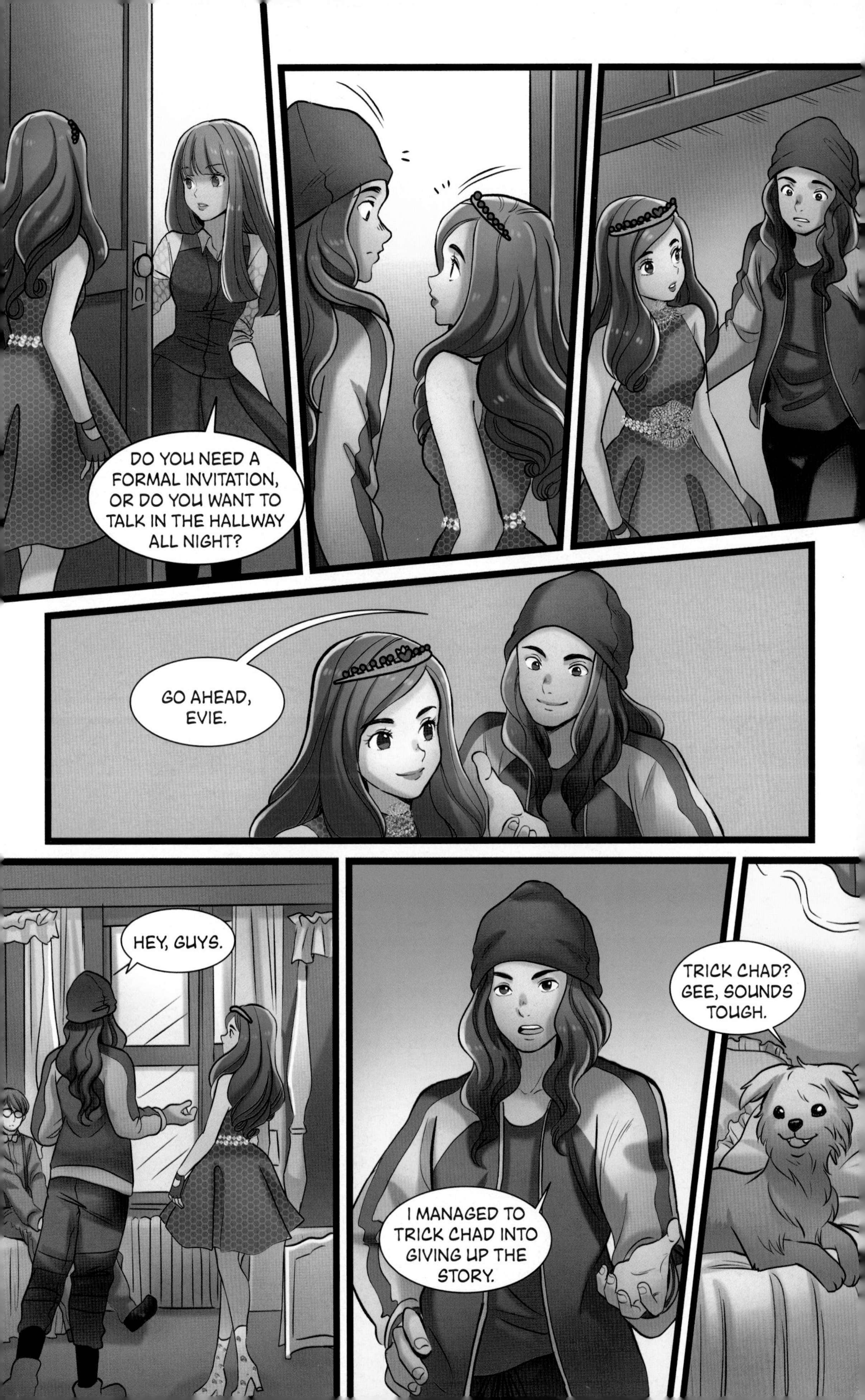
DO YOU NEED A FORMAL INVITATION, OR DO YOU WANT TO TALK IN THE HALLWAY ALL NIGHT?
GO AHEAD, EVIE.
HEY, GUYS.
I MANAGED TO TRICK CHAD INTO GIVING UP THE STORY.
TRICK CHAD? GEE, SOUNDS TOUGH.

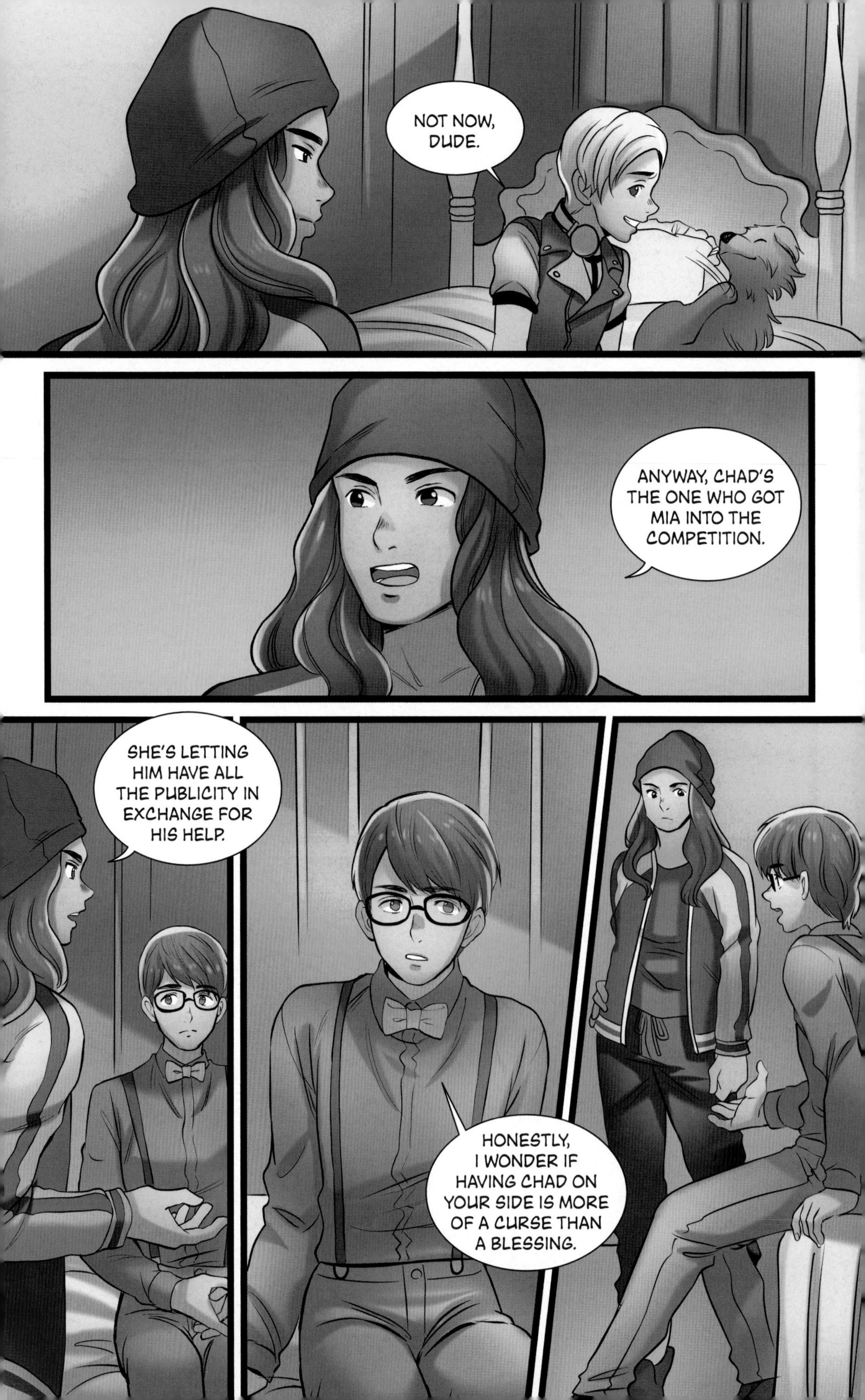
NOT NOW, DUDE.
ANYWAY, CHAD'S THE ONE WHO GOT MIA INTO THE COMPETITION.
SHE'S LETTING HIM HAVE ALL THE PUBLICITY IN EXCHANGE FOR HIS HELP.
HONESTLY, I WONDER IF HAVING CHAD ON YOUR SIDE IS MORE OF A CURSE THAN A BLESSING.

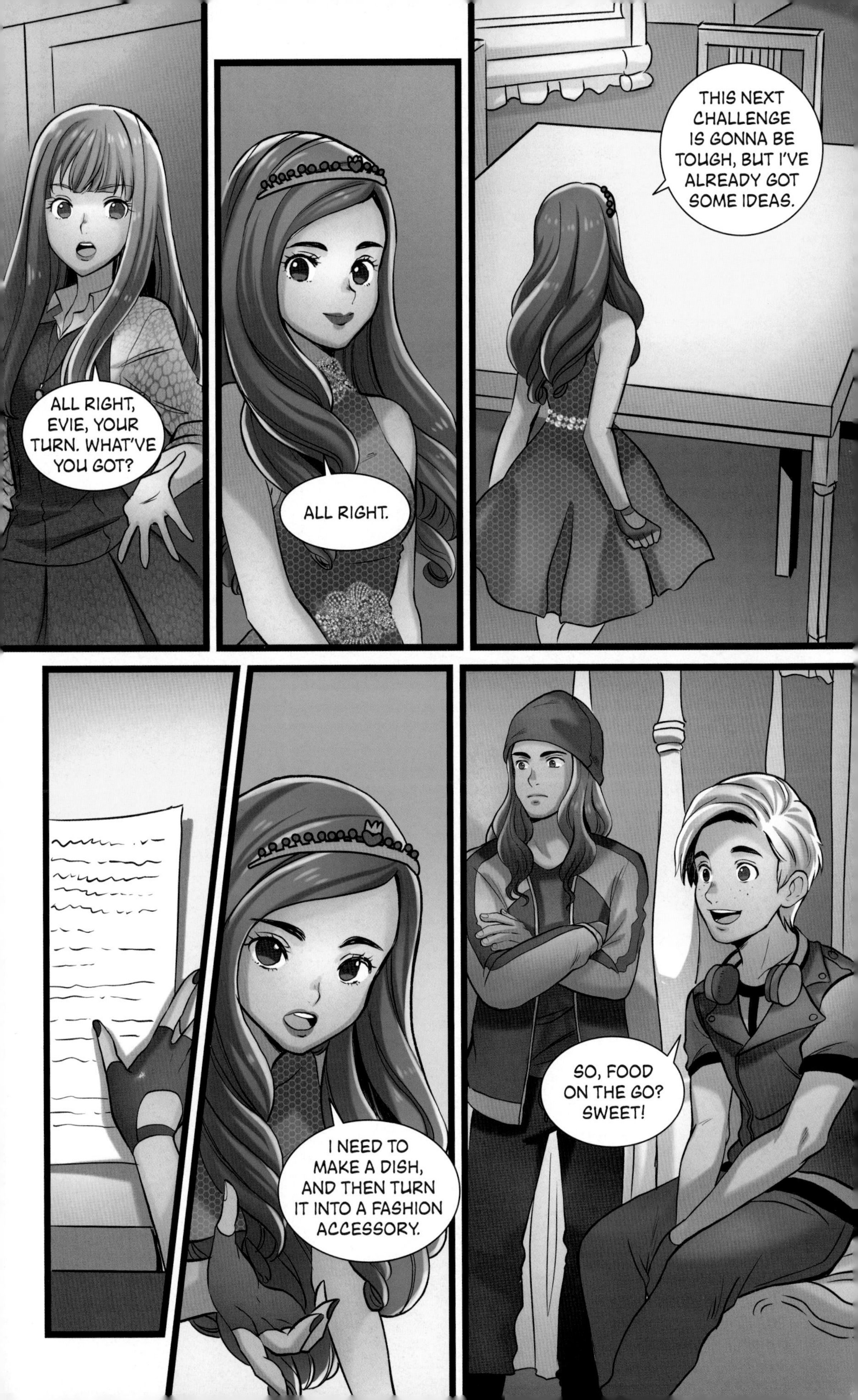
ALL RIGHT, EVIE, YOUR TURN. WHAT'VE YOU GOT?
ALL RIGHT.
THIS NEXT CHALLENGE IS GONNA BE TOUGH, BUT I'VE ALREADY GOT SOME IDEAS.
I NEED TO MAKE A DISH, AND THEN TURN IT INTO A FASHION ACCESSORY.
SO, FOOD ON THE GO? SWEET!

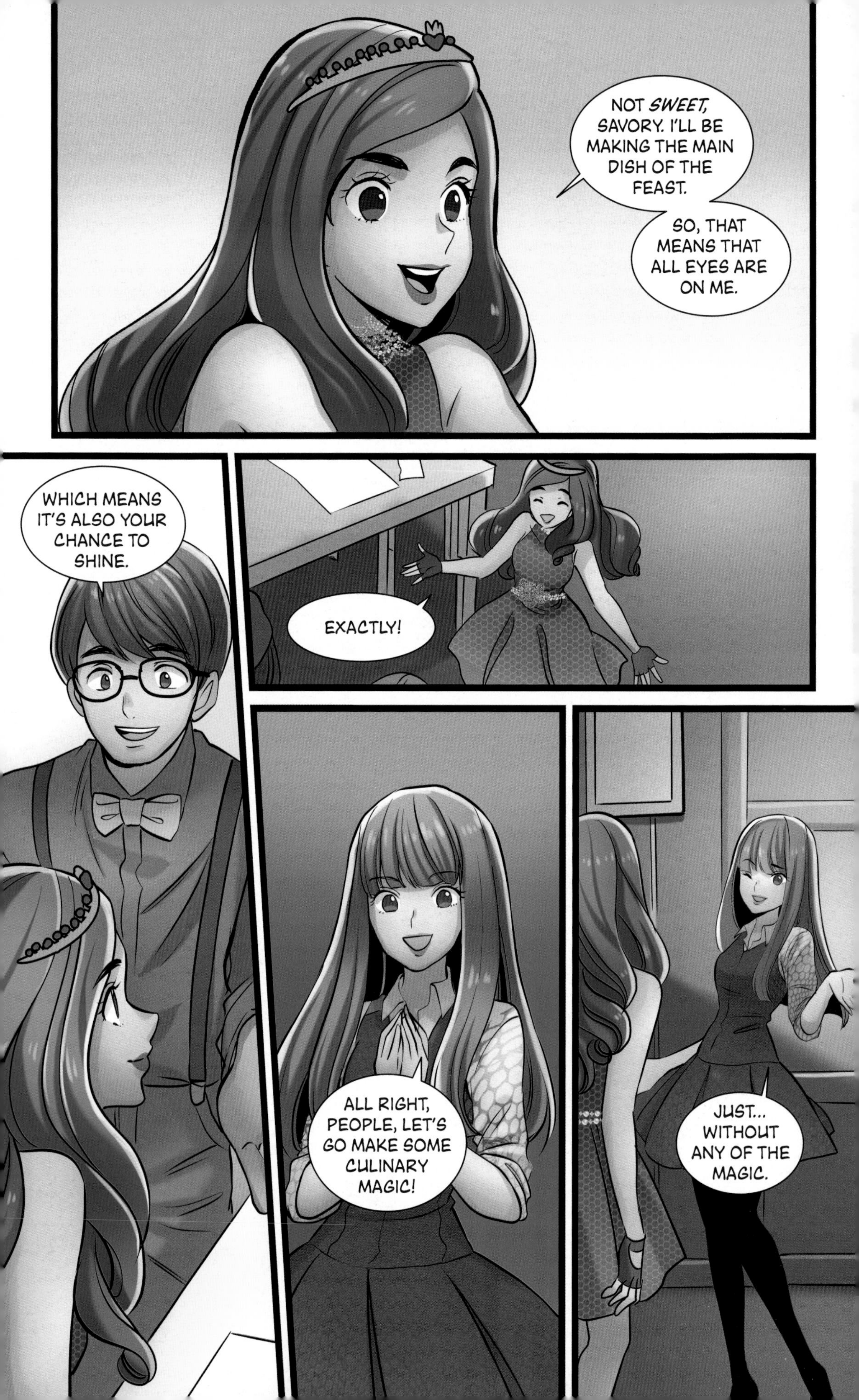
NOT *SWEET,* SAVORY. I'LL BE MAKING THE MAIN DISH OF THE FEAST.
SO, THAT MEANS THAT ALL EYES ARE ON ME.
WHICH MEANS IT'S ALSO YOUR CHANCE TO SHINE.
EXACTLY!
ALL RIGHT, PEOPLE, LET'S GO MAKE SOME CULINARY MAGIC!
JUST... WITHOUT ANY OF THE MAGIC.

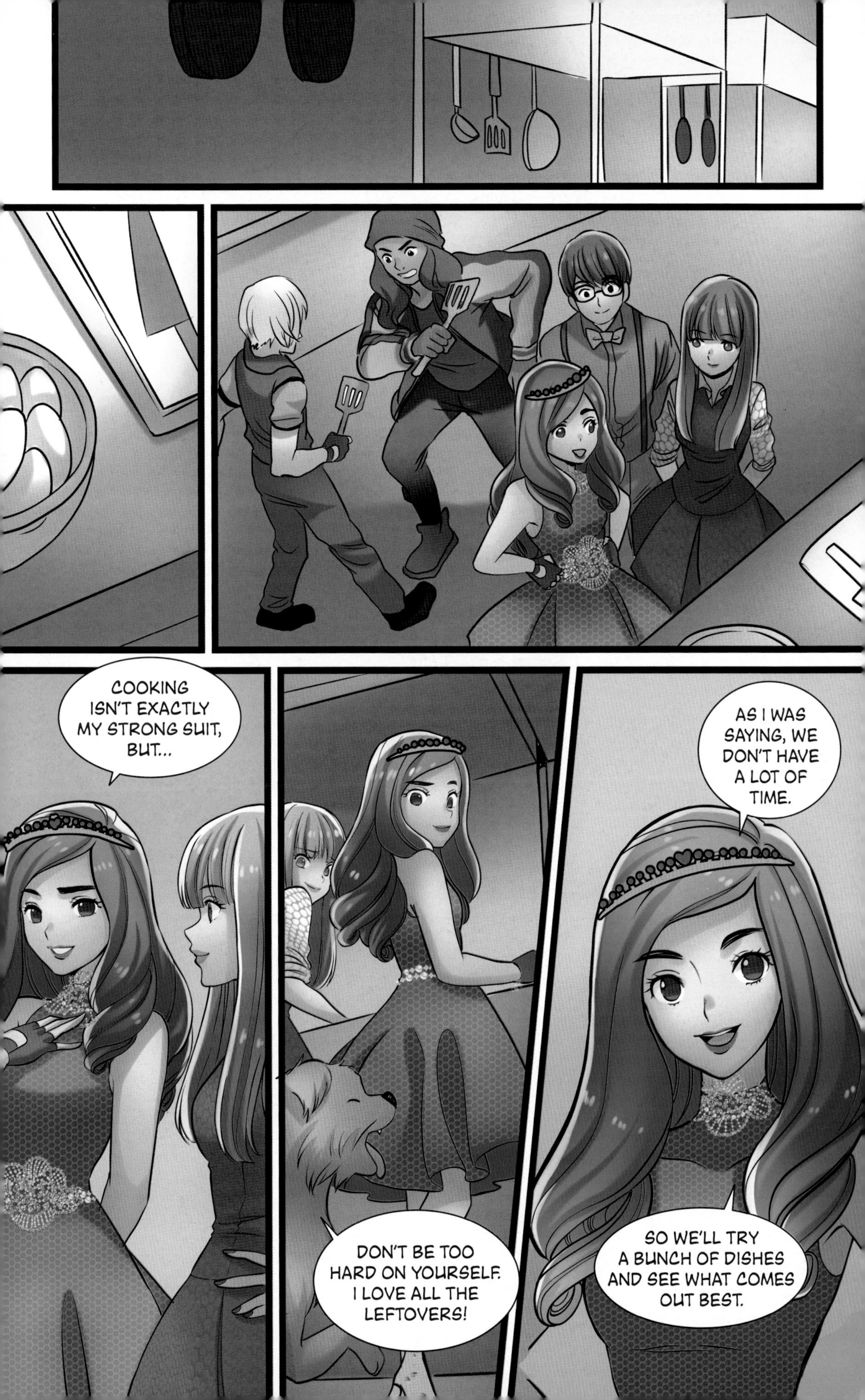
COOKING ISN'T EXACTLY MY STRONG SUIT, BUT...
DON'T BE TOO HARD ON YOURSELF. I LOVE ALL THE LEFTOVERS!
AS I WAS SAYING, WE DON'T HAVE A LOT OF TIME.
SO WE'LL TRY A BUNCH OF DISHES AND SEE WHAT COMES OUT BEST.

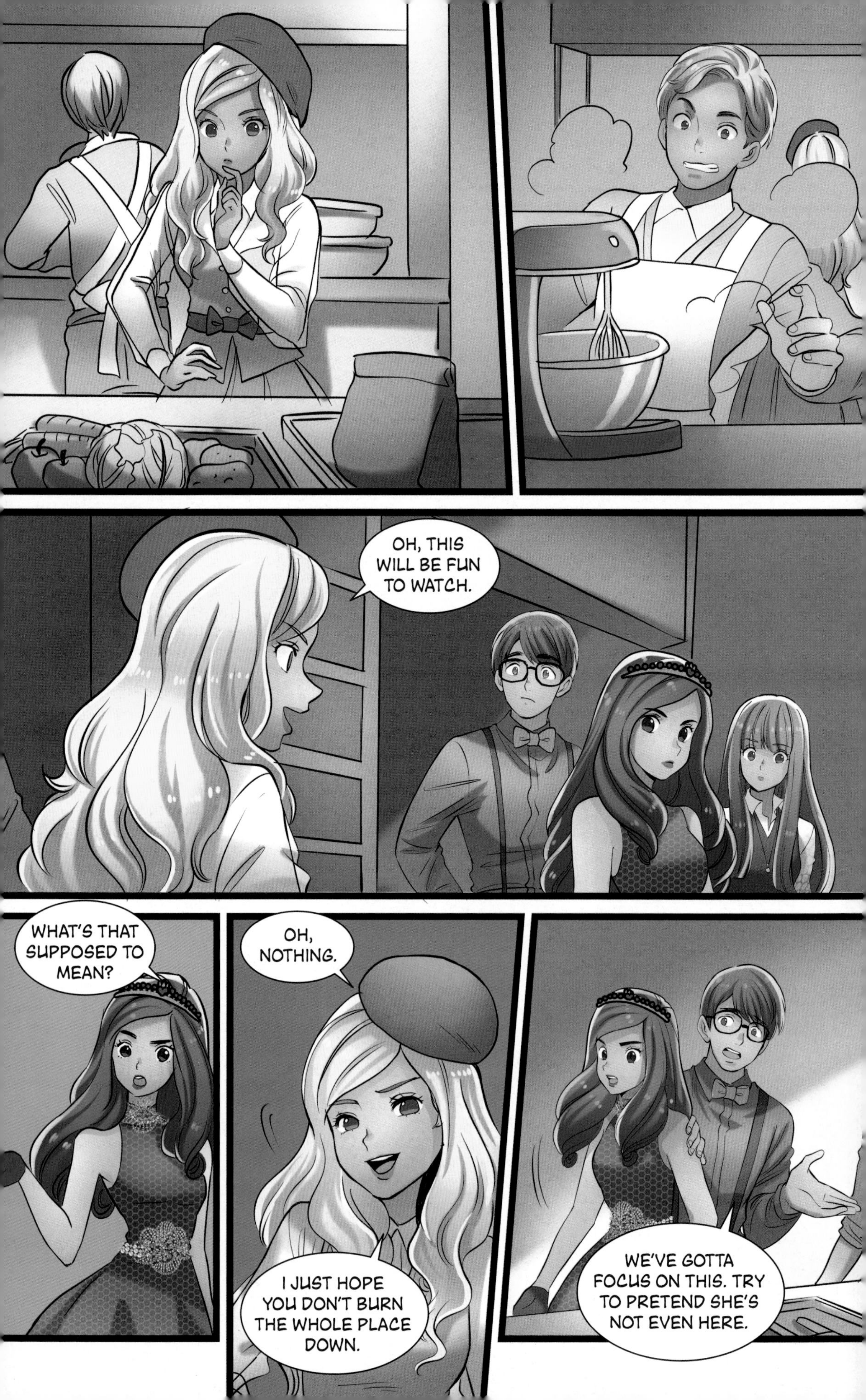
OH, THIS WILL BE FUN TO WATCH.
WHAT'S THAT SUPPOSED TO MEAN?
OH, NOTHING.
I JUST HOPE YOU DON'T BURN THE WHOLE PLACE DOWN.
WE'VE GOTTA FOCUS ON THIS. TRY TO PRETEND SHE'S NOT EVEN HERE.

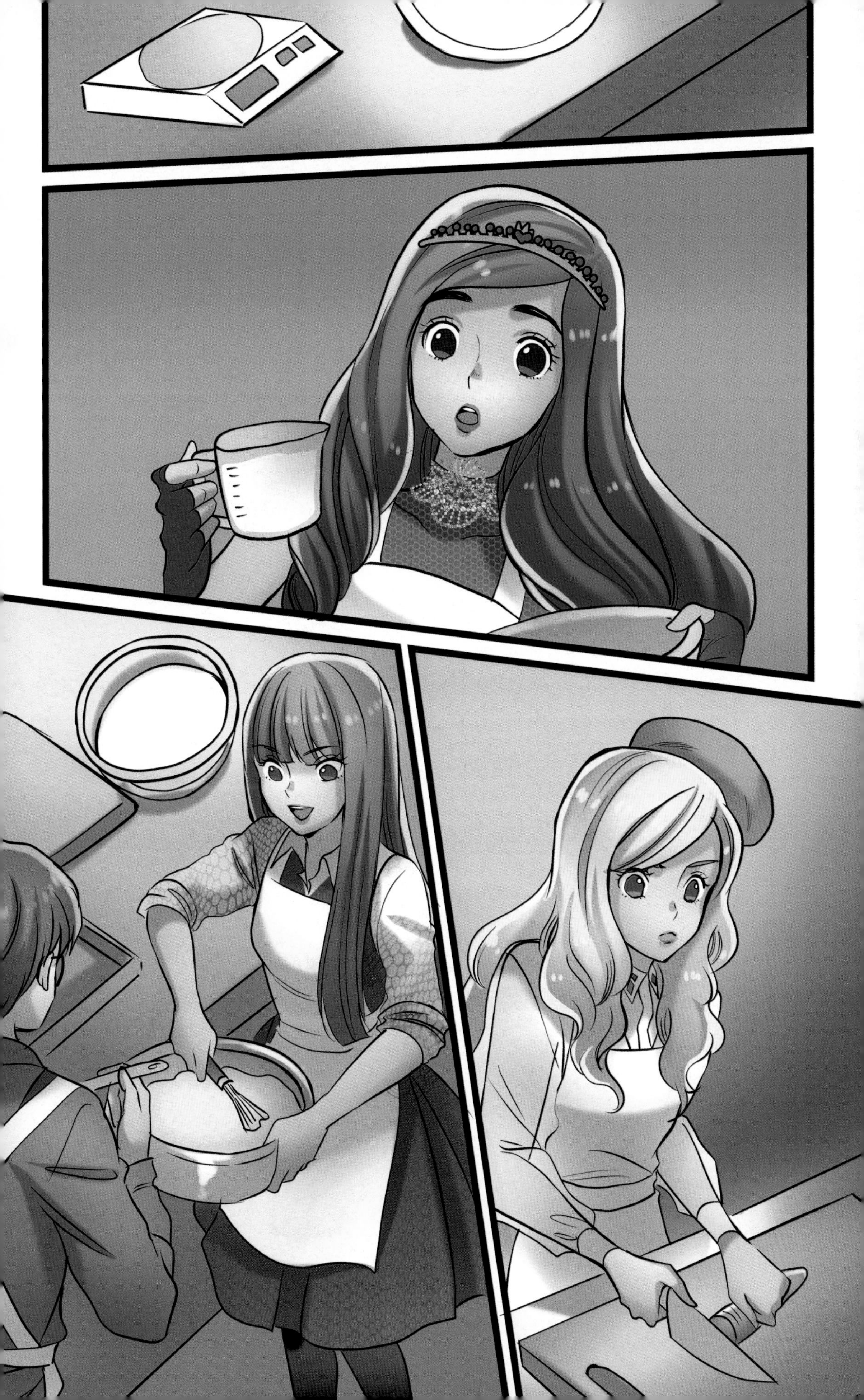

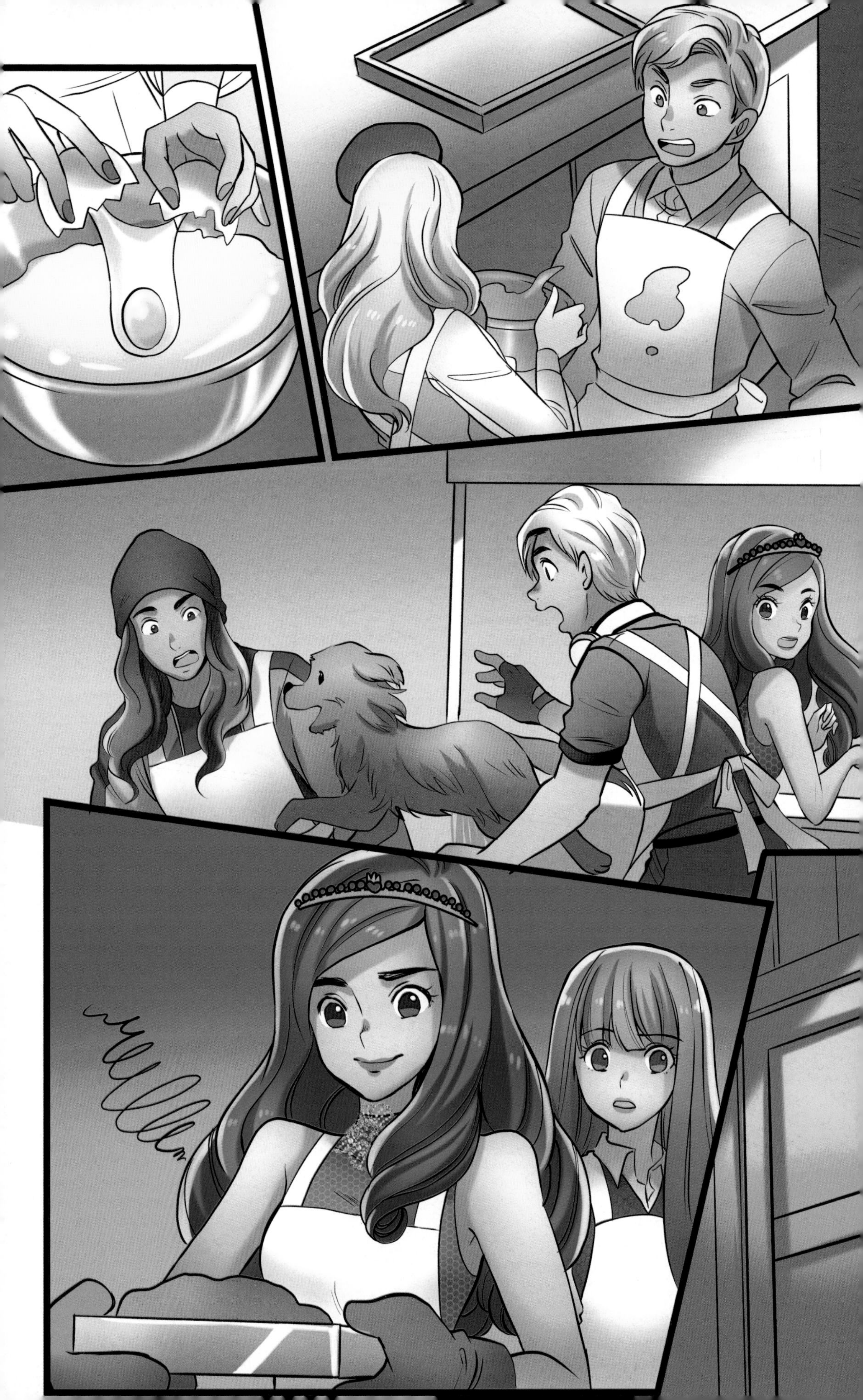

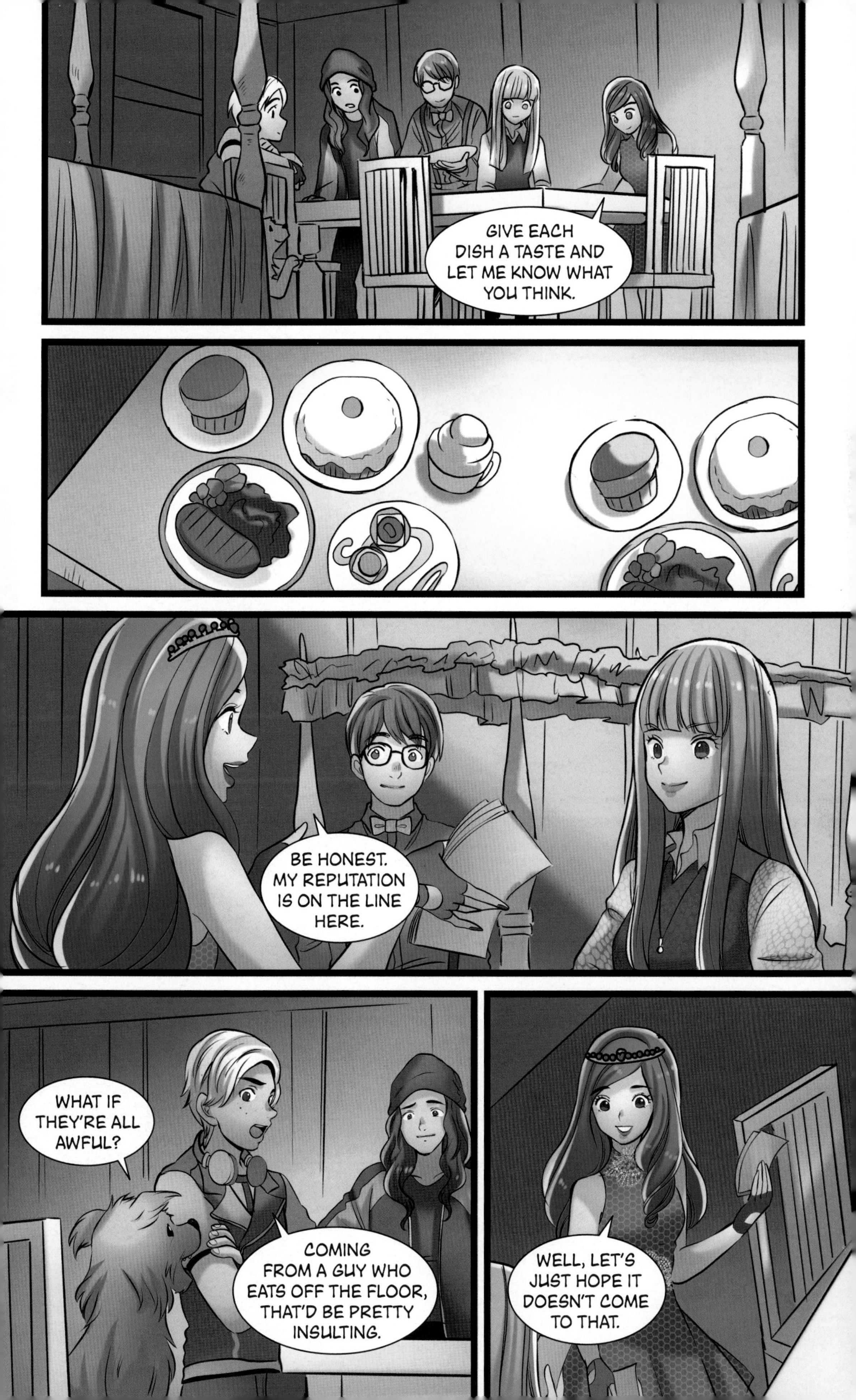
GIVE EACH DISH A TASTE AND LET ME KNOW WHAT YOU THINK.
BE HONEST. MY REPUTATION IS ON THE LINE HERE.
WHAT IF THEY'RE ALL AWFUL?
COMING FROM A GUY WHO EATS OFF THE FLOOR, THAT'D BE PRETTY INSULTING.
WELL, LET'S JUST HOPE IT DOESN'T COME TO THAT.

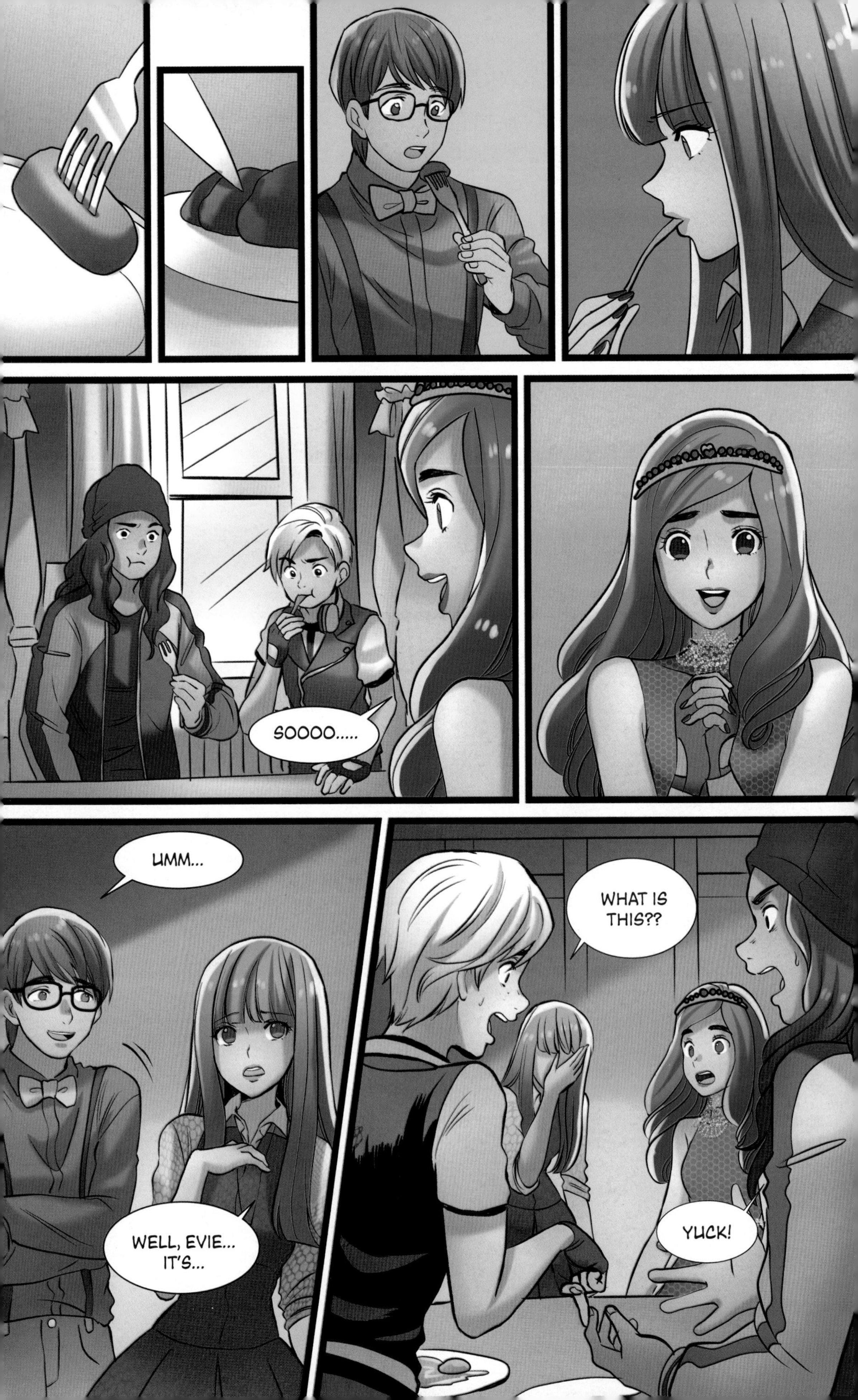
SOOOO.....
UMM...
WELL, EVIE... IT'S...
WHAT IS THIS??
YUCK!

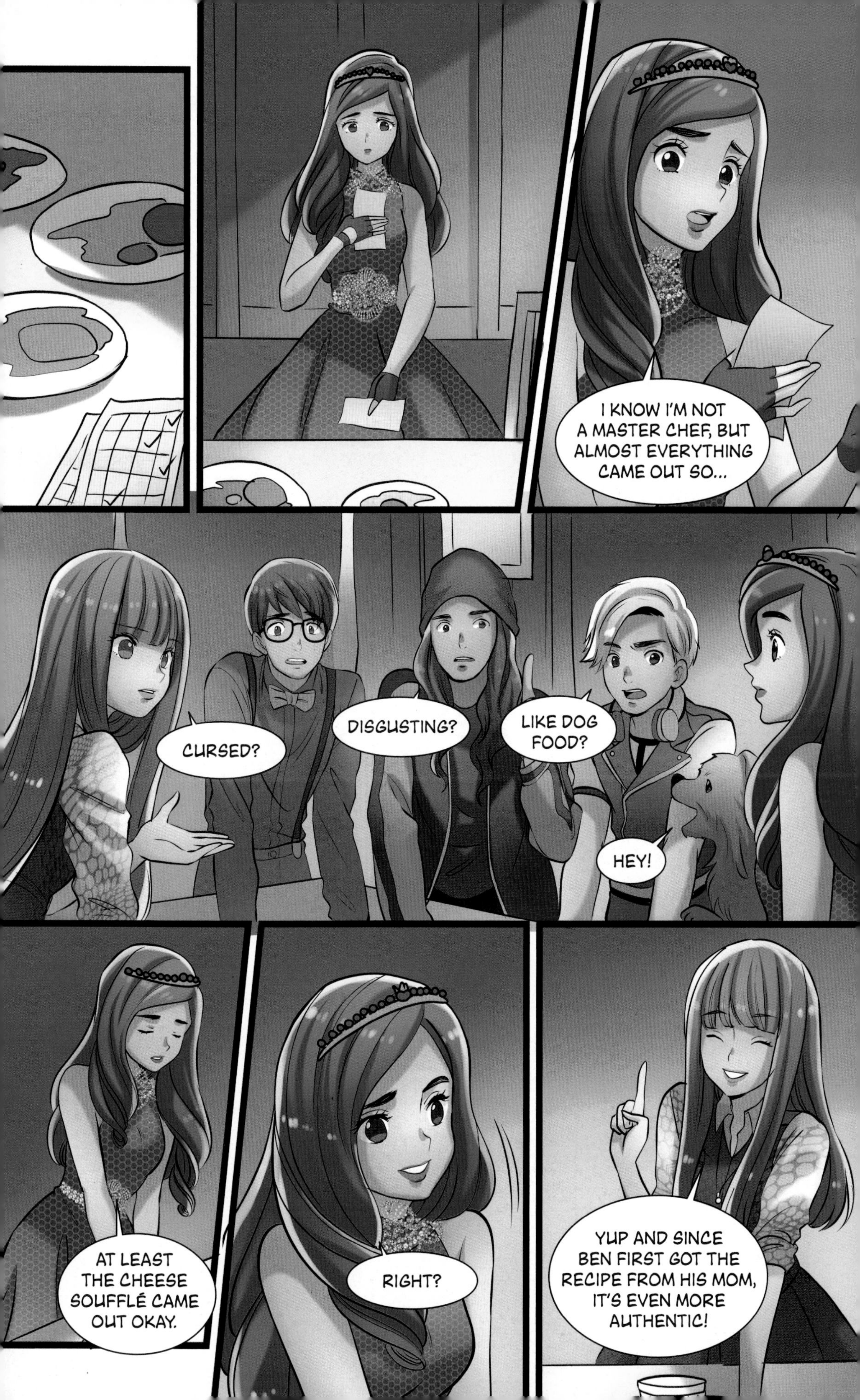
I KNOW I'M NOT A MASTER CHEF, BUT ALMOST EVERYTHING CAME OUT SO...
CURSED?
DISGUSTING?
LIKE DOG FOOD?
HEY!
AT LEAST THE CHEESE SOUFFLÉ CAME OUT OKAY.
RIGHT?
YUP AND SINCE BEN FIRST GOT THE RECIPE FROM HIS MOM, IT'S EVEN MORE AUTHENTIC!

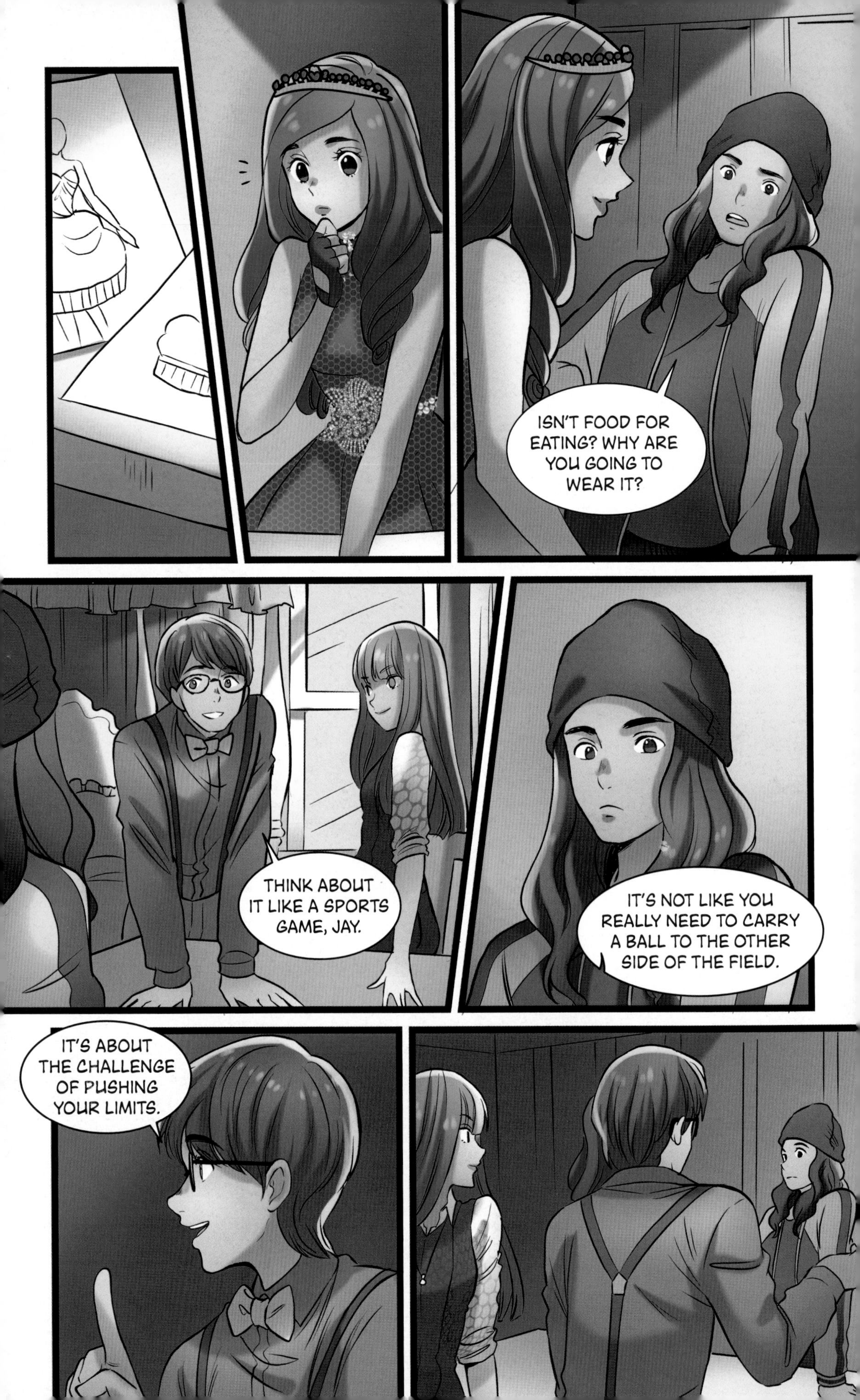
ISN'T FOOD FOR EATING? WHY ARE YOU GOING TO WEAR IT?
THINK ABOUT IT LIKE A SPORTS GAME, JAY.
IT'S NOT LIKE YOU REALLY NEED TO CARRY A BALL TO THE OTHER SIDE OF THE FIELD.
IT'S ABOUT THE CHALLENGE OF PUSHING YOUR LIMITS.

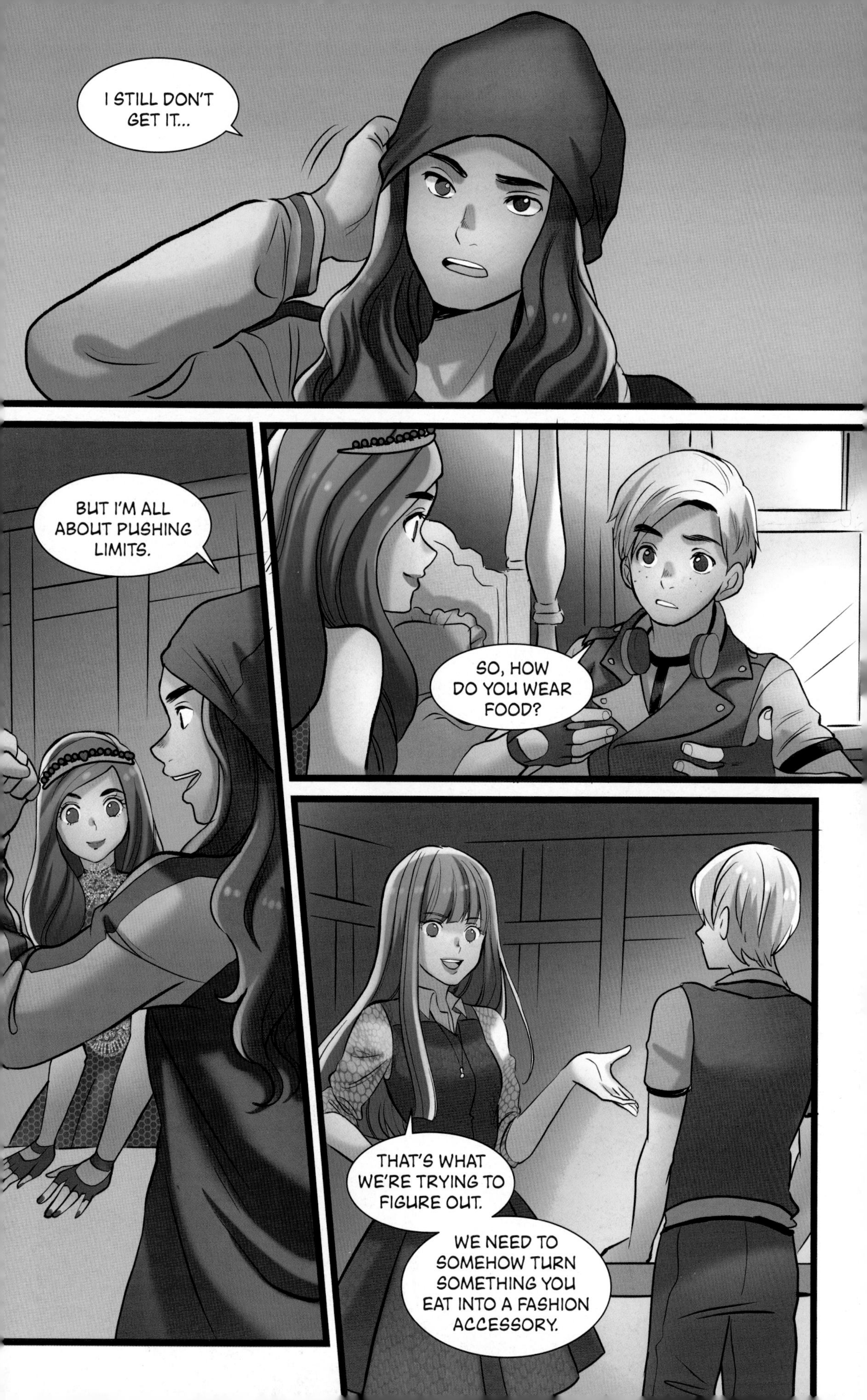
I STILL DON'T GET IT...
BUT I'M ALL ABOUT PUSHING LIMITS.
SO, HOW DO YOU WEAR FOOD?
THAT'S WHAT WE'RE TRYING TO FIGURE OUT.
WE NEED TO SOMEHOW TURN SOMETHING YOU EAT INTO A FASHION ACCESSORY.

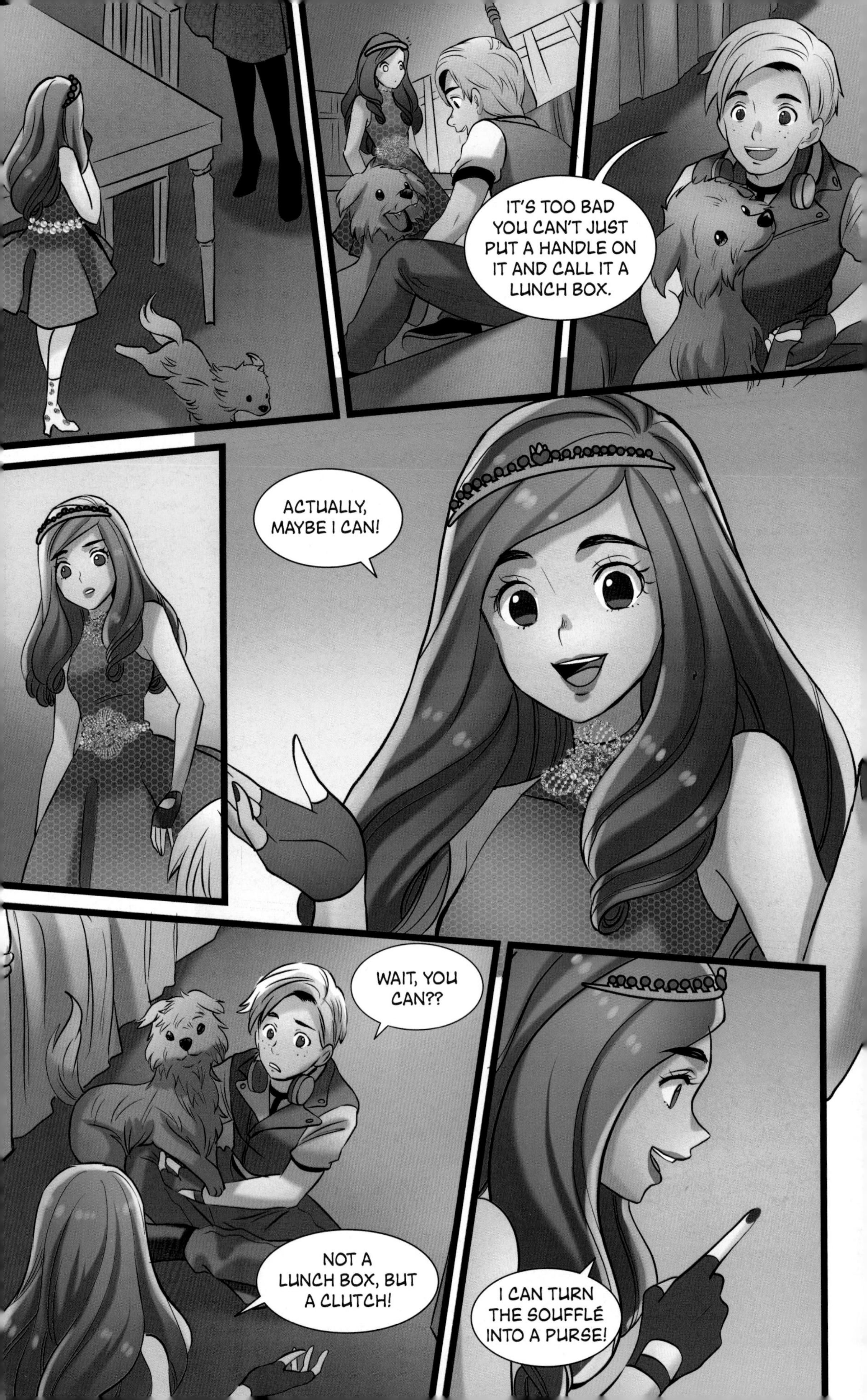
IT'S TOO BAD YOU CAN'T JUST PUT A HANDLE ON IT AND CALL IT A LUNCH BOX.
ACTUALLY, MAYBE I CAN!
WAIT, YOU CAN??
NOT A LUNCH BOX, BUT A CLUTCH!
I CAN TURN THE SOUFFLÉ INTO A PURSE!

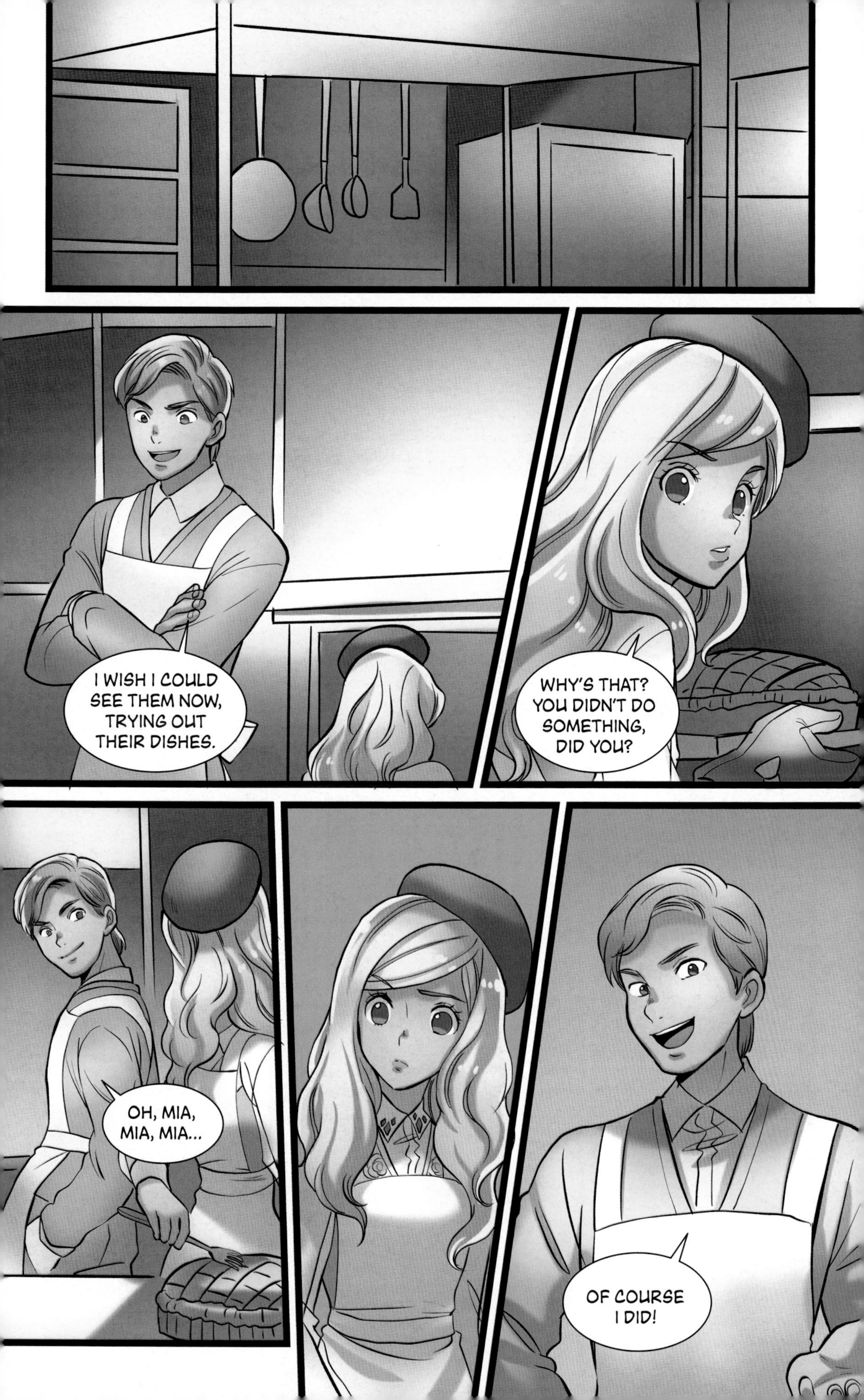
I WISH I COULD SEE THEM NOW, TRYING OUT THEIR DISHES.
WHY'S THAT? YOU DIDN'T DO SOMETHING, DID YOU?
OH, MIA, MIA, MIA...
OF COURSE I DID!

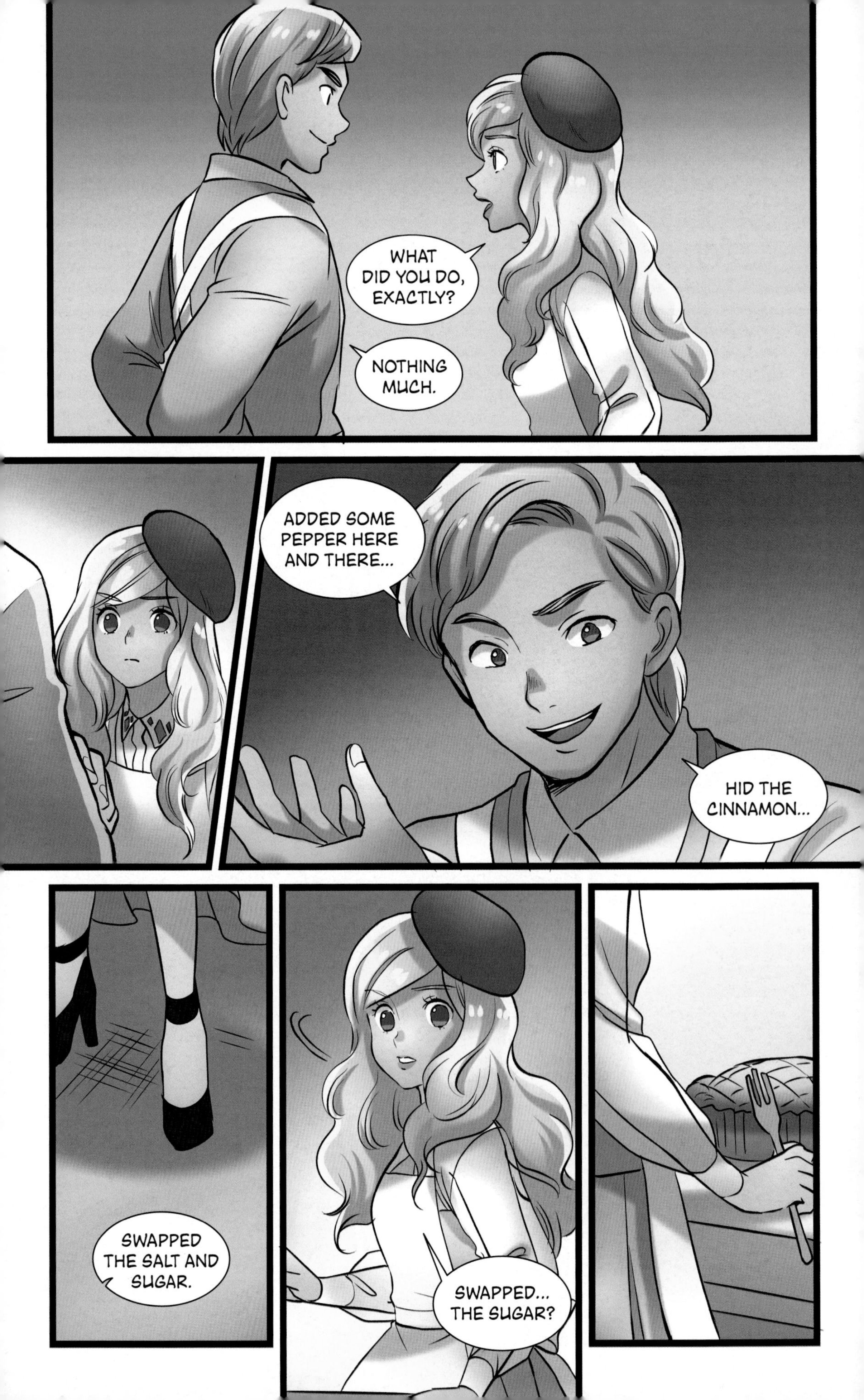
WHAT DID YOU DO, EXACTLY?
NOTHING MUCH.
ADDED SOME PEPPER HERE AND THERE...
HID THE CINNAMON...
SWAPPED THE SALT AND SUGAR.
SWAPPED... THE SUGAR?

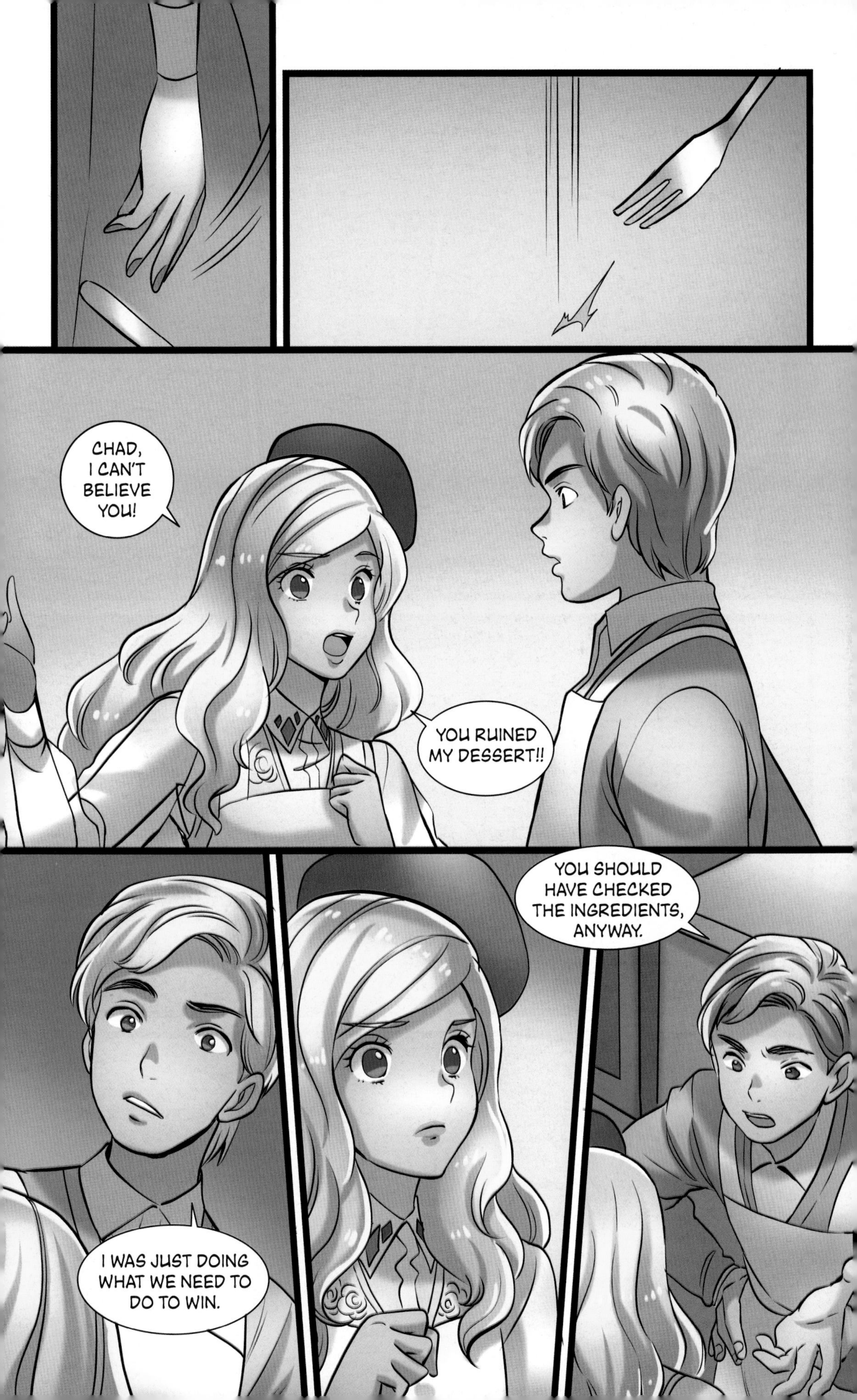
CHAD, I CAN'T BELIEVE YOU!
YOU RUINED MY DESSERT!!
I WAS JUST DOING WHAT WE NEED TO DO TO WIN.
YOU SHOULD HAVE CHECKED THE INGREDIENTS, ANYWAY.

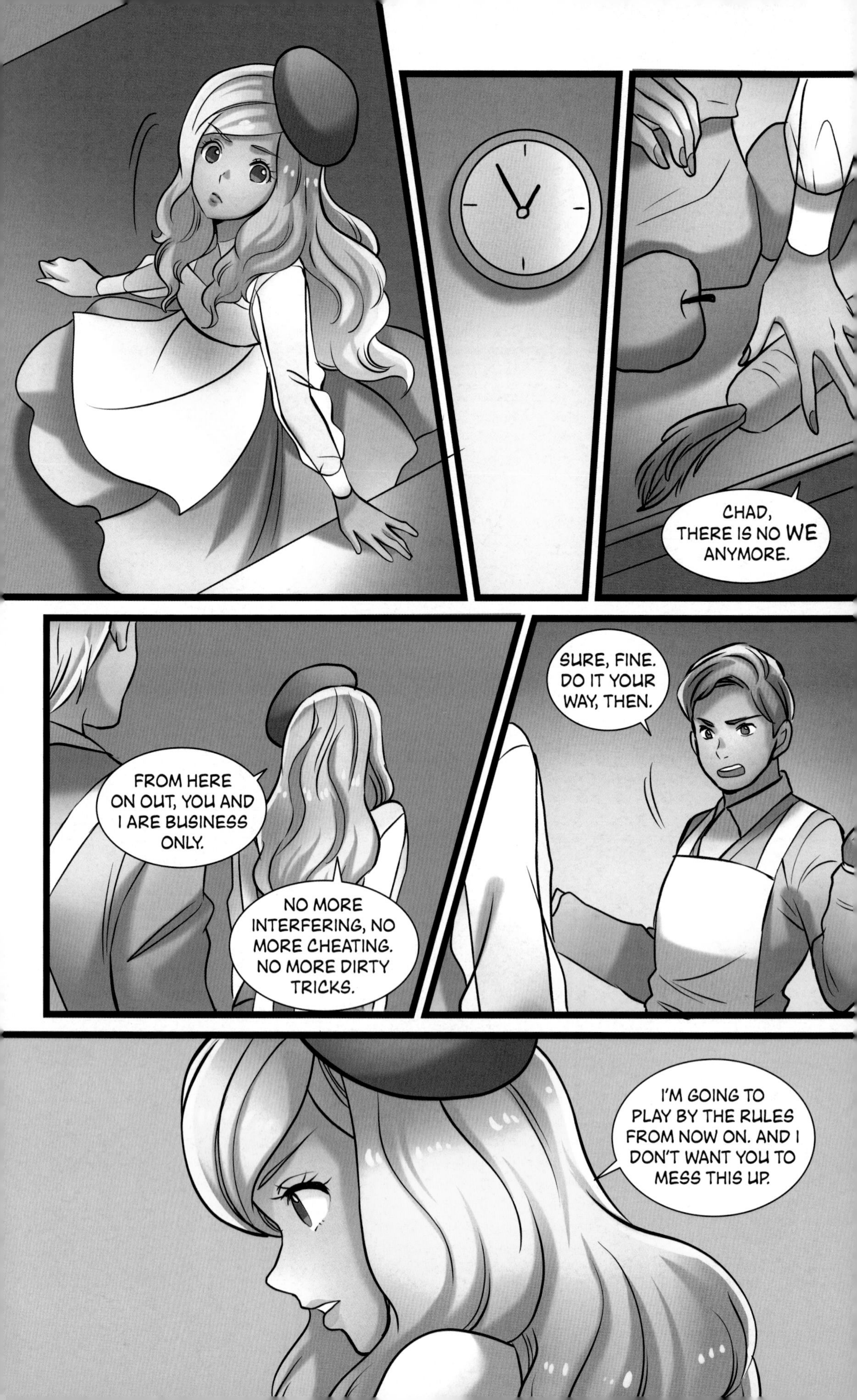
CHAD, THERE IS NO WE ANYMORE.
FROM HERE ON OUT, YOU AND I ARE BUSINESS ONLY.
NO MORE INTERFERING, NO MORE CHEATING. NO MORE DIRTY TRICKS.
SURE, FINE. DO IT YOUR WAY, THEN.
I'M GOING TO PLAY BY THE RULES FROM NOW ON. AND I DON'T WANT YOU TO MESS THIS UP.

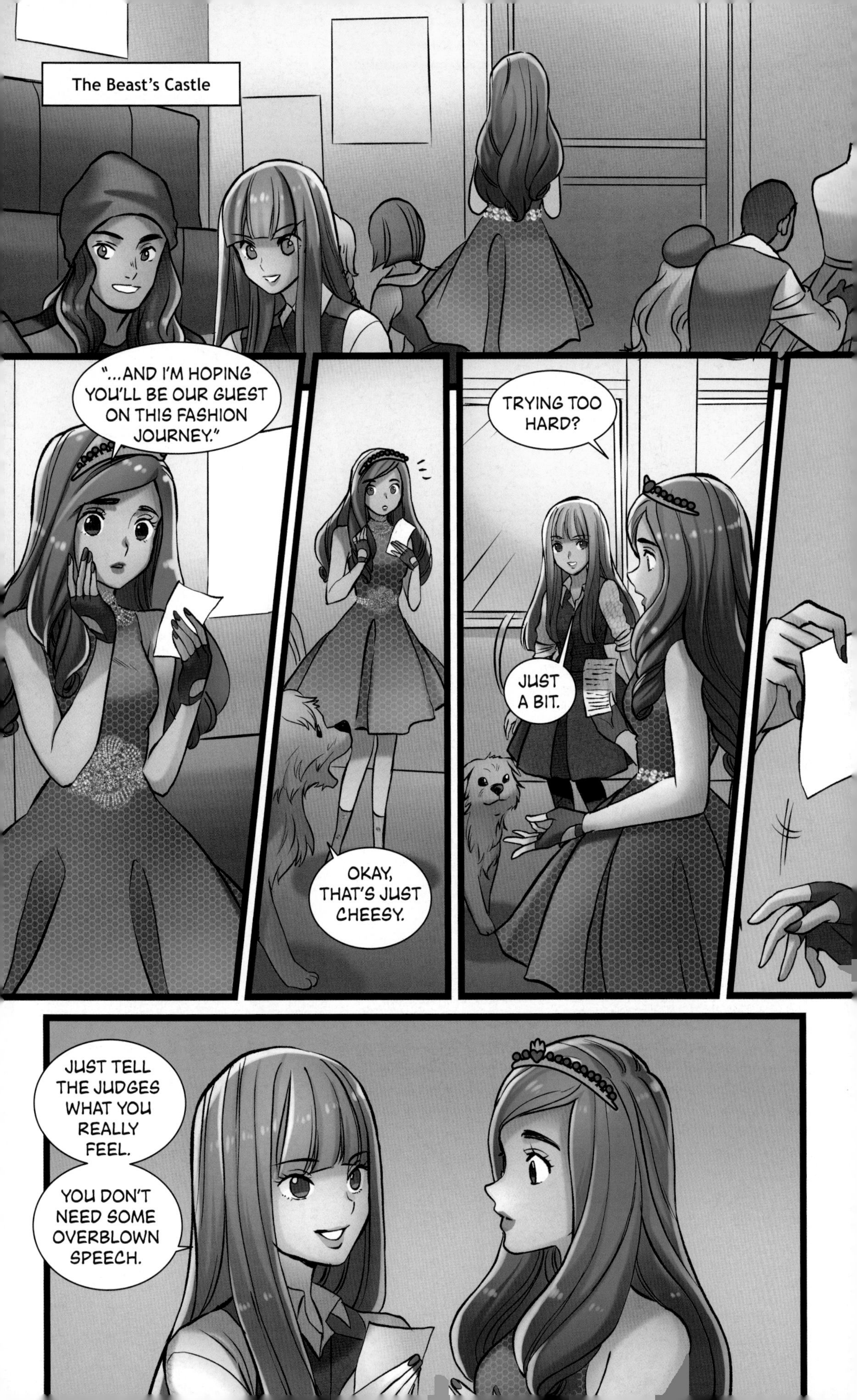
The Beast's Castle
"...AND I'M HOPING YOU'LL BE OUR GUEST ON THIS FASHION JOURNEY."
OKAY, THAT'S JUST CHEESY.
TRYING TOO HARD?
JUST A BIT.
JUST TELL THE JUDGES WHAT YOU REALLY FEEL.
YOU DON'T NEED SOME OVERBLOWN SPEECH.

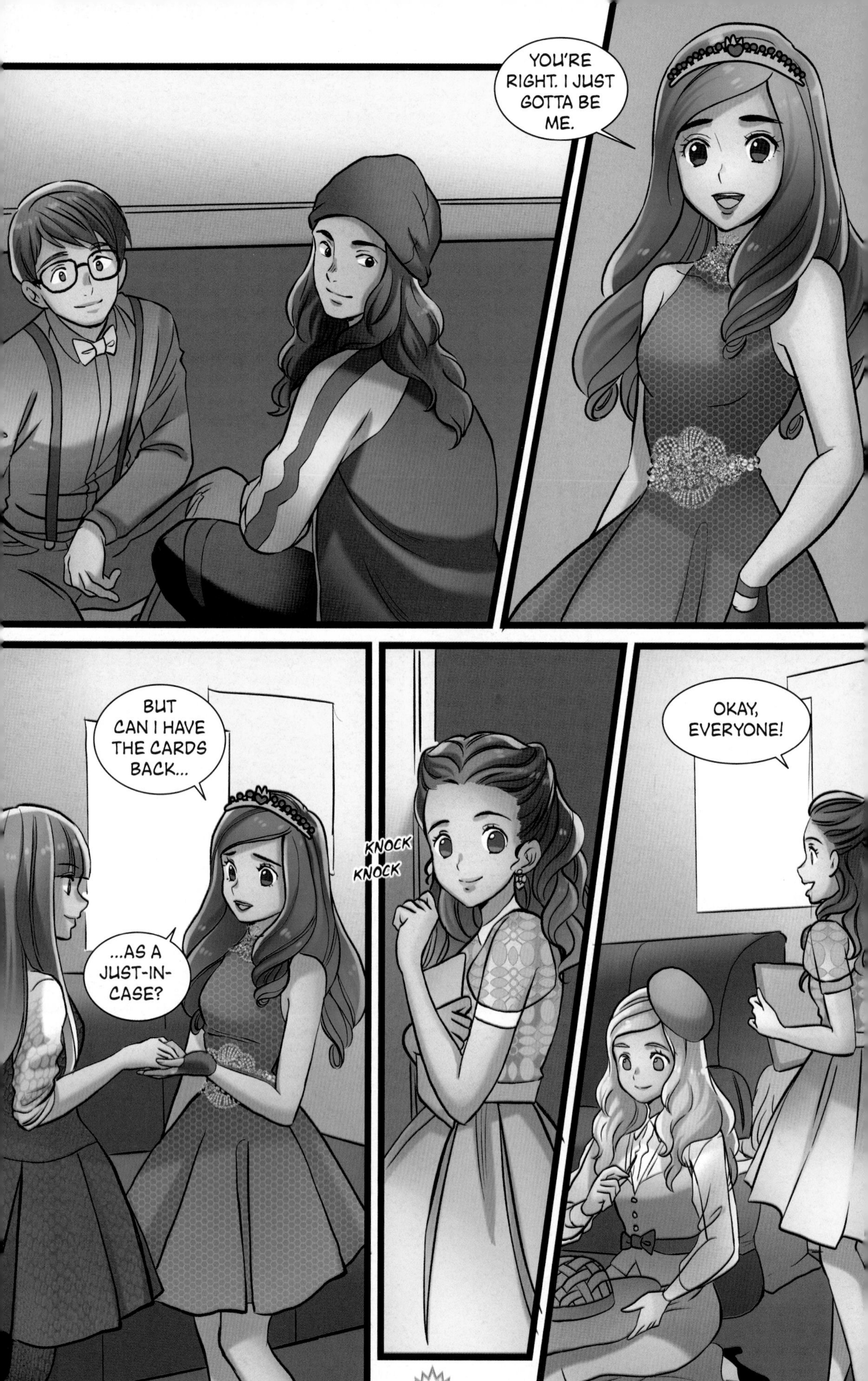
YOU'RE RIGHT. I JUST GOTTA BE ME.
BUT CAN I HAVE THE CARDS BACK...
...AS A JUST-IN-CASE?
KNOCK KNOCK
OKAY, EVERYONE!

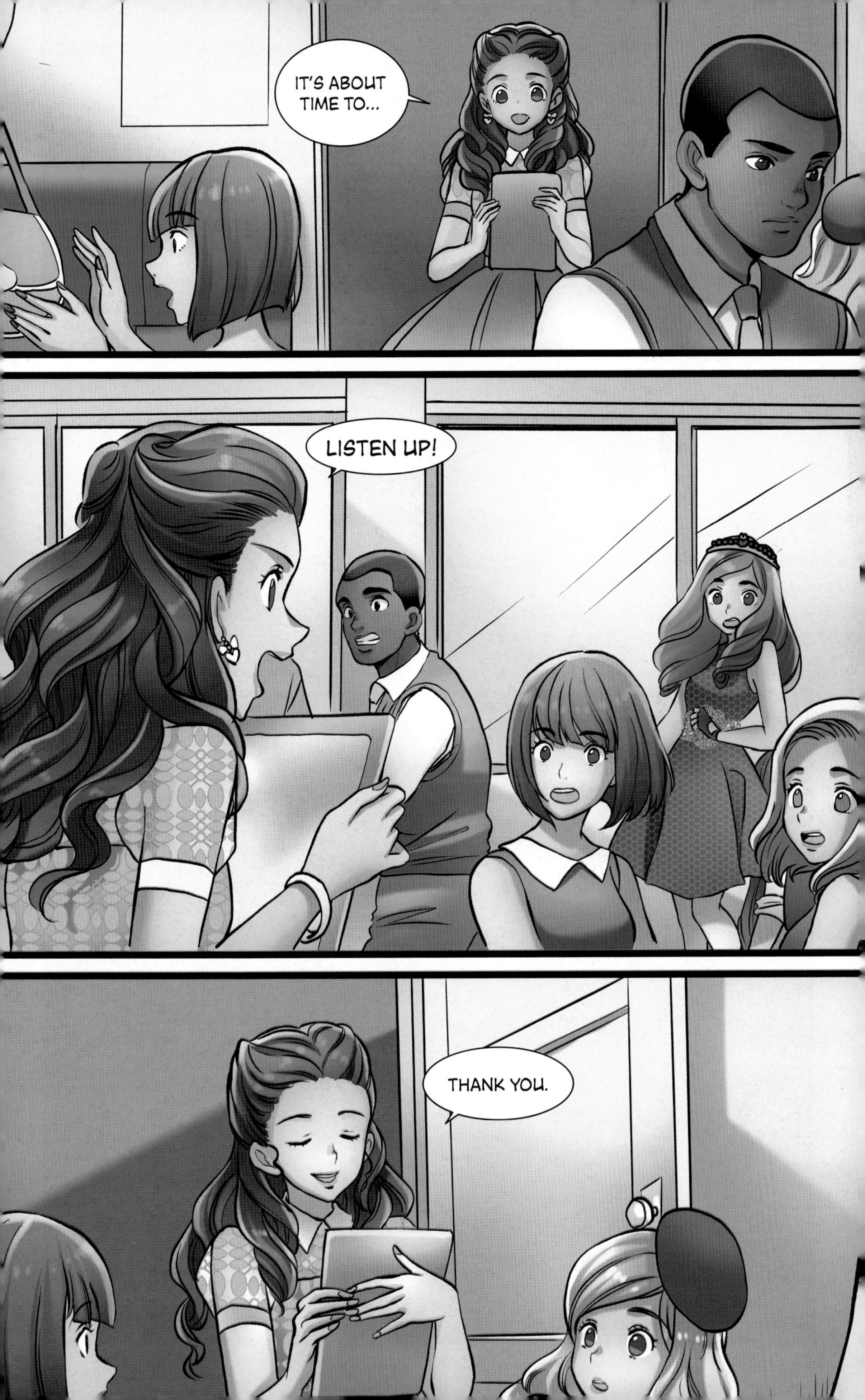
IT'S ABOUT TIME TO...
LISTEN UP!
THANK YOU.

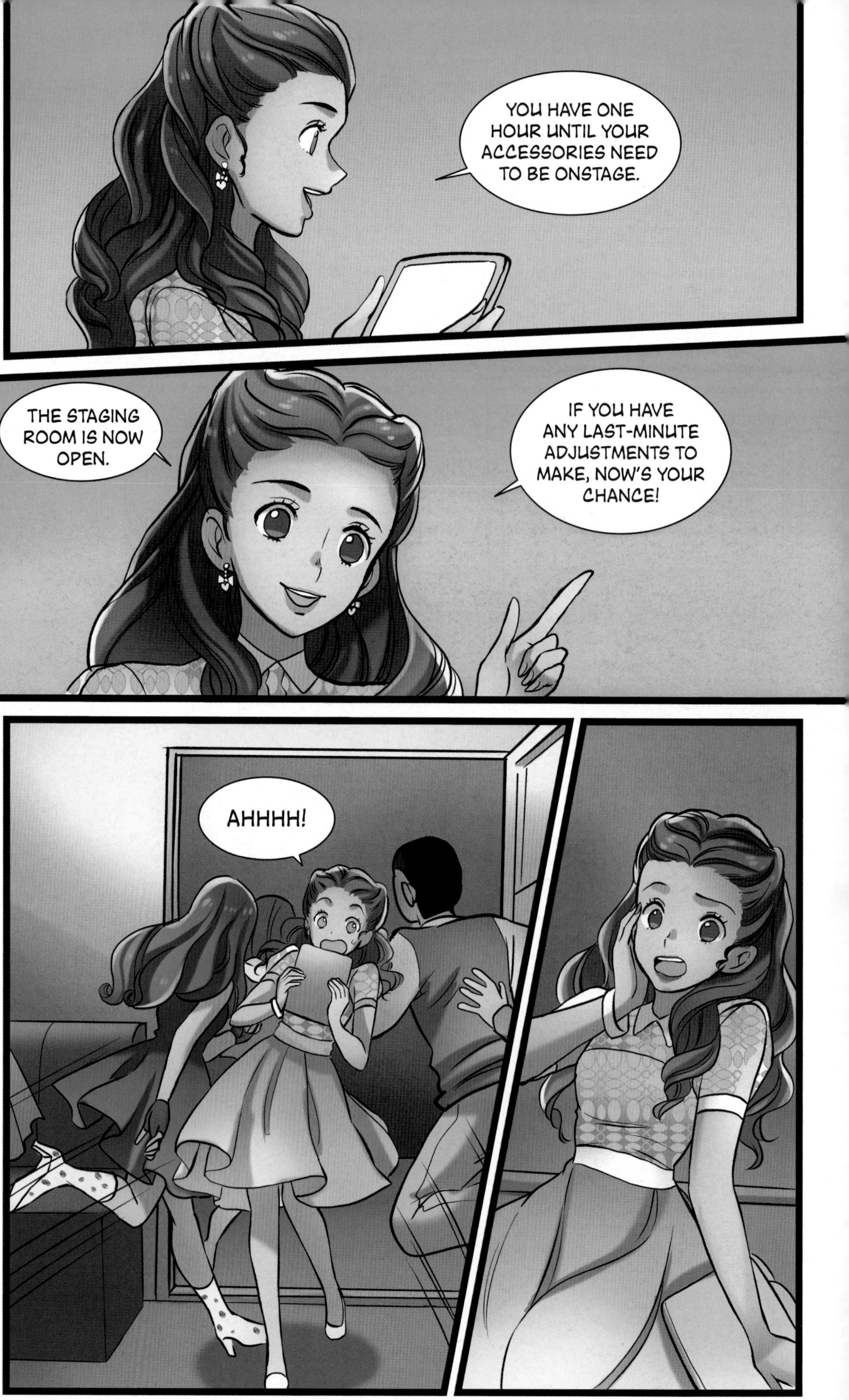
YOU HAVE ONE HOUR UNTIL YOUR ACCESSORIES NEED TO BE ONSTAGE.
THE STAGING ROOM IS NOW OPEN.
IF YOU HAVE ANY LAST-MINUTE ADJUSTMENTS TO MAKE, NOW'S YOUR CHANCE!
AHHHH!

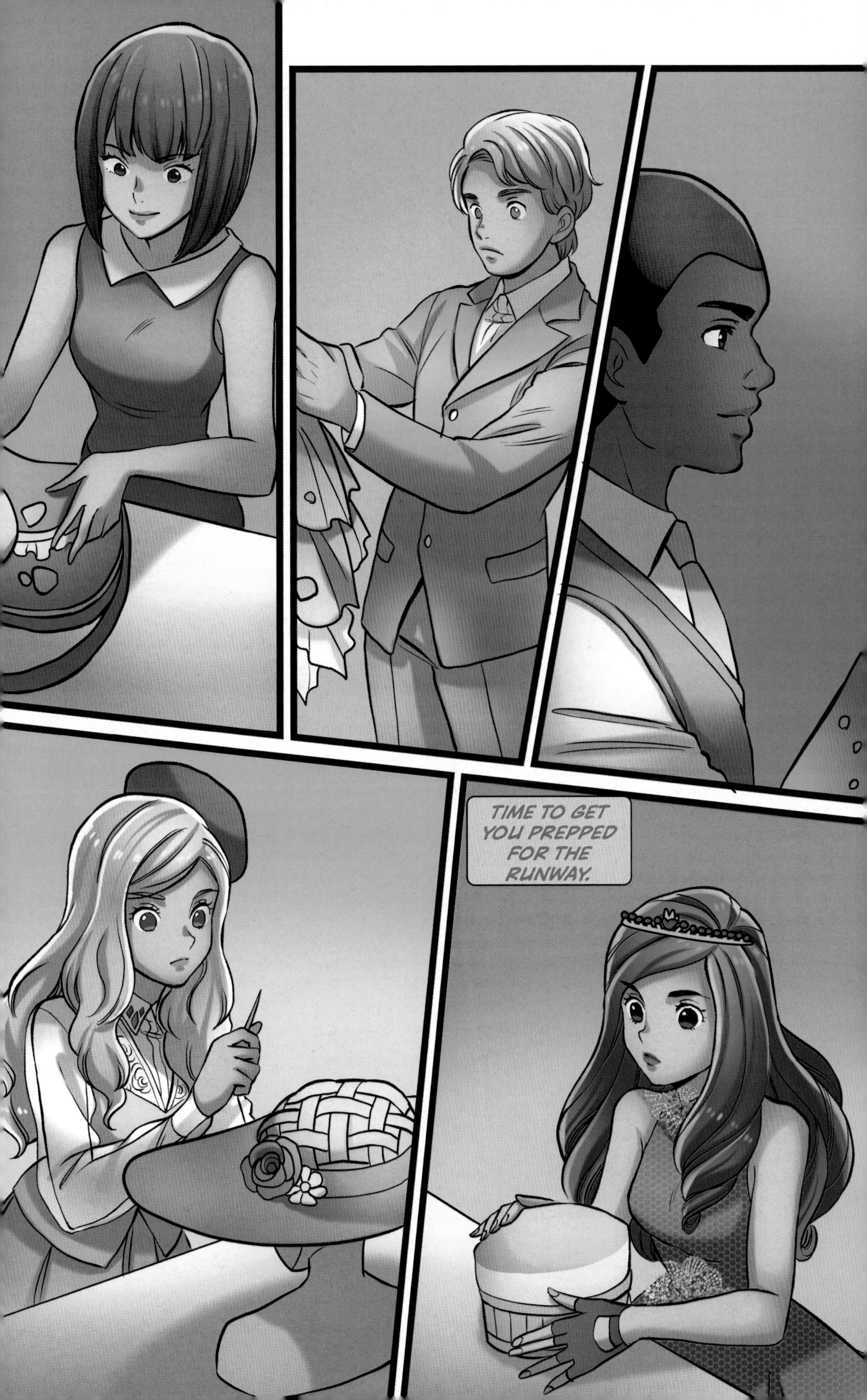
TIME TO GET
YOU PREPPED
FOR THE
RUNWAY.

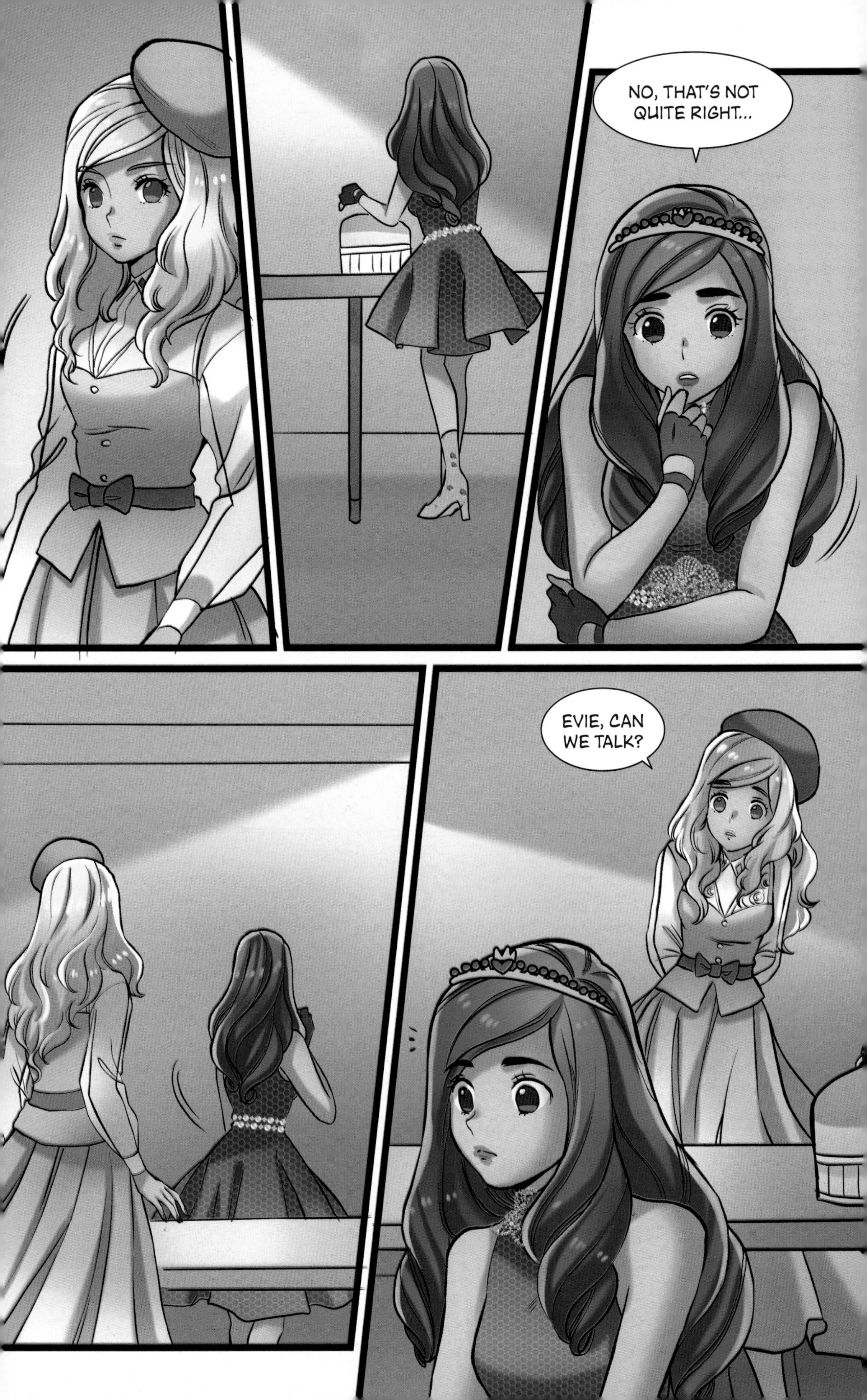
NO, THAT'S NOT QUITE RIGHT...
EVIE, CAN WE TALK?

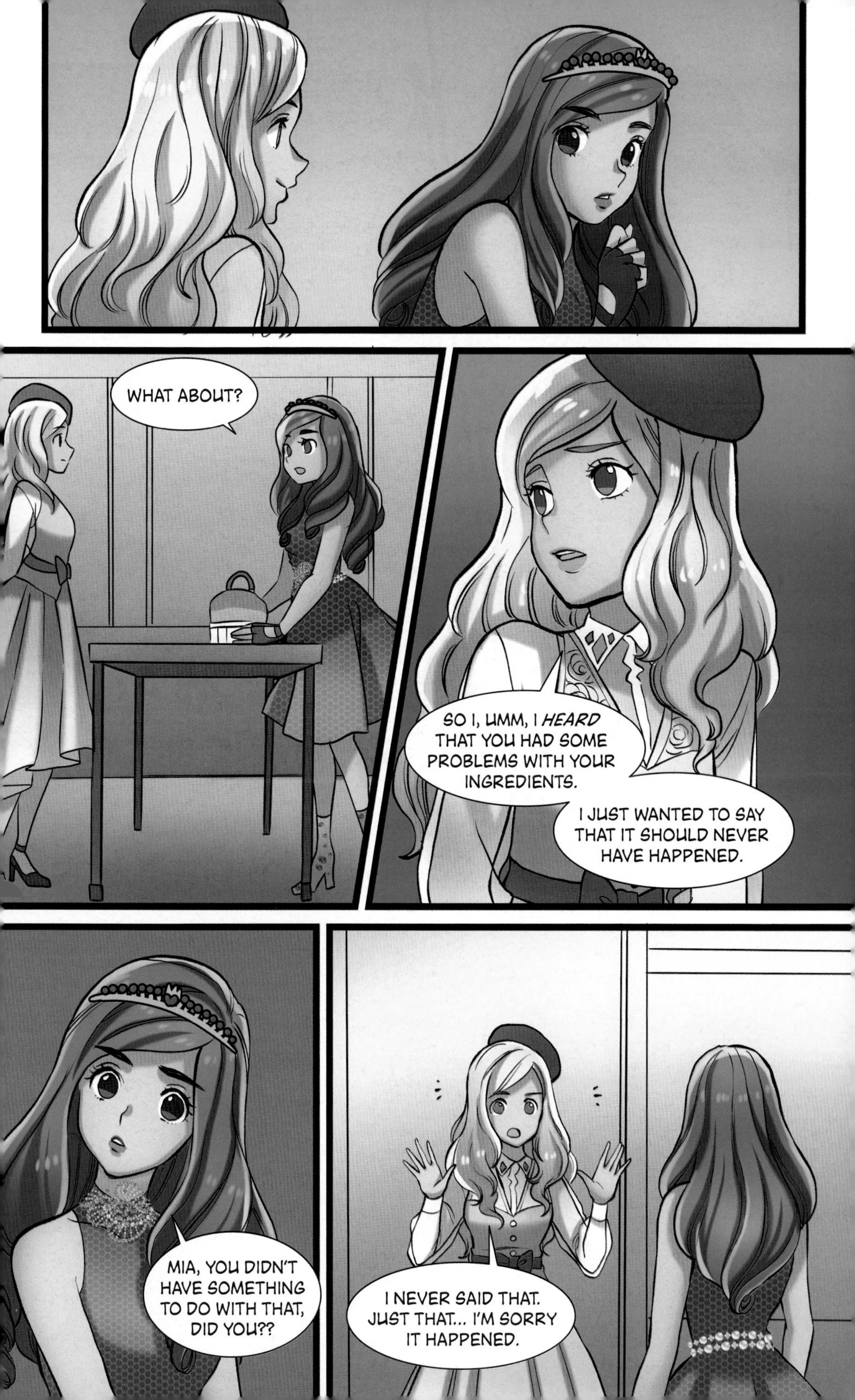
WHAT ABOUT?
SO I, UMM, I *HEARD* THAT YOU HAD SOME PROBLEMS WITH YOUR INGREDIENTS.
I JUST WANTED TO SAY THAT IT SHOULD NEVER HAVE HAPPENED.
MIA, YOU DIDN'T HAVE SOMETHING TO DO WITH THAT, DID YOU??
I NEVER SAID THAT. JUST THAT... I'M SORRY IT HAPPENED.

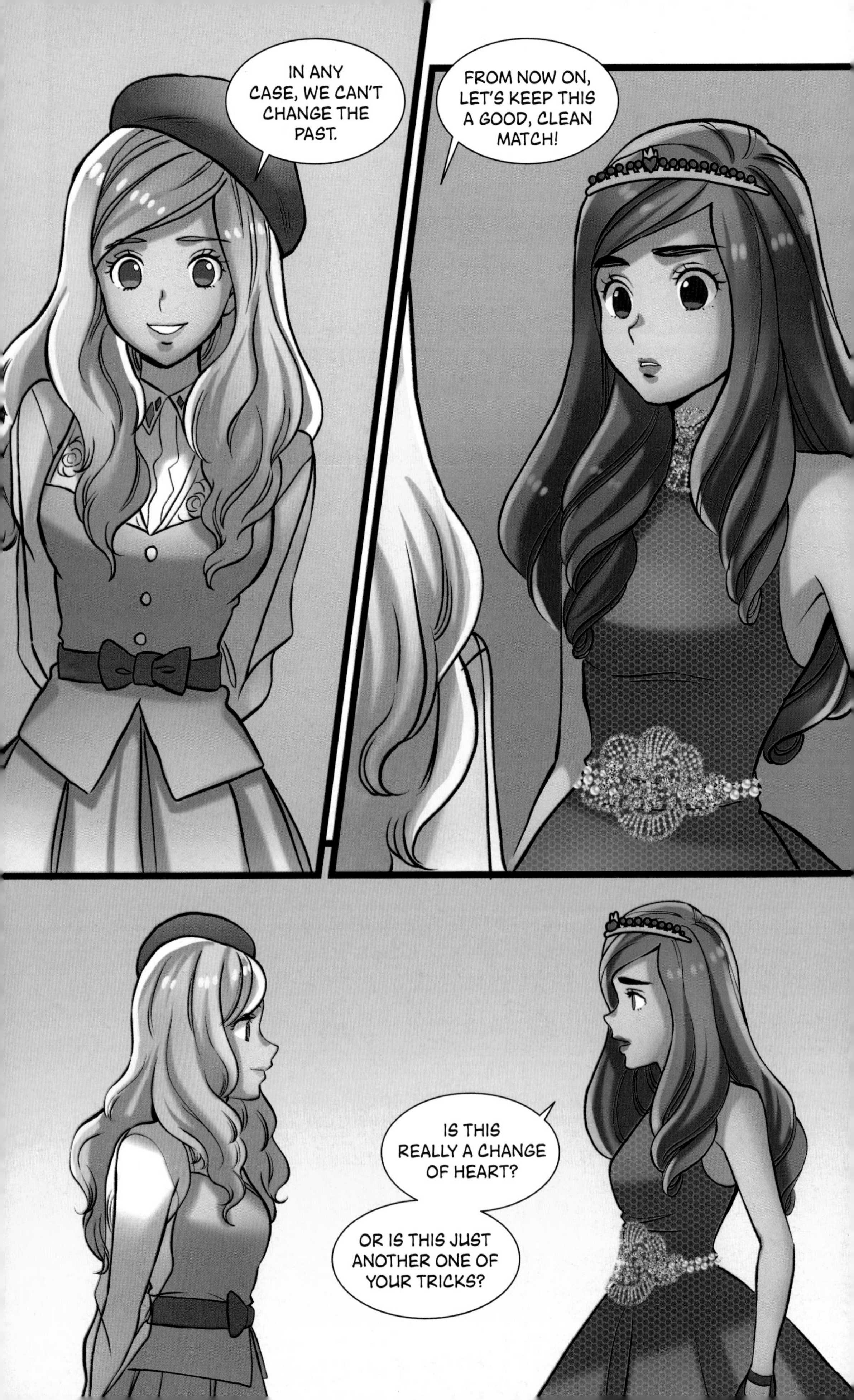
IN ANY CASE, WE CAN'T CHANGE THE PAST.
FROM NOW ON, LET'S KEEP THIS A GOOD, CLEAN MATCH!
IS THIS REALLY A CHANGE OF HEART?
OR IS THIS JUST ANOTHER ONE OF YOUR TRICKS?

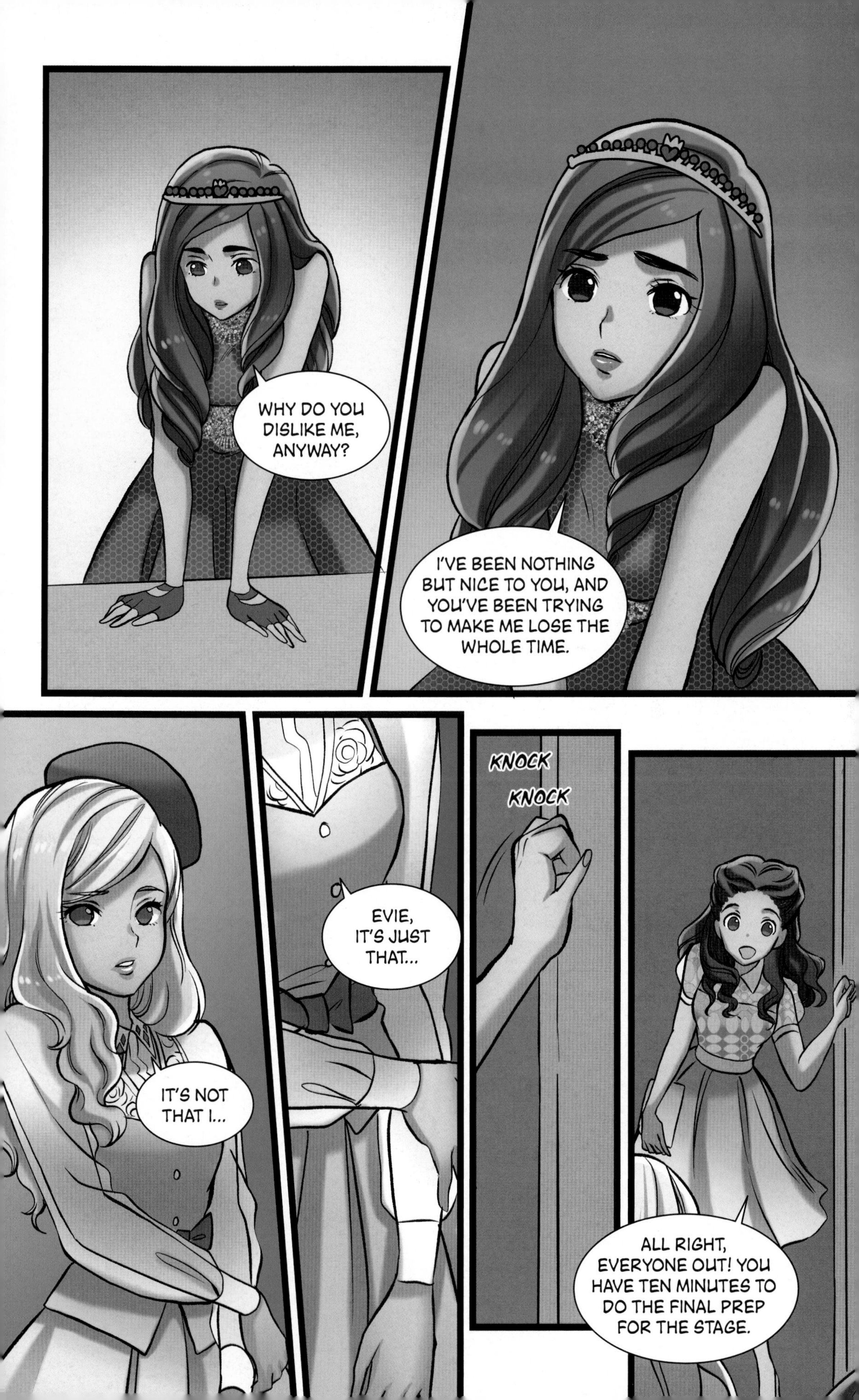
WHY DO YOU DISLIKE ME, ANYWAY?
I'VE BEEN NOTHING BUT NICE TO YOU, AND YOU'VE BEEN TRYING TO MAKE ME LOSE THE WHOLE TIME.
IT'S NOT THAT I...
EVIE, IT'S JUST THAT...
KNOCK
KNOCK
ALL RIGHT, EVERYONE OUT! YOU HAVE TEN MINUTES TO DO THE FINAL PREP FOR THE STAGE.

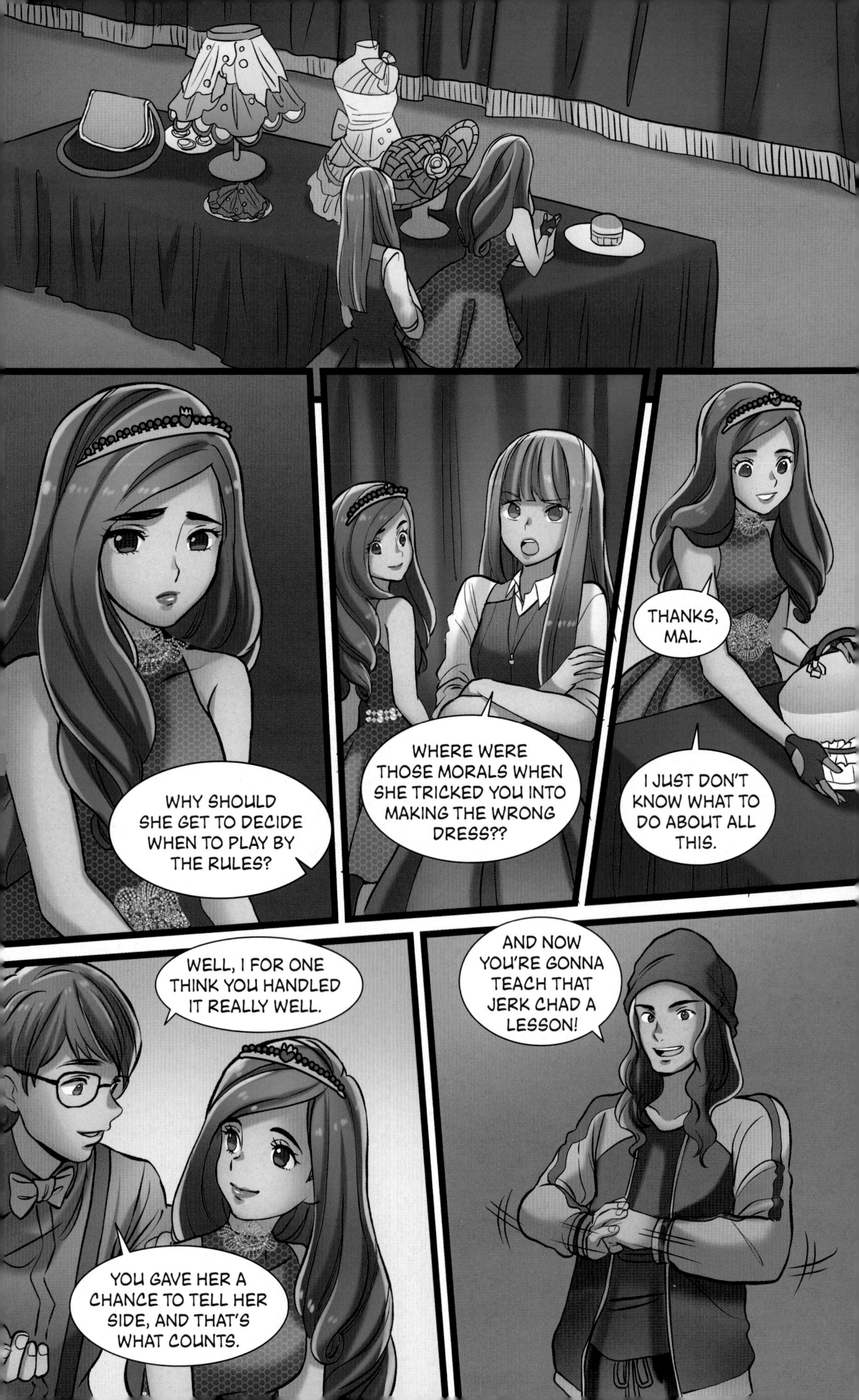
WHY SHOULD SHE GET TO DECIDE WHEN TO PLAY BY THE RULES?
WHERE WERE THOSE MORALS WHEN SHE TRICKED YOU INTO MAKING THE WRONG DRESS??
THANKS, MAL.
I JUST DON'T KNOW WHAT TO DO ABOUT ALL THIS.
WELL, I FOR ONE THINK YOU HANDLED IT REALLY WELL.
YOU GAVE HER A CHANCE TO TELL HER SIDE, AND THAT'S WHAT COUNTS.
AND NOW YOU'RE GONNA TEACH THAT JERK CHAD A LESSON!

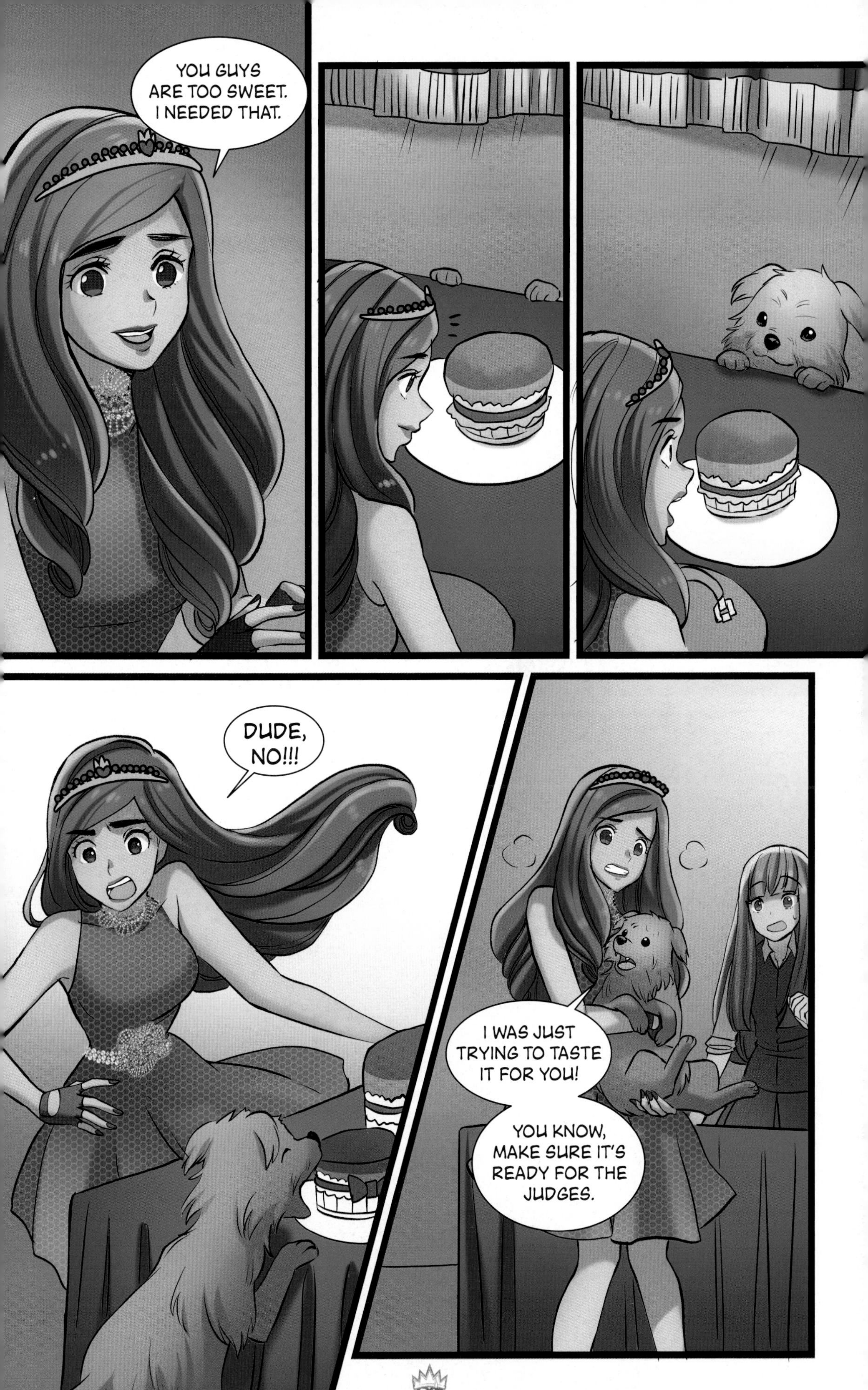
YOU GUYS ARE TOO SWEET. I NEEDED THAT.
DUDE, NO!!!
I WAS JUST TRYING TO TASTE IT FOR YOU!
YOU KNOW, MAKE SURE IT'S READY FOR THE JUDGES.

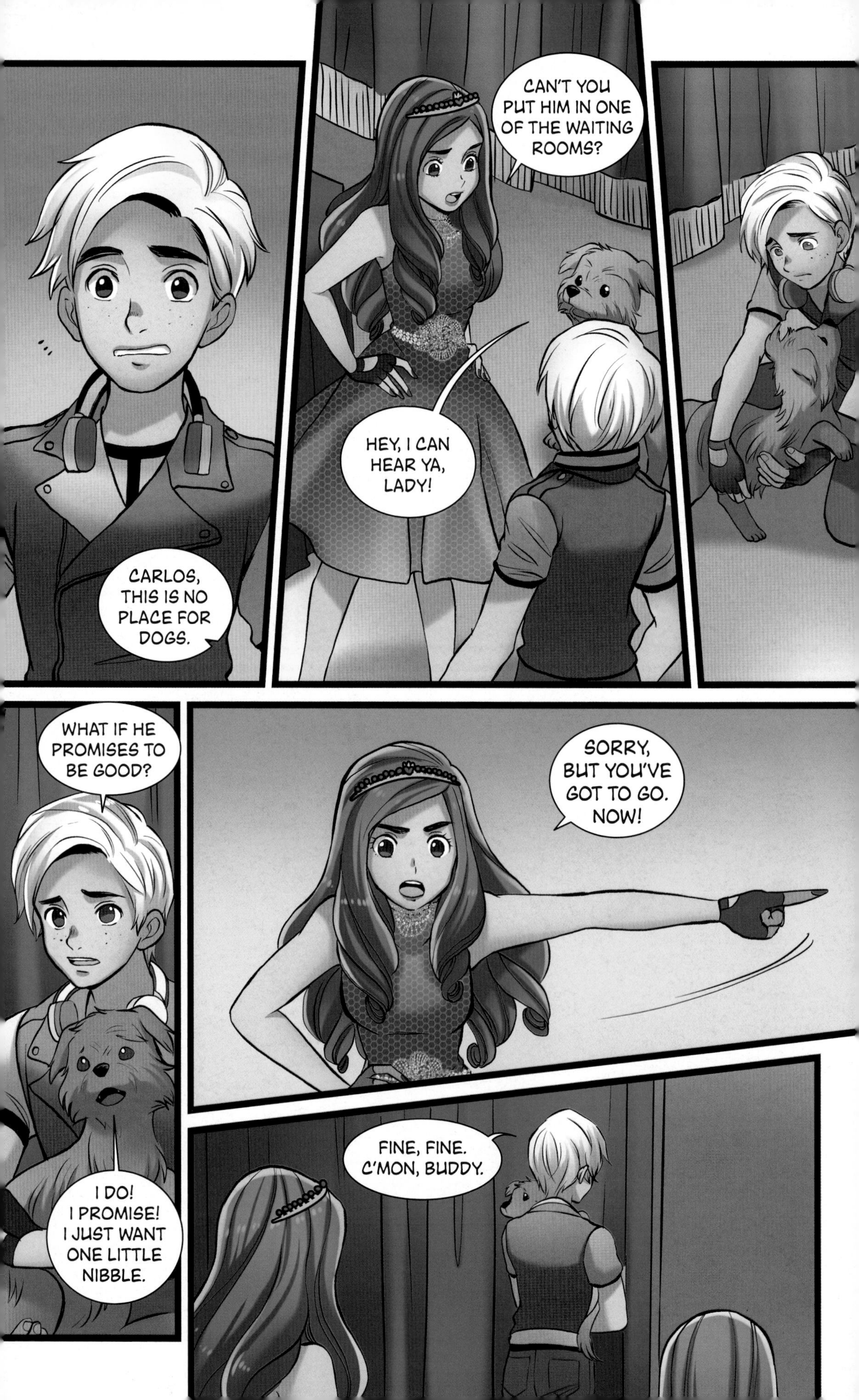
CARLOS, THIS IS NO PLACE FOR DOGS.
CAN'T YOU PUT HIM IN ONE OF THE WAITING ROOMS?
HEY, I CAN HEAR YA, LADY!
WHAT IF HE PROMISES TO BE GOOD?
I DO! I PROMISE! I JUST WANT ONE LITTLE NIBBLE.
SORRY, BUT YOU'VE GOT TO GO. NOW!
FINE, FINE. C'MON, BUDDY.

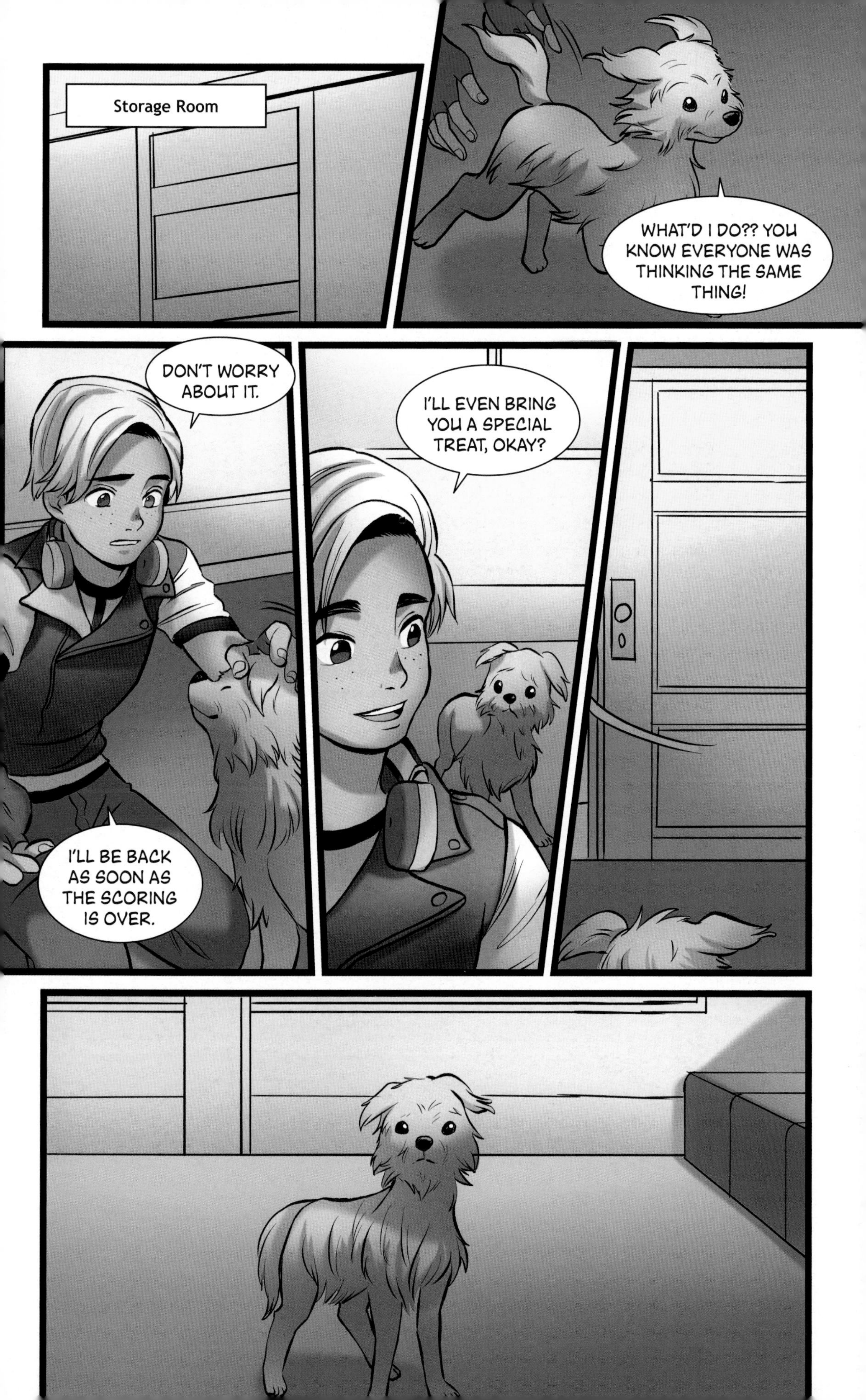
Storage Room
WHAT'D I DO?? YOU KNOW EVERYONE WAS THINKING THE SAME THING!
DON'T WORRY ABOUT IT.
I'LL BE BACK AS SOON AS THE SCORING IS OVER.
I'LL EVEN BRING YOU A SPECIAL TREAT, OKAY?

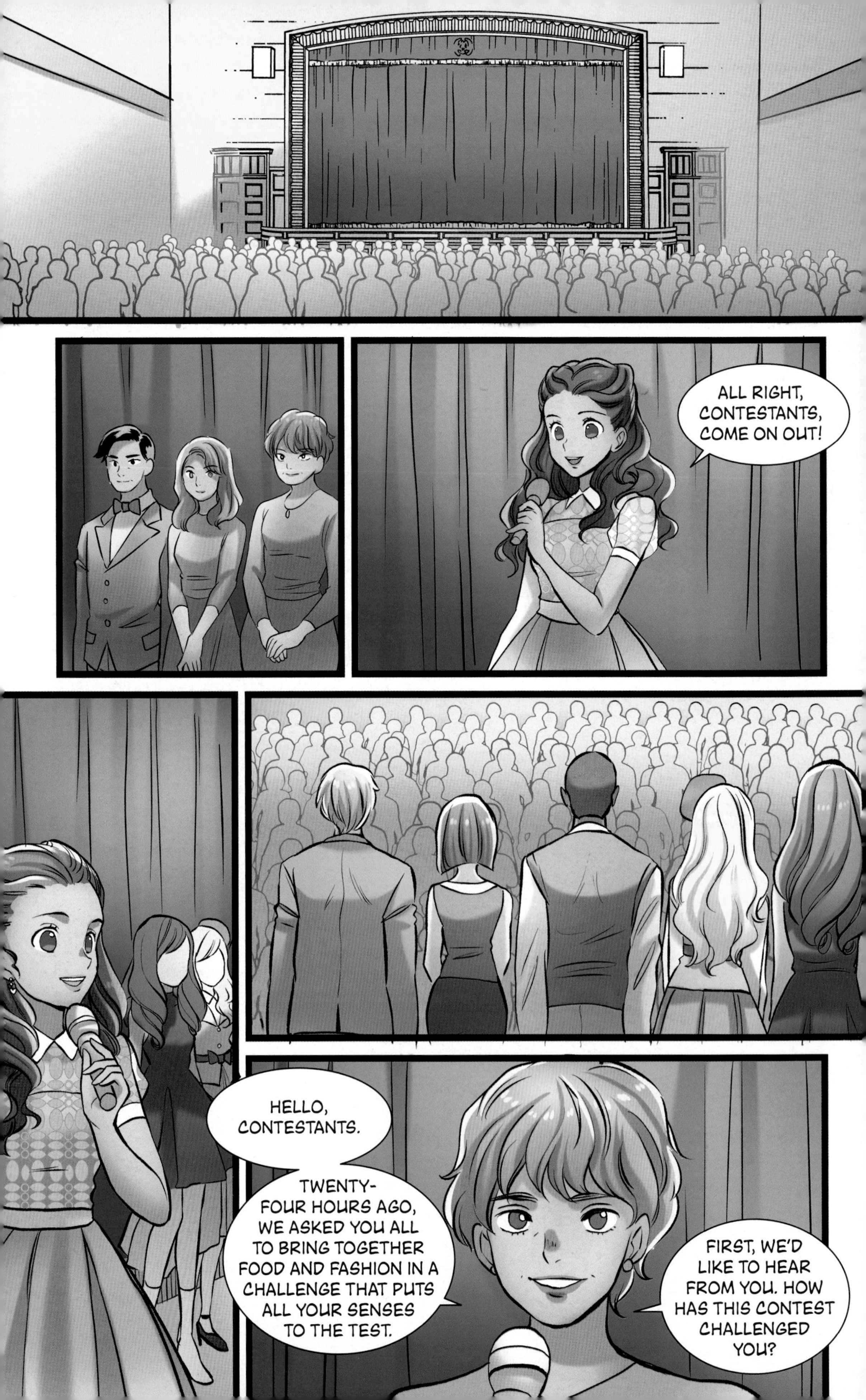
ALL RIGHT, CONTESTANTS, COME ON OUT!
HELLO, CONTESTANTS.
TWENTY-FOUR HOURS AGO, WE ASKED YOU ALL TO BRING TOGETHER FOOD AND FASHION IN A CHALLENGE THAT PUTS ALL YOUR SENSES TO THE TEST.
FIRST, WE'D LIKE TO HEAR FROM YOU. HOW HAS THIS CONTEST CHALLENGED YOU?

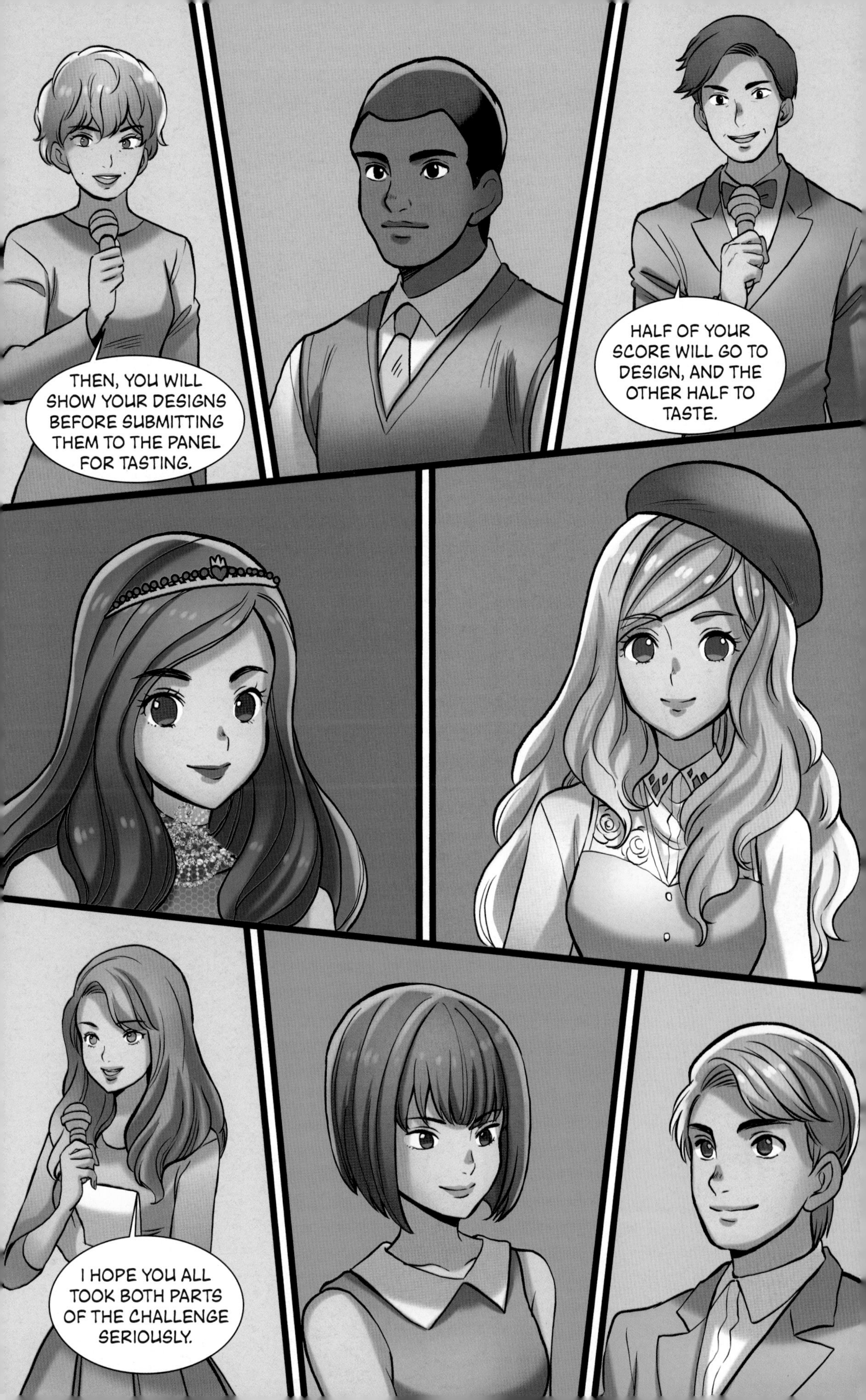
THEN, YOU WILL SHOW YOUR DESIGNS BEFORE SUBMITTING THEM TO THE PANEL FOR TASTING.
HALF OF YOUR SCORE WILL GO TO DESIGN, AND THE OTHER HALF TO TASTE.
I HOPE YOU ALL TOOK BOTH PARTS OF THE CHALLENGE SERIOUSLY.

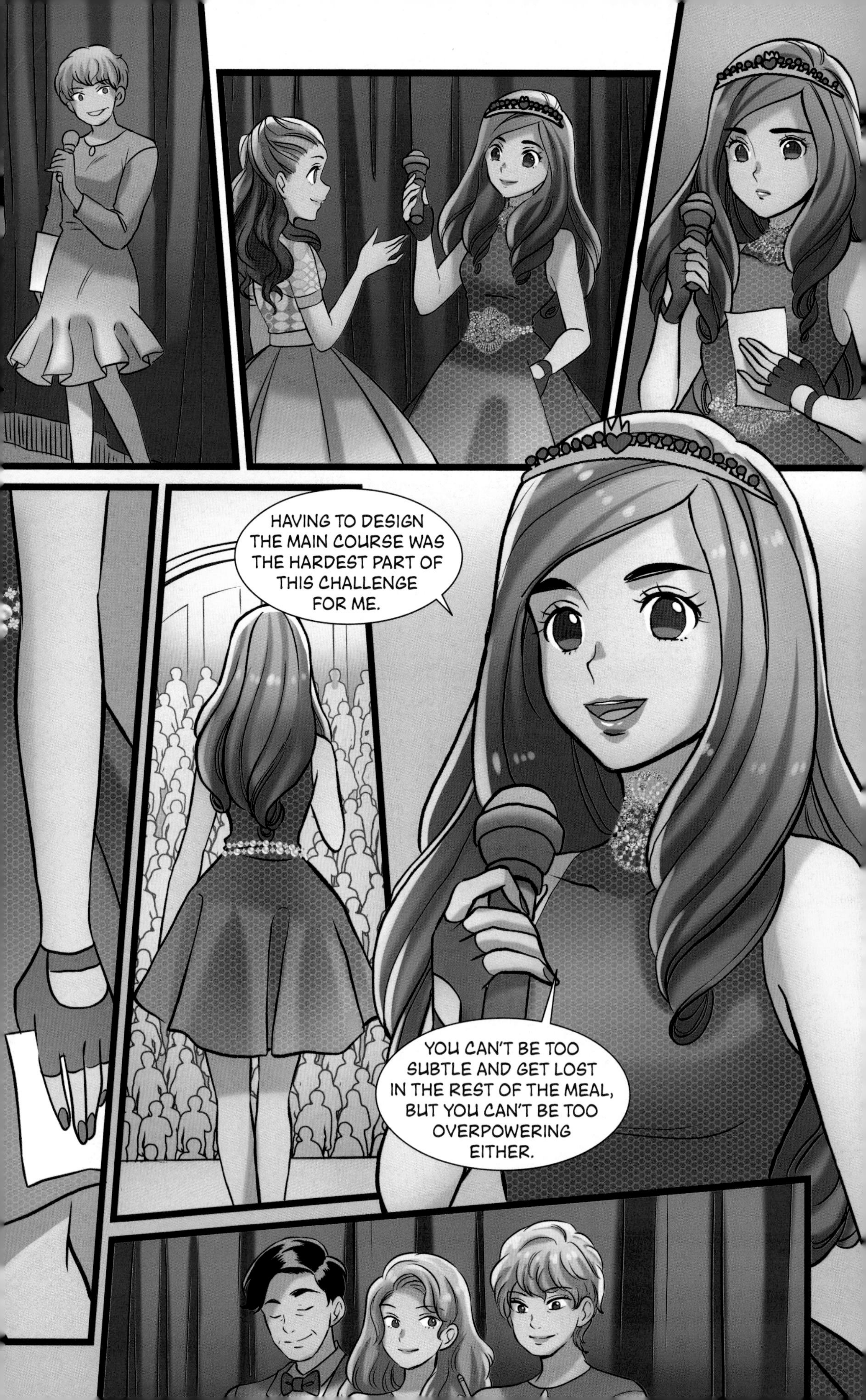
HAVING TO DESIGN THE MAIN COURSE WAS THE HARDEST PART OF THIS CHALLENGE FOR ME.
YOU CAN'T BE TOO SUBTLE AND GET LOST IN THE REST OF THE MEAL, BUT YOU CAN'T BE TOO OVERPOWERING EITHER.

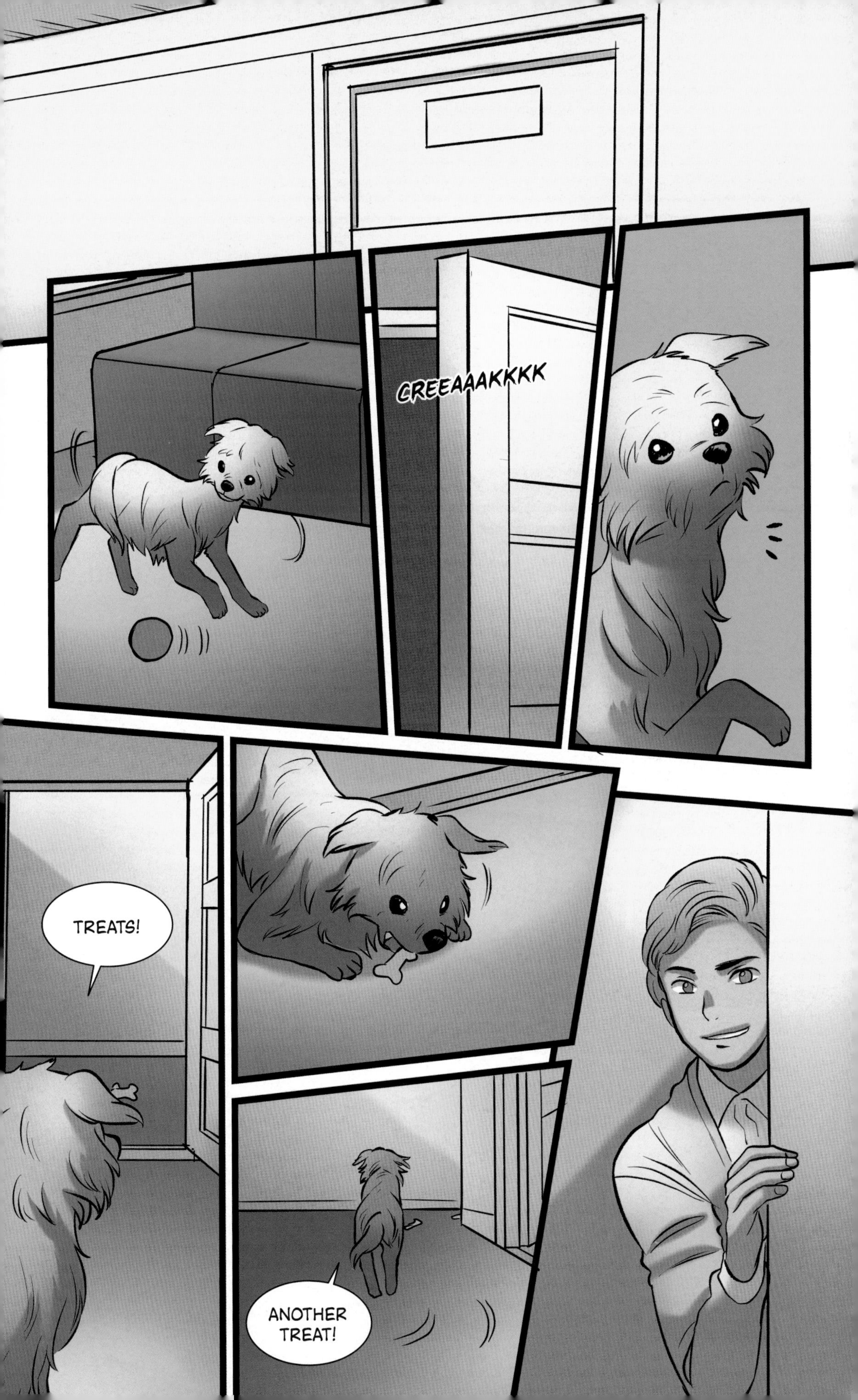
CREEAAAKKKK
TREATS!
ANOTHER TREAT!

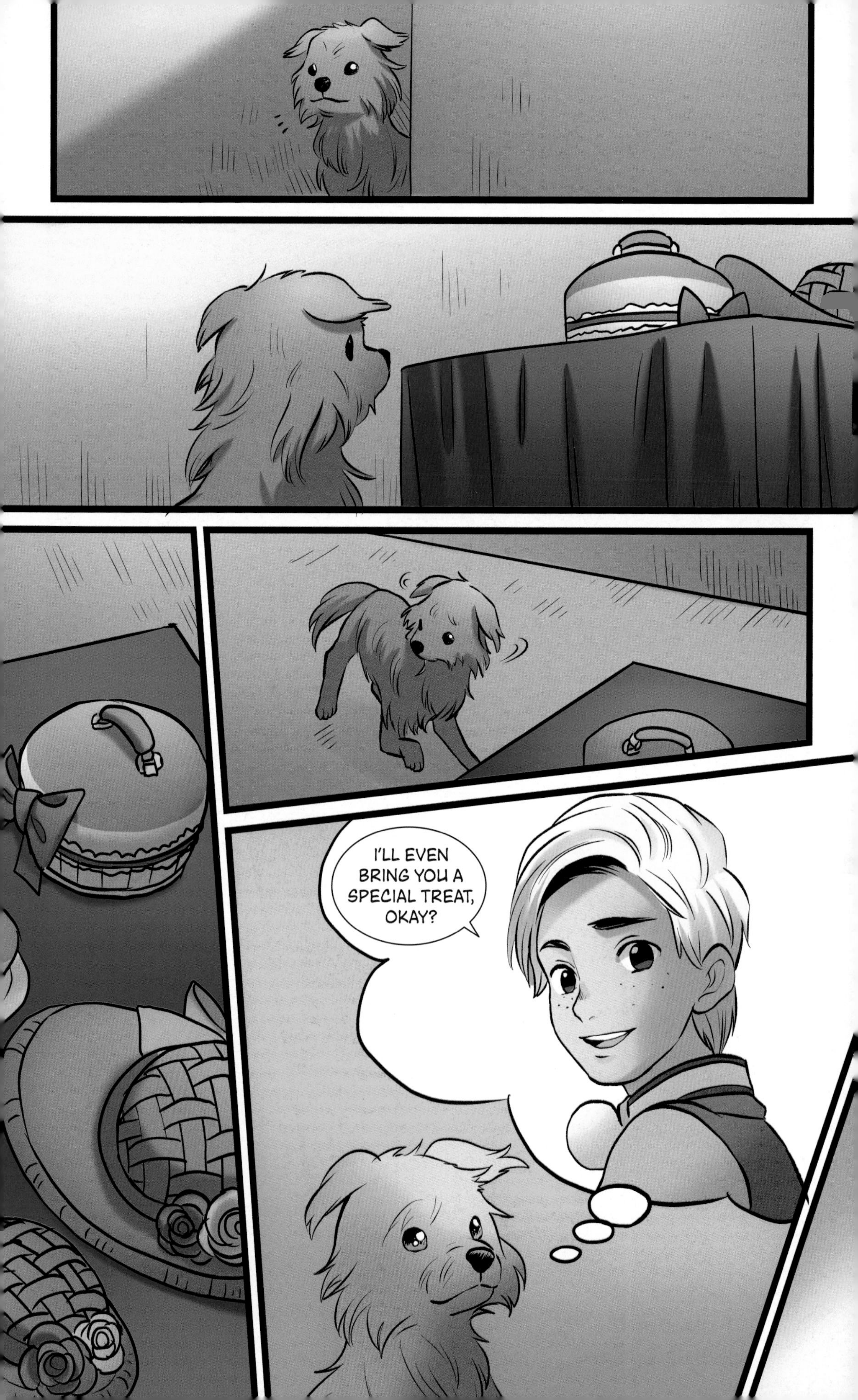
I'LL EVEN BRING YOU A SPECIAL TREAT, OKAY?

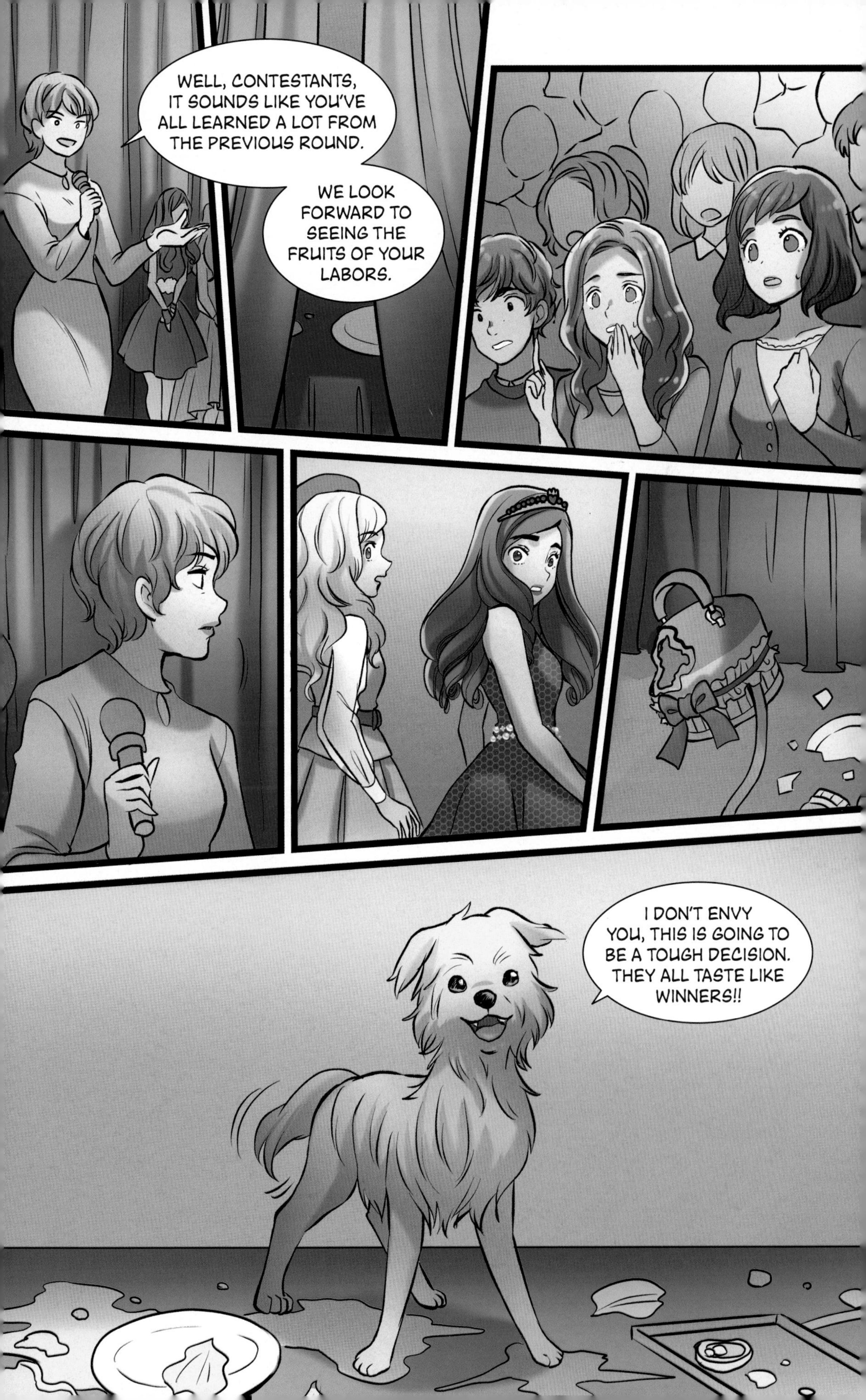
WELL, CONTESTANTS, IT SOUNDS LIKE YOU'VE ALL LEARNED A LOT FROM THE PREVIOUS ROUND.
WE LOOK FORWARD TO SEEING THE FRUITS OF YOUR LABORS.
I DON'T ENVY YOU, THIS IS GOING TO BE A TOUGH DECISION. THEY ALL TASTE LIKE WINNERS!!

EVIE'S WICKED RUNWAY

BOOK 2

THIS... CAN'T BE. AFTER ALL MY HARD WORK, IS THIS HOW IT ENDS?

I WAS SO HAPPY TO GET ACCEPTED INTO THE INTERSCHOLASTIC AURADON FASHION CONTEST, BUT IT'S JUST BEEN ONE DISASTER AFTER THE NEXT.

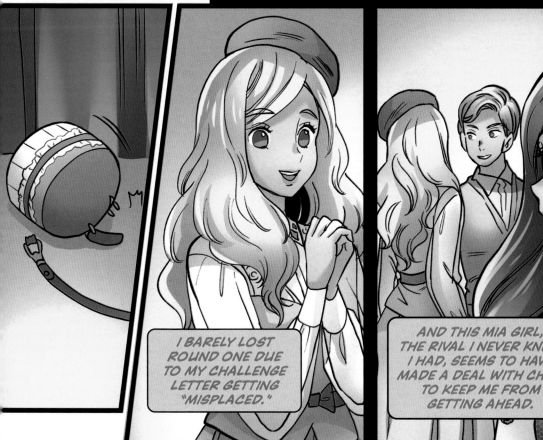

I BARELY LOST ROUND ONE DUE TO MY CHALLENGE LETTER GETTING "MISPLACED."

AND THIS MIA GIRL, THE RIVAL I NEVER KNEW I HAD, SEEMS TO HAVE MADE A DEAL WITH CHAD TO KEEP ME FROM GETTING AHEAD.

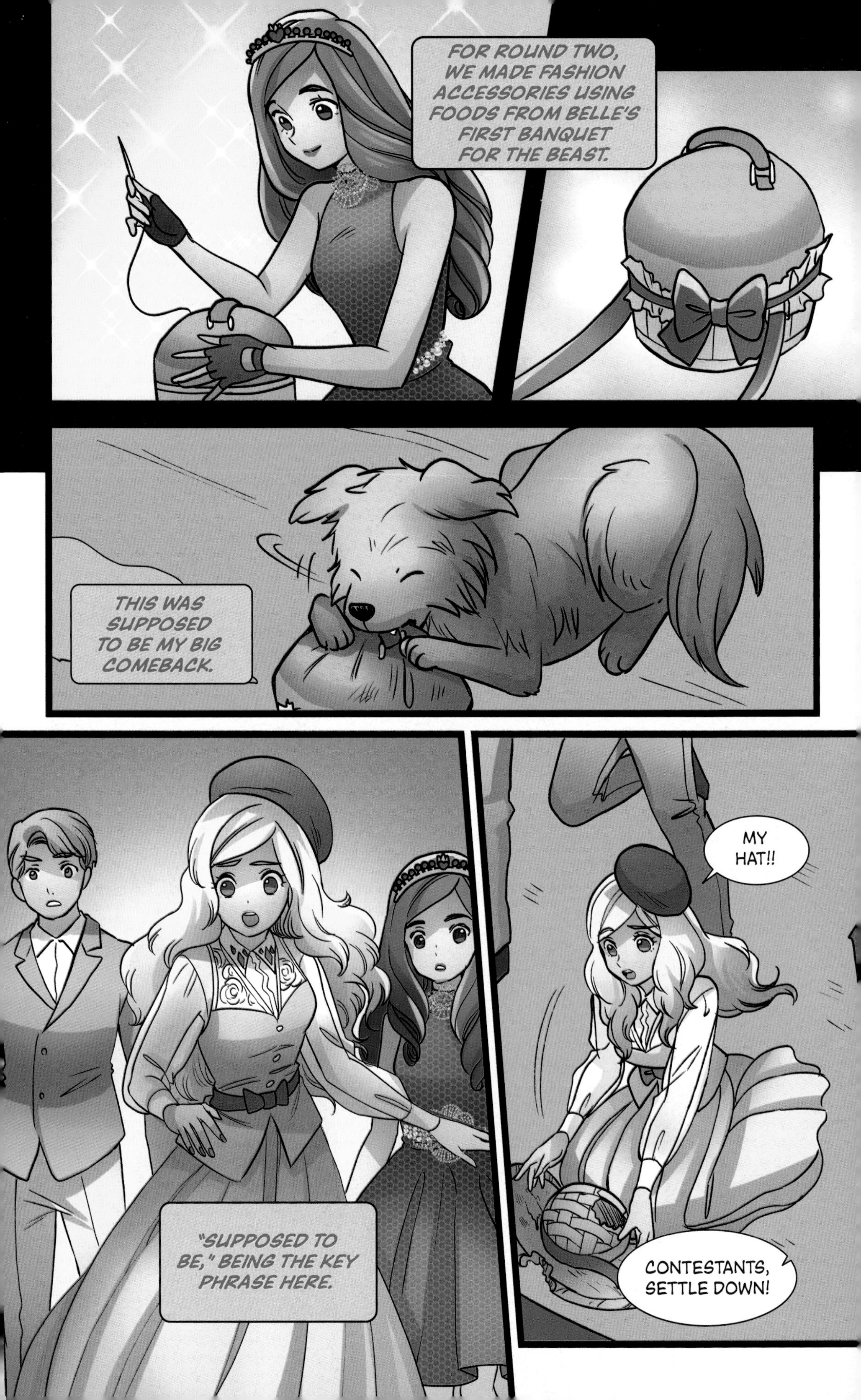
FOR ROUND TWO, WE MADE FASHION ACCESSORIES USING FOODS FROM BELLE'S FIRST BANQUET FOR THE BEAST.
THIS WAS SUPPOSED TO BE MY BIG COMEBACK.
"SUPPOSED TO BE," BEING THE KEY PHRASE HERE.
MY HAT!!
CONTESTANTS, SETTLE DOWN!

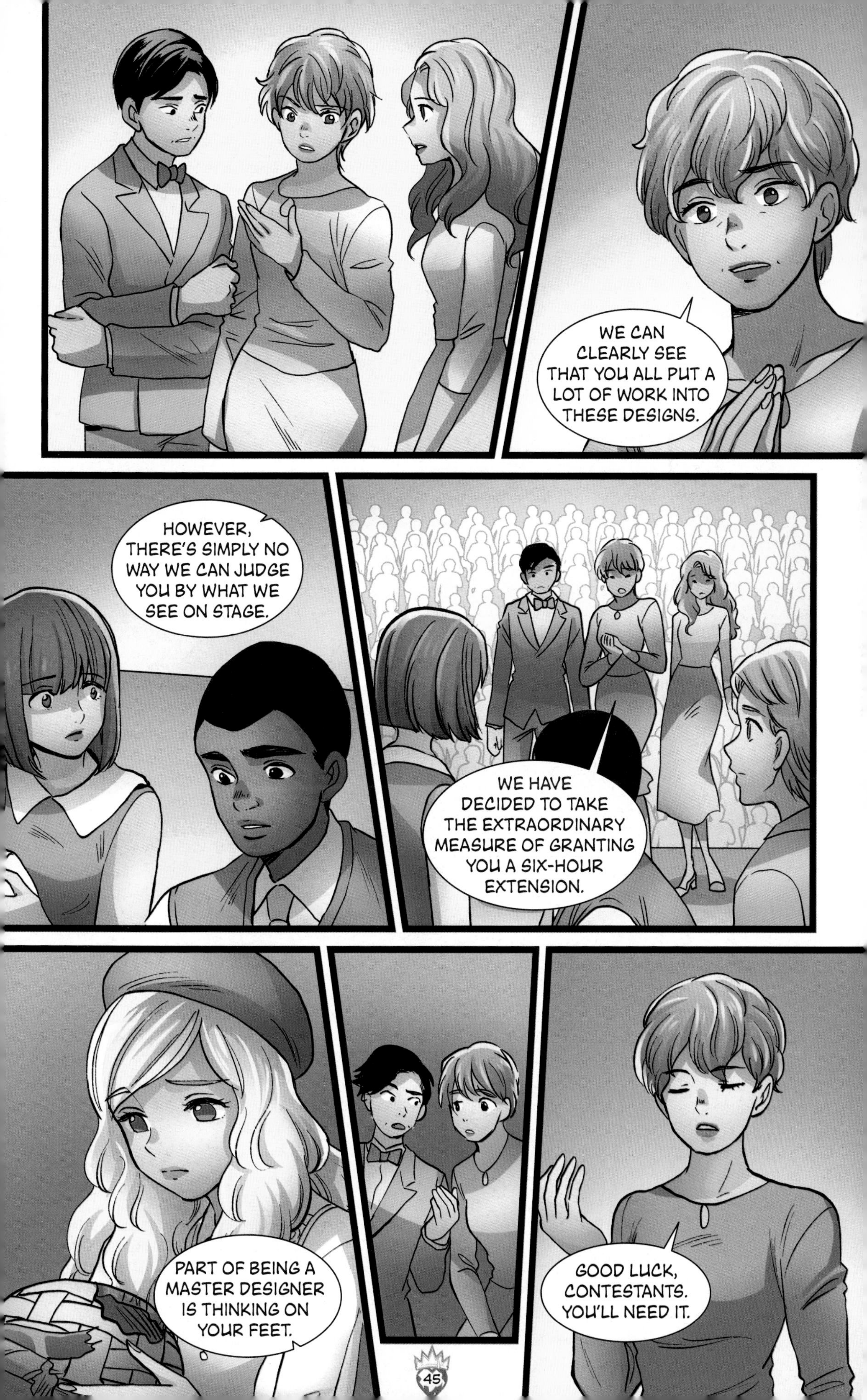
WE CAN CLEARLY SEE THAT YOU ALL PUT A LOT OF WORK INTO THESE DESIGNS.
HOWEVER, THERE'S SIMPLY NO WAY WE CAN JUDGE YOU BY WHAT WE SEE ON STAGE.
WE HAVE DECIDED TO TAKE THE EXTRAORDINARY MEASURE OF GRANTING YOU A SIX-HOUR EXTENSION.
PART OF BEING A MASTER DESIGNER IS THINKING ON YOUR FEET.
GOOD LUCK, CONTESTANTS. YOU'LL NEED IT.

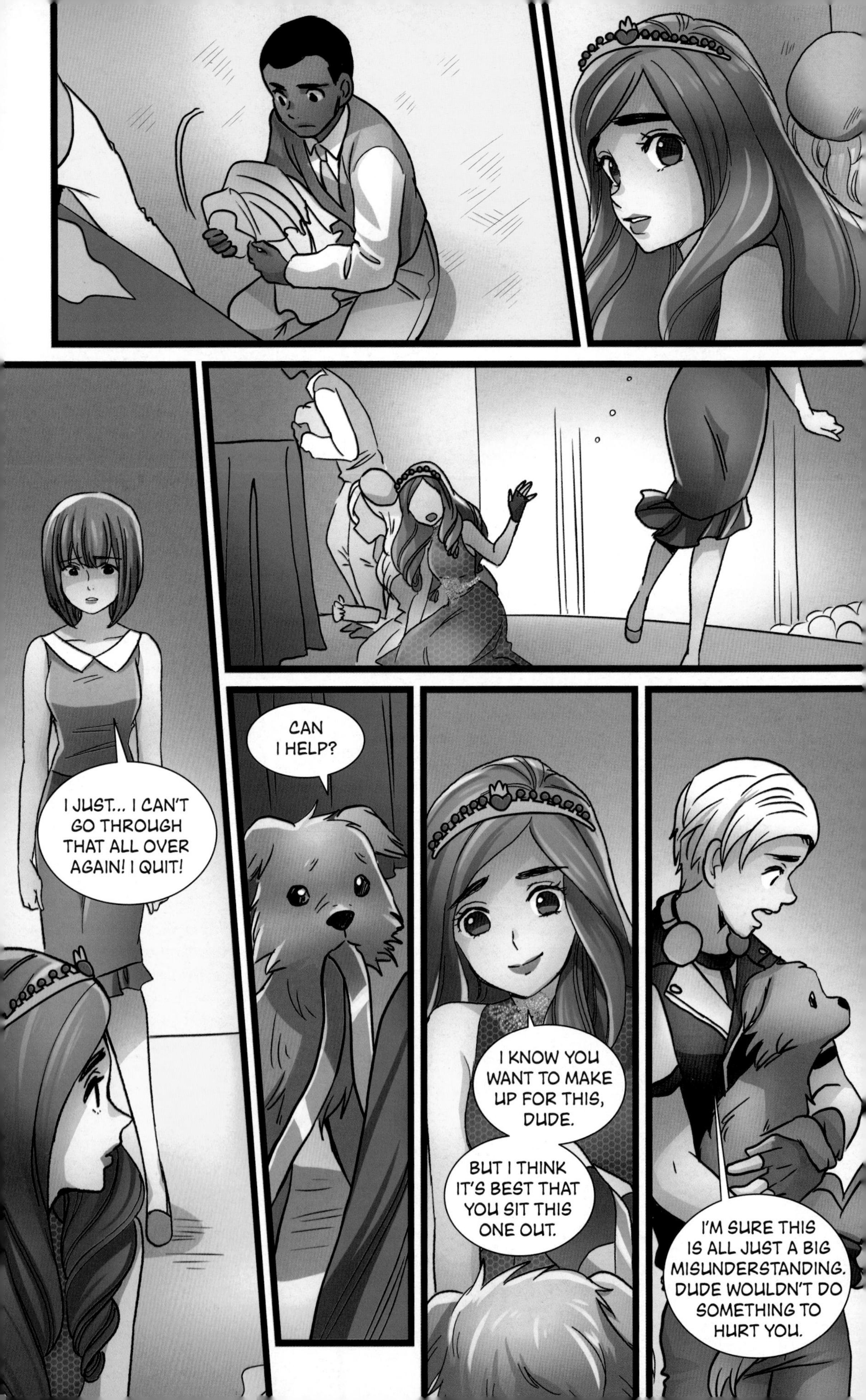
I JUST... I CAN'T GO THROUGH THAT ALL OVER AGAIN! I QUIT!
CAN I HELP?
I KNOW YOU WANT TO MAKE UP FOR THIS, DUDE.
BUT I THINK IT'S BEST THAT YOU SIT THIS ONE OUT.
I'M SURE THIS IS ALL JUST A BIG MISUNDERSTANDING. DUDE WOULDN'T DO SOMETHING TO HURT YOU.

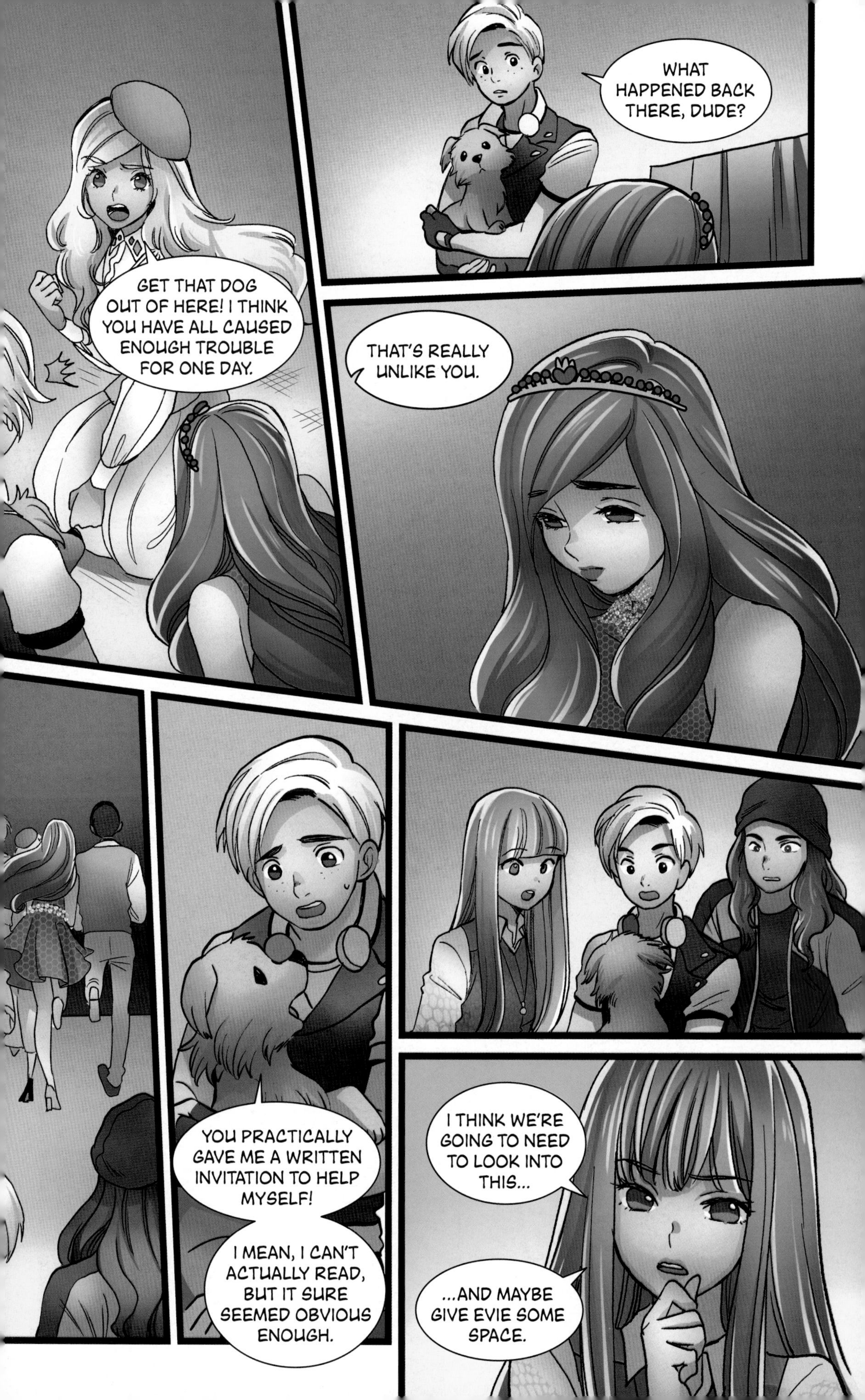
GET THAT DOG OUT OF HERE! I THINK YOU HAVE ALL CAUSED ENOUGH TROUBLE FOR ONE DAY.
WHAT HAPPENED BACK THERE, DUDE?
THAT'S REALLY UNLIKE YOU.
YOU PRACTICALLY GAVE ME A WRITTEN INVITATION TO HELP MYSELF!
I MEAN, I CAN'T ACTUALLY READ, BUT IT SURE SEEMED OBVIOUS ENOUGH.
I THINK WE'RE GOING TO NEED TO LOOK INTO THIS...
...AND MAYBE GIVE EVIE SOME SPACE.

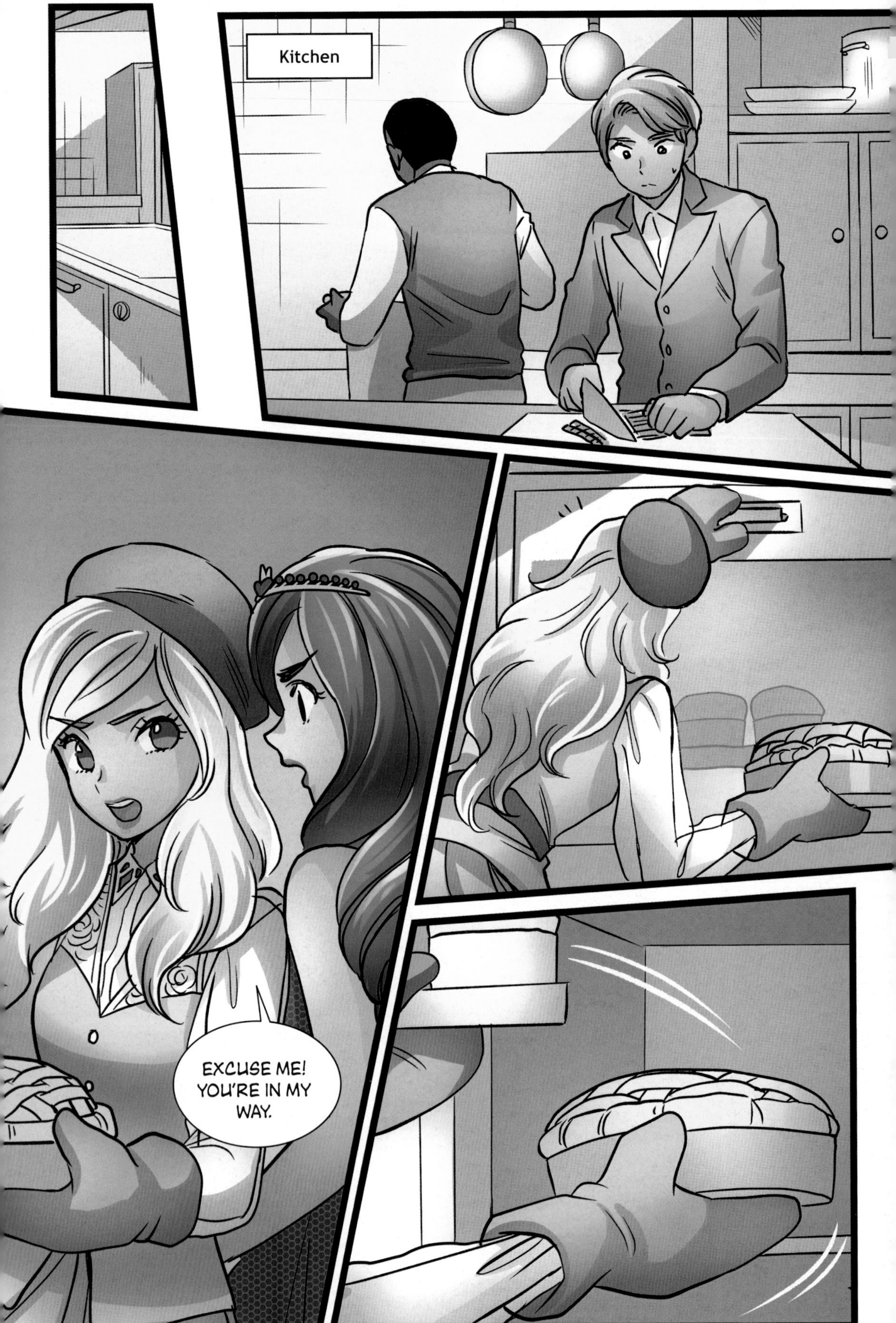
Kitchen
EXCUSE ME! YOU'RE IN MY WAY.

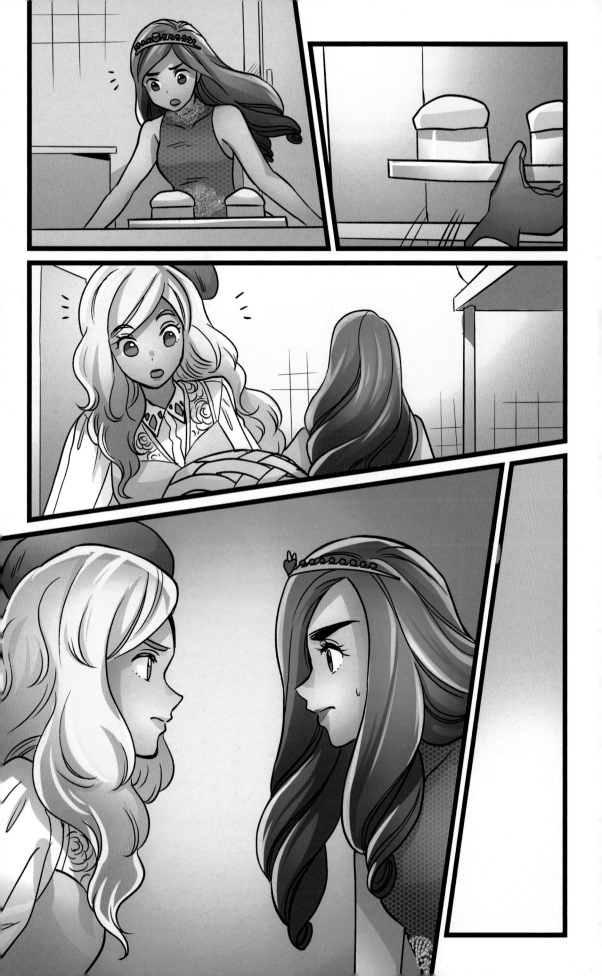

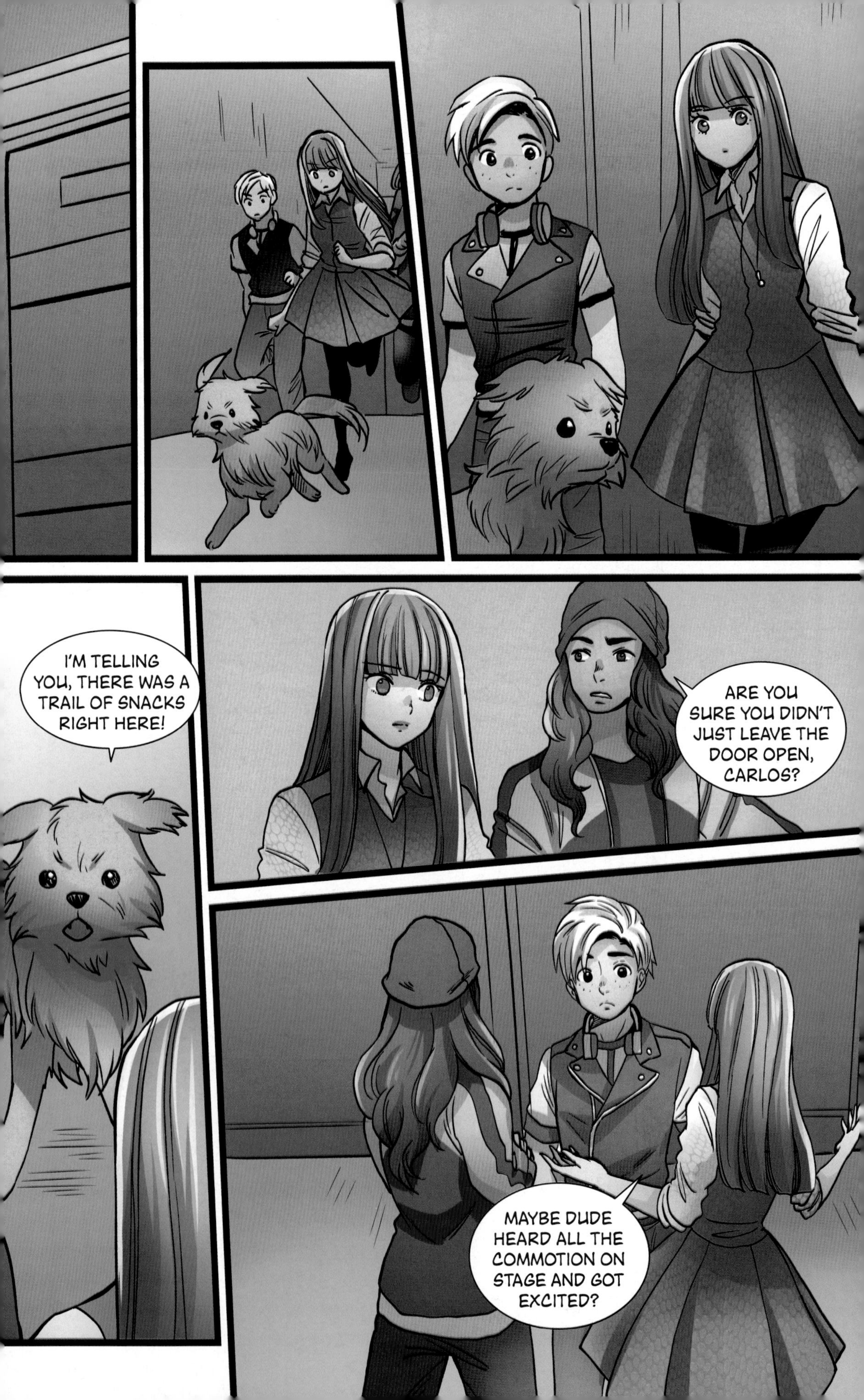
I'M TELLING YOU, THERE WAS A TRAIL OF SNACKS RIGHT HERE!
ARE YOU SURE YOU DIDN'T JUST LEAVE THE DOOR OPEN, CARLOS?
MAYBE DUDE HEARD ALL THE COMMOTION ON STAGE AND GOT EXCITED?

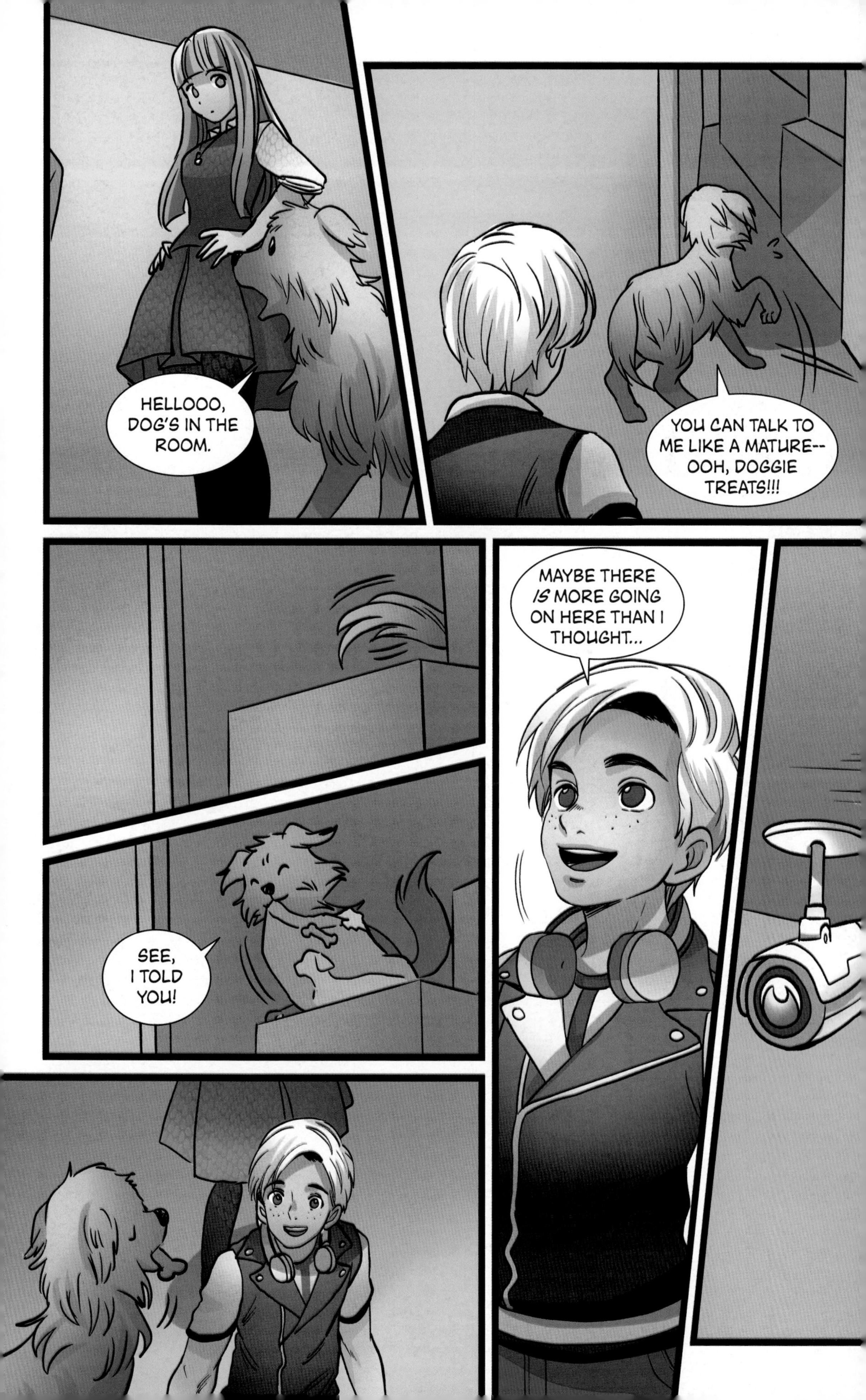
HELLOOO, DOG'S IN THE ROOM.
YOU CAN TALK TO ME LIKE A MATURE-- OOH, DOGGIE TREATS!!!
SEE, I TOLD YOU!
MAYBE THERE *IS* MORE GOING ON HERE THAN I THOUGHT...

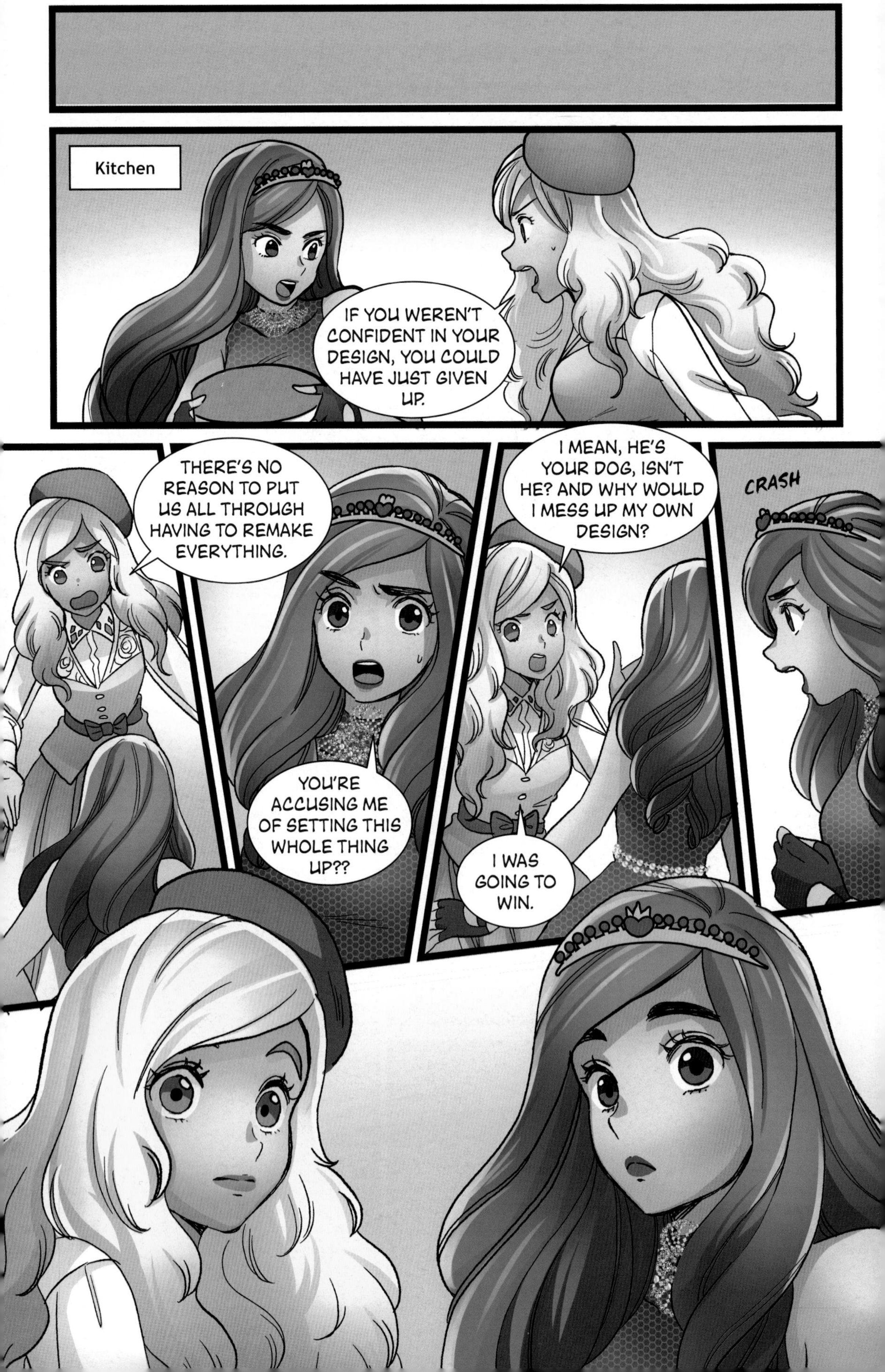
Kitchen
IF YOU WEREN'T CONFIDENT IN YOUR DESIGN, YOU COULD HAVE JUST GIVEN UP.
THERE'S NO REASON TO PUT US ALL THROUGH HAVING TO REMAKE EVERYTHING.
YOU'RE ACCUSING ME OF SETTING THIS WHOLE THING UP??
I MEAN, HE'S YOUR DOG, ISN'T HE? AND WHY WOULD I MESS UP MY OWN DESIGN?
I WAS GOING TO WIN.
CRASH

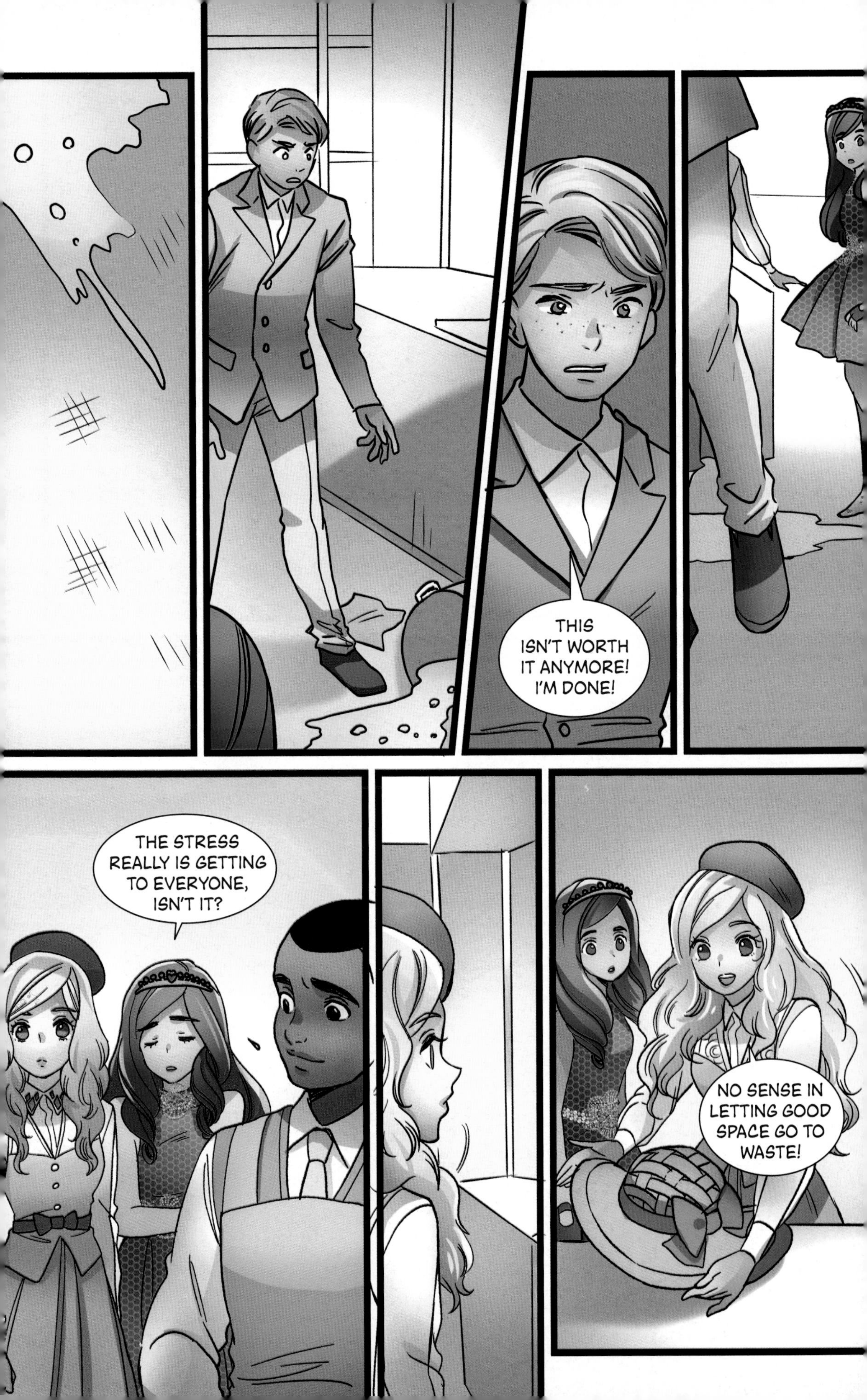
THIS ISN'T WORTH IT ANYMORE! I'M DONE!
THE STRESS REALLY IS GETTING TO EVERYONE, ISN'T IT?
NO SENSE IN LETTING GOOD SPACE GO TO WASTE!

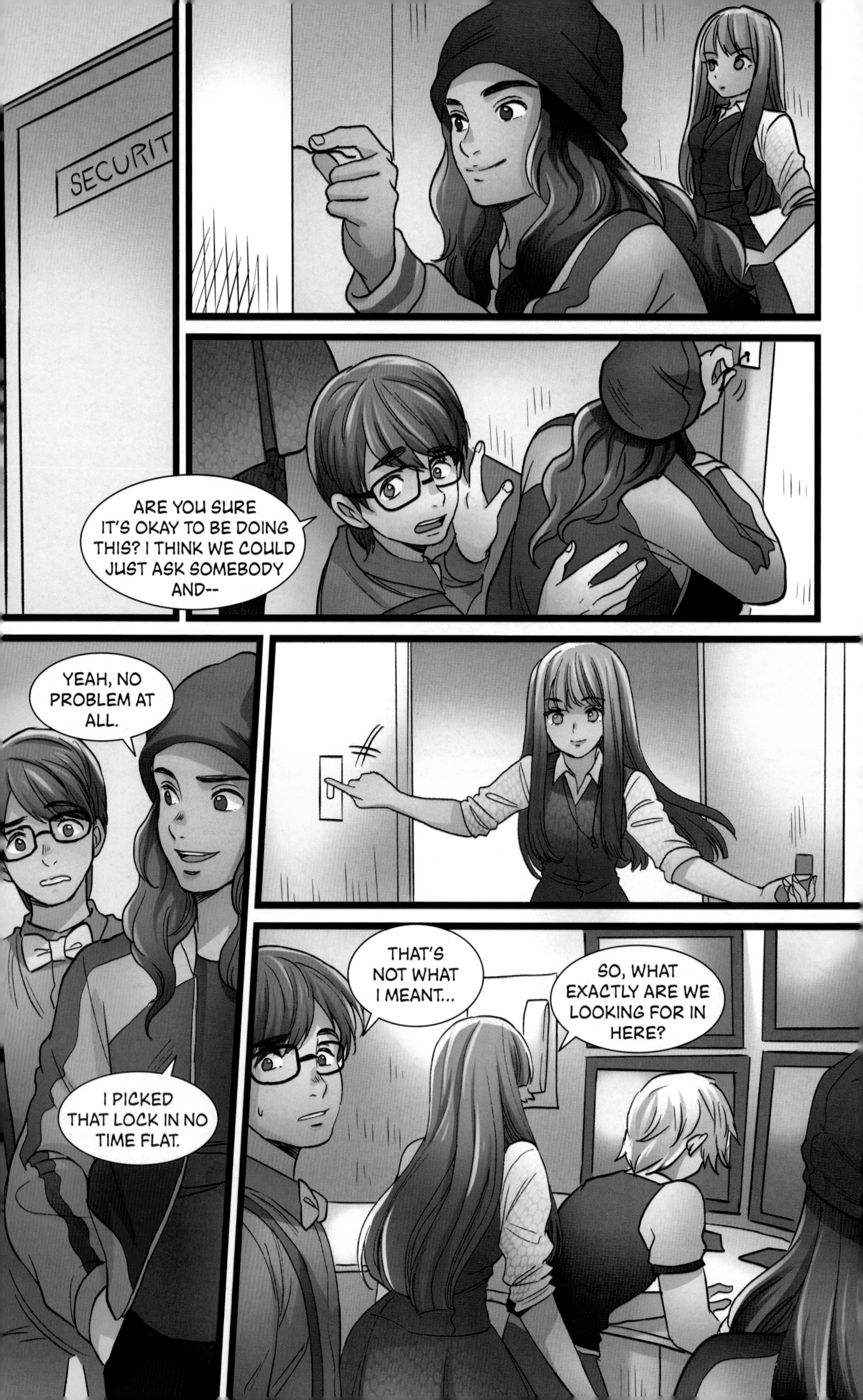
SECURIT
ARE YOU SURE IT'S OKAY TO BE DOING THIS? I THINK WE COULD JUST ASK SOMEBODY AND--
YEAH, NO PROBLEM AT ALL.
I PICKED THAT LOCK IN NO TIME FLAT.
THAT'S NOT WHAT I MEANT...
SO, WHAT EXACTLY ARE WE LOOKING FOR IN HERE?

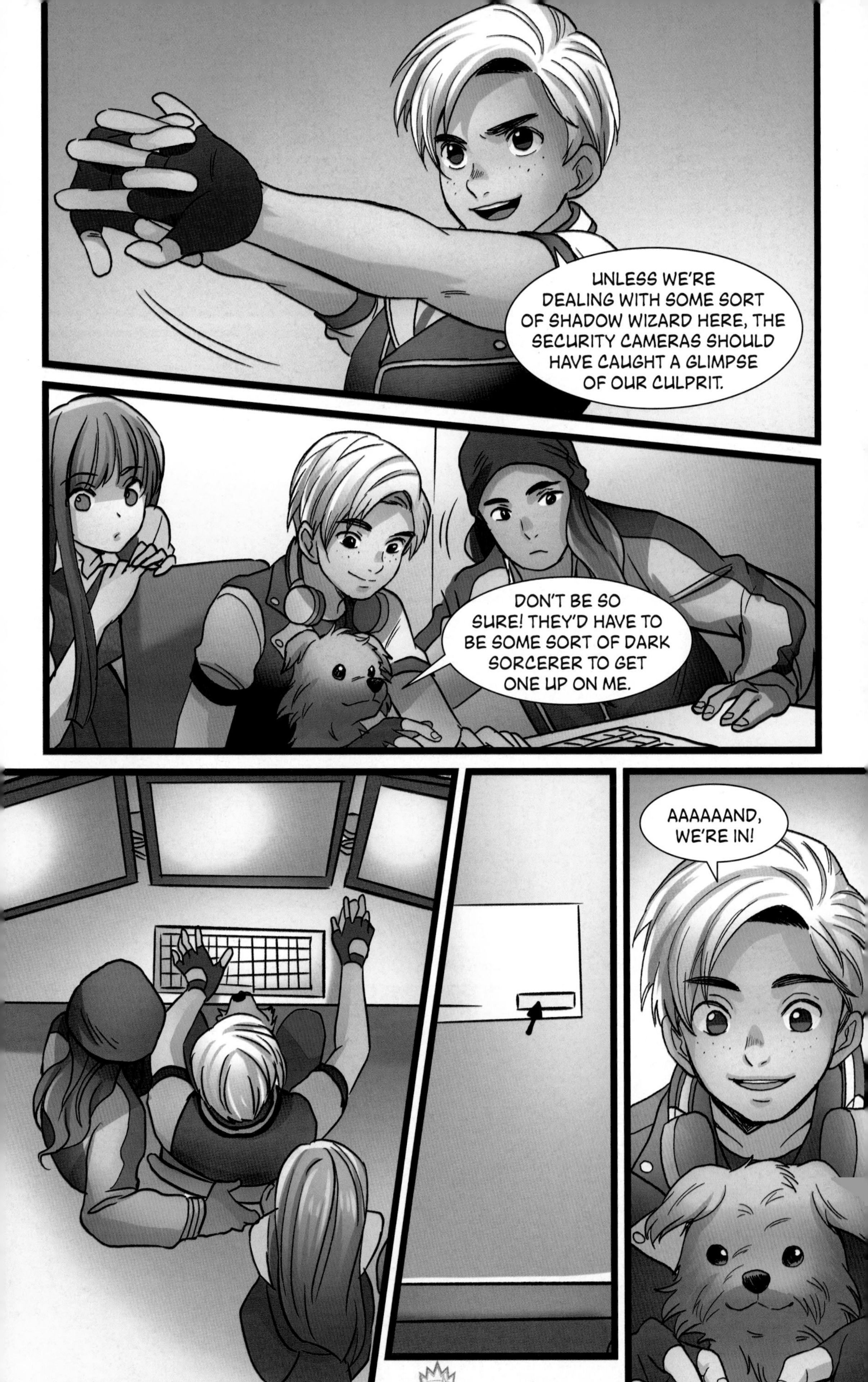
UNLESS WE'RE DEALING WITH SOME SORT OF SHADOW WIZARD HERE, THE SECURITY CAMERAS SHOULD HAVE CAUGHT A GLIMPSE OF OUR CULPRIT.
DON'T BE SO SURE! THEY'D HAVE TO BE SOME SORT OF DARK SORCERER TO GET ONE UP ON ME.
AAAAAAND, WE'RE IN!

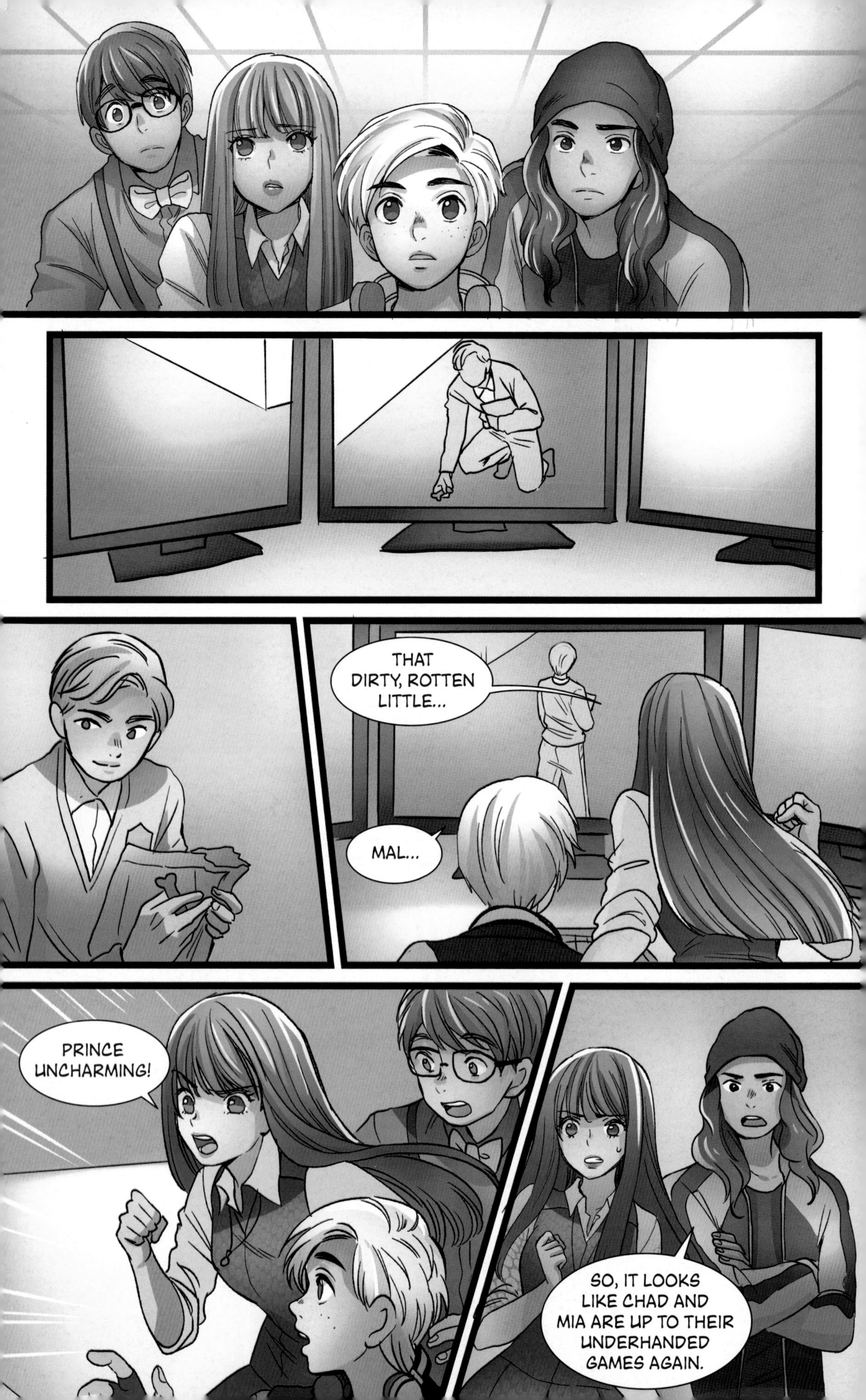
THAT DIRTY, ROTTEN LITTLE...
MAL...
PRINCE UNCHARMING!
SO, IT LOOKS LIKE CHAD AND MIA ARE UP TO THEIR UNDERHANDED GAMES AGAIN.

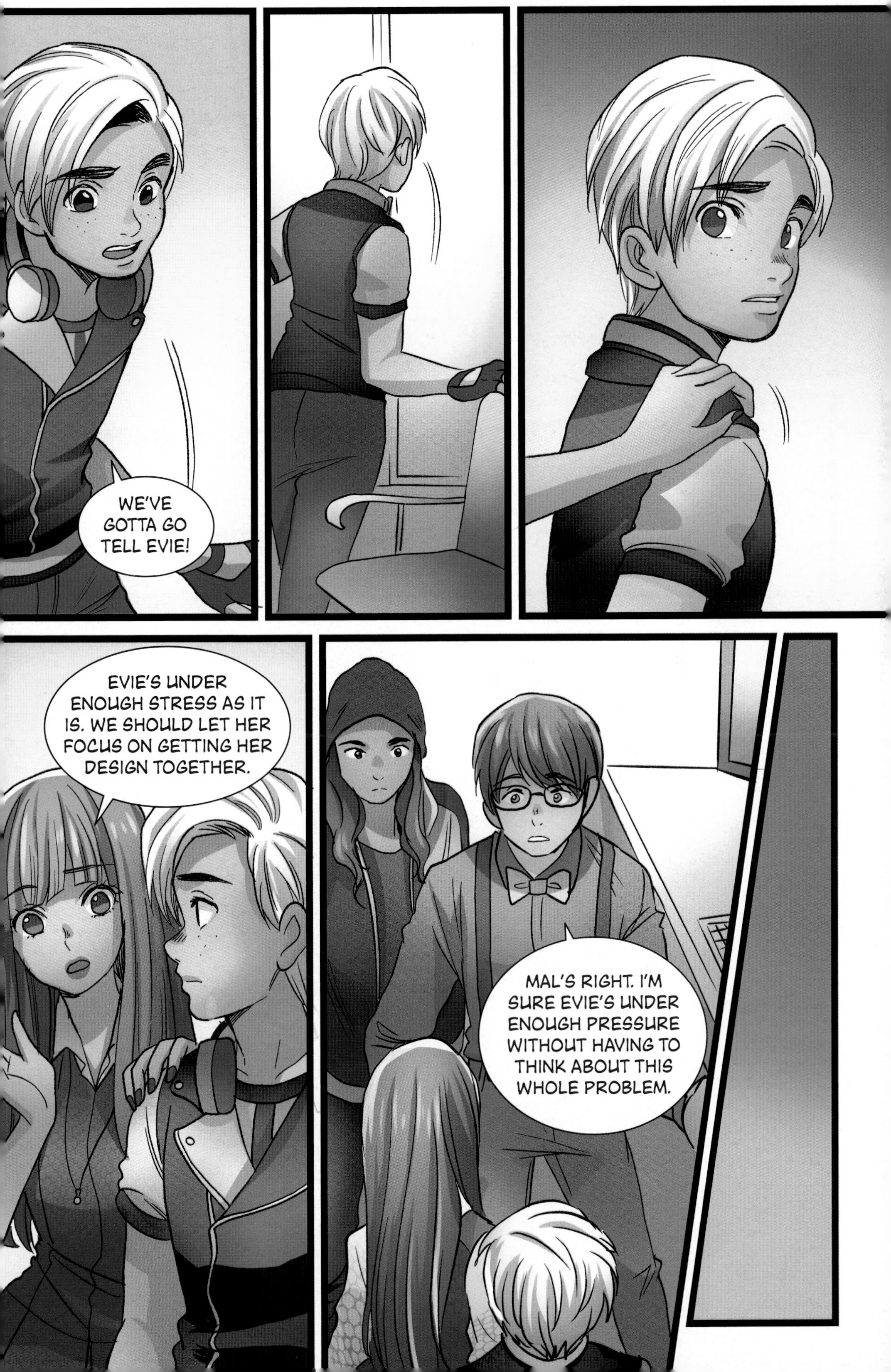
WE'VE GOTTA GO TELL EVIE!
EVIE'S UNDER ENOUGH STRESS AS IT IS. WE SHOULD LET HER FOCUS ON GETTING HER DESIGN TOGETHER.
MAL'S RIGHT. I'M SURE EVIE'S UNDER ENOUGH PRESSURE WITHOUT HAVING TO THINK ABOUT THIS WHOLE PROBLEM.

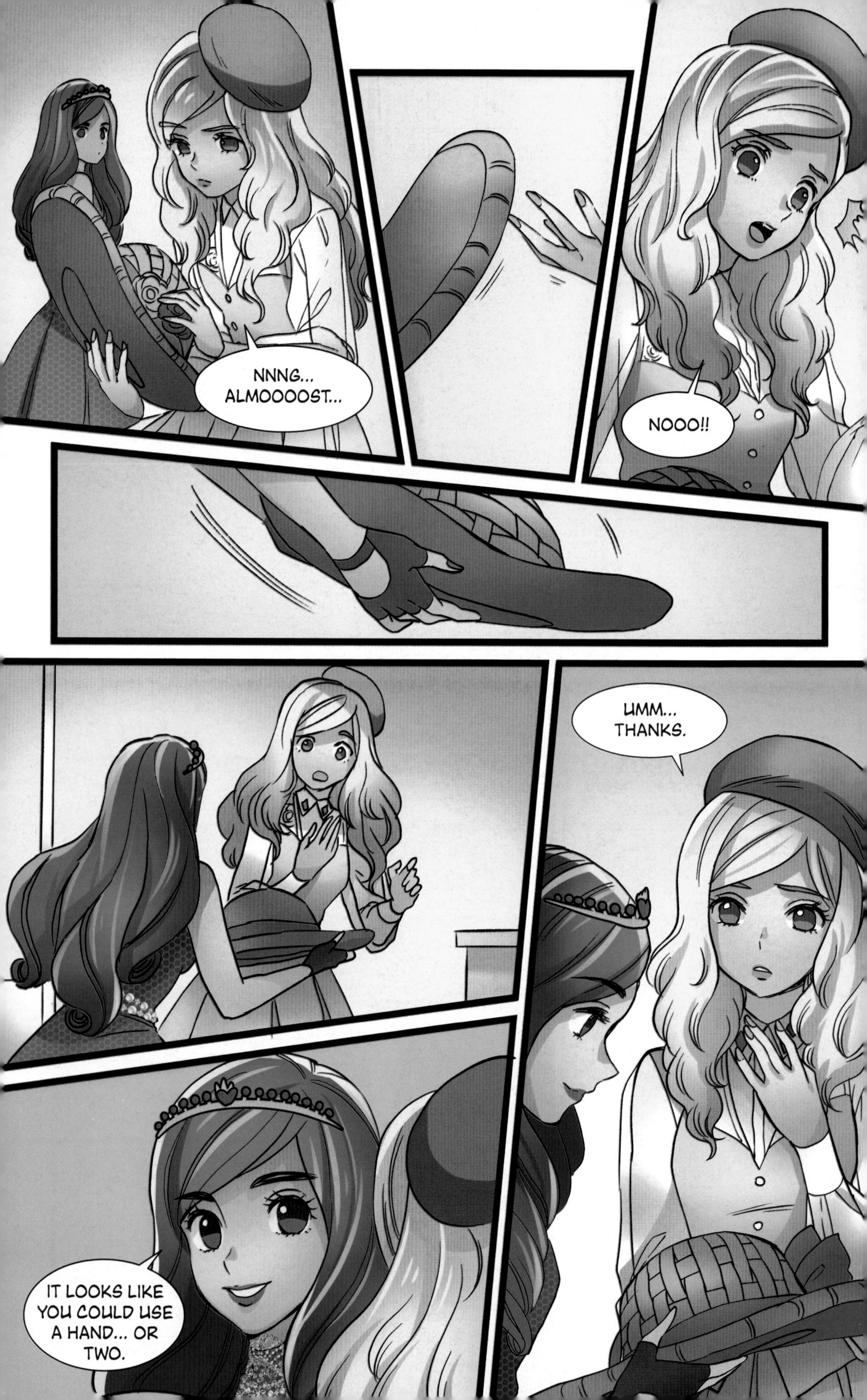
NNNG... ALMOOOOST...
NOOO!!
UMM... THANKS.
IT LOOKS LIKE YOU COULD USE A HAND... OR TWO.

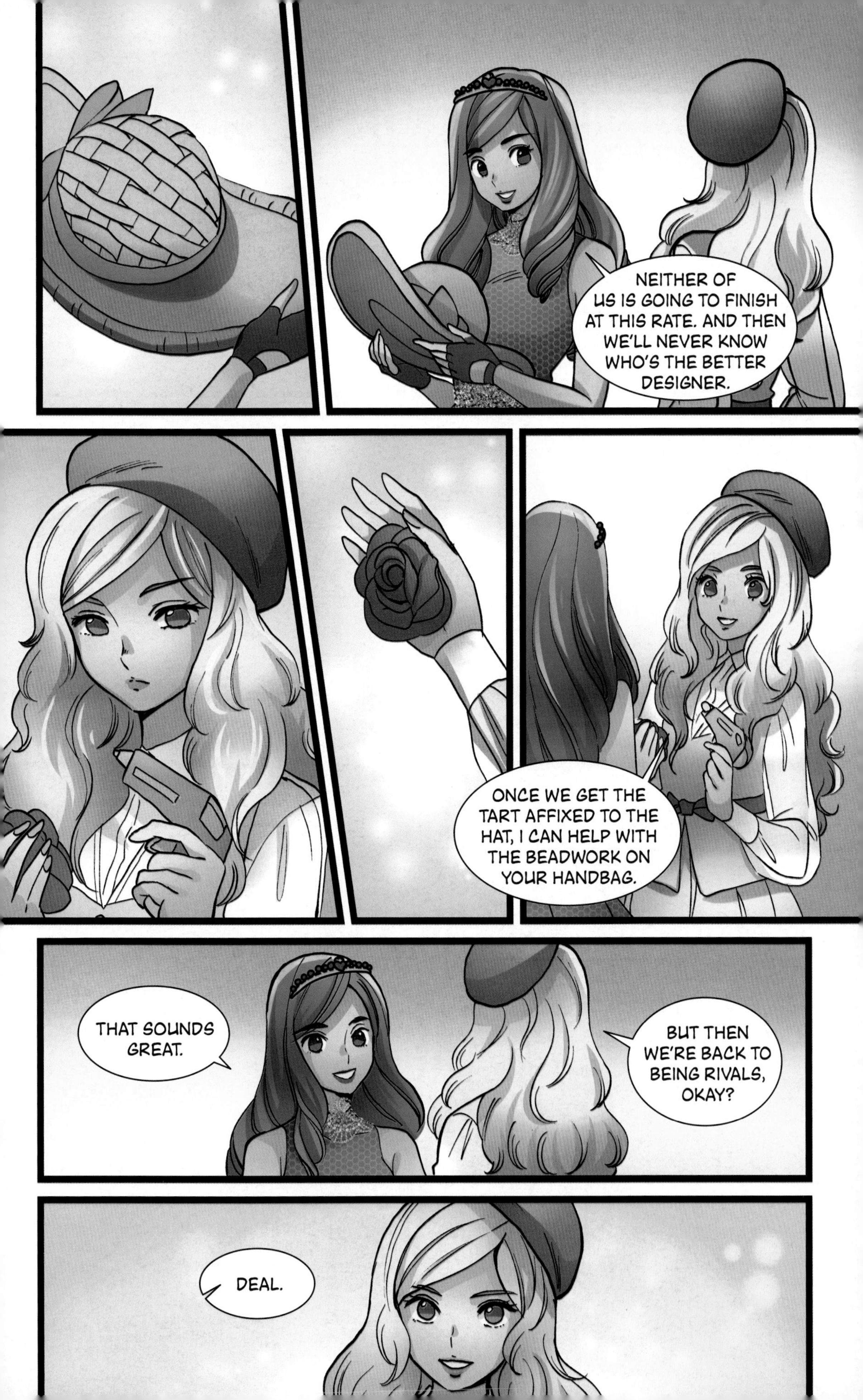
NEITHER OF US IS GOING TO FINISH AT THIS RATE. AND THEN WE'LL NEVER KNOW WHO'S THE BETTER DESIGNER.
ONCE WE GET THE TART AFFIXED TO THE HAT, I CAN HELP WITH THE BEADWORK ON YOUR HANDBAG.
THAT SOUNDS GREAT.
BUT THEN WE'RE BACK TO BEING RIVALS, OKAY?
DEAL.

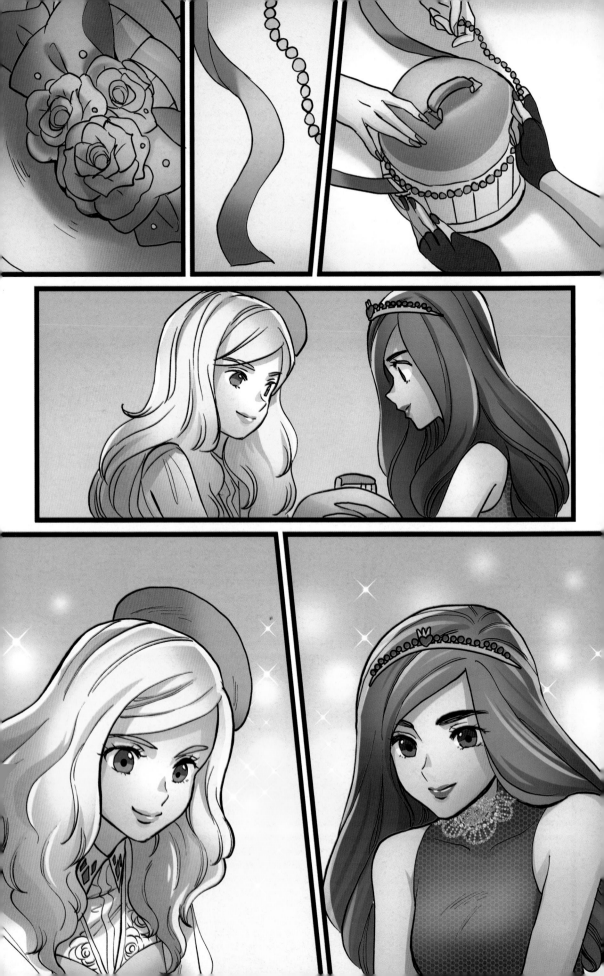

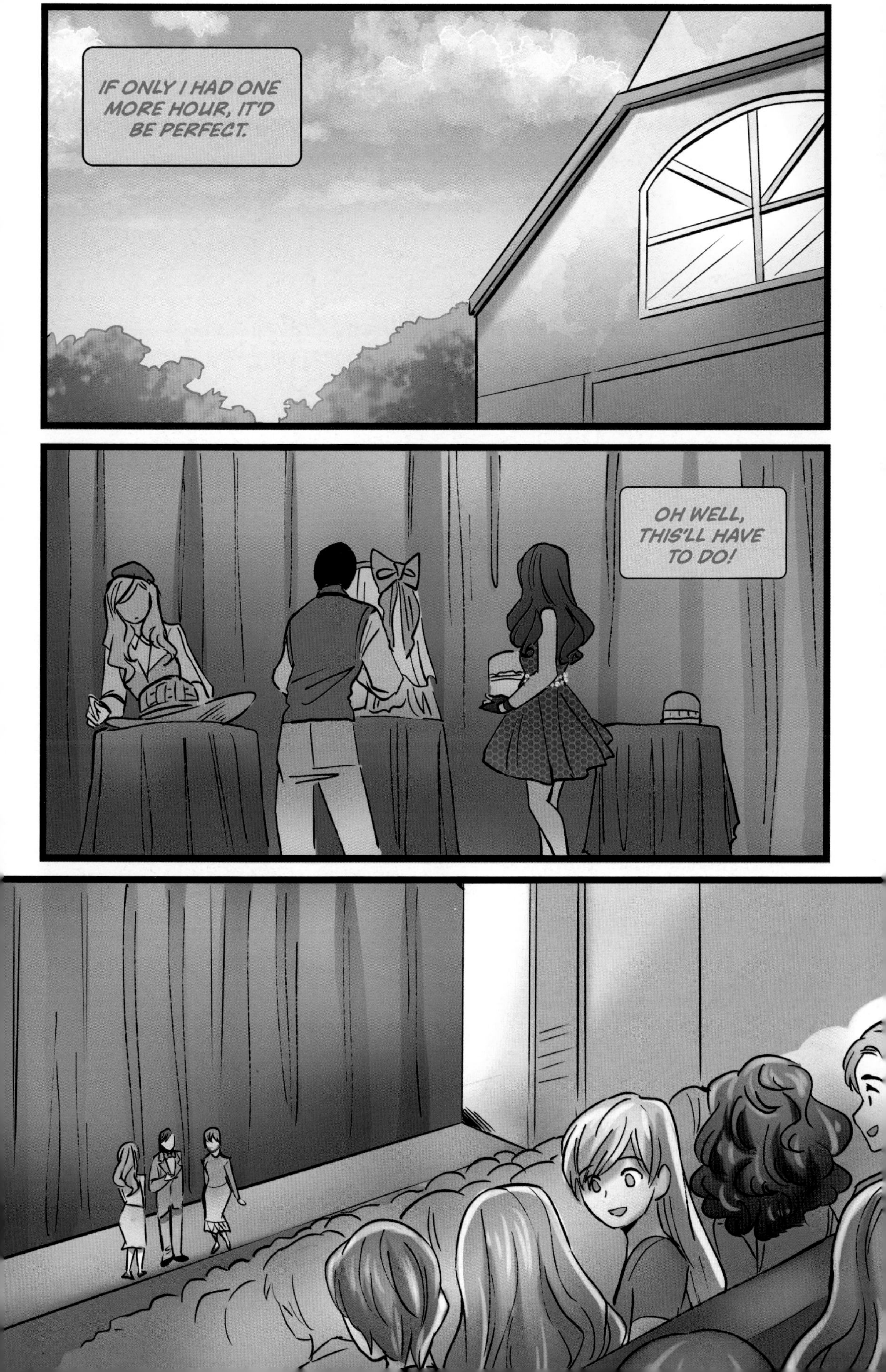
IF ONLY I HAD ONE MORE HOUR, IT'D BE PERFECT.
OH WELL, THIS'LL HAVE TO DO!

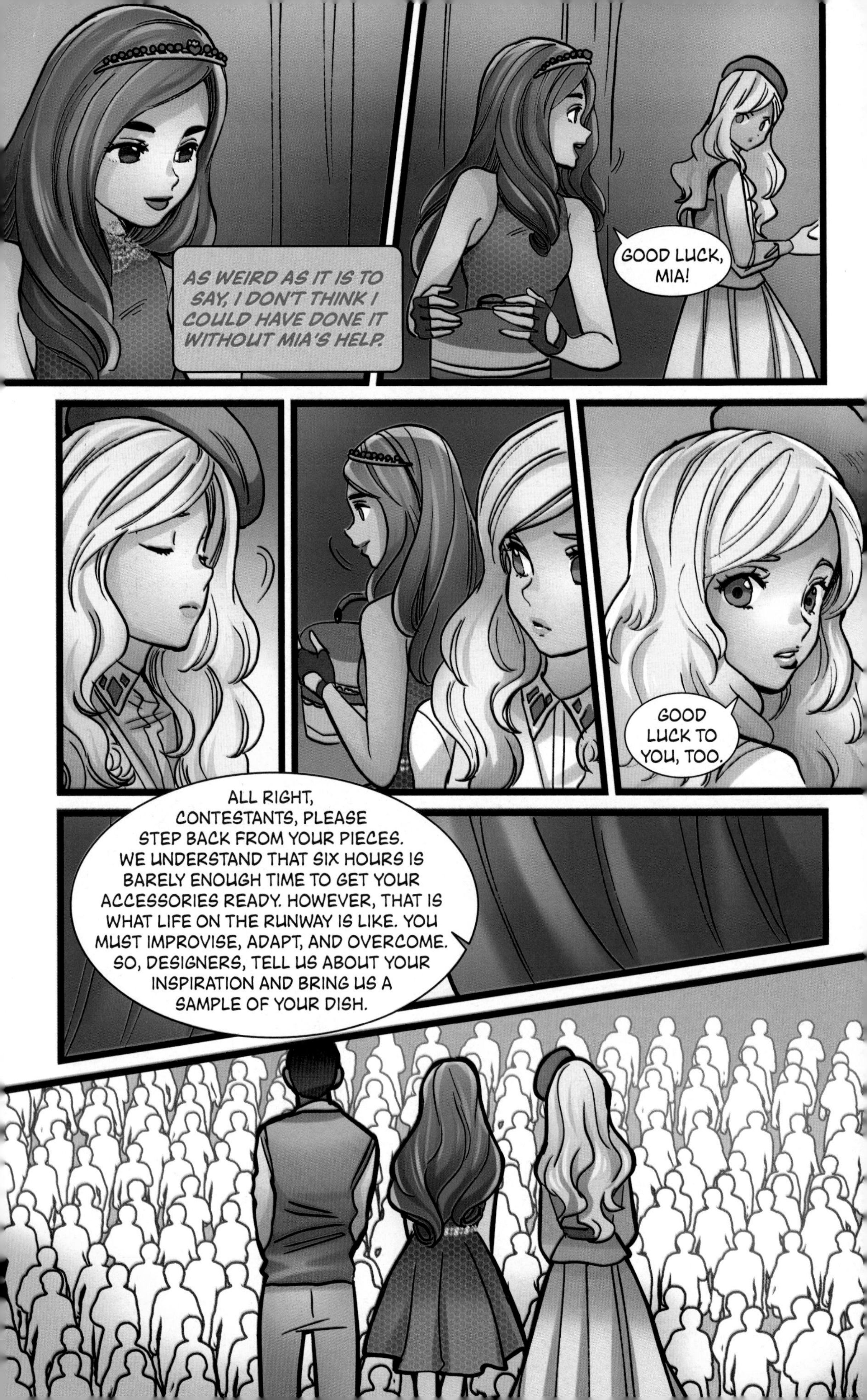
AS WEIRD AS IT IS TO SAY, I DON'T THINK I COULD HAVE DONE IT WITHOUT MIA'S HELP.
GOOD LUCK, MIA!
GOOD LUCK TO YOU, TOO.
ALL RIGHT, CONTESTANTS, PLEASE STEP BACK FROM YOUR PIECES. WE UNDERSTAND THAT SIX HOURS IS BARELY ENOUGH TIME TO GET YOUR ACCESSORIES READY. HOWEVER, THAT IS WHAT LIFE ON THE RUNWAY IS LIKE. YOU MUST IMPROVISE, ADAPT, AND OVERCOME. SO, DESIGNERS, TELL US ABOUT YOUR INSPIRATION AND BRING US A SAMPLE OF YOUR DISH.

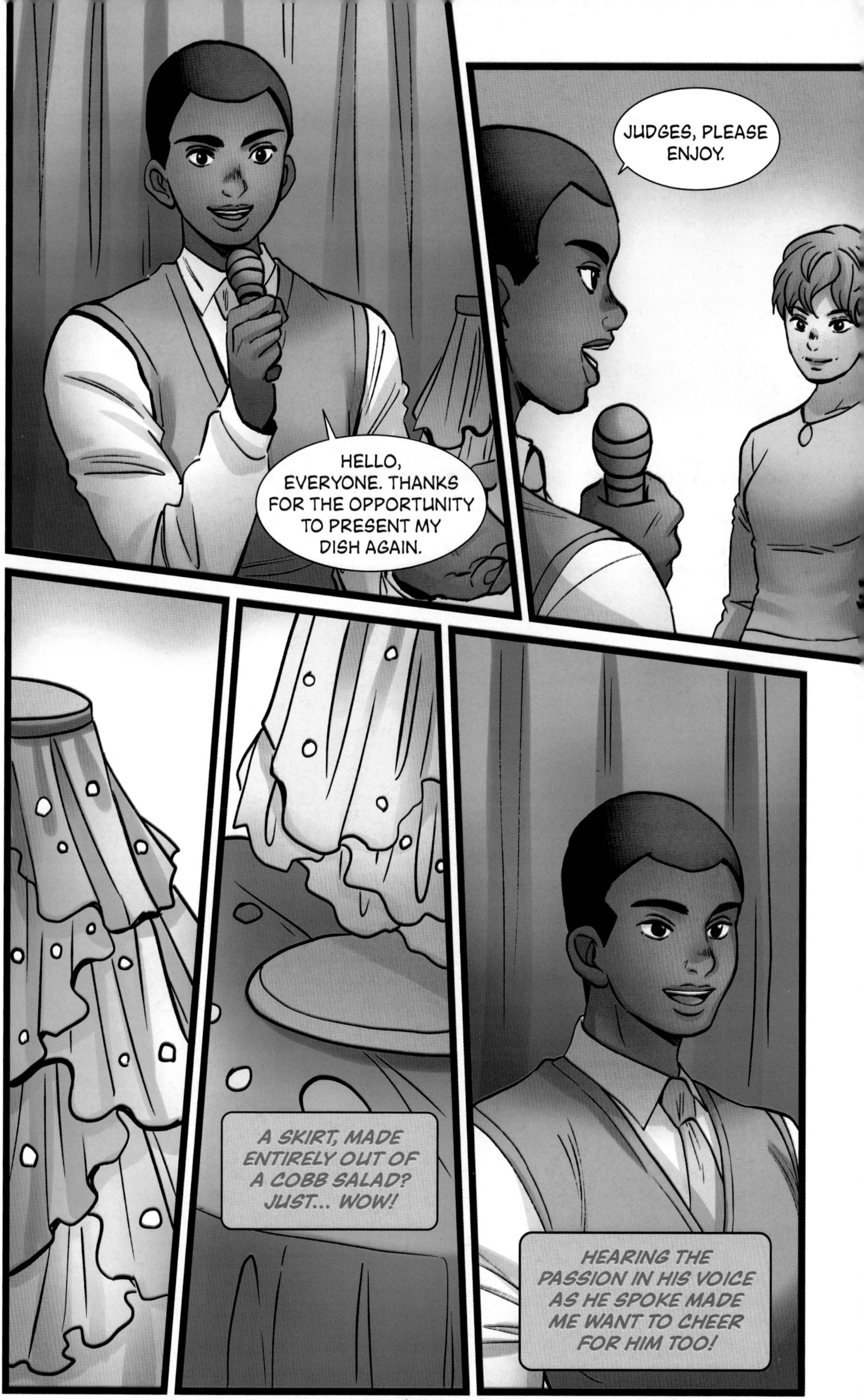
HELLO, EVERYONE. THANKS FOR THE OPPORTUNITY TO PRESENT MY DISH AGAIN.
JUDGES, PLEASE ENJOY.
A SKIRT, MADE ENTIRELY OUT OF A COBB SALAD? JUST... WOW!
HEARING THE PASSION IN HIS VOICE AS HE SPOKE MADE ME WANT TO CHEER FOR HIM TOO!

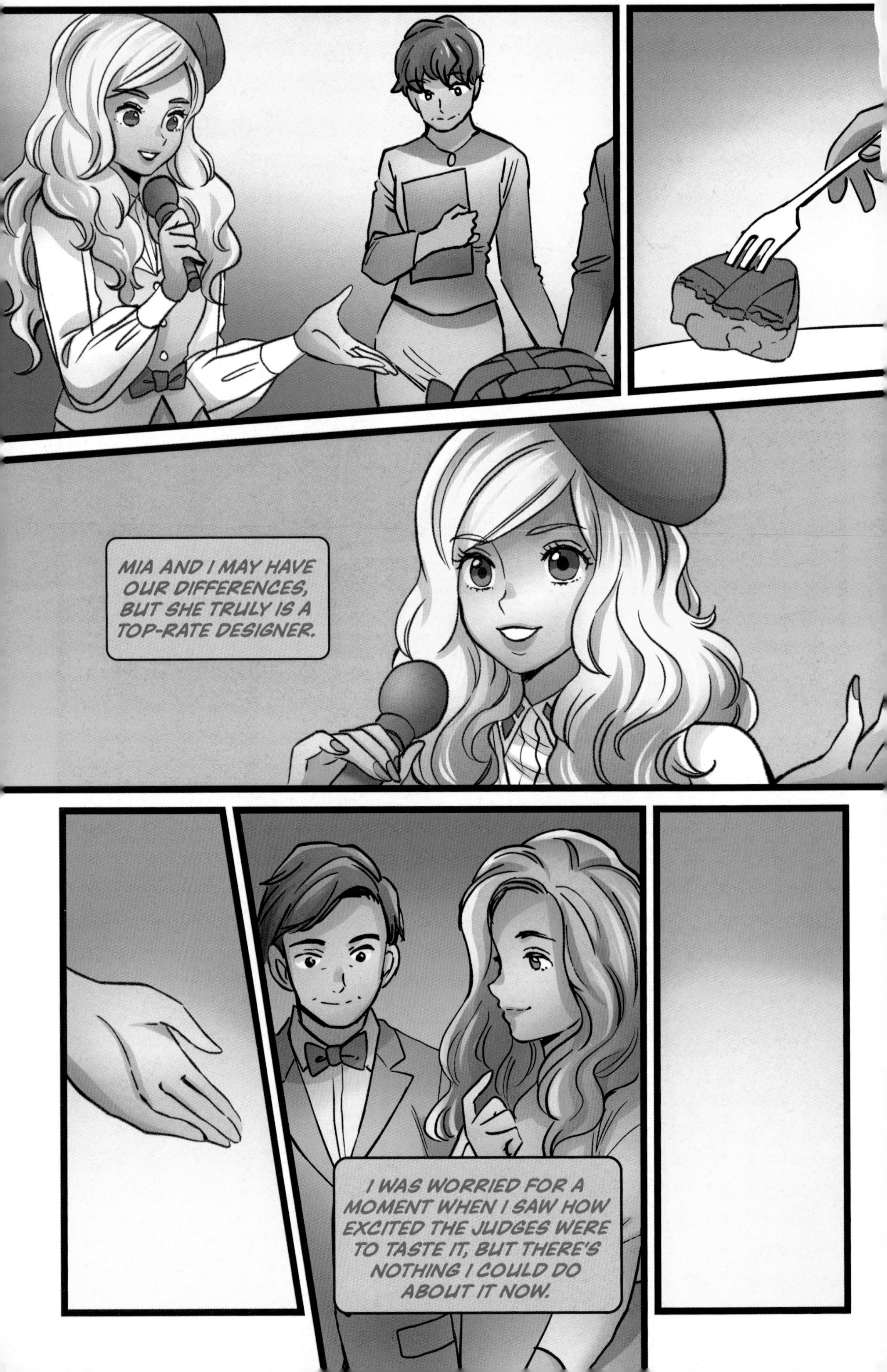
MIA AND I MAY HAVE OUR DIFFERENCES, BUT SHE TRULY IS A TOP-RATE DESIGNER.
I WAS WORRIED FOR A MOMENT WHEN I SAW HOW EXCITED THE JUDGES WERE TO TASTE IT, BUT THERE'S NOTHING I COULD DO ABOUT IT NOW.

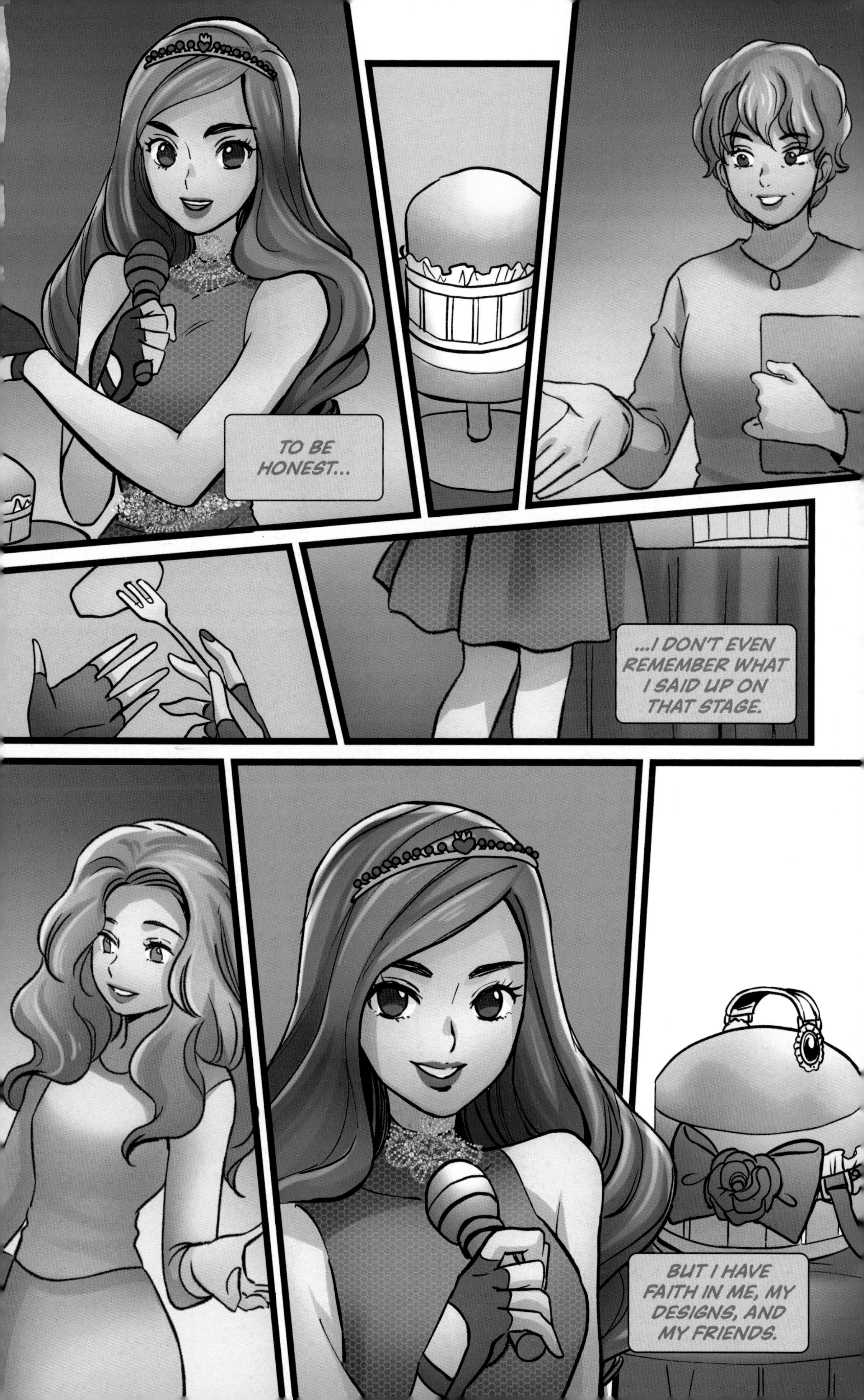
TO BE HONEST...
...I DON'T EVEN REMEMBER WHAT I SAID UP ON THAT STAGE.
BUT I HAVE FAITH IN ME, MY DESIGNS, AND MY FRIENDS.

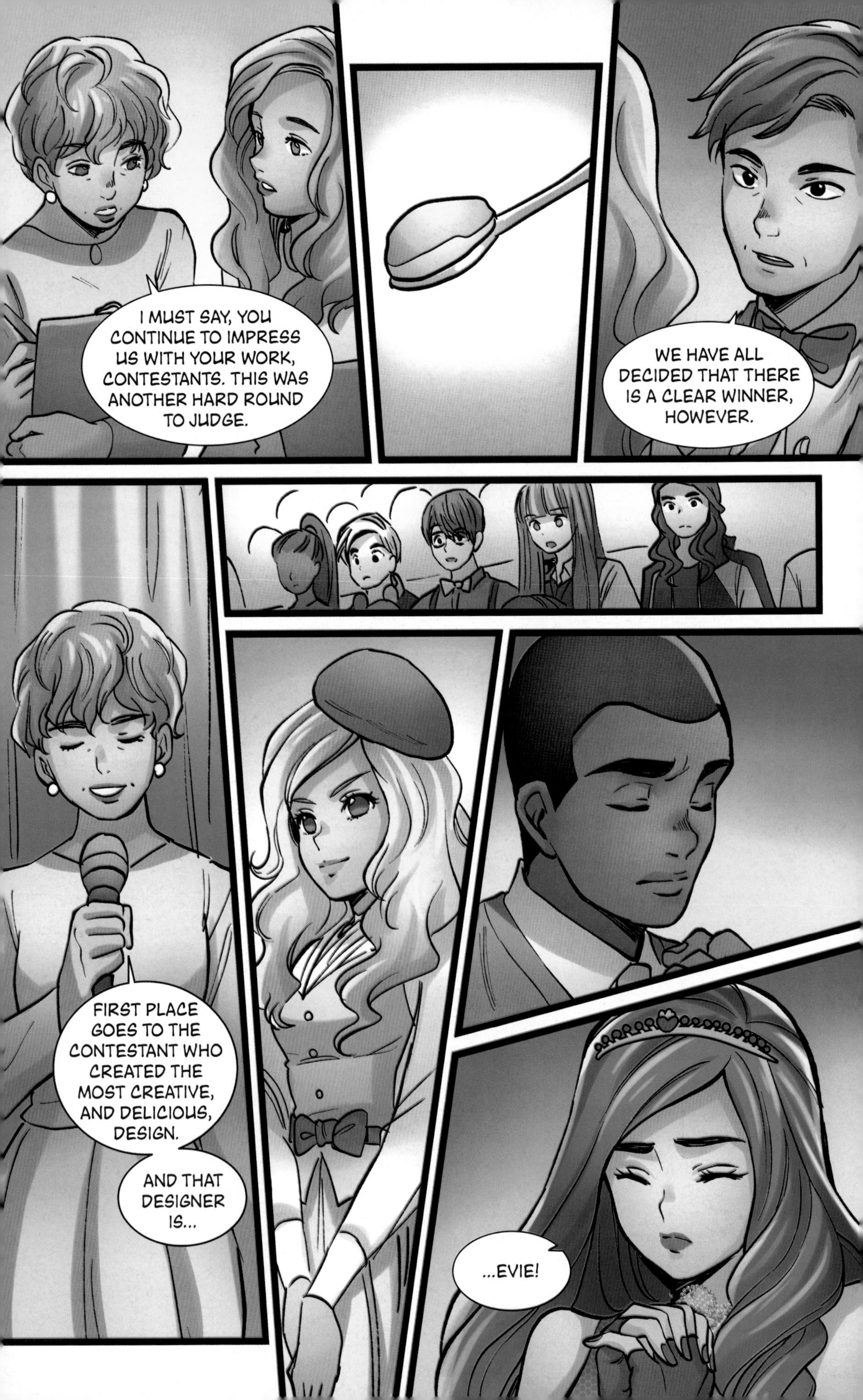
I MUST SAY, YOU CONTINUE TO IMPRESS US WITH YOUR WORK, CONTESTANTS. THIS WAS ANOTHER HARD ROUND TO JUDGE.
WE HAVE ALL DECIDED THAT THERE IS A CLEAR WINNER, HOWEVER.
FIRST PLACE GOES TO THE CONTESTANT WHO CREATED THE MOST CREATIVE, AND DELICIOUS, DESIGN.
AND THAT DESIGNER IS...
...EVIE!

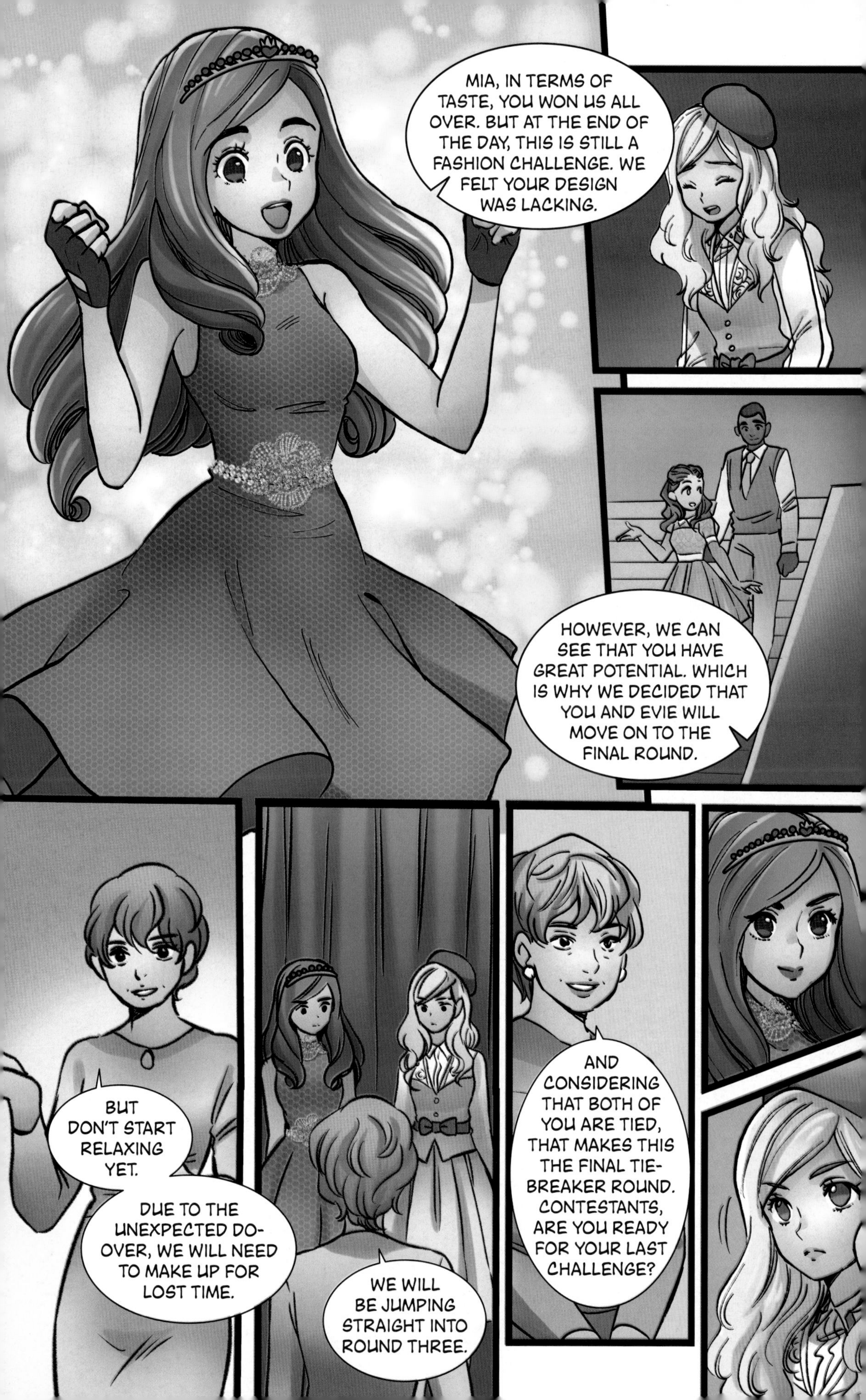
MIA, IN TERMS OF TASTE, YOU WON US ALL OVER. BUT AT THE END OF THE DAY, THIS IS STILL A FASHION CHALLENGE. WE FELT YOUR DESIGN WAS LACKING.
HOWEVER, WE CAN SEE THAT YOU HAVE GREAT POTENTIAL. WHICH IS WHY WE DECIDED THAT YOU AND EVIE WILL MOVE ON TO THE FINAL ROUND.
BUT DON'T START RELAXING YET.
DUE TO THE UNEXPECTED DO-OVER, WE WILL NEED TO MAKE UP FOR LOST TIME.
WE WILL BE JUMPING STRAIGHT INTO ROUND THREE.
AND CONSIDERING THAT BOTH OF YOU ARE TIED, THAT MAKES THIS THE FINAL TIE-BREAKER ROUND. CONTESTANTS, ARE YOU READY FOR YOUR LAST CHALLENGE?

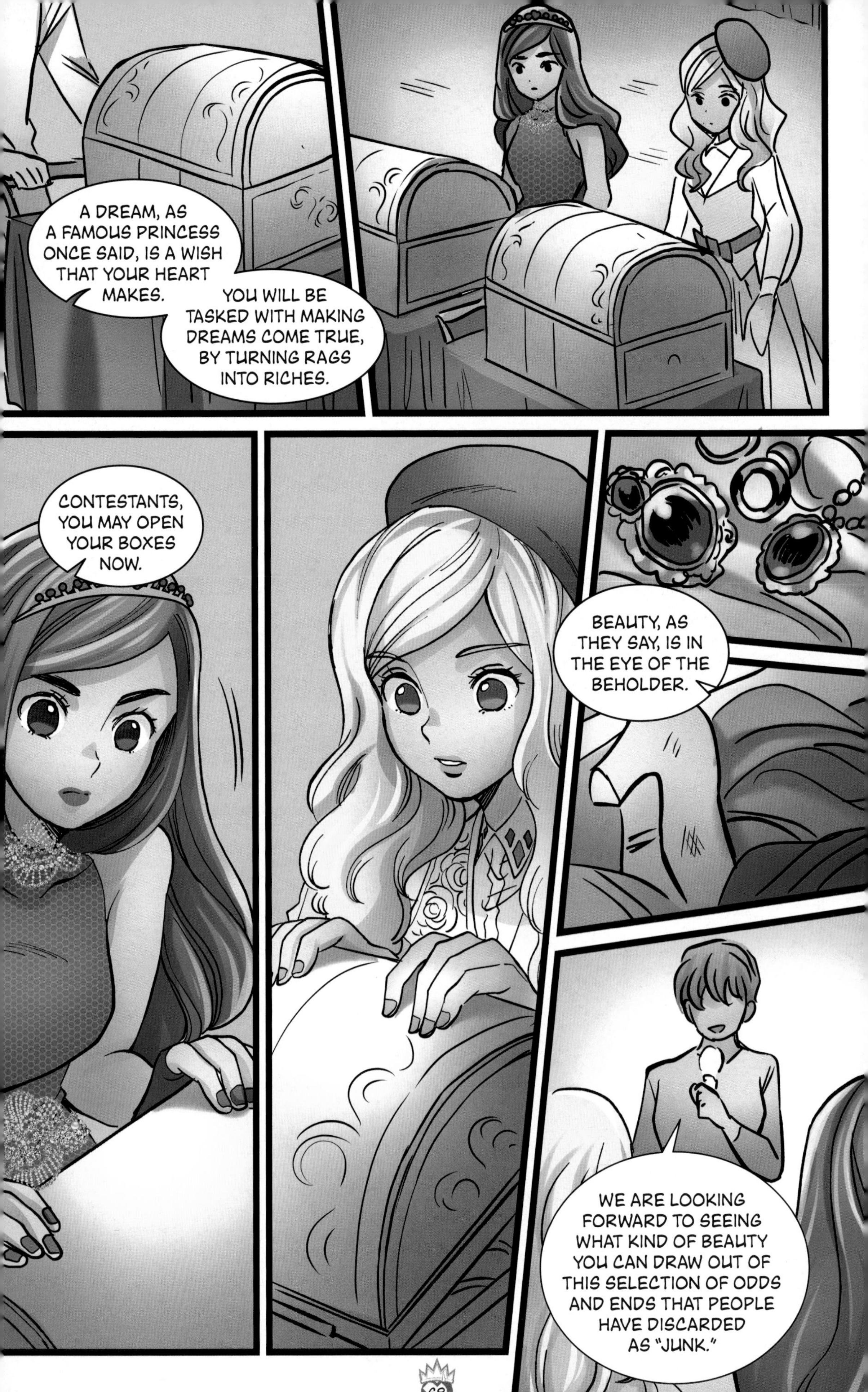
A DREAM, AS A FAMOUS PRINCESS ONCE SAID, IS A WISH THAT YOUR HEART MAKES.
YOU WILL BE TASKED WITH MAKING DREAMS COME TRUE, BY TURNING RAGS INTO RICHES.
CONTESTANTS, YOU MAY OPEN YOUR BOXES NOW.
BEAUTY, AS THEY SAY, IS IN THE EYE OF THE BEHOLDER.
WE ARE LOOKING FORWARD TO SEEING WHAT KIND OF BEAUTY YOU CAN DRAW OUT OF THIS SELECTION OF ODDS AND ENDS THAT PEOPLE HAVE DISCARDED AS "JUNK."

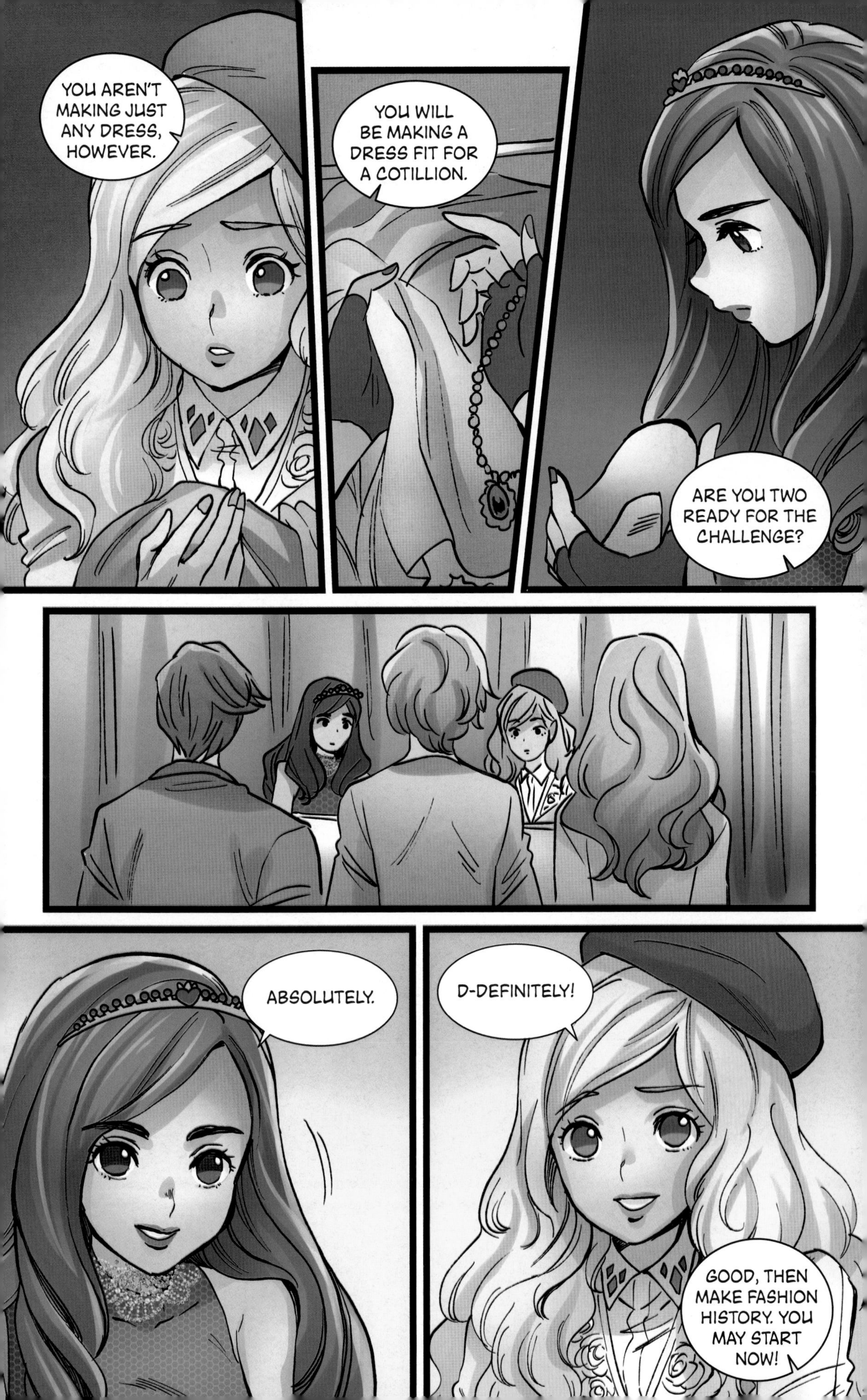
YOU AREN'T MAKING JUST ANY DRESS, HOWEVER.
YOU WILL BE MAKING A DRESS FIT FOR A COTILLION.
ARE YOU TWO READY FOR THE CHALLENGE?
ABSOLUTELY.
D-DEFINITELY!
GOOD, THEN MAKE FASHION HISTORY. YOU MAY START NOW!

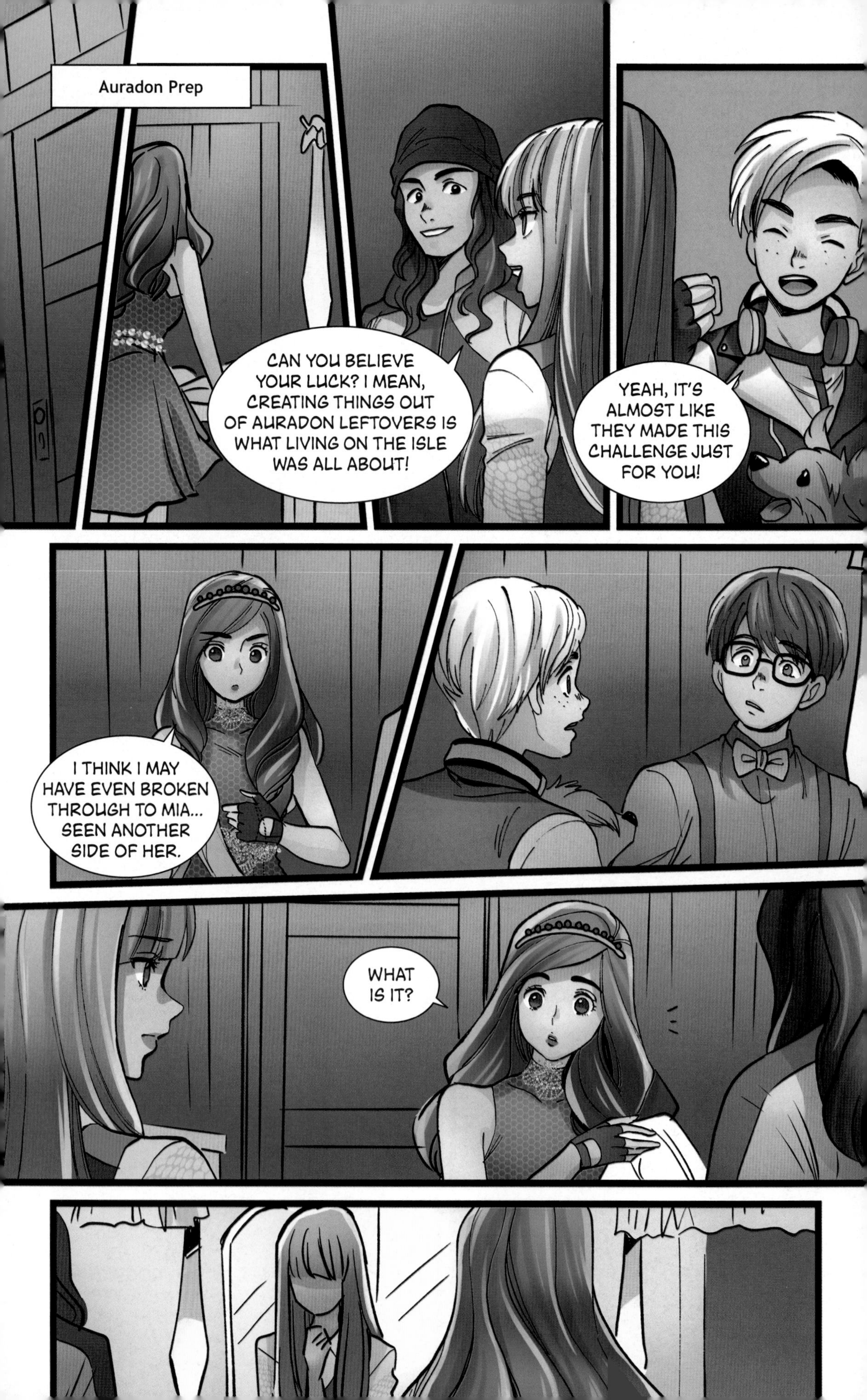
Auradon Prep
CAN YOU BELIEVE YOUR LUCK? I MEAN, CREATING THINGS OUT OF AURADON LEFTOVERS IS WHAT LIVING ON THE ISLE WAS ALL ABOUT!
YEAH, IT'S ALMOST LIKE THEY MADE THIS CHALLENGE JUST FOR YOU!
I THINK I MAY HAVE EVEN BROKEN THROUGH TO MIA... SEEN ANOTHER SIDE OF HER.
WHAT IS IT?

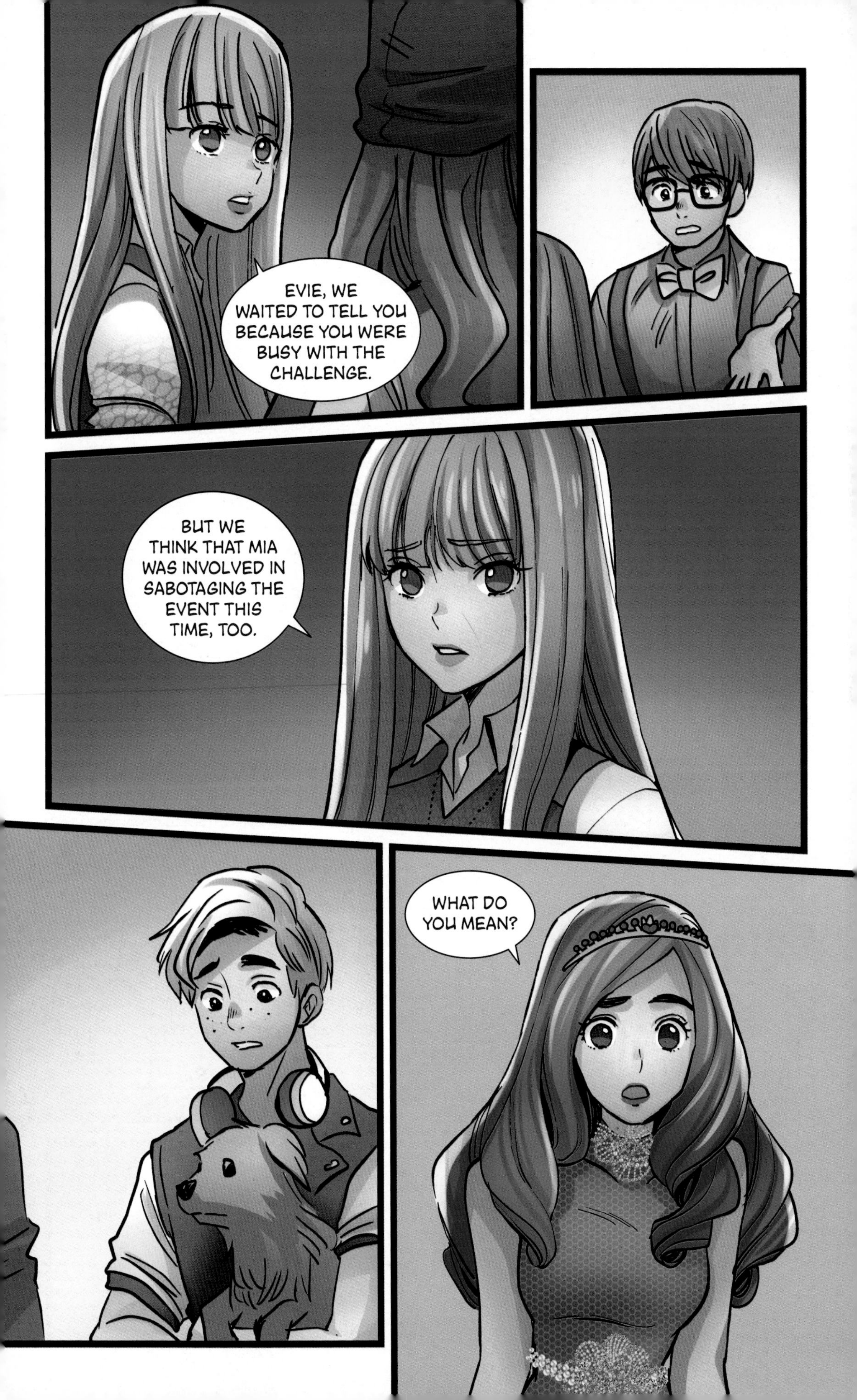
EVIE, WE WAITED TO TELL YOU BECAUSE YOU WERE BUSY WITH THE CHALLENGE.
BUT WE THINK THAT MIA WAS INVOLVED IN SABOTAGING THE EVENT THIS TIME, TOO.
WHAT DO YOU MEAN?

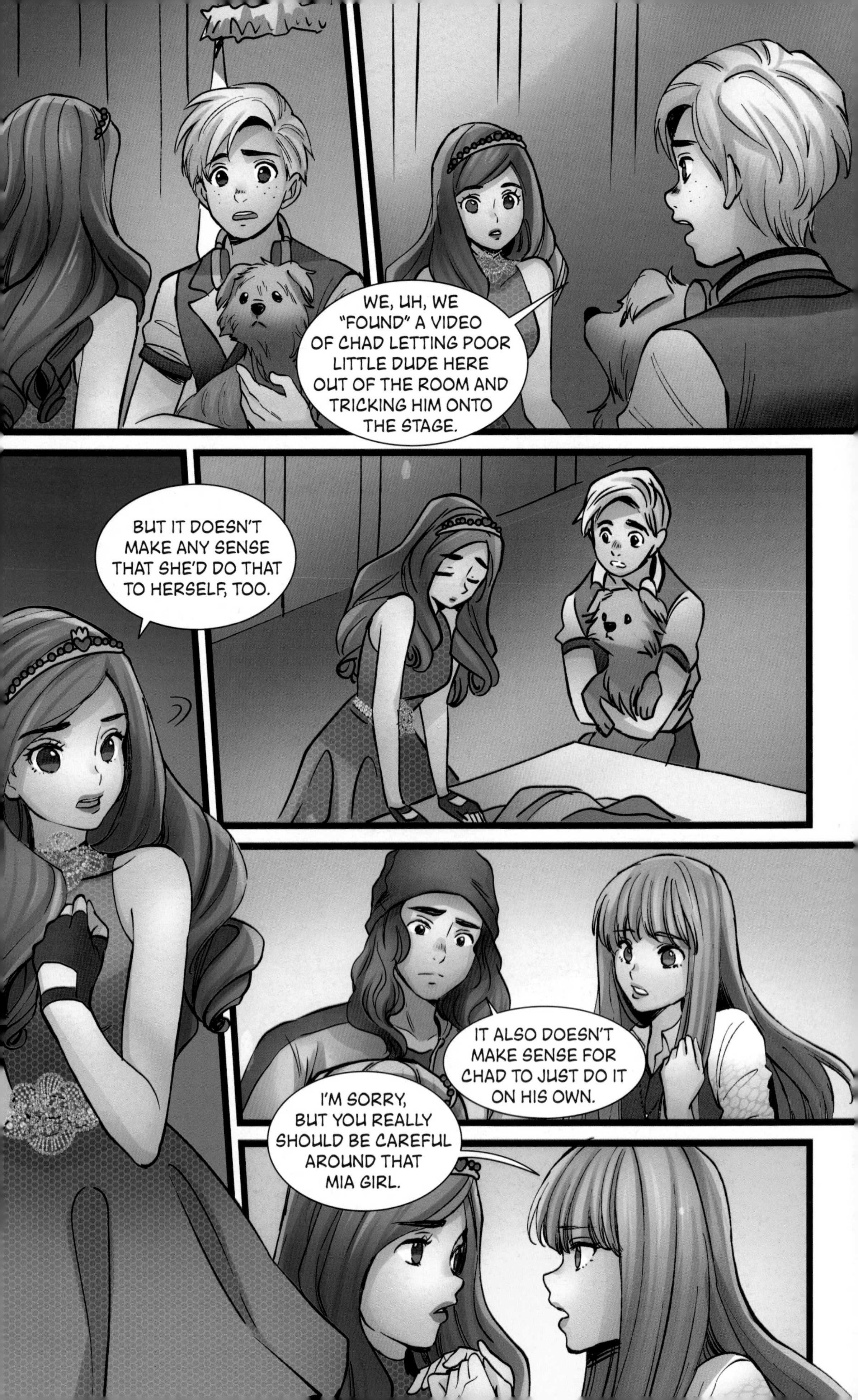
WE, UH, WE "FOUND" A VIDEO OF CHAD LETTING POOR LITTLE DUDE HERE OUT OF THE ROOM AND TRICKING HIM ONTO THE STAGE.
BUT IT DOESN'T MAKE ANY SENSE THAT SHE'D DO THAT TO HERSELF, TOO.
IT ALSO DOESN'T MAKE SENSE FOR CHAD TO JUST DO IT ON HIS OWN.
I'M SORRY, BUT YOU REALLY SHOULD BE CAREFUL AROUND THAT MIA GIRL.

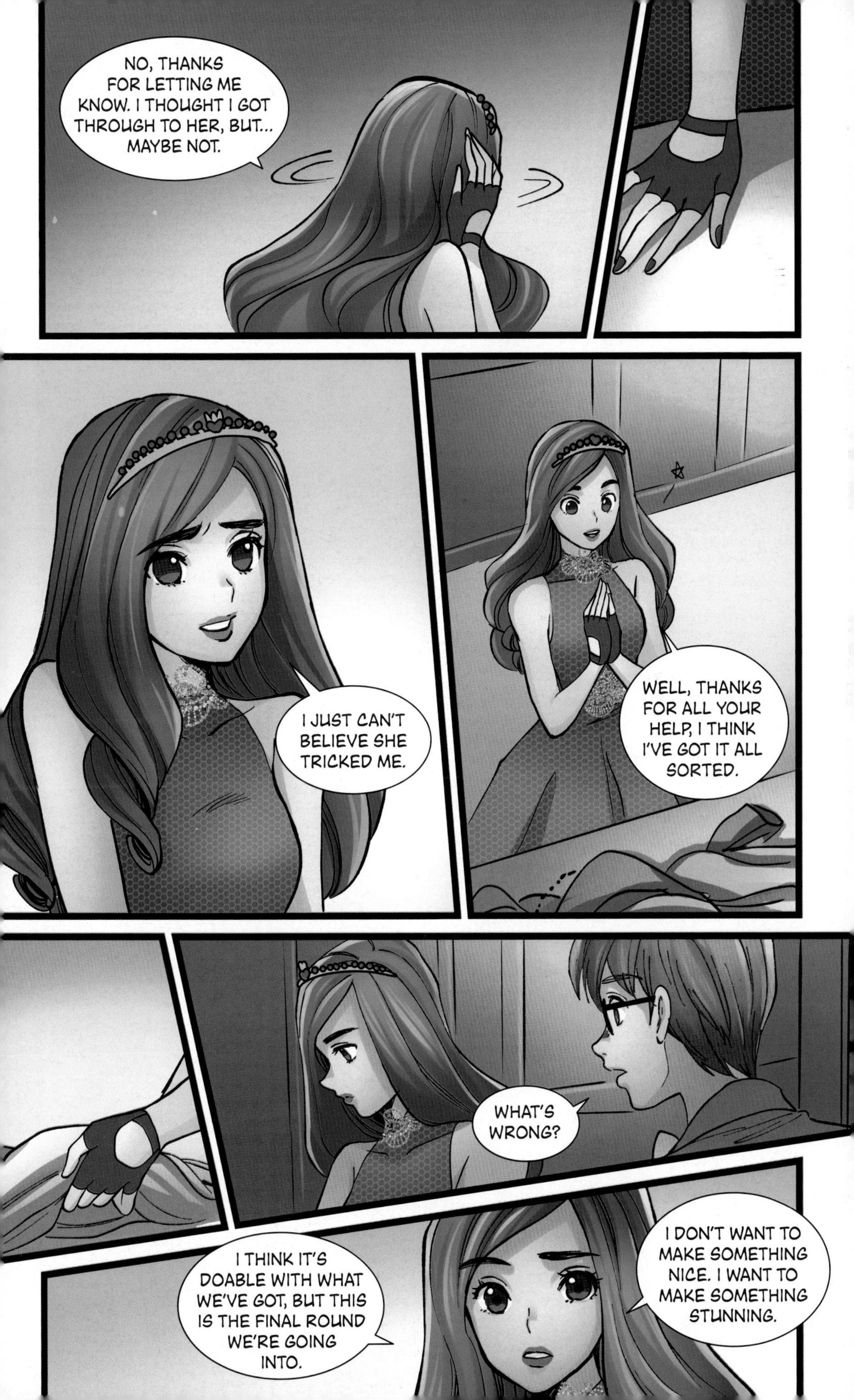
NO, THANKS FOR LETTING ME KNOW. I THOUGHT I GOT THROUGH TO HER, BUT... MAYBE NOT.
I JUST CAN'T BELIEVE SHE TRICKED ME.
WELL, THANKS FOR ALL YOUR HELP, I THINK I'VE GOT IT ALL SORTED.
WHAT'S WRONG?
I THINK IT'S DOABLE WITH WHAT WE'VE GOT, BUT THIS IS THE FINAL ROUND WE'RE GOING INTO.
I DON'T WANT TO MAKE SOMETHING NICE. I WANT TO MAKE SOMETHING STUNNING.

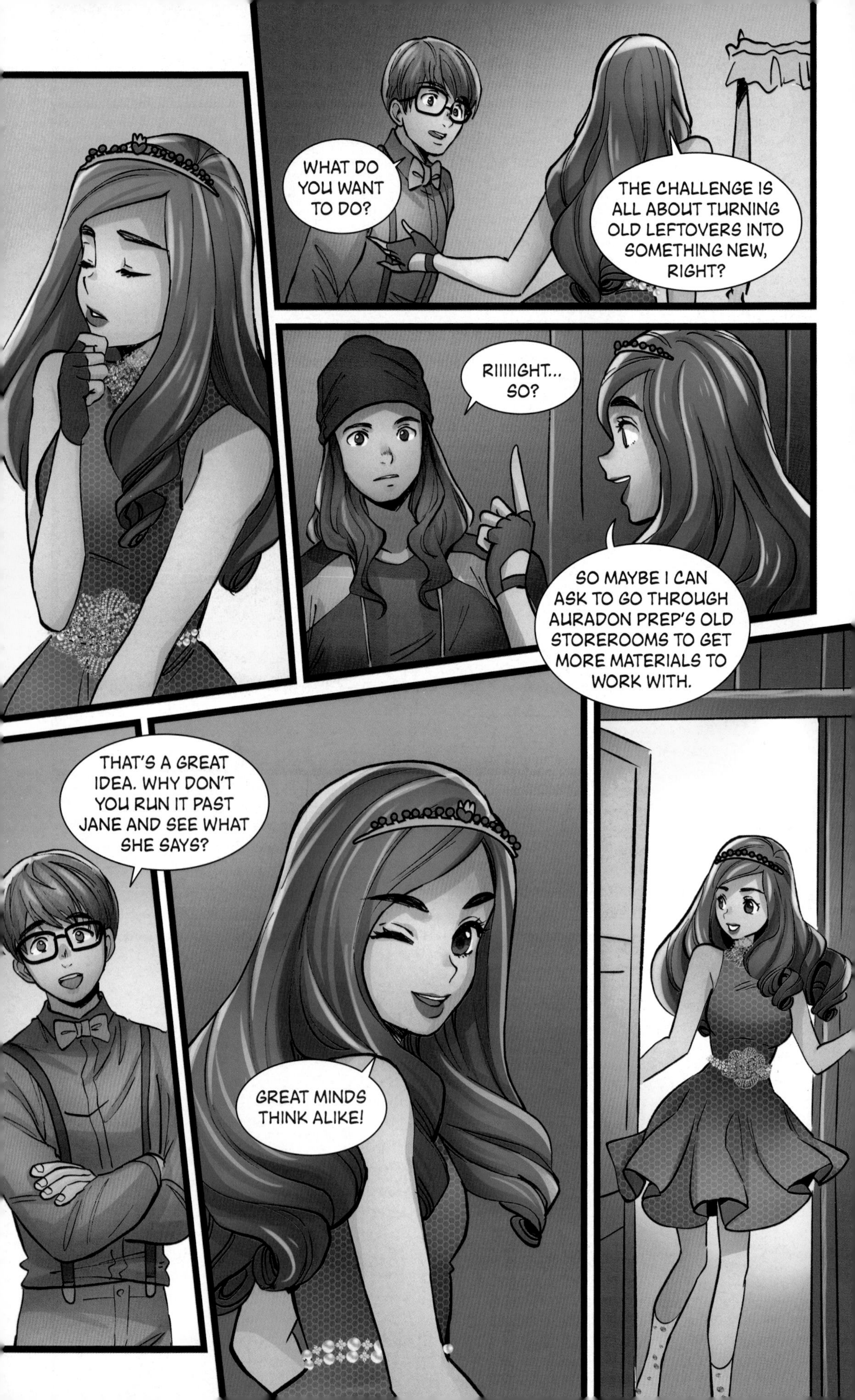
WHAT DO YOU WANT TO DO?
THE CHALLENGE IS ALL ABOUT TURNING OLD LEFTOVERS INTO SOMETHING NEW, RIGHT?
RIIIIGHT... SO?
SO MAYBE I CAN ASK TO GO THROUGH AURADON PREP'S OLD STOREROOMS TO GET MORE MATERIALS TO WORK WITH.
THAT'S A GREAT IDEA. WHY DON'T YOU RUN IT PAST JANE AND SEE WHAT SHE SAYS?
GREAT MINDS THINK ALIKE!

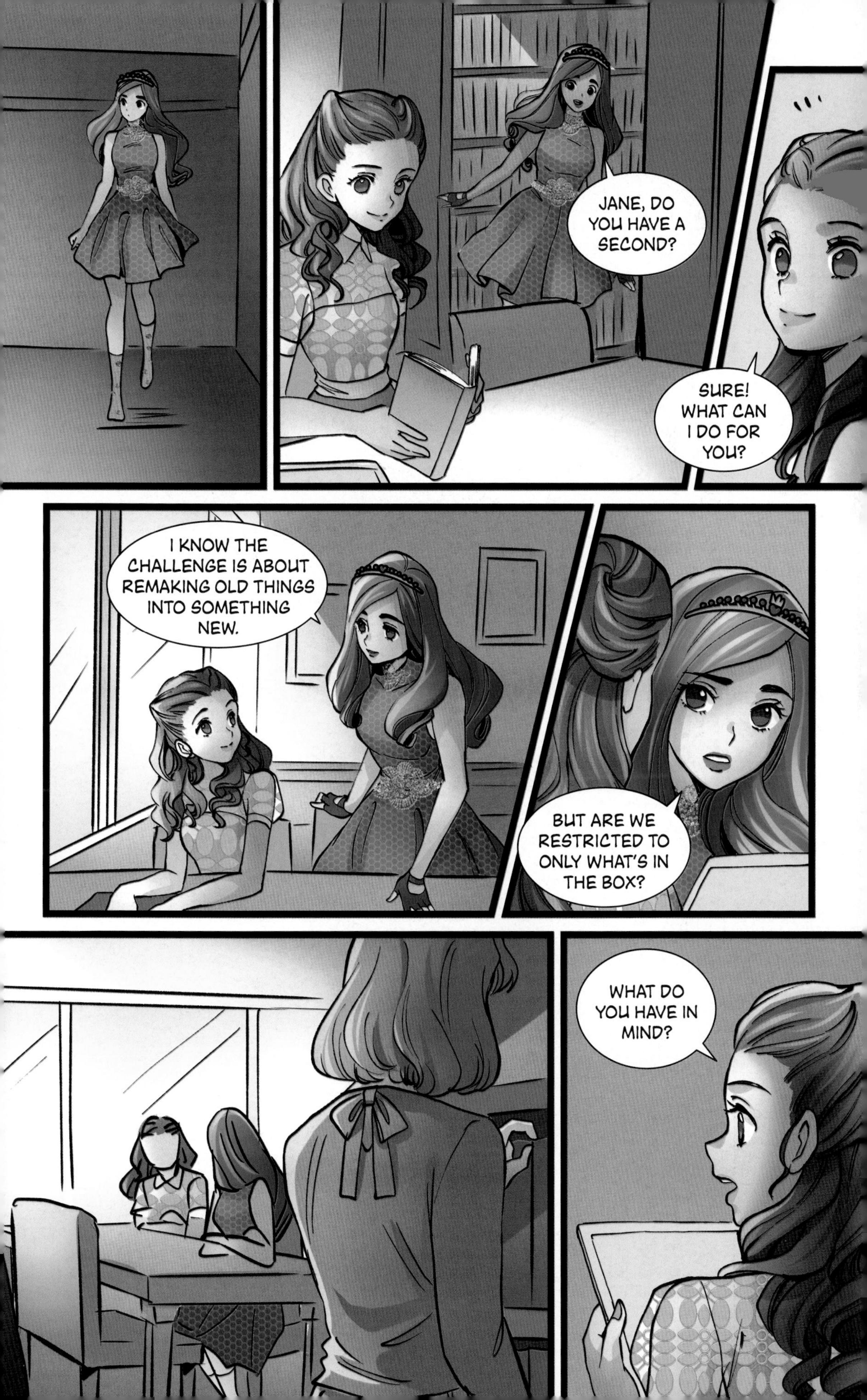
JANE, DO YOU HAVE A SECOND?
SURE! WHAT CAN I DO FOR YOU?
I KNOW THE CHALLENGE IS ABOUT REMAKING OLD THINGS INTO SOMETHING NEW.
BUT ARE WE RESTRICTED TO ONLY WHAT'S IN THE BOX?
WHAT DO YOU HAVE IN MIND?

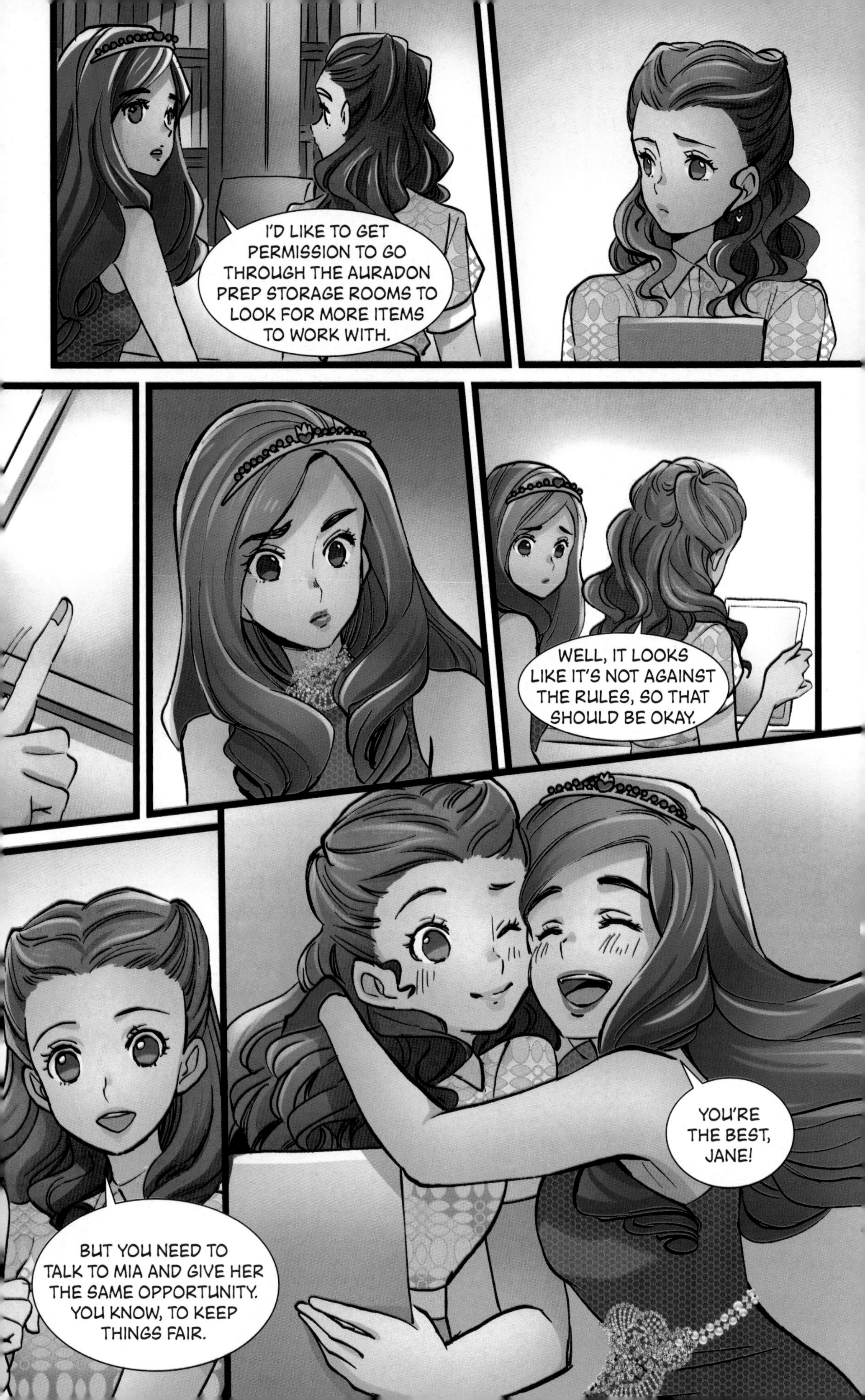
I'D LIKE TO GET PERMISSION TO GO THROUGH THE AURADON PREP STORAGE ROOMS TO LOOK FOR MORE ITEMS TO WORK WITH.
WELL, IT LOOKS LIKE IT'S NOT AGAINST THE RULES, SO THAT SHOULD BE OKAY.
BUT YOU NEED TO TALK TO MIA AND GIVE HER THE SAME OPPORTUNITY. YOU KNOW, TO KEEP THINGS FAIR.
YOU'RE THE BEST, JANE!

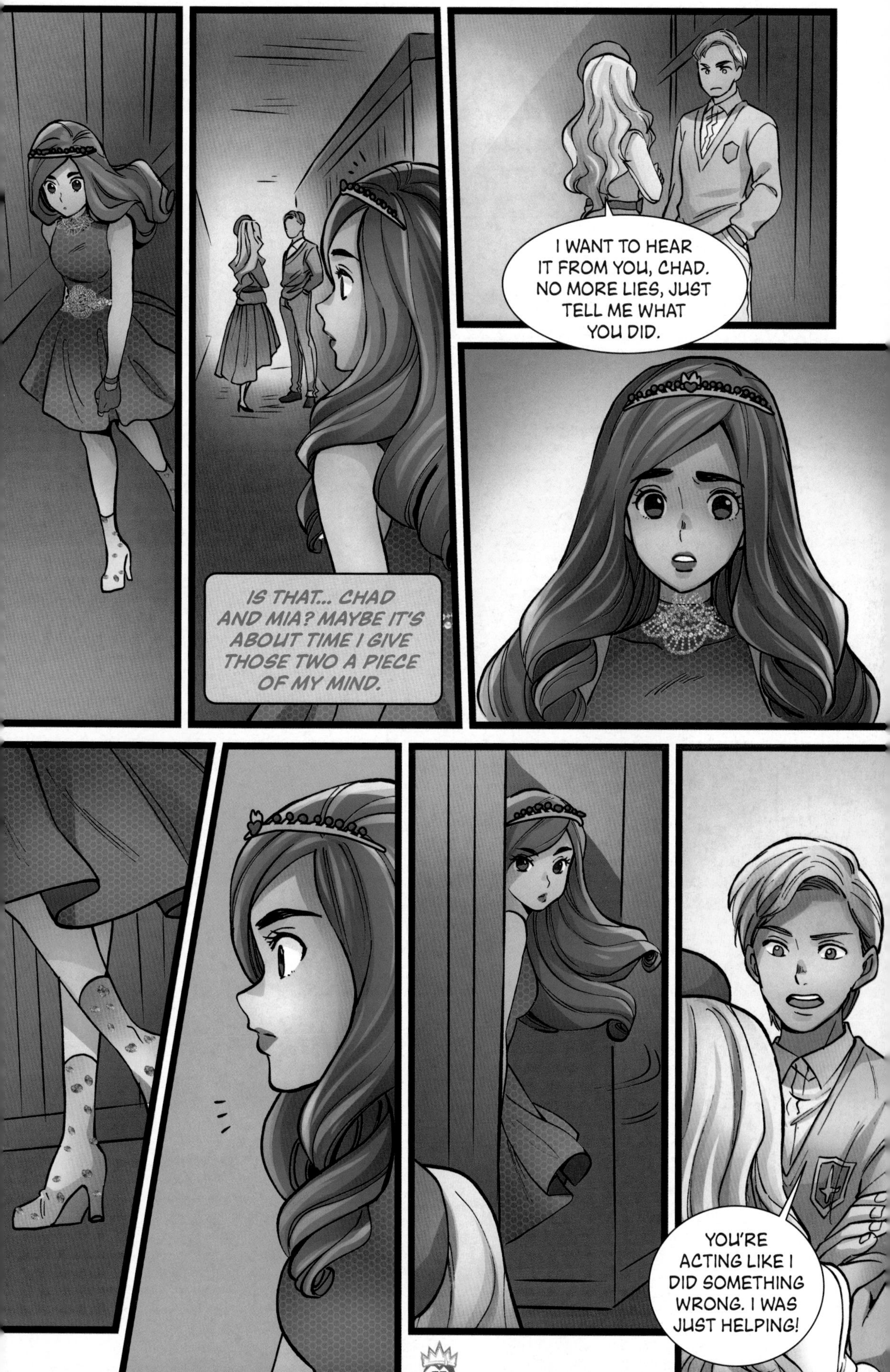
IS THAT... CHAD AND MIA? MAYBE IT'S ABOUT TIME I GIVE THOSE TWO A PIECE OF MY MIND.
I WANT TO HEAR IT FROM YOU, CHAD. NO MORE LIES, JUST TELL ME WHAT YOU DID.
YOU'RE ACTING LIKE I DID SOMETHING WRONG. I WAS JUST HELPING!

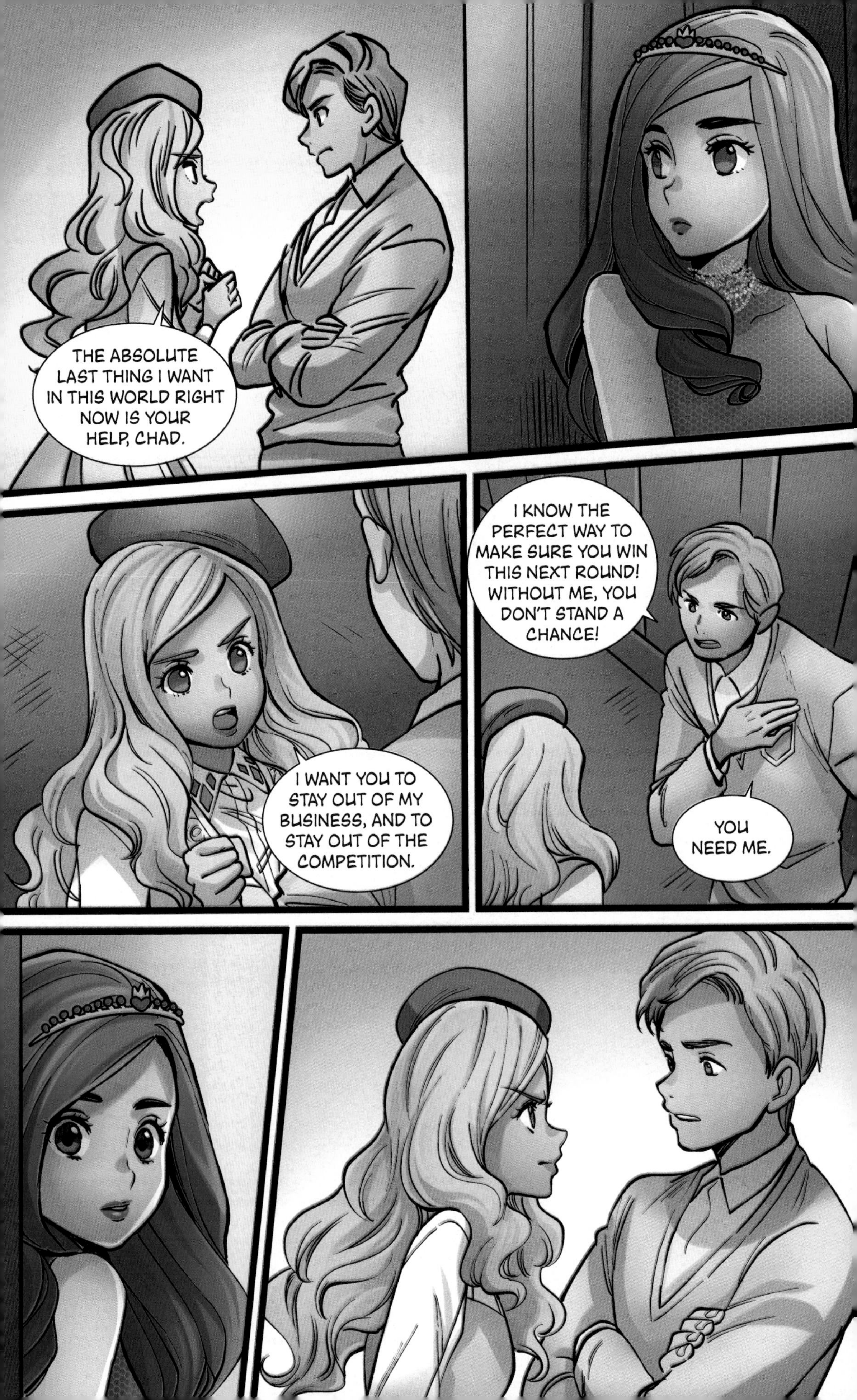
THE ABSOLUTE LAST THING I WANT IN THIS WORLD RIGHT NOW IS YOUR HELP, CHAD.
I WANT YOU TO STAY OUT OF MY BUSINESS, AND TO STAY OUT OF THE COMPETITION.
I KNOW THE PERFECT WAY TO MAKE SURE YOU WIN THIS NEXT ROUND! WITHOUT ME, YOU DON'T STAND A CHANCE!
YOU NEED ME.

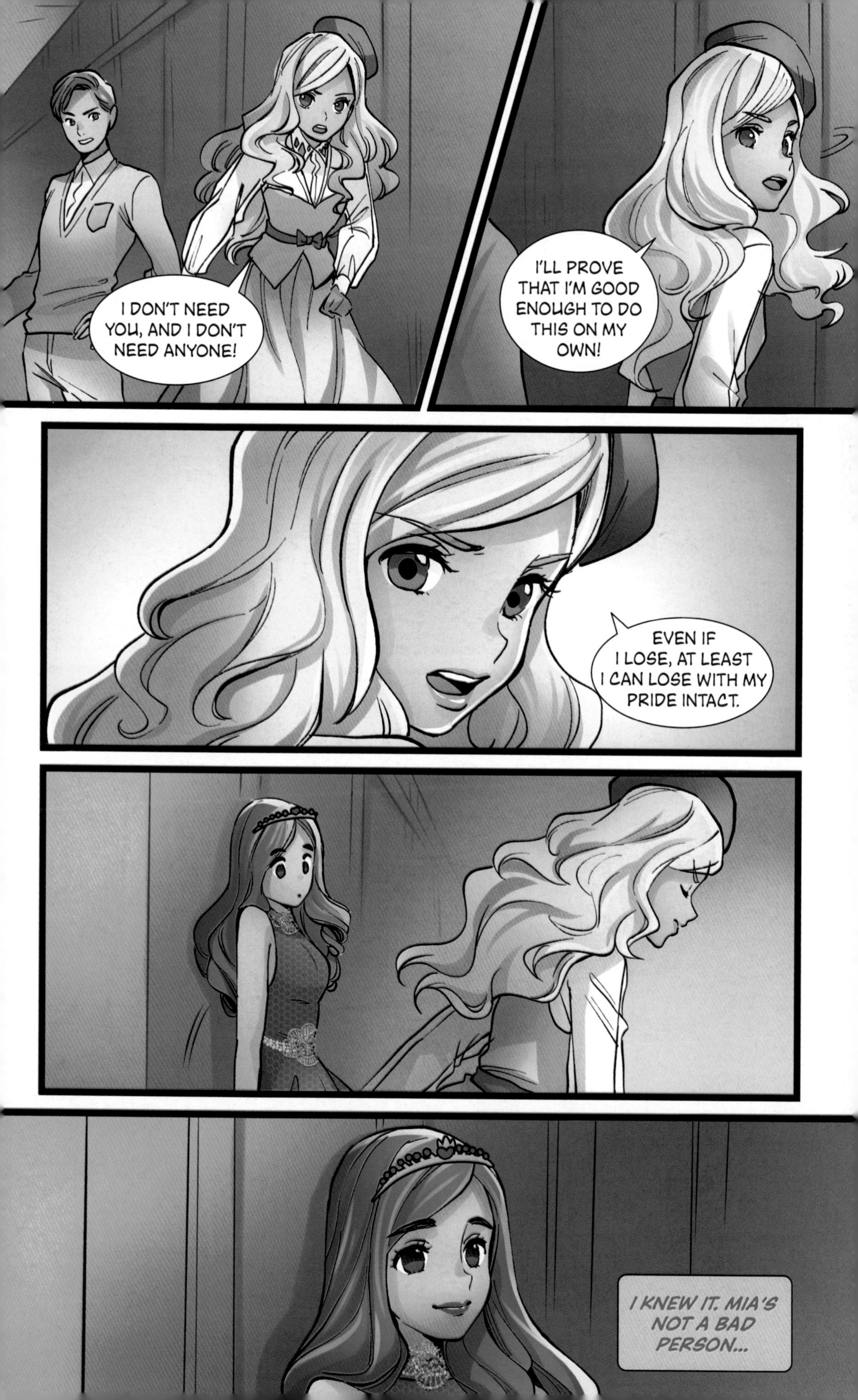
I DON'T NEED YOU, AND I DON'T NEED ANYONE!
I'LL PROVE THAT I'M GOOD ENOUGH TO DO THIS ON MY OWN!
EVEN IF I LOSE, AT LEAST I CAN LOSE WITH MY PRIDE INTACT.
I KNEW IT. MIA'S NOT A BAD PERSON...

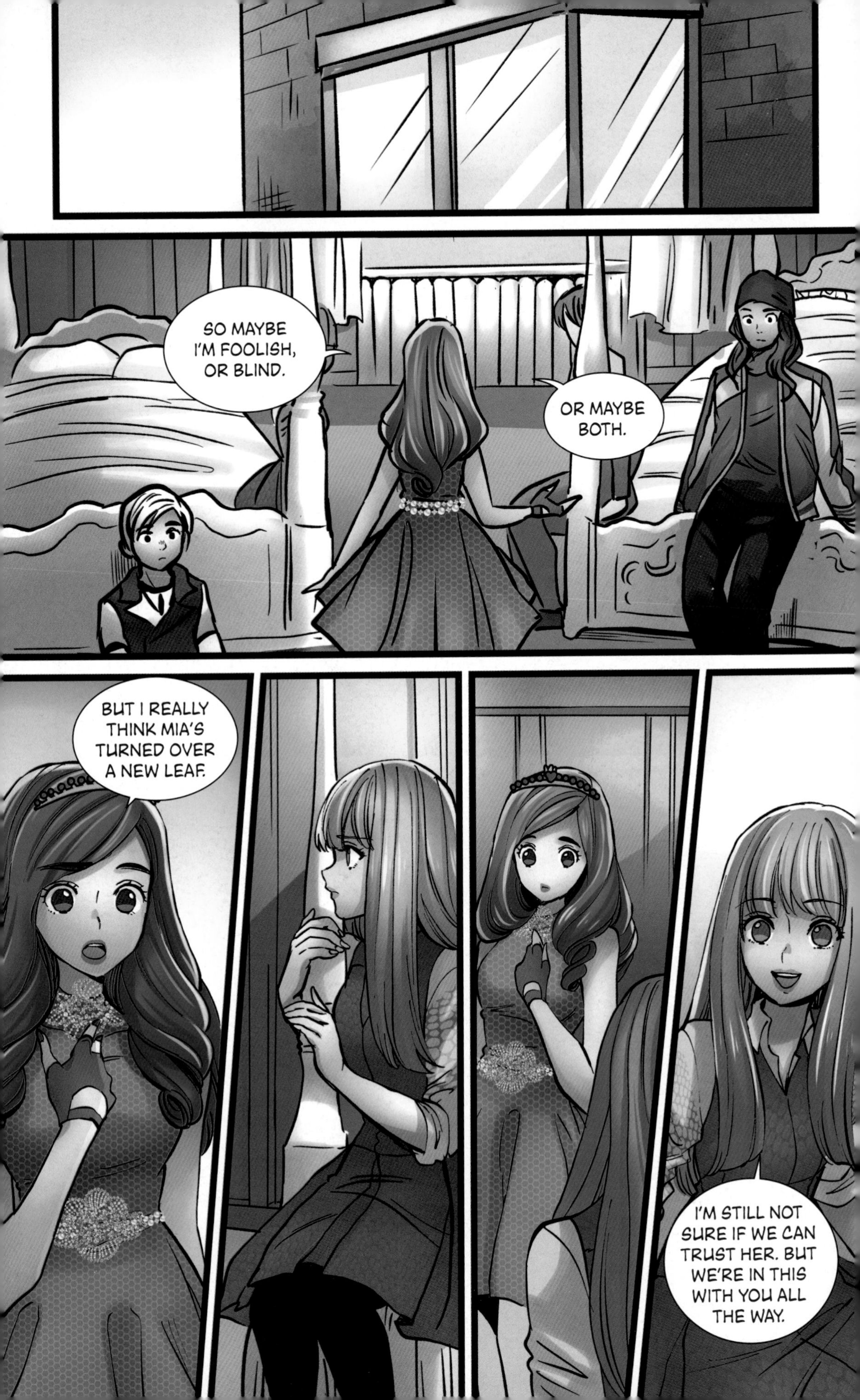
SO MAYBE I'M FOOLISH, OR BLIND.
OR MAYBE BOTH.
BUT I REALLY THINK MIA'S TURNED OVER A NEW LEAF.
I'M STILL NOT SURE IF WE CAN TRUST HER. BUT WE'RE IN THIS WITH YOU ALL THE WAY.

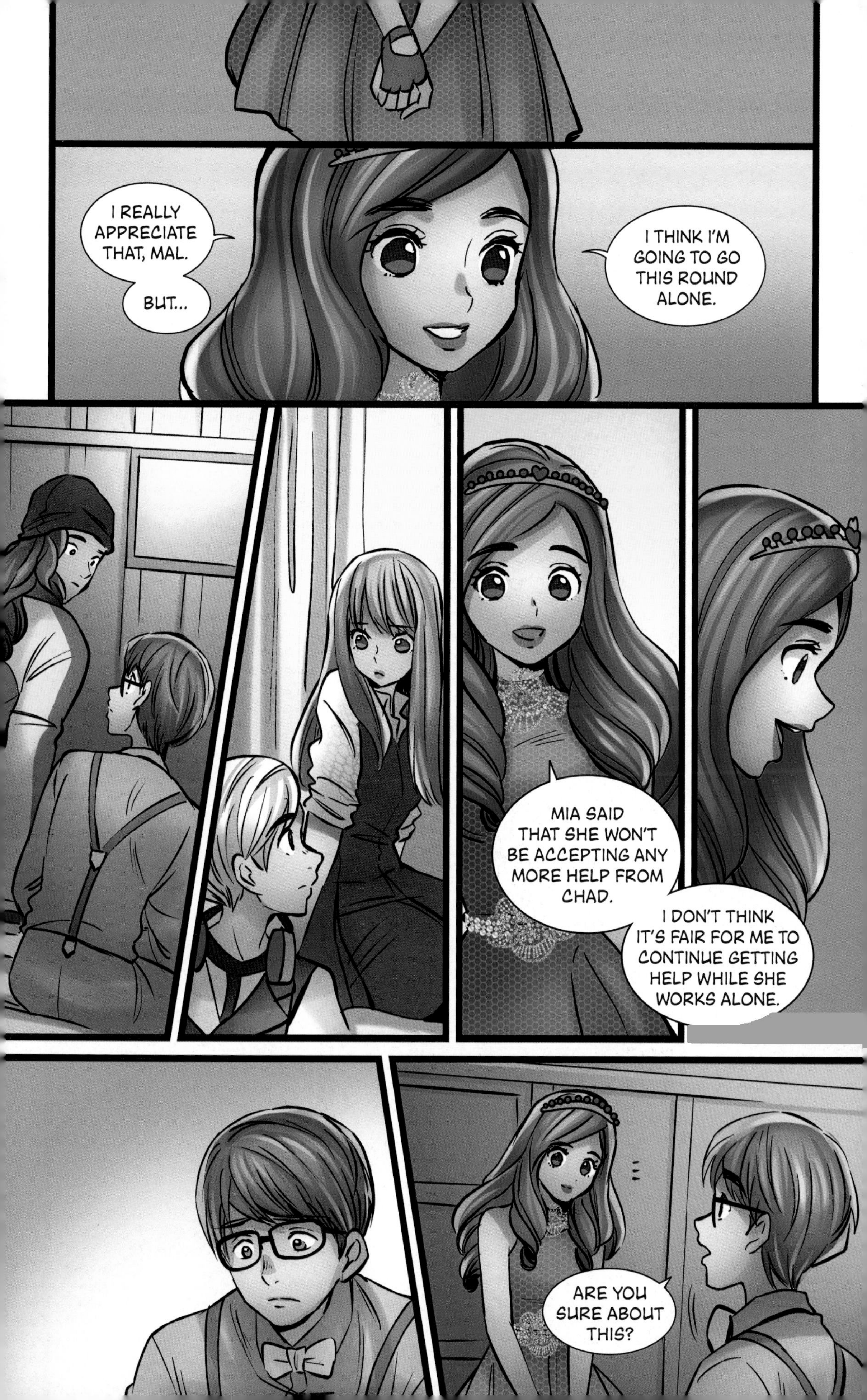
I REALLY APPRECIATE THAT, MAL.
BUT...
I THINK I'M GOING TO GO THIS ROUND ALONE.
MIA SAID THAT SHE WON'T BE ACCEPTING ANY MORE HELP FROM CHAD.
I DON'T THINK IT'S FAIR FOR ME TO CONTINUE GETTING HELP WHILE SHE WORKS ALONE.
...
ARE YOU SURE ABOUT THIS?

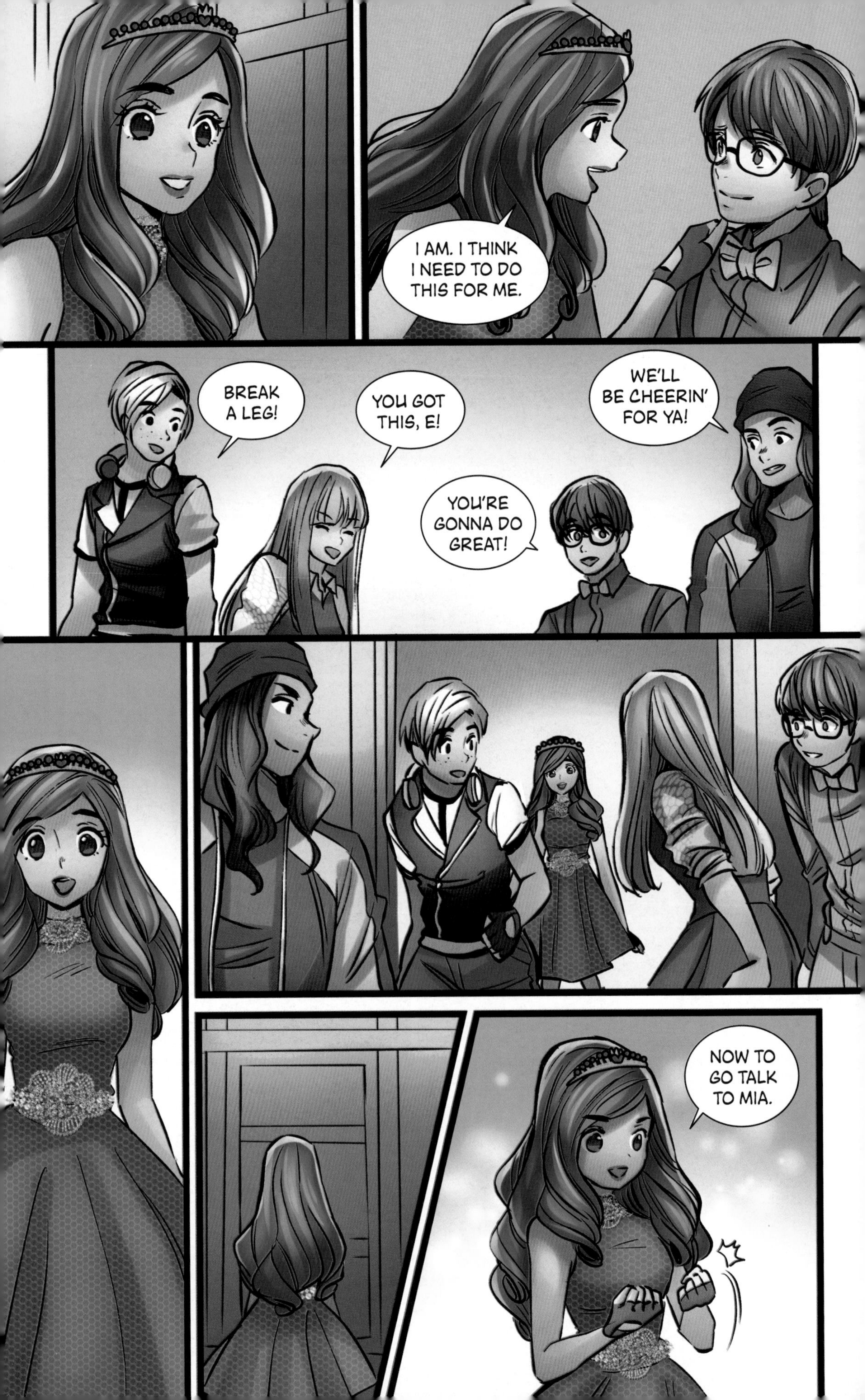
I AM. I THINK I NEED TO DO THIS FOR ME.
WE'LL BE CHEERIN' FOR YA!
YOU GOT THIS, E!
BREAK A LEG!
YOU'RE GONNA DO GREAT!
NOW TO GO TALK TO MIA.

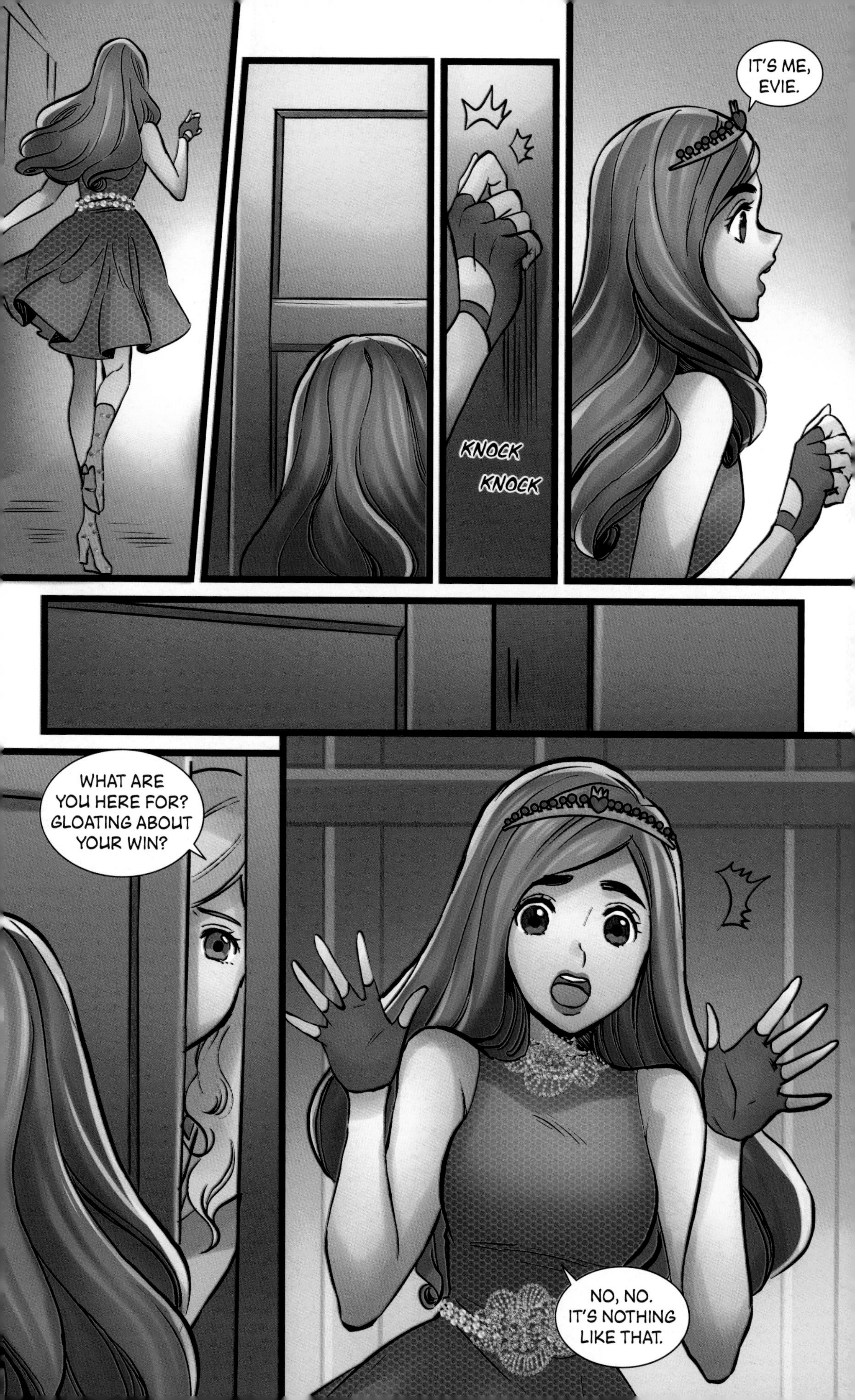
KNOCK
KNOCK
IT'S ME, EVIE.
WHAT ARE YOU HERE FOR? GLOATING ABOUT YOUR WIN?
NO, NO. IT'S NOTHING LIKE THAT.

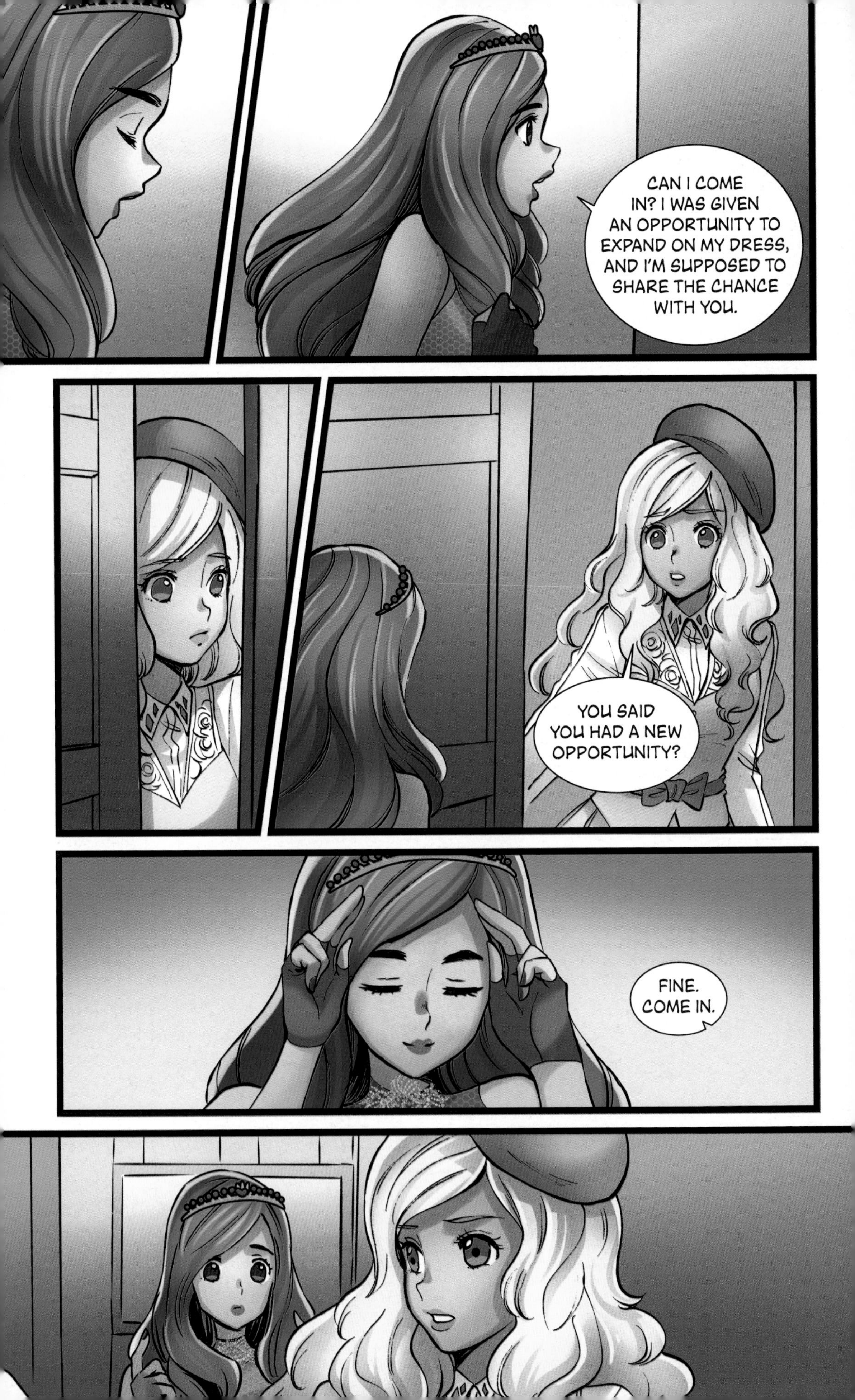
CAN I COME IN? I WAS GIVEN AN OPPORTUNITY TO EXPAND ON MY DRESS, AND I'M SUPPOSED TO SHARE THE CHANCE WITH YOU.
YOU SAID YOU HAD A NEW OPPORTUNITY?
FINE. COME IN.

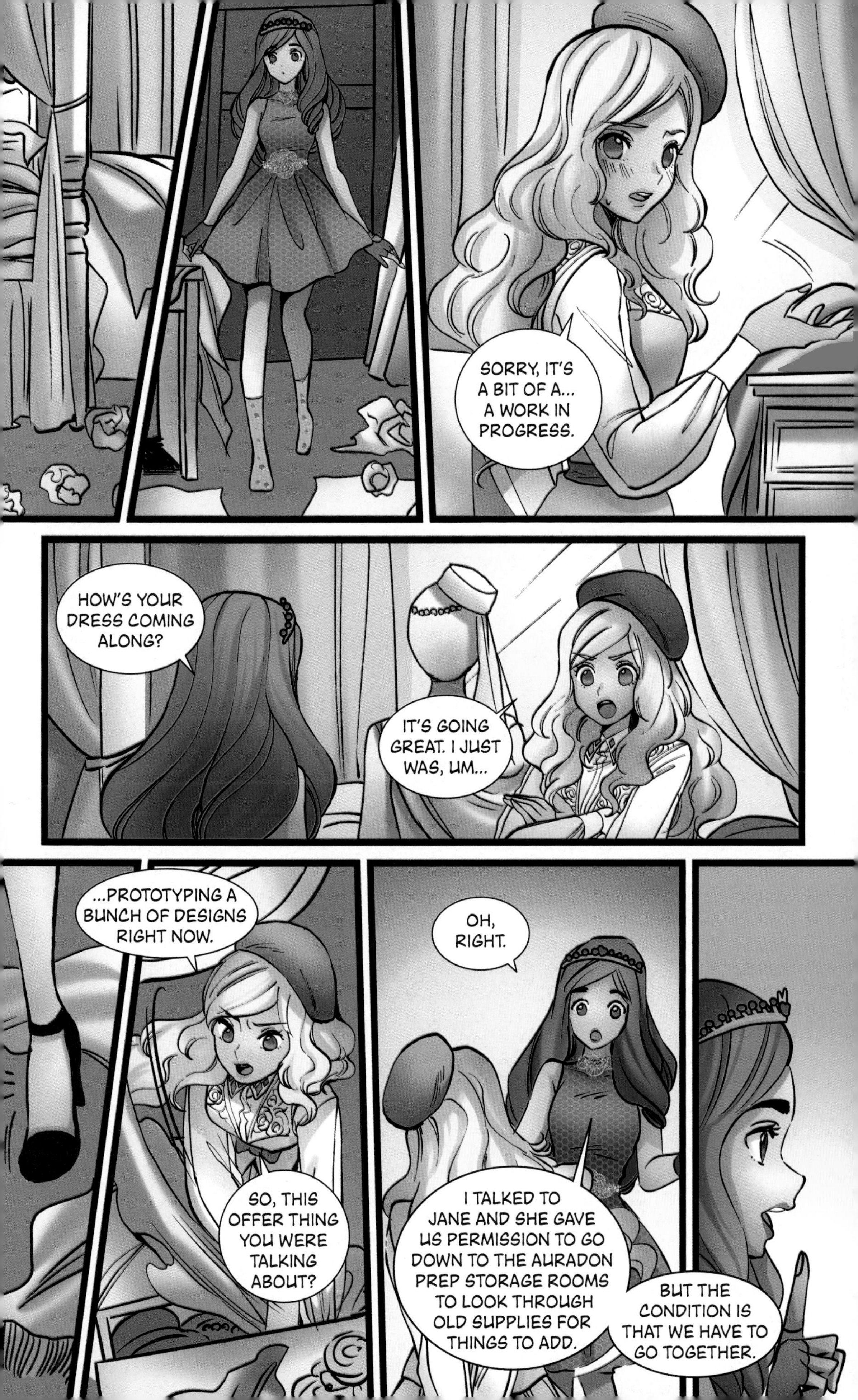
SORRY, IT'S A BIT OF A... A WORK IN PROGRESS.
HOW'S YOUR DRESS COMING ALONG?
IT'S GOING GREAT. I JUST WAS, UM...
...PROTOTYPING A BUNCH OF DESIGNS RIGHT NOW.
SO, THIS OFFER THING YOU WERE TALKING ABOUT?
OH, RIGHT.
I TALKED TO JANE AND SHE GAVE US PERMISSION TO GO DOWN TO THE AURADON PREP STORAGE ROOMS TO LOOK THROUGH OLD SUPPLIES FOR THINGS TO ADD.
BUT THE CONDITION IS THAT WE HAVE TO GO TOGETHER.

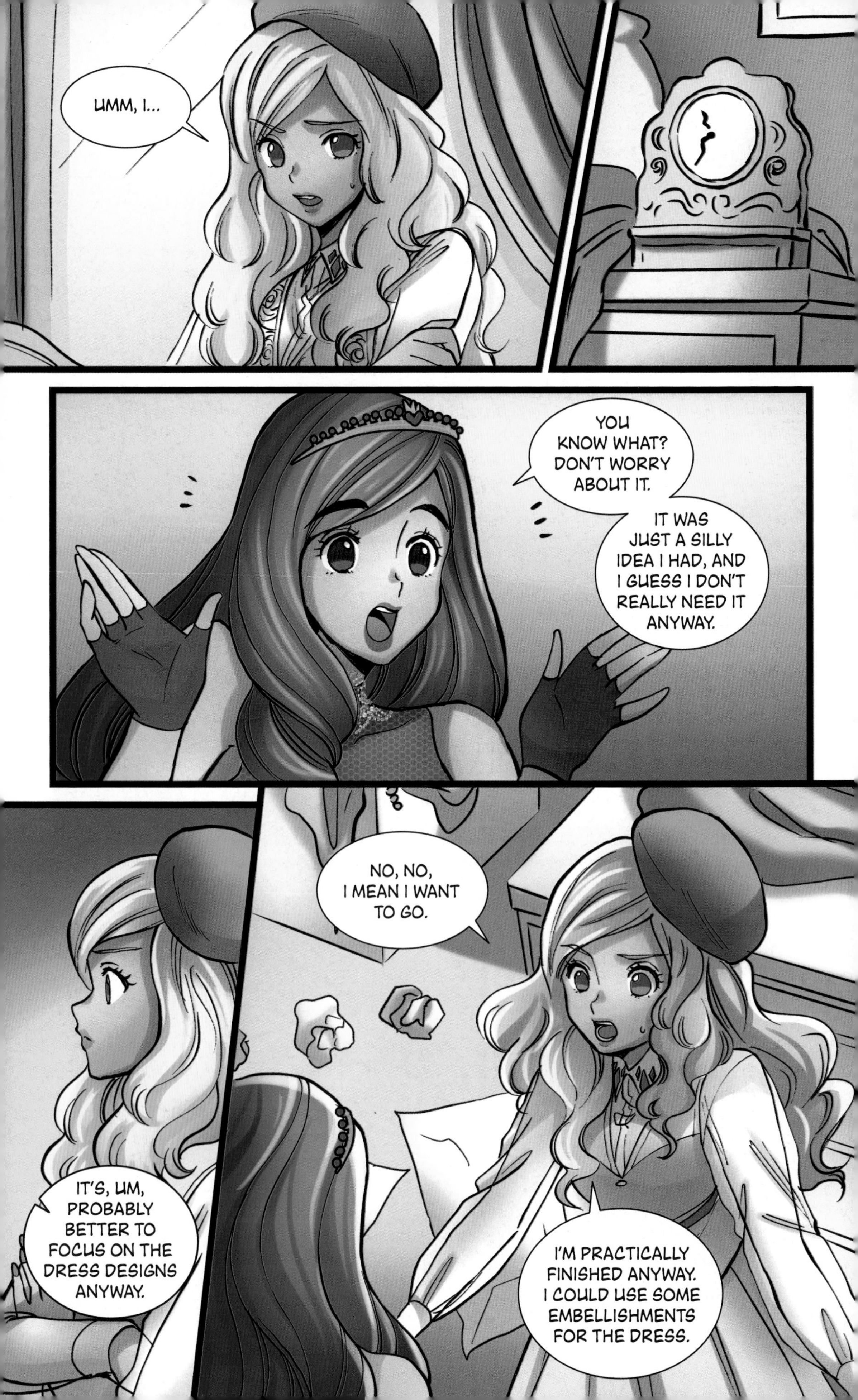
UMM, I...
YOU KNOW WHAT? DON'T WORRY ABOUT IT.
IT WAS JUST A SILLY IDEA I HAD, AND I GUESS I DON'T REALLY NEED IT ANYWAY.
IT'S, UM, PROBABLY BETTER TO FOCUS ON THE DRESS DESIGNS ANYWAY.
NO, NO, I MEAN I WANT TO GO.
I'M PRACTICALLY FINISHED ANYWAY. I COULD USE SOME EMBELLISHMENTS FOR THE DRESS.

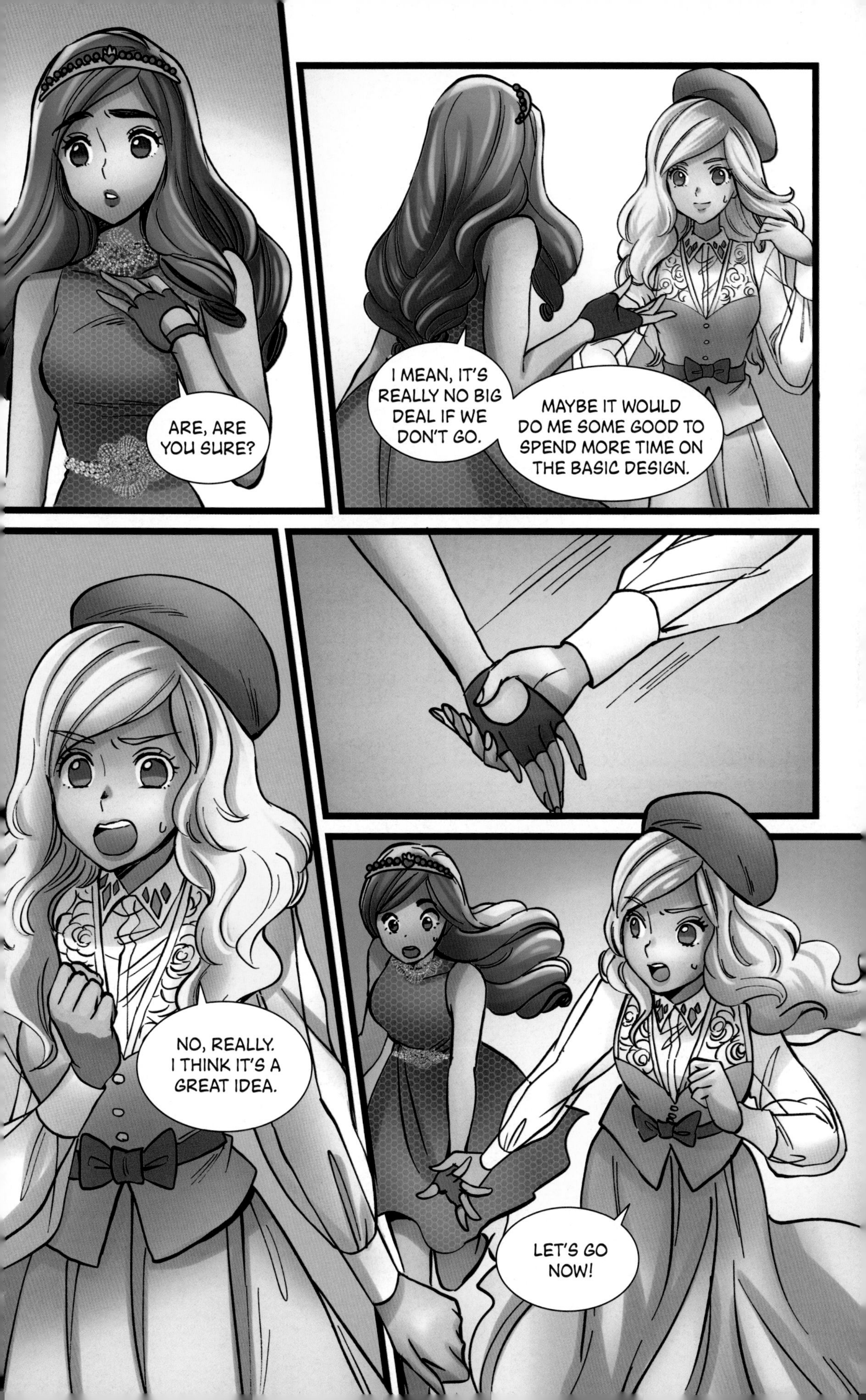
ARE, ARE YOU SURE?
I MEAN, IT'S REALLY NO BIG DEAL IF WE DON'T GO.
MAYBE IT WOULD DO ME SOME GOOD TO SPEND MORE TIME ON THE BASIC DESIGN.
NO, REALLY. I THINK IT'S A GREAT IDEA.
LET'S GO NOW!

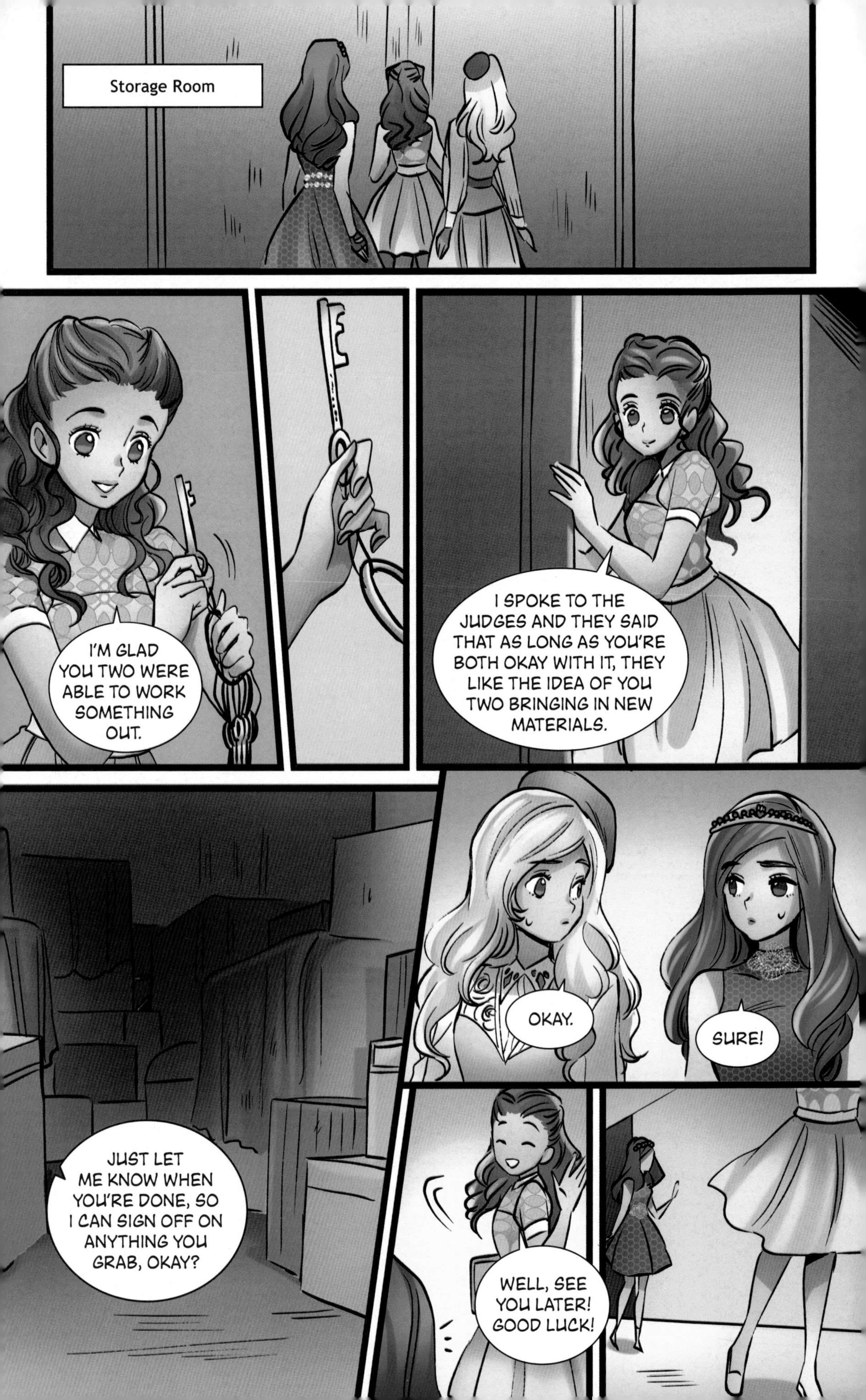
Storage Room
I'M GLAD YOU TWO WERE ABLE TO WORK SOMETHING OUT.
I SPOKE TO THE JUDGES AND THEY SAID THAT AS LONG AS YOU'RE BOTH OKAY WITH IT, THEY LIKE THE IDEA OF YOU TWO BRINGING IN NEW MATERIALS.
JUST LET ME KNOW WHEN YOU'RE DONE, SO I CAN SIGN OFF ON ANYTHING YOU GRAB, OKAY?
OKAY.
SURE!
WELL, SEE YOU LATER! GOOD LUCK!

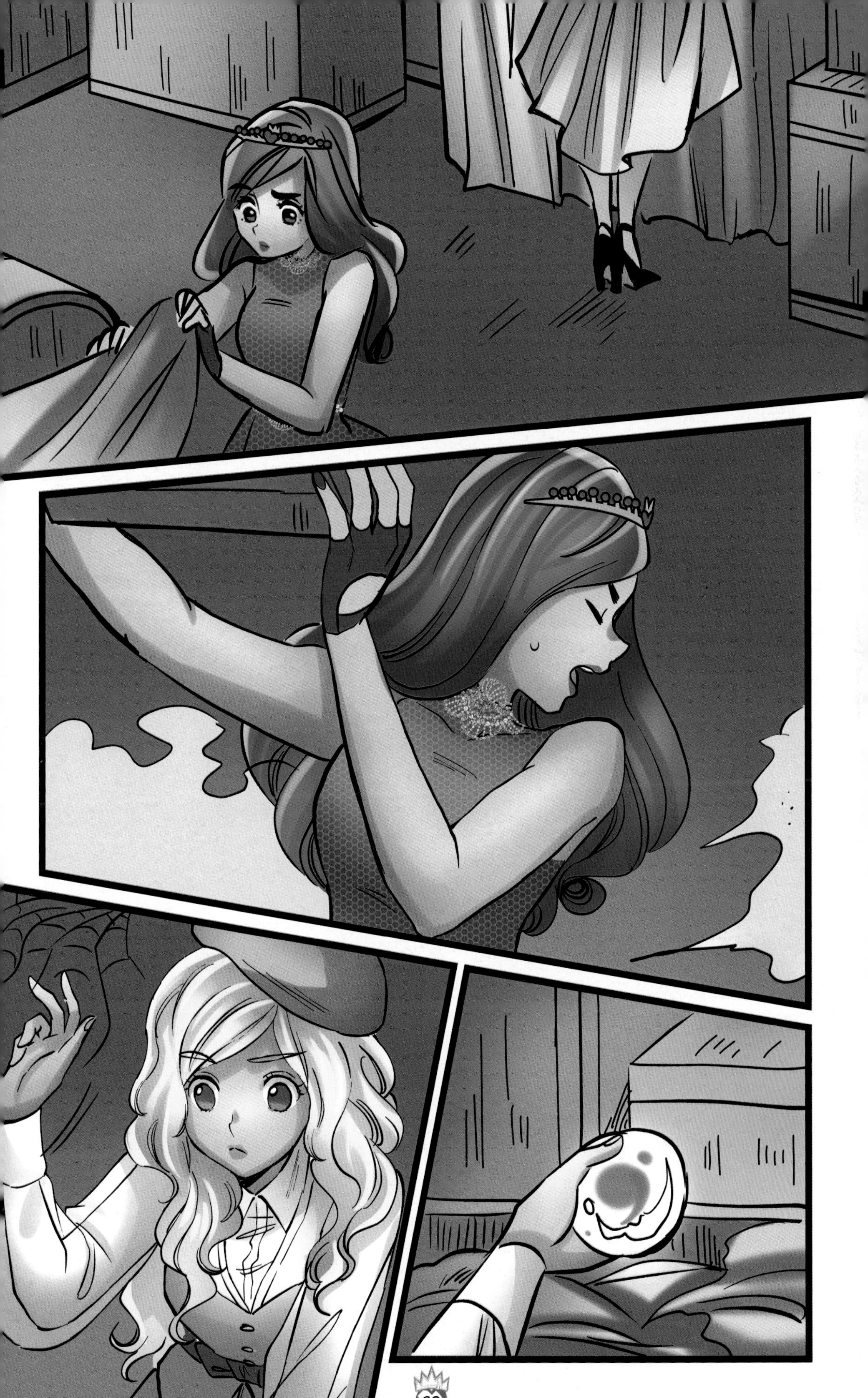

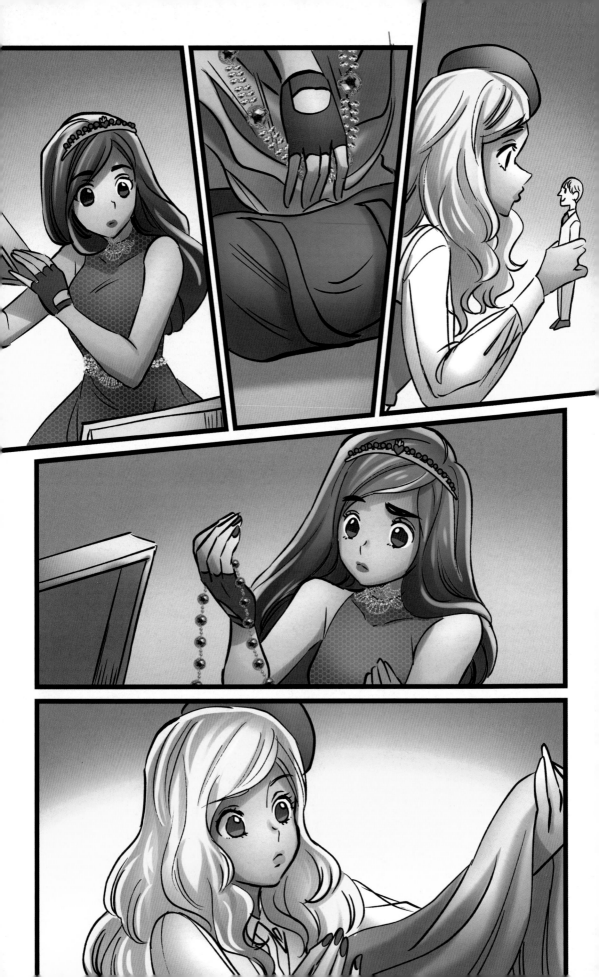

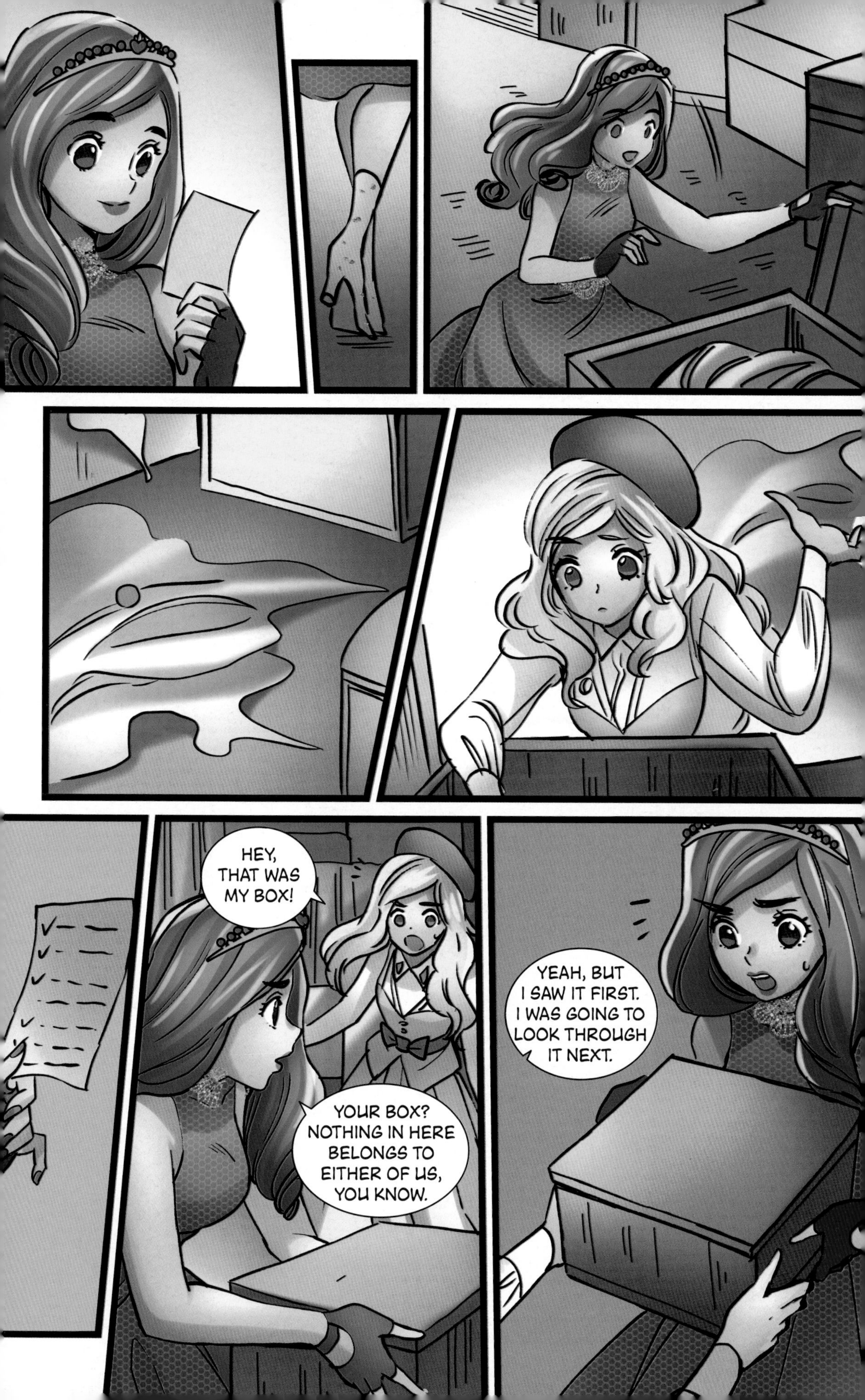
HEY, THAT WAS MY BOX!
YOUR BOX? NOTHING IN HERE BELONGS TO EITHER OF US, YOU KNOW.
YEAH, BUT I SAW IT FIRST. I WAS GOING TO LOOK THROUGH IT NEXT.

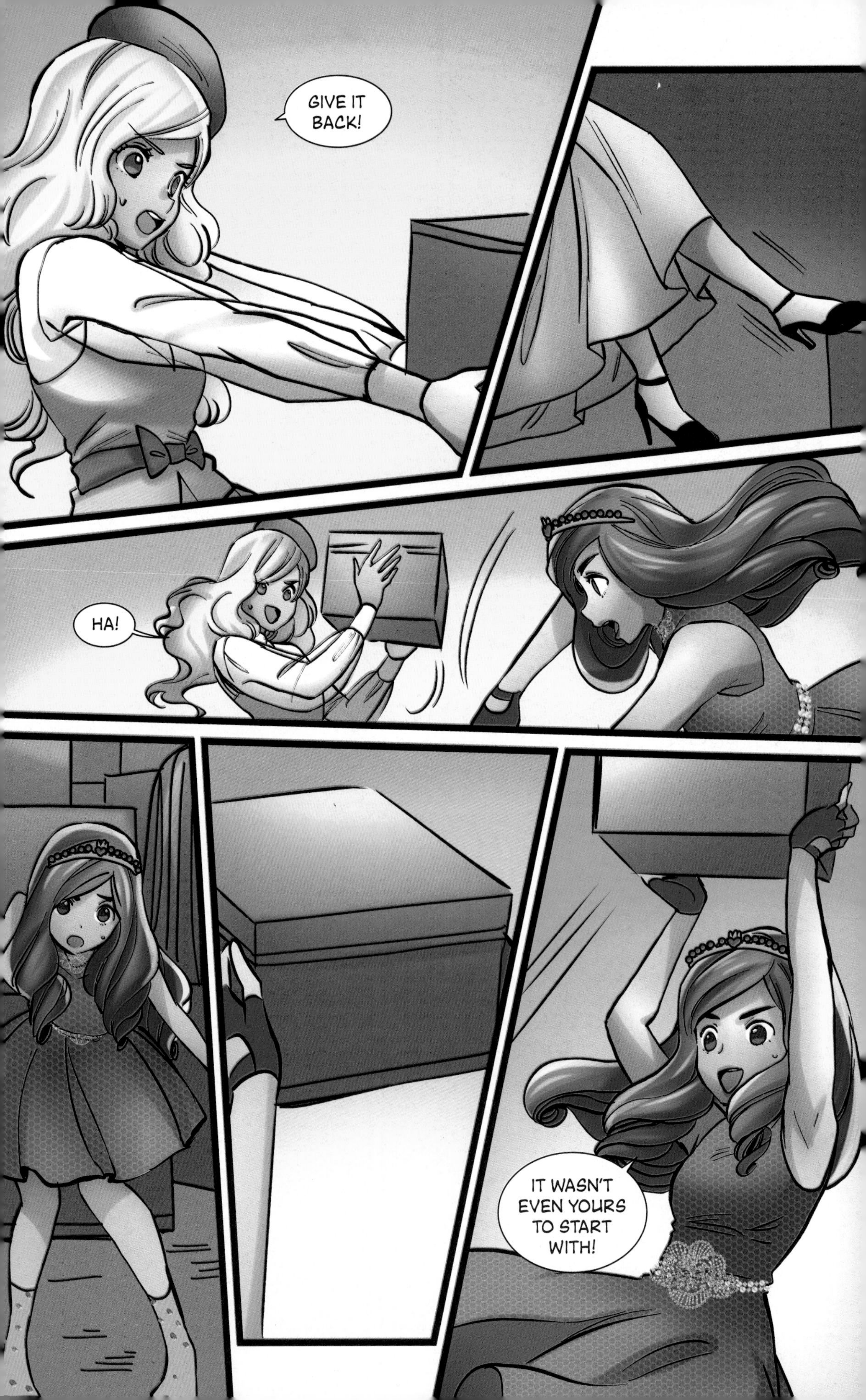
GIVE IT BACK!
HA!
IT WASN'T EVEN YOURS TO START WITH!

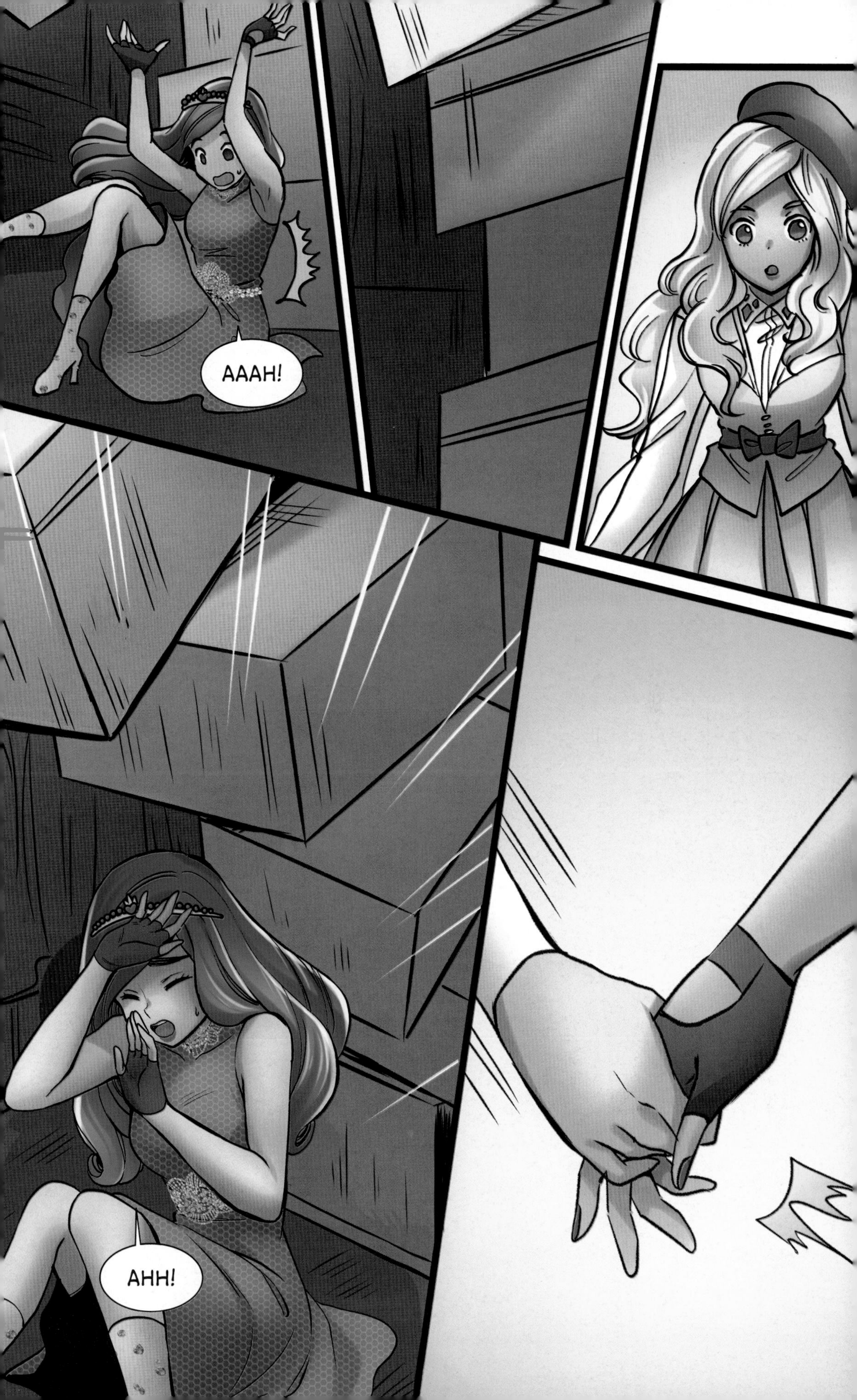
AAAH!
AHH!

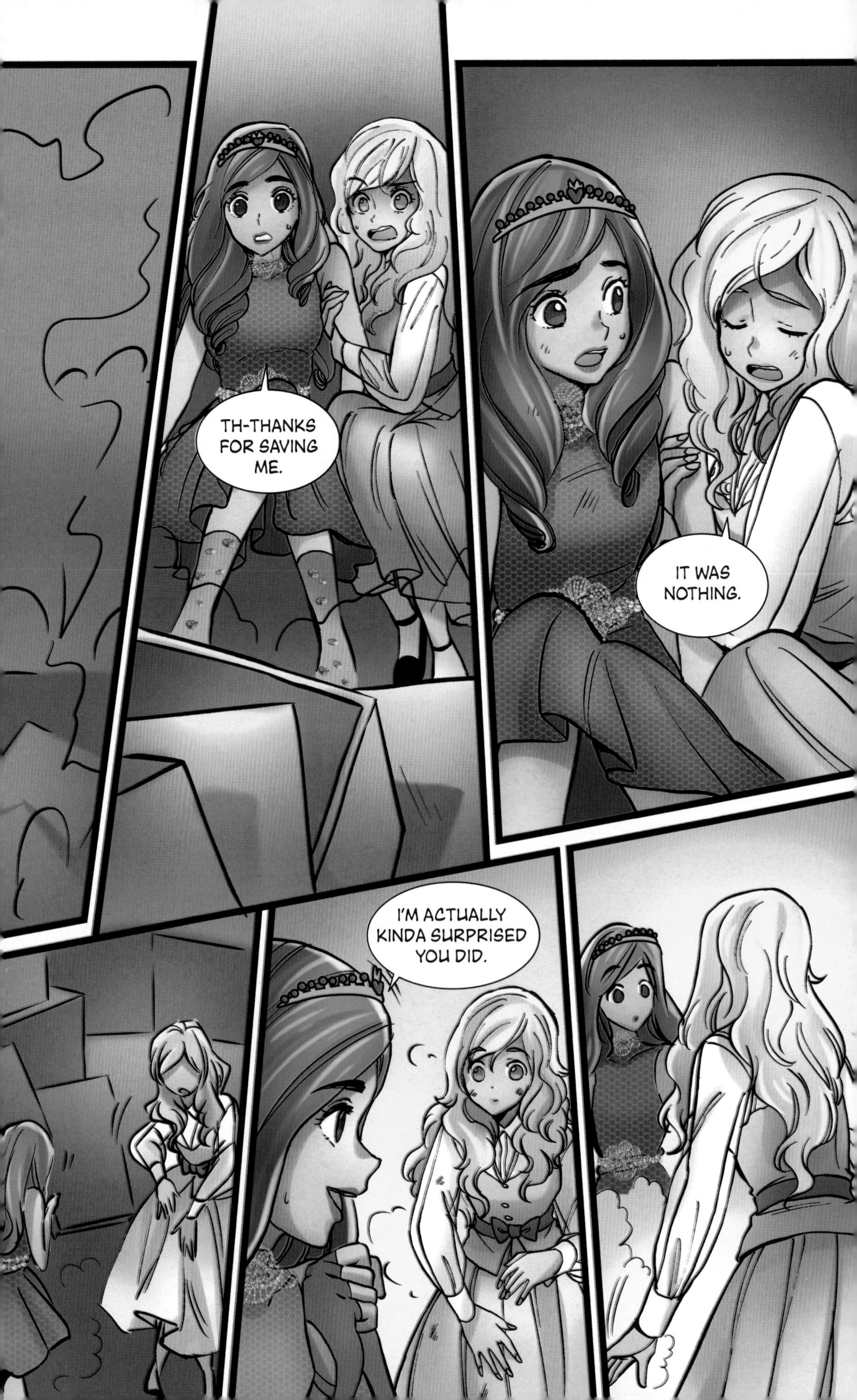
TH-THANKS FOR SAVING ME.
IT WAS NOTHING.
I'M ACTUALLY KINDA SURPRISED YOU DID.

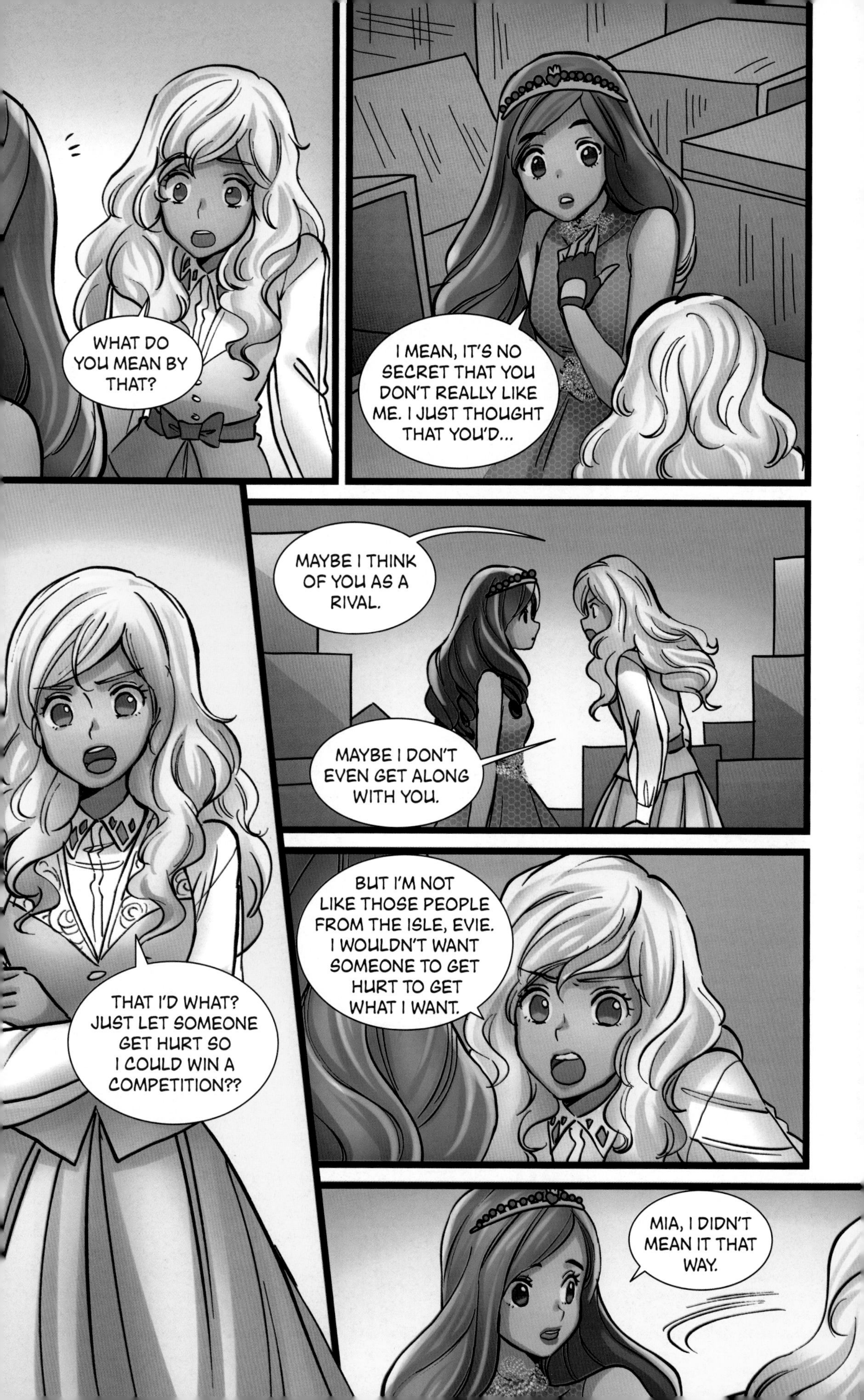
WHAT DO YOU MEAN BY THAT?
I MEAN, IT'S NO SECRET THAT YOU DON'T REALLY LIKE ME. I JUST THOUGHT THAT YOU'D...
THAT I'D WHAT? JUST LET SOMEONE GET HURT SO I COULD WIN A COMPETITION??
MAYBE I THINK OF YOU AS A RIVAL.
MAYBE I DON'T EVEN GET ALONG WITH YOU.
BUT I'M NOT LIKE THOSE PEOPLE FROM THE ISLE, EVIE. I WOULDN'T WANT SOMEONE TO GET HURT TO GET WHAT I WANT.
MIA, I DIDN'T MEAN IT THAT WAY.

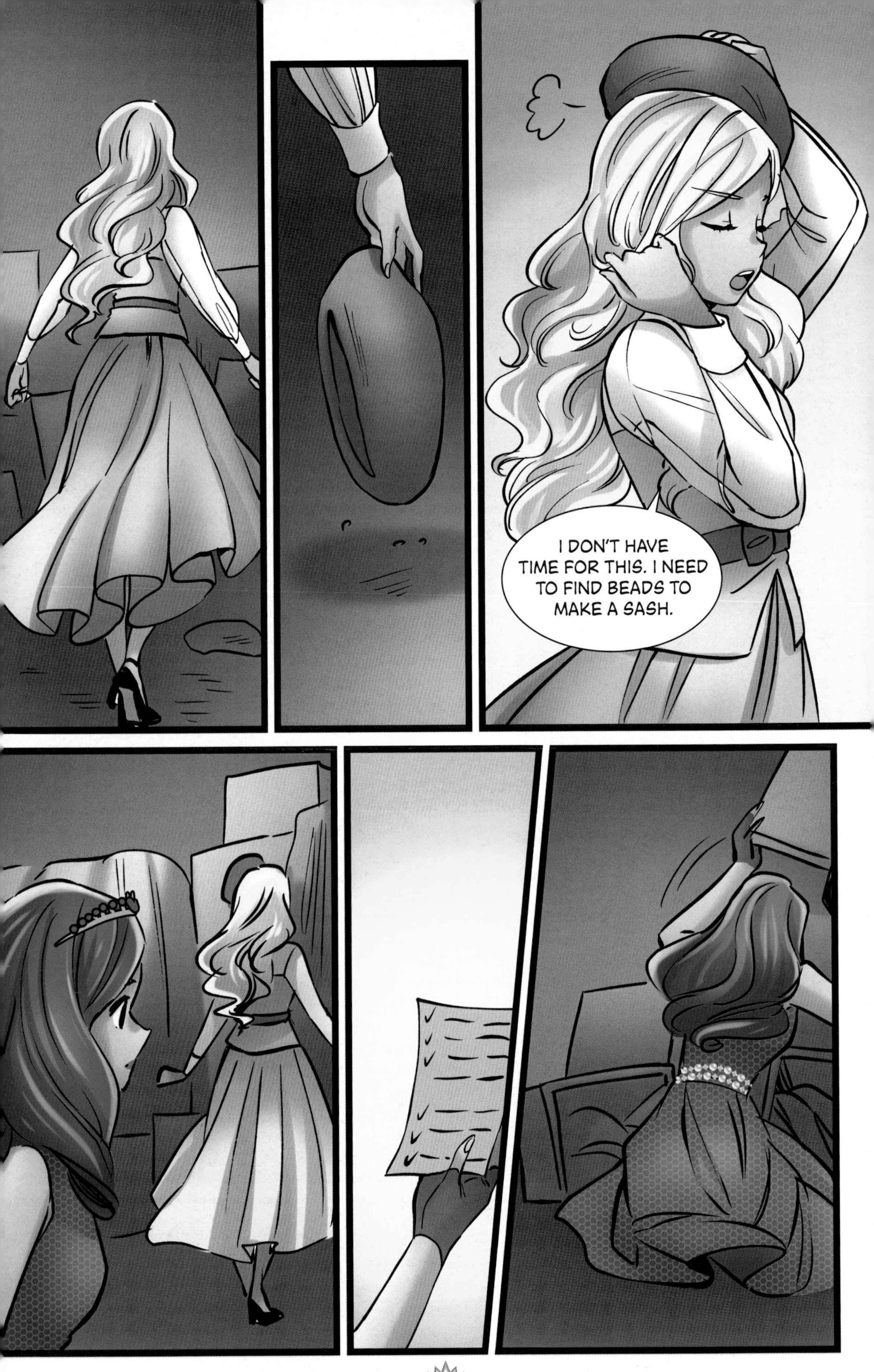
I DON'T HAVE TIME FOR THIS. I NEED TO FIND BEADS TO MAKE A SASH.

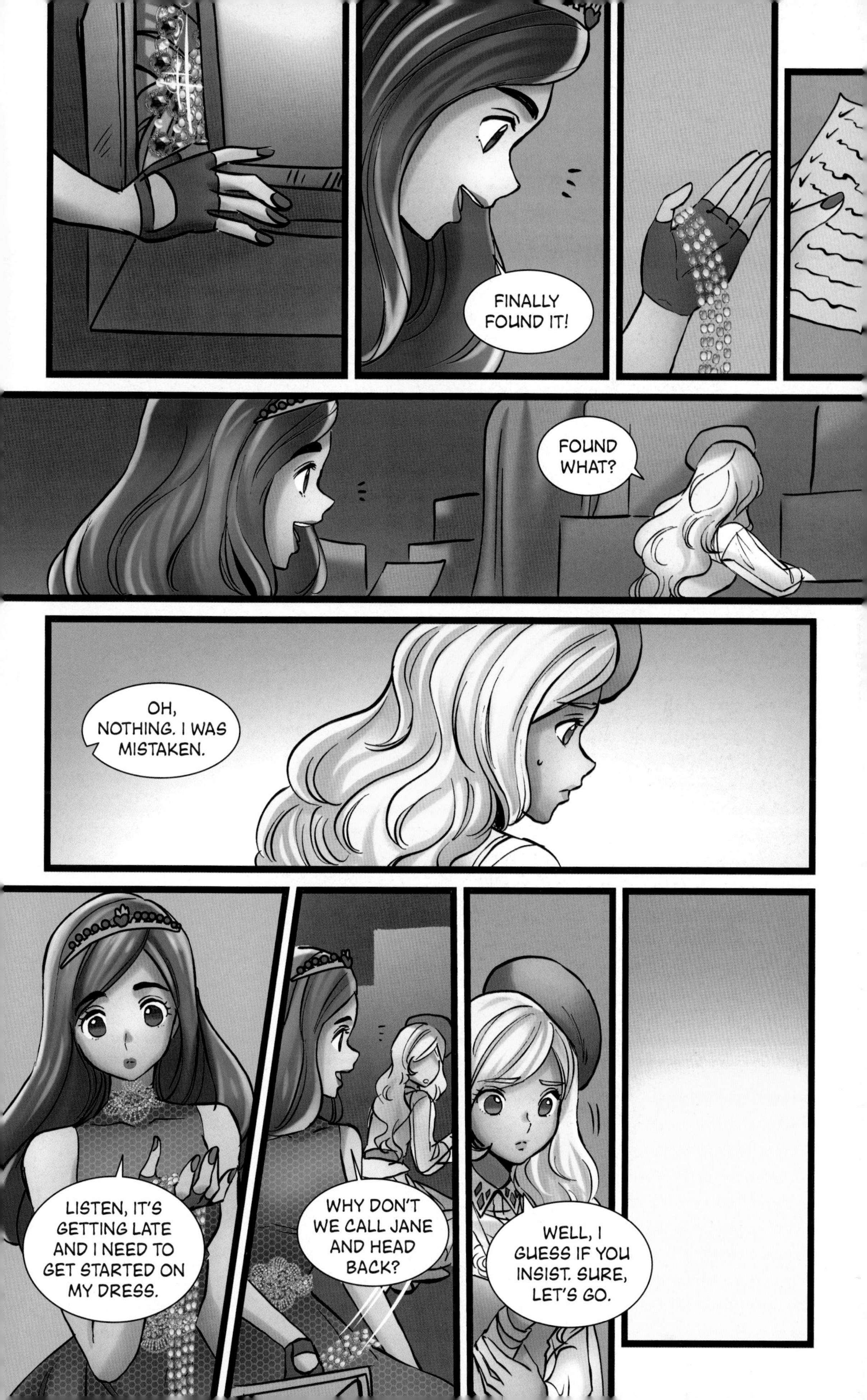
FINALLY FOUND IT!
FOUND WHAT?
OH, NOTHING. I WAS MISTAKEN.
LISTEN, IT'S GETTING LATE AND I NEED TO GET STARTED ON MY DRESS.
WHY DON'T WE CALL JANE AND HEAD BACK?
WELL, I GUESS IF YOU INSIST. SURE, LET'S GO.

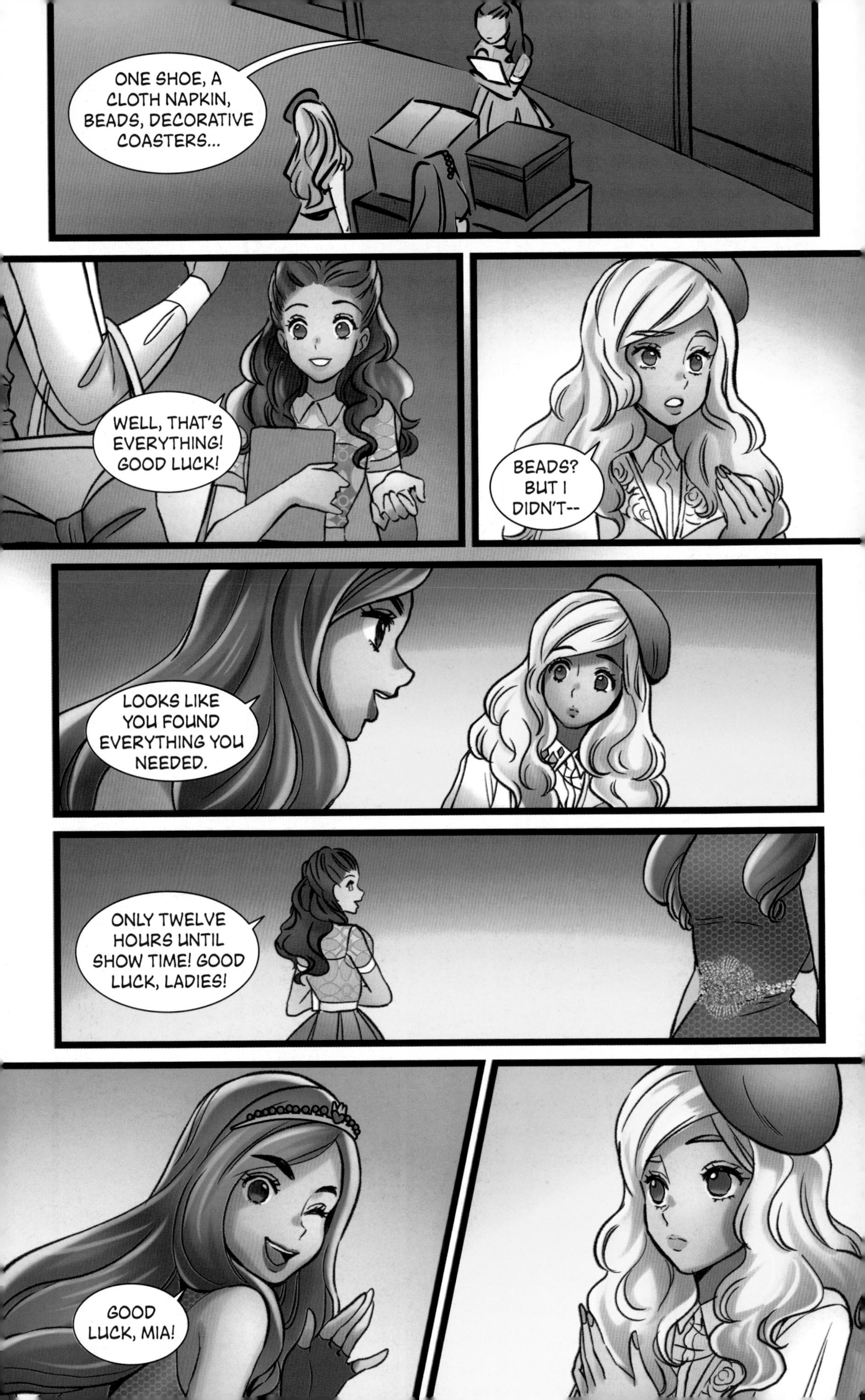
ONE SHOE, A CLOTH NAPKIN, BEADS, DECORATIVE COASTERS...
WELL, THAT'S EVERYTHING! GOOD LUCK!
BEADS? BUT I DIDN'T--
LOOKS LIKE YOU FOUND EVERYTHING YOU NEEDED.
ONLY TWELVE HOURS UNTIL SHOW TIME! GOOD LUCK, LADIES!
GOOD LUCK, MIA!

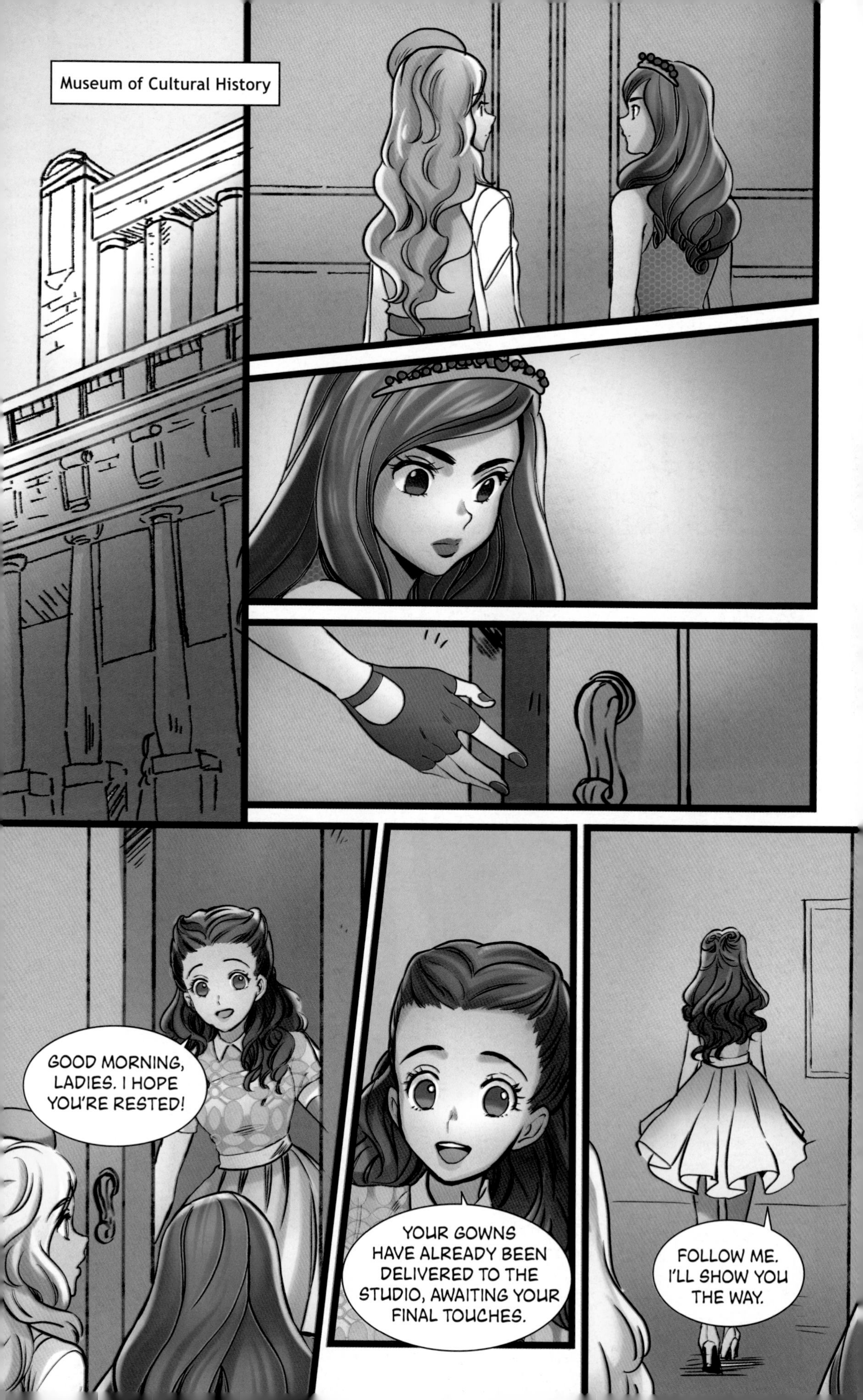
Museum of Cultural History
GOOD MORNING, LADIES. I HOPE YOU'RE RESTED!
YOUR GOWNS HAVE ALREADY BEEN DELIVERED TO THE STUDIO, AWAITING YOUR FINAL TOUCHES.
FOLLOW ME. I'LL SHOW YOU THE WAY.

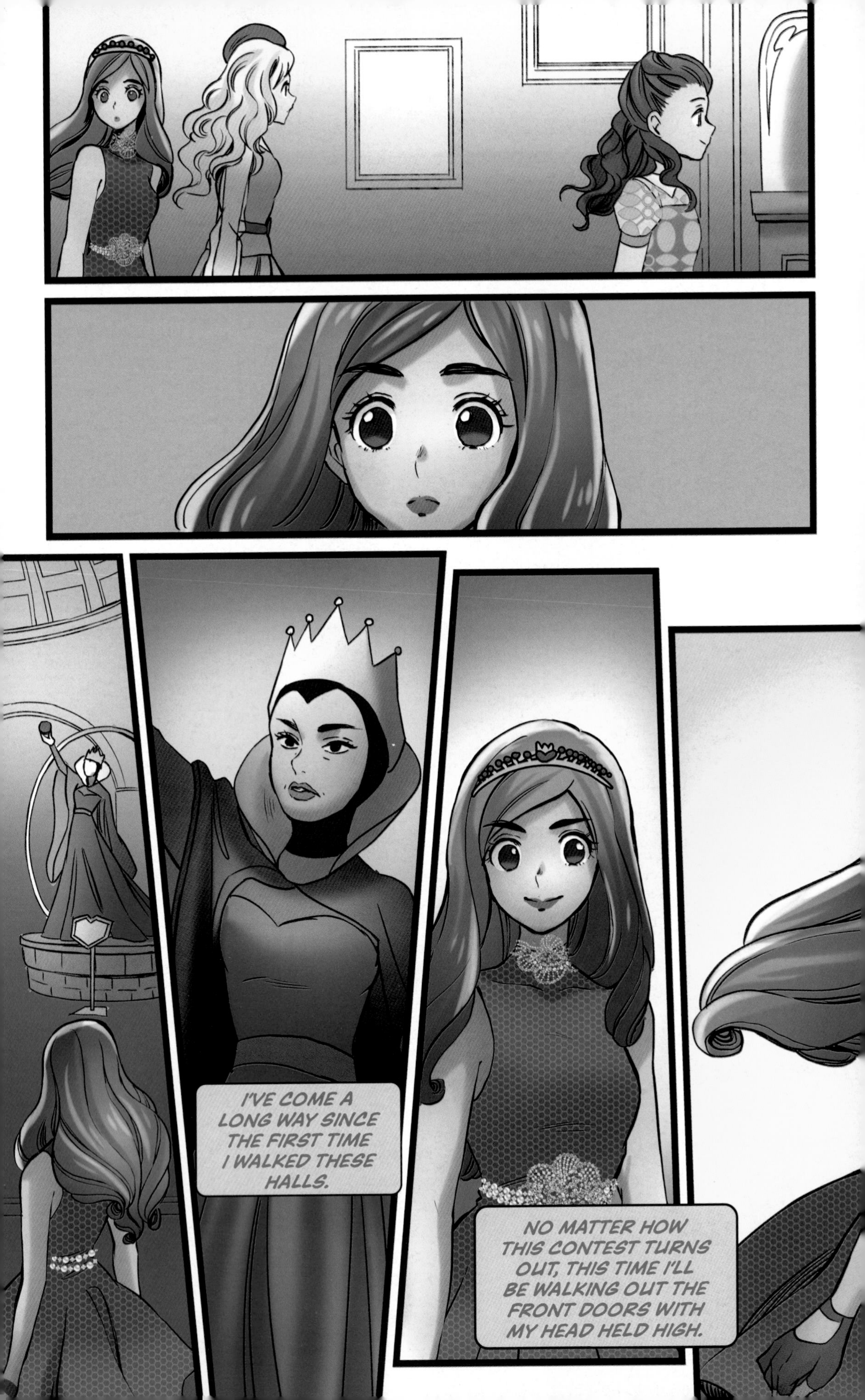
I'VE COME A LONG WAY SINCE THE FIRST TIME I WALKED THESE HALLS.
NO MATTER HOW THIS CONTEST TURNS OUT, THIS TIME I'LL BE WALKING OUT THE FRONT DOORS WITH MY HEAD HELD HIGH.

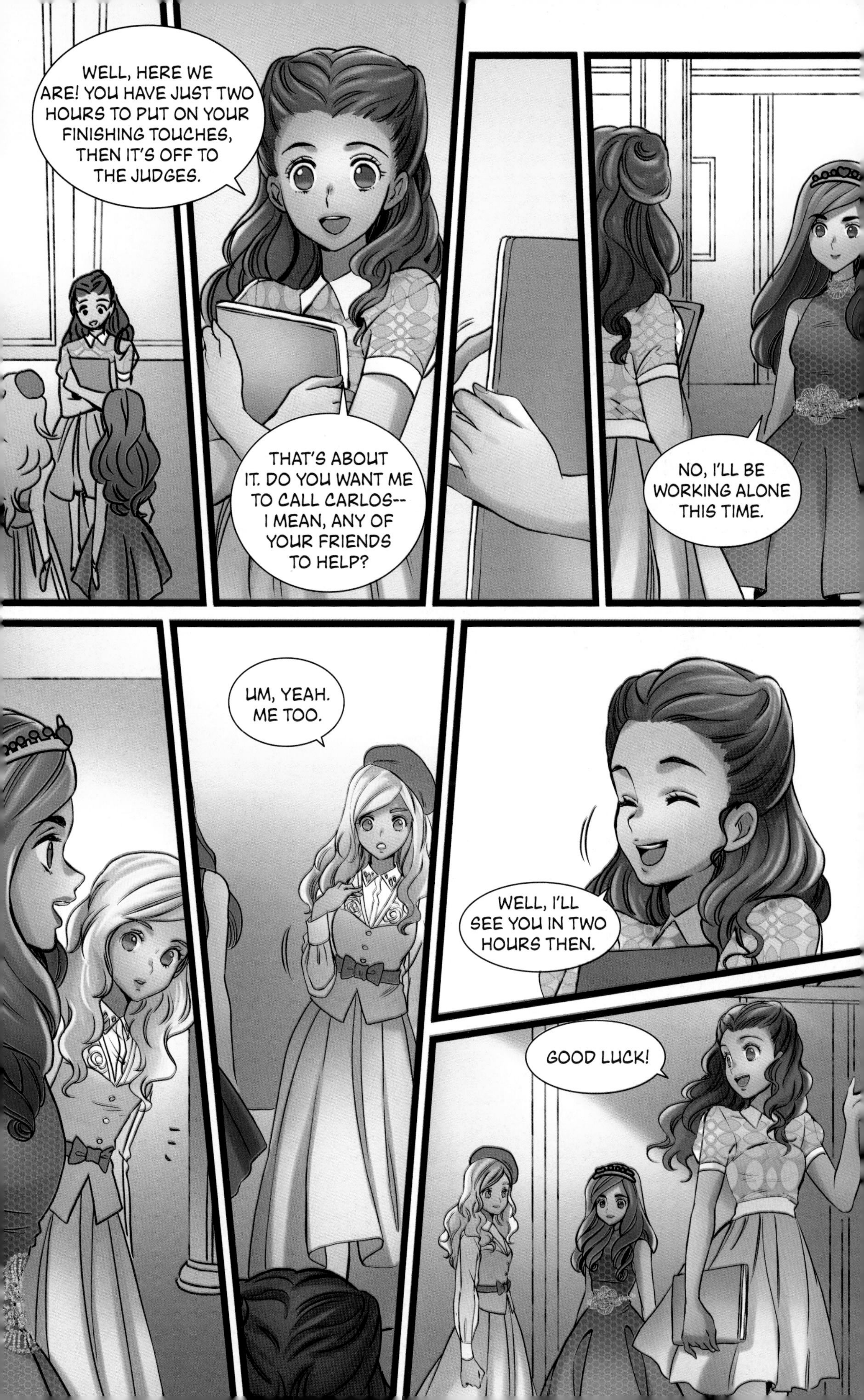
WELL, HERE WE ARE! YOU HAVE JUST TWO HOURS TO PUT ON YOUR FINISHING TOUCHES, THEN IT'S OFF TO THE JUDGES.
THAT'S ABOUT IT. DO YOU WANT ME TO CALL CARLOS-- I MEAN, ANY OF YOUR FRIENDS TO HELP?
NO, I'LL BE WORKING ALONE THIS TIME.
UM, YEAH. ME TOO.
WELL, I'LL SEE YOU IN TWO HOURS THEN.
GOOD LUCK!

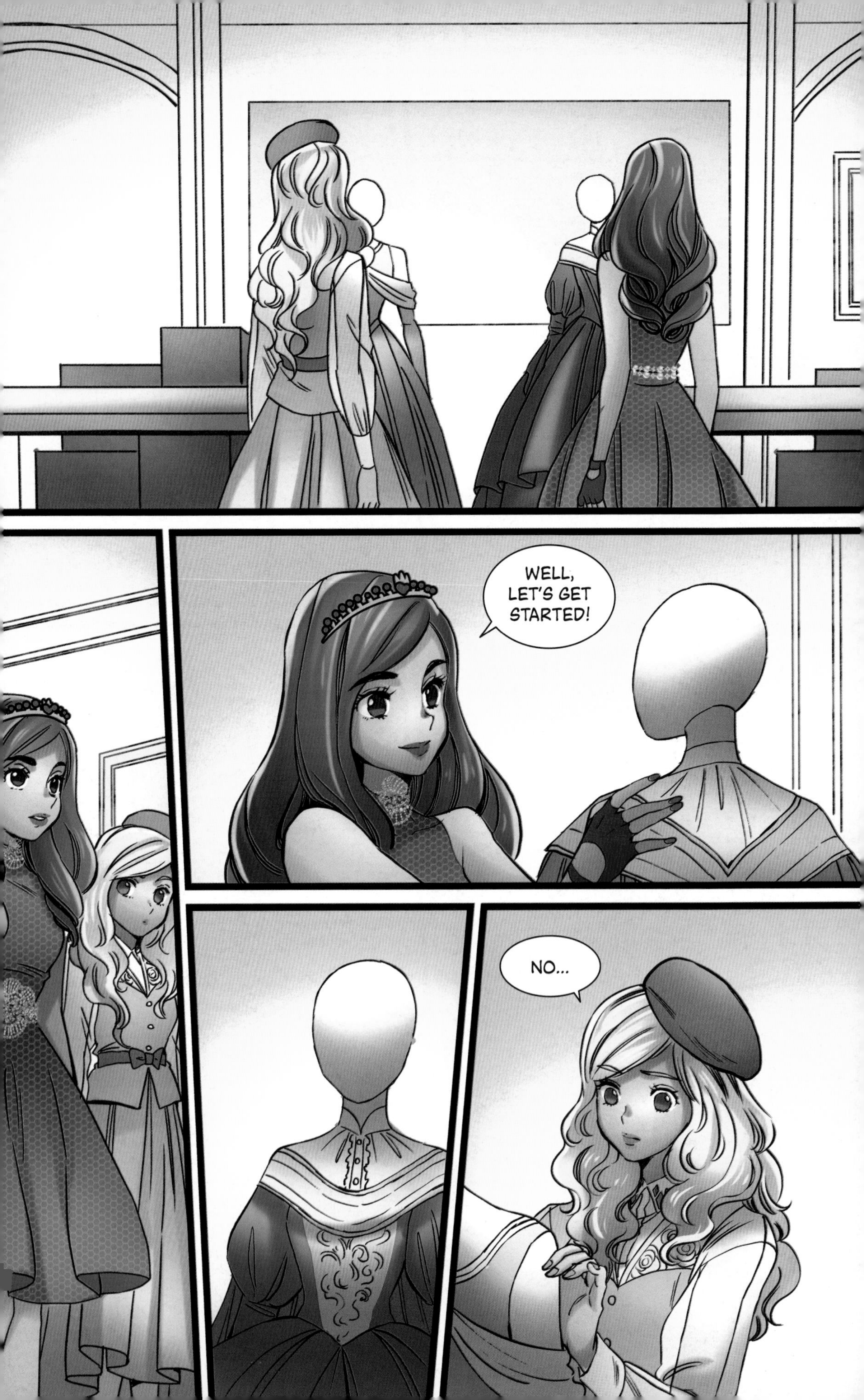
WELL, LET'S GET STARTED!
NO...

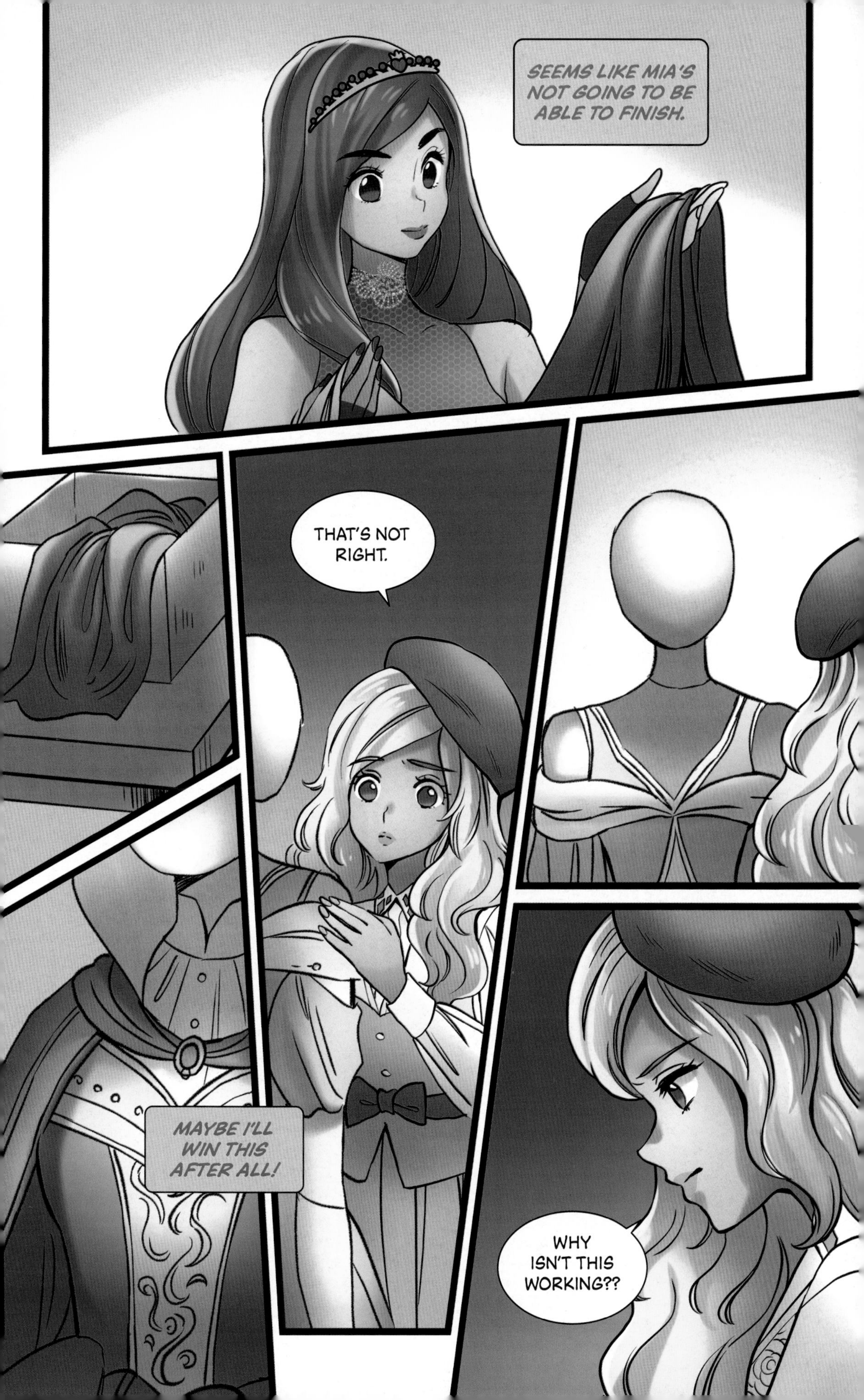
SEEMS LIKE MIA'S NOT GOING TO BE ABLE TO FINISH.
MAYBE I'LL WIN THIS AFTER ALL!
THAT'S NOT RIGHT.
WHY ISN'T THIS WORKING??

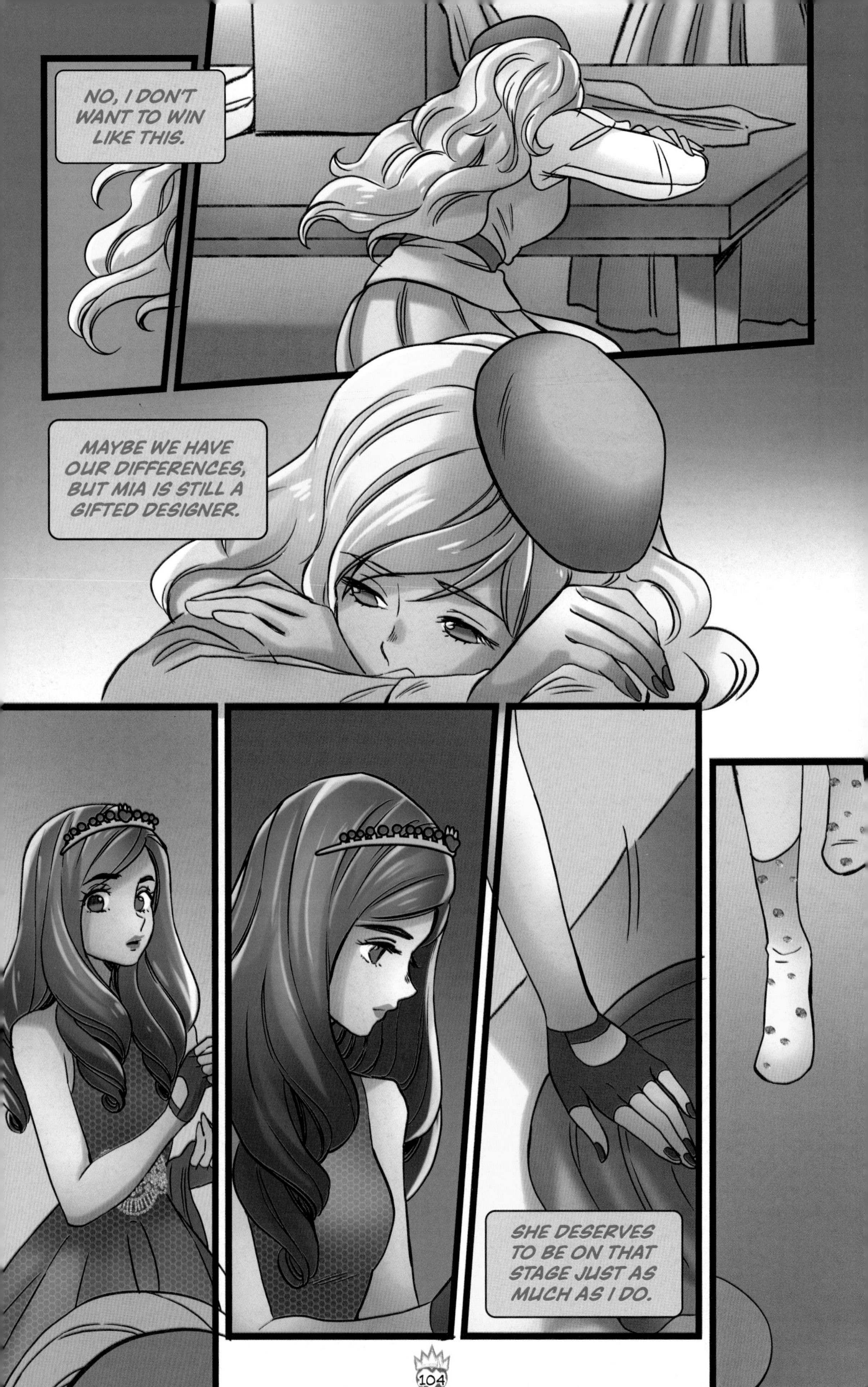
NO, I DON'T WANT TO WIN LIKE THIS.
MAYBE WE HAVE OUR DIFFERENCES, BUT MIA IS STILL A GIFTED DESIGNER.
SHE DESERVES TO BE ON THAT STAGE JUST AS MUCH AS I DO.

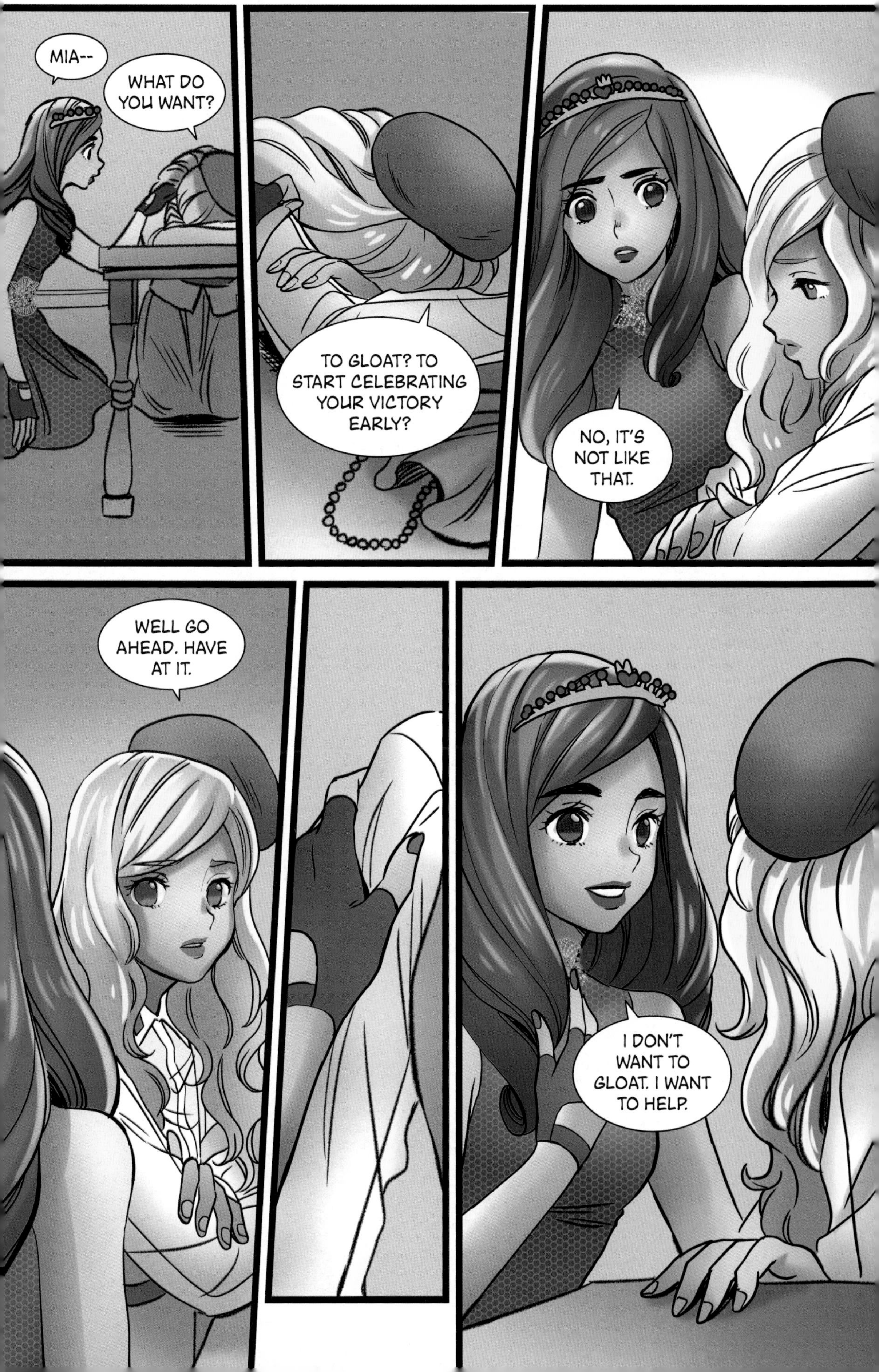
MIA--
WHAT DO YOU WANT?
TO GLOAT? TO START CELEBRATING YOUR VICTORY EARLY?
NO, IT'S NOT LIKE THAT.
WELL GO AHEAD. HAVE AT IT.
I DON'T WANT TO GLOAT. I WANT TO HELP.

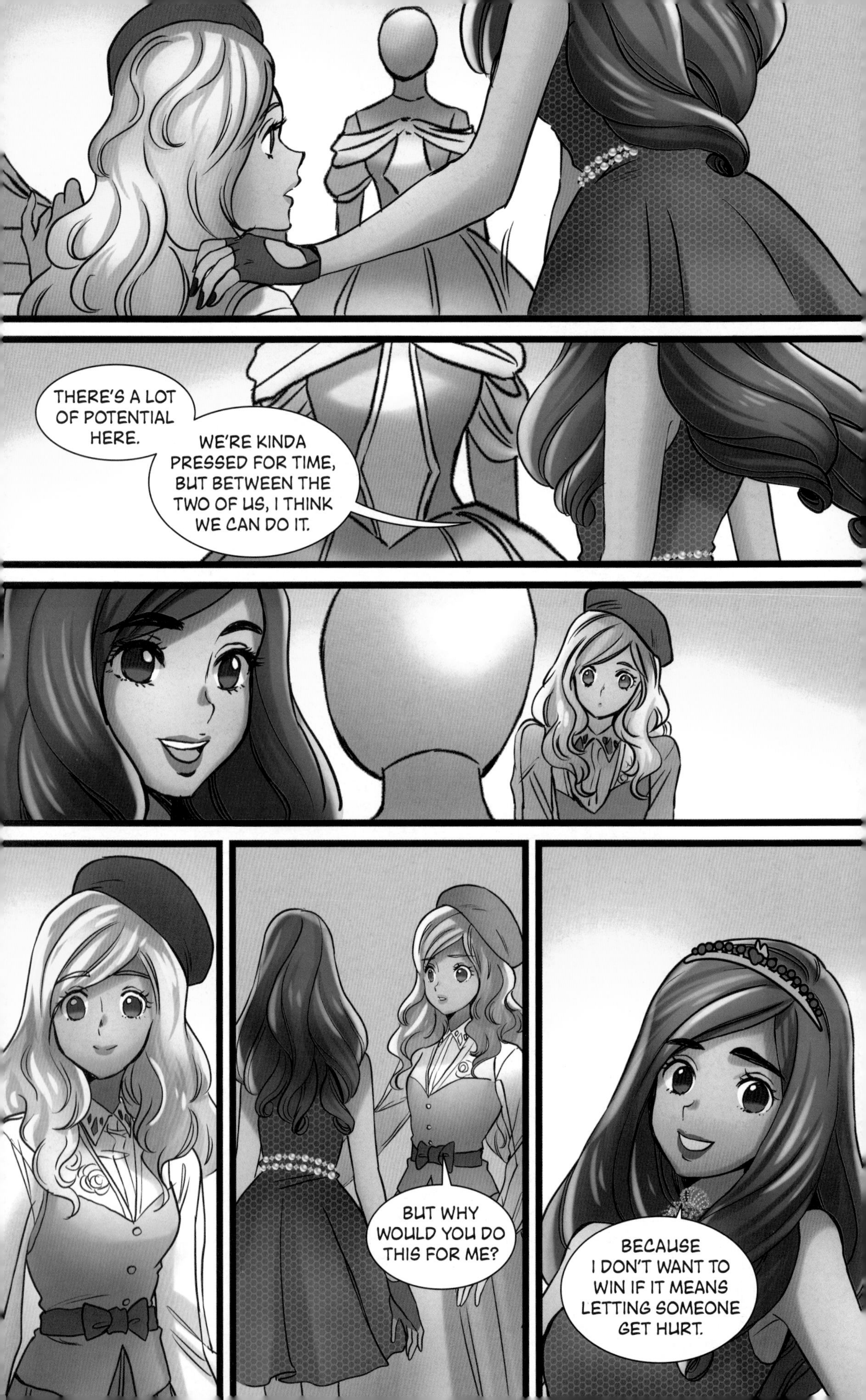
THERE'S A LOT OF POTENTIAL HERE.
WE'RE KINDA PRESSED FOR TIME, BUT BETWEEN THE TWO OF US, I THINK WE CAN DO IT.
BUT WHY WOULD YOU DO THIS FOR ME?
BECAUSE I DON'T WANT TO WIN IF IT MEANS LETTING SOMEONE GET HURT.

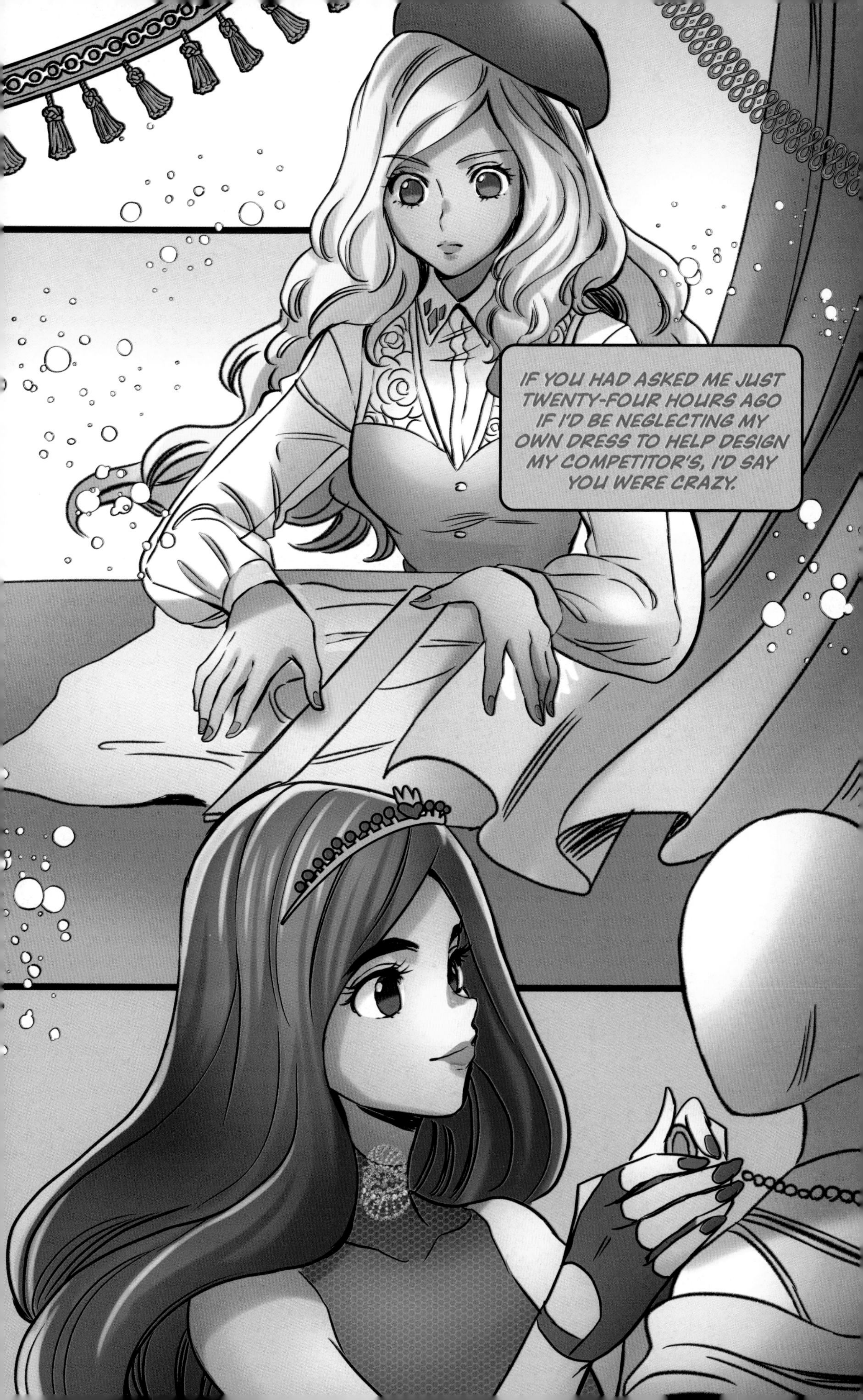
IF YOU HAD ASKED ME JUST TWENTY-FOUR HOURS AGO IF I'D BE NEGLECTING MY OWN DRESS TO HELP DESIGN MY COMPETITOR'S, I'D SAY YOU WERE CRAZY.

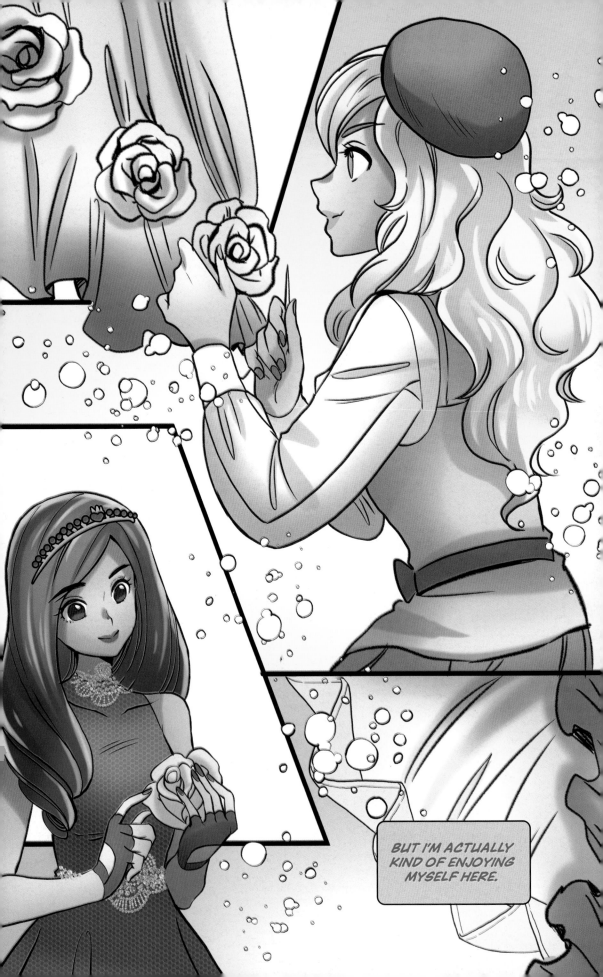

BUT I'M ACTUALLY
KIND OF ENJOYING
MYSELF HERE.

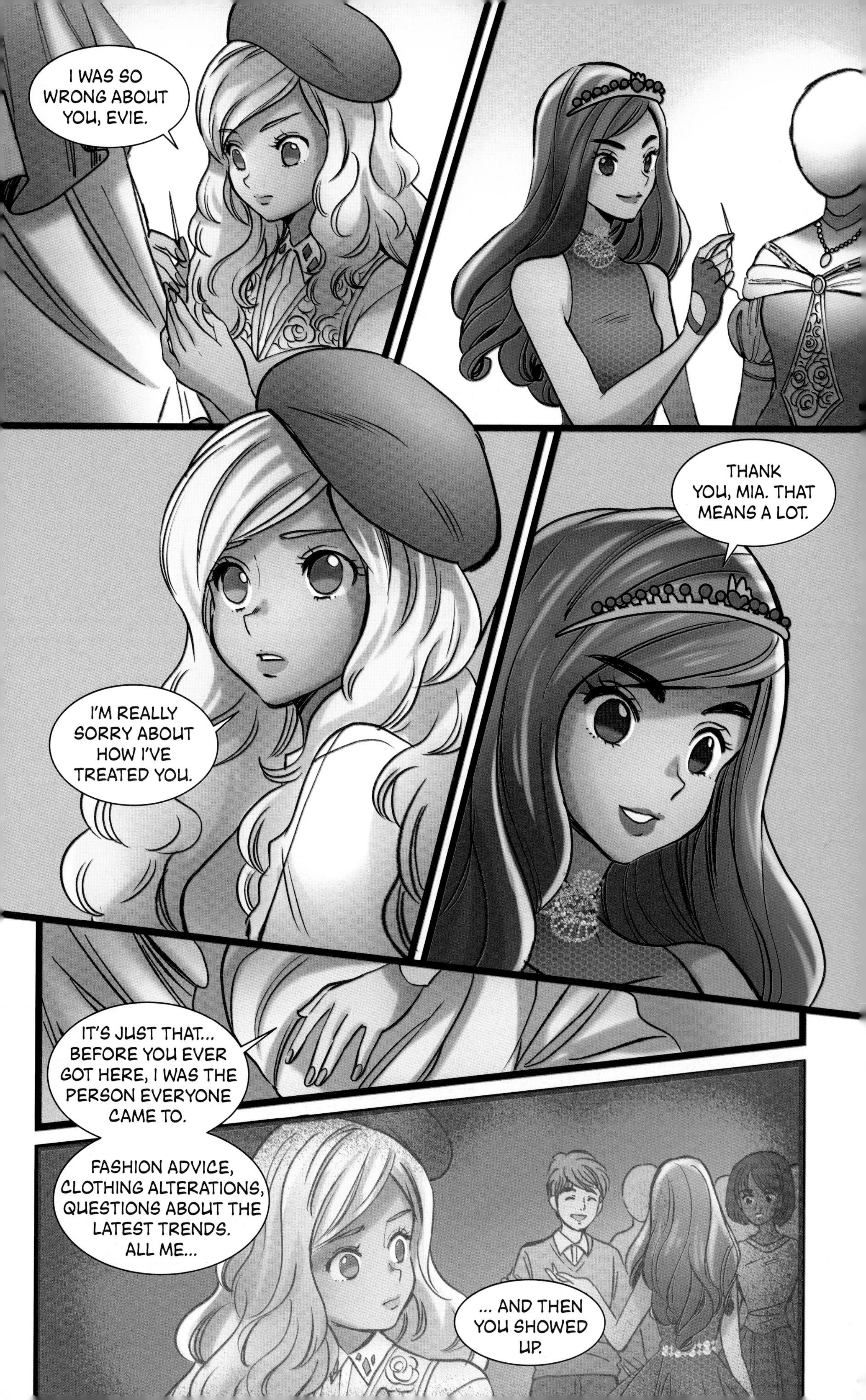
I WAS SO WRONG ABOUT YOU, EVIE.
I'M REALLY SORRY ABOUT HOW I'VE TREATED YOU.
THANK YOU, MIA. THAT MEANS A LOT.
IT'S JUST THAT... BEFORE YOU EVER GOT HERE, I WAS THE PERSON EVERYONE CAME TO.
FASHION ADVICE, CLOTHING ALTERATIONS, QUESTIONS ABOUT THE LATEST TRENDS. ALL ME...
... AND THEN YOU SHOWED UP.

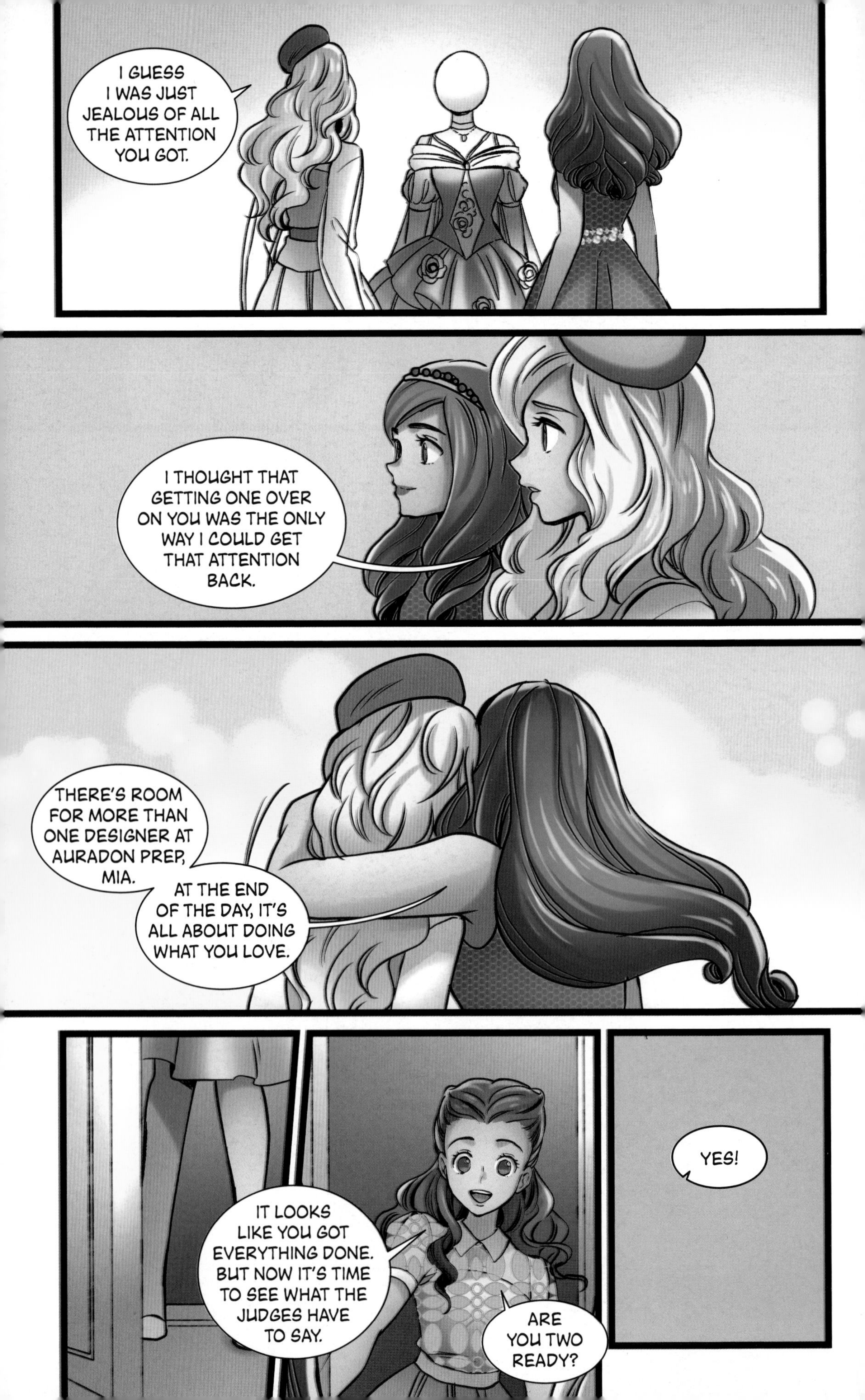
I GUESS I WAS JUST JEALOUS OF ALL THE ATTENTION YOU GOT.
I THOUGHT THAT GETTING ONE OVER ON YOU WAS THE ONLY WAY I COULD GET THAT ATTENTION BACK.
THERE'S ROOM FOR MORE THAN ONE DESIGNER AT AURADON PREP, MIA.
AT THE END OF THE DAY, IT'S ALL ABOUT DOING WHAT YOU LOVE.
IT LOOKS LIKE YOU GOT EVERYTHING DONE. BUT NOW IT'S TIME TO SEE WHAT THE JUDGES HAVE TO SAY.
ARE YOU TWO READY?
YES!

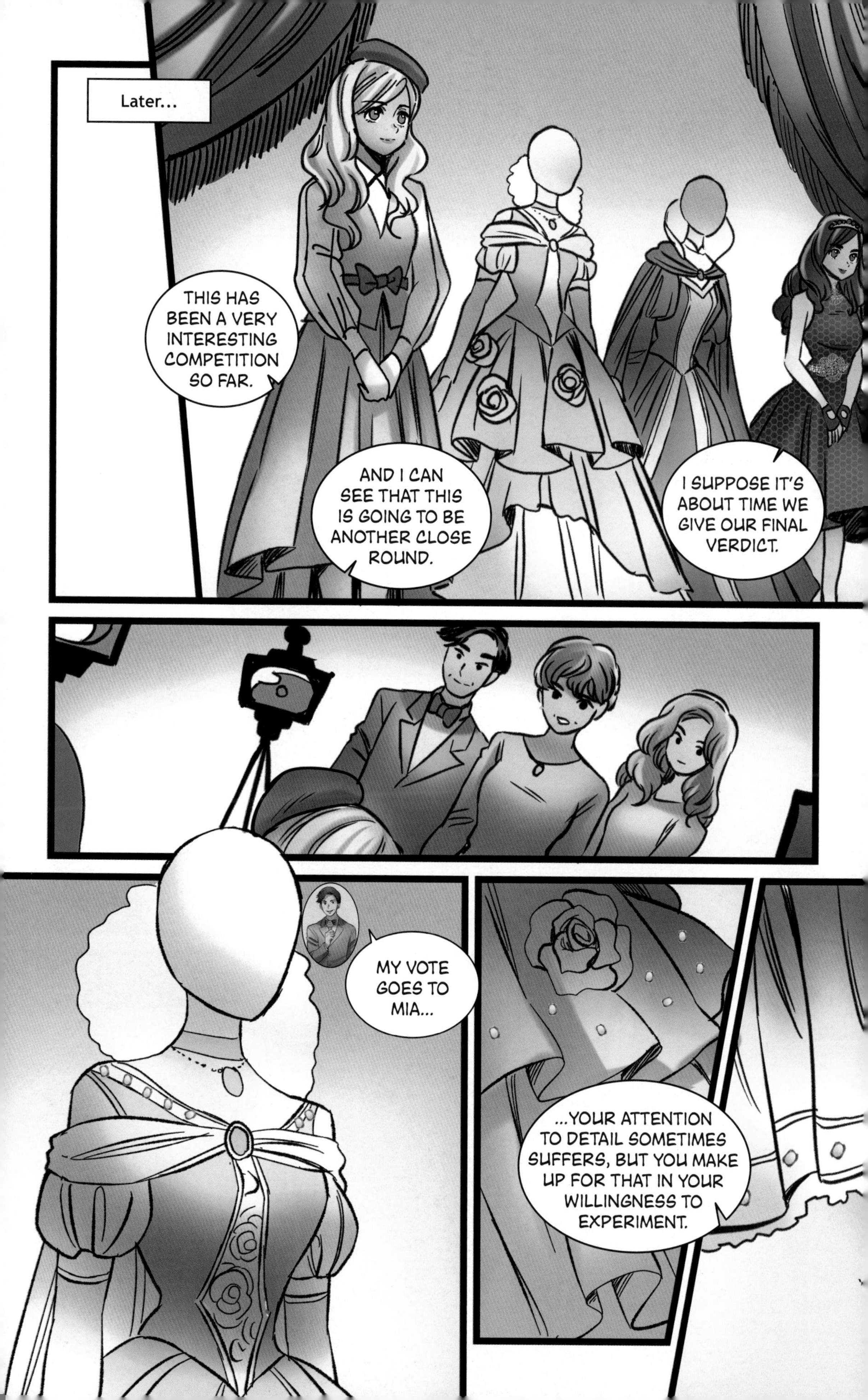
Later...
THIS HAS BEEN A VERY INTERESTING COMPETITION SO FAR.
AND I CAN SEE THAT THIS IS GOING TO BE ANOTHER CLOSE ROUND.
I SUPPOSE IT'S ABOUT TIME WE GIVE OUR FINAL VERDICT.
MY VOTE GOES TO MIA...
...YOUR ATTENTION TO DETAIL SOMETIMES SUFFERS, BUT YOU MAKE UP FOR THAT IN YOUR WILLINGNESS TO EXPERIMENT.

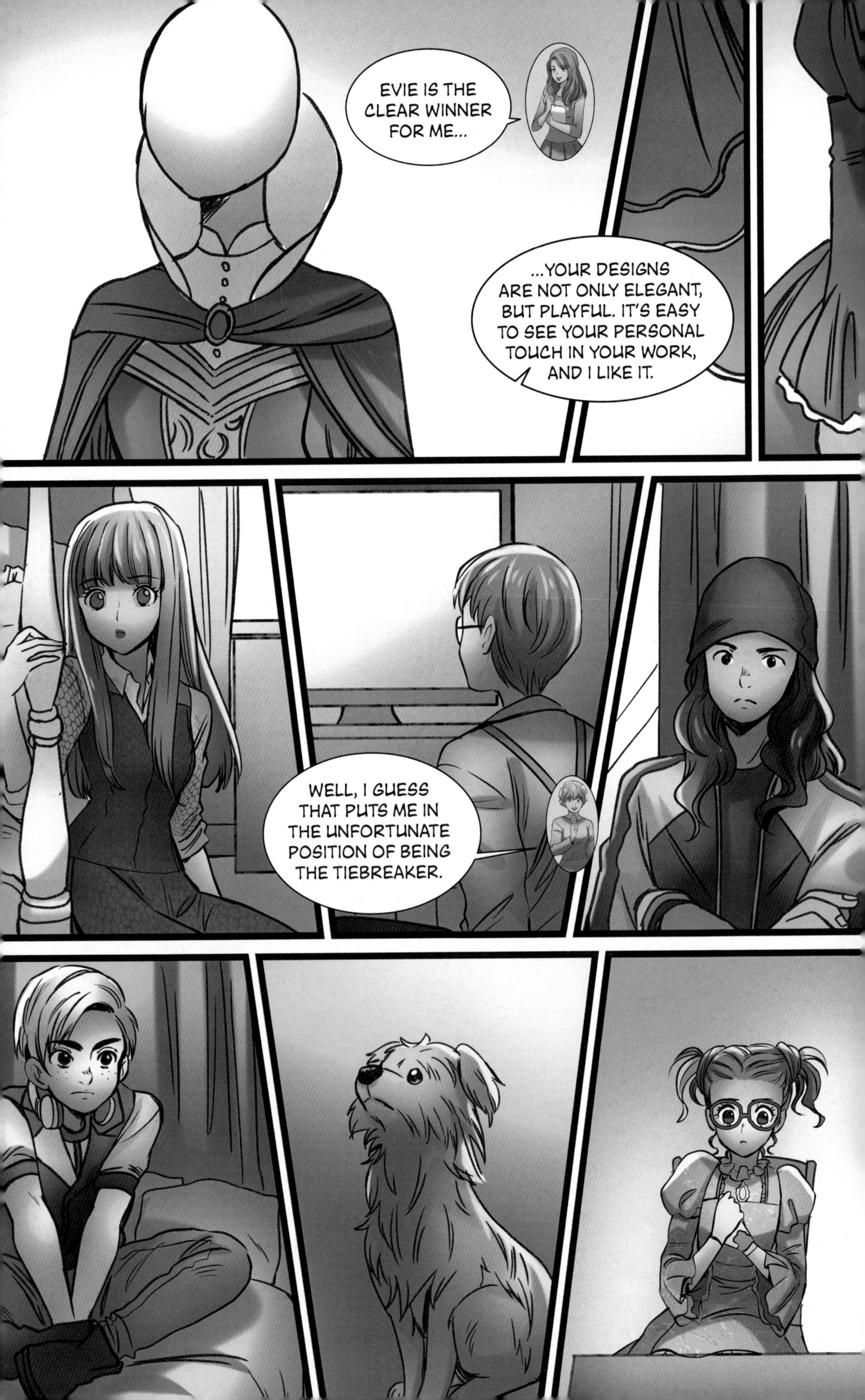
EVIE IS THE CLEAR WINNER FOR ME...
...YOUR DESIGNS ARE NOT ONLY ELEGANT, BUT PLAYFUL. IT'S EASY TO SEE YOUR PERSONAL TOUCH IN YOUR WORK, AND I LIKE IT.
WELL, I GUESS THAT PUTS ME IN THE UNFORTUNATE POSITION OF BEING THE TIEBREAKER.

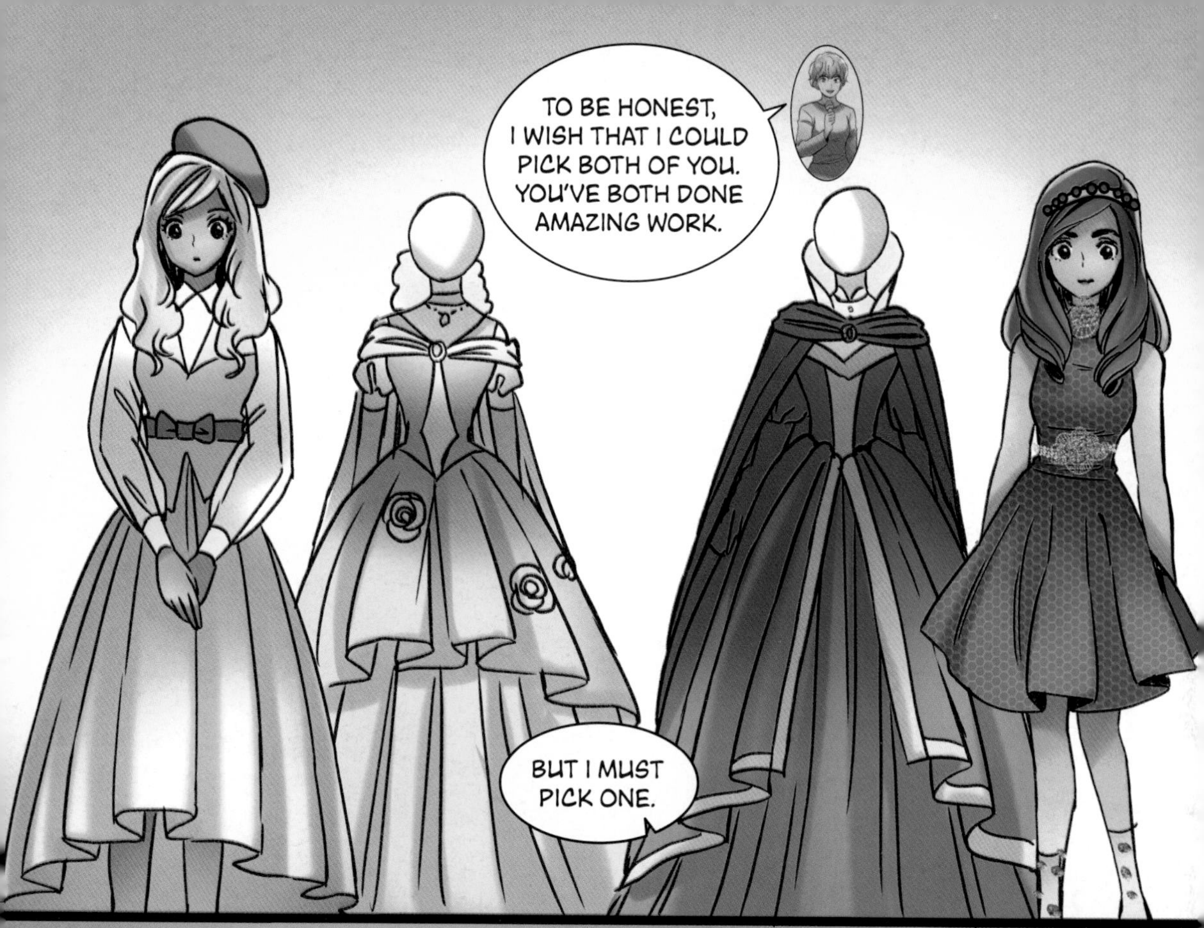
TO BE HONEST, I WISH THAT I COULD PICK BOTH OF YOU. YOU'VE BOTH DONE AMAZING WORK.
BUT I MUST PICK ONE.

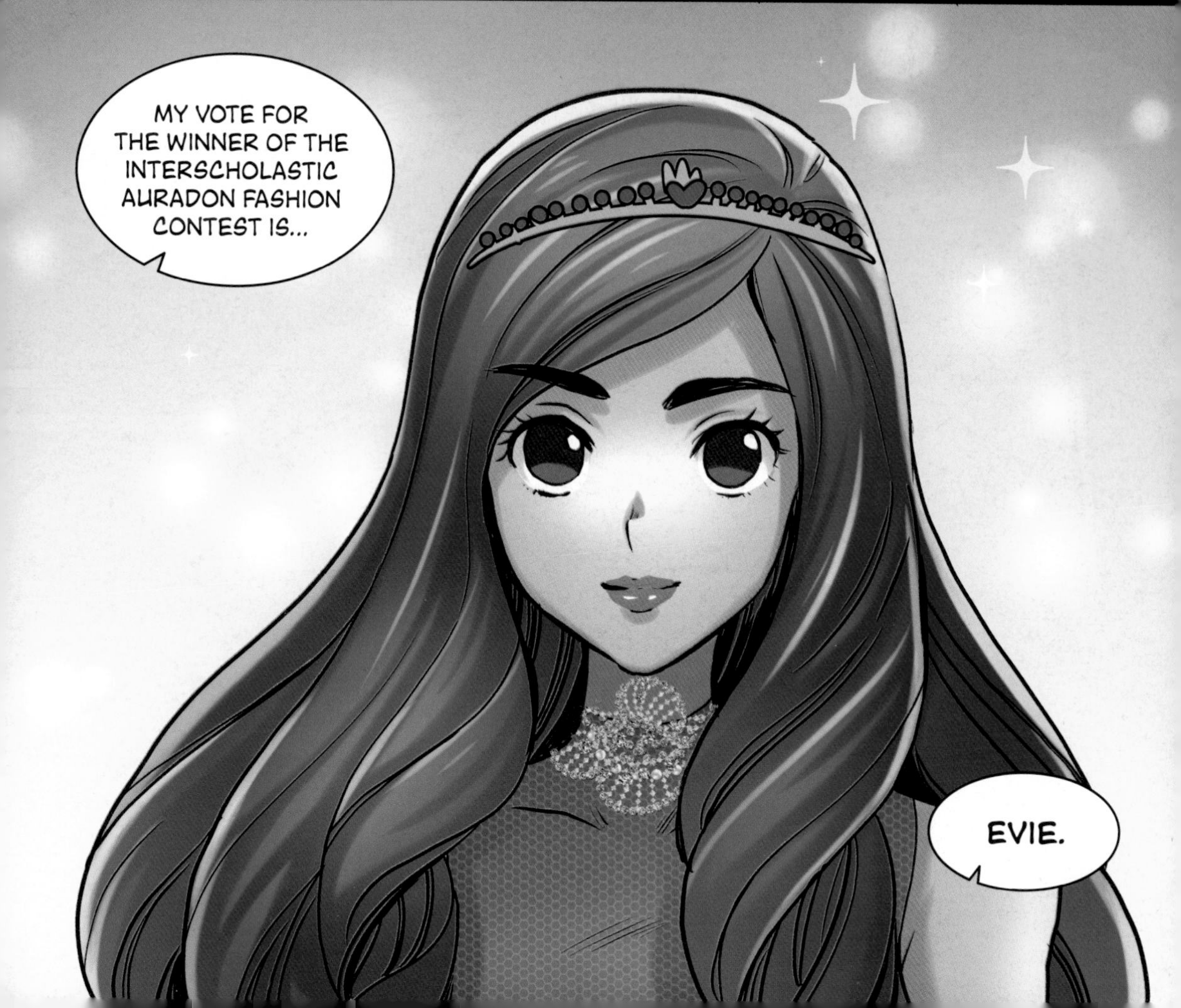
MY VOTE FOR THE WINNER OF THE INTERSCHOLASTIC AURADON FASHION CONTEST IS...
EVIE.

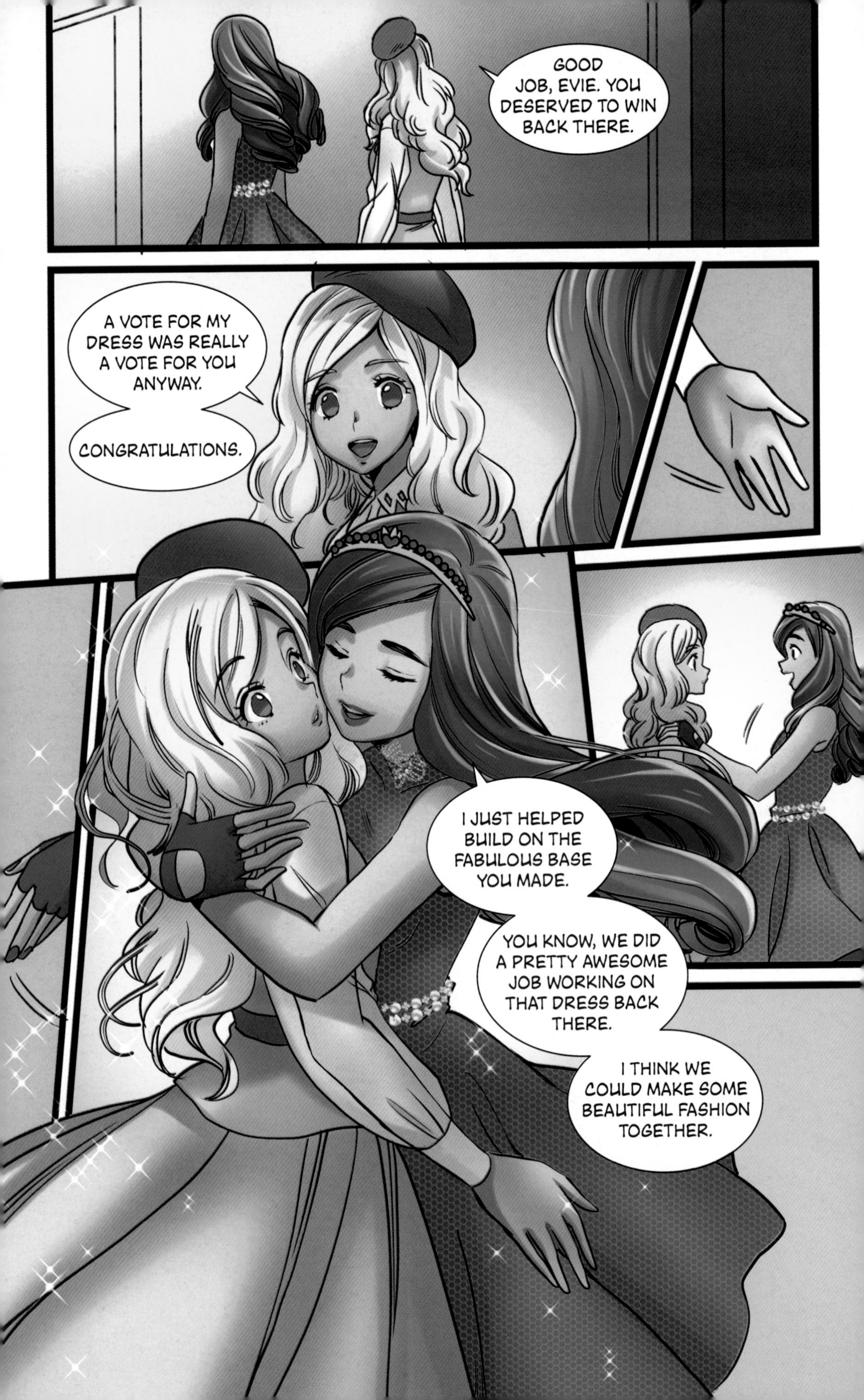
GOOD JOB, EVIE. YOU DESERVED TO WIN BACK THERE.
A VOTE FOR MY DRESS WAS REALLY A VOTE FOR YOU ANYWAY.
CONGRATULATIONS.
I JUST HELPED BUILD ON THE FABULOUS BASE YOU MADE.
YOU KNOW, WE DID A PRETTY AWESOME JOB WORKING ON THAT DRESS BACK THERE.
I THINK WE COULD MAKE SOME BEAUTIFUL FASHION TOGETHER.

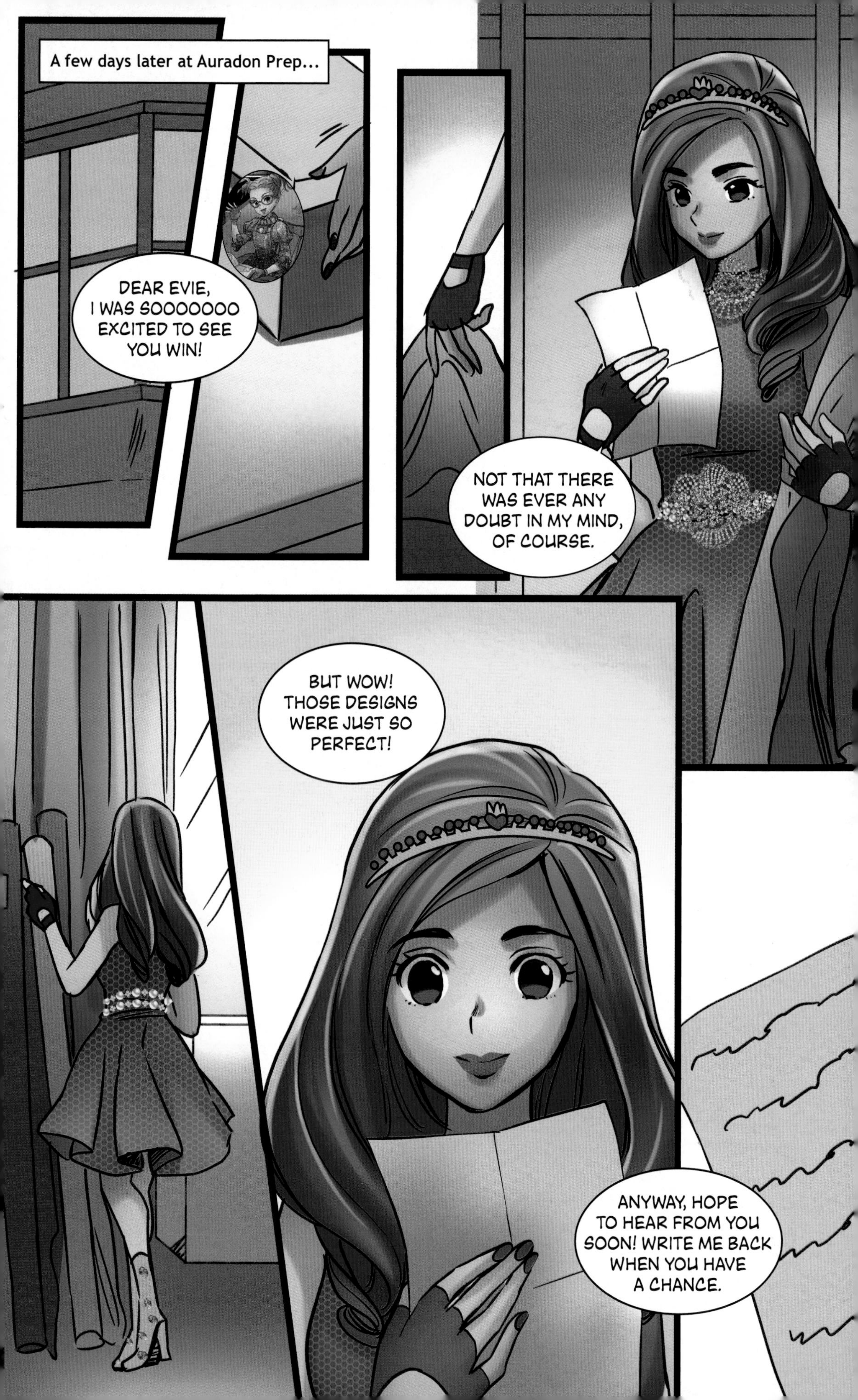
A few days later at Auradon Prep…
DEAR EVIE, I WAS SOOOOOOO EXCITED TO SEE YOU WIN!
NOT THAT THERE WAS EVER ANY DOUBT IN MY MIND, OF COURSE.
BUT WOW! THOSE DESIGNS WERE JUST SO PERFECT!
ANYWAY, HOPE TO HEAR FROM YOU SOON! WRITE ME BACK WHEN YOU HAVE A CHANCE.

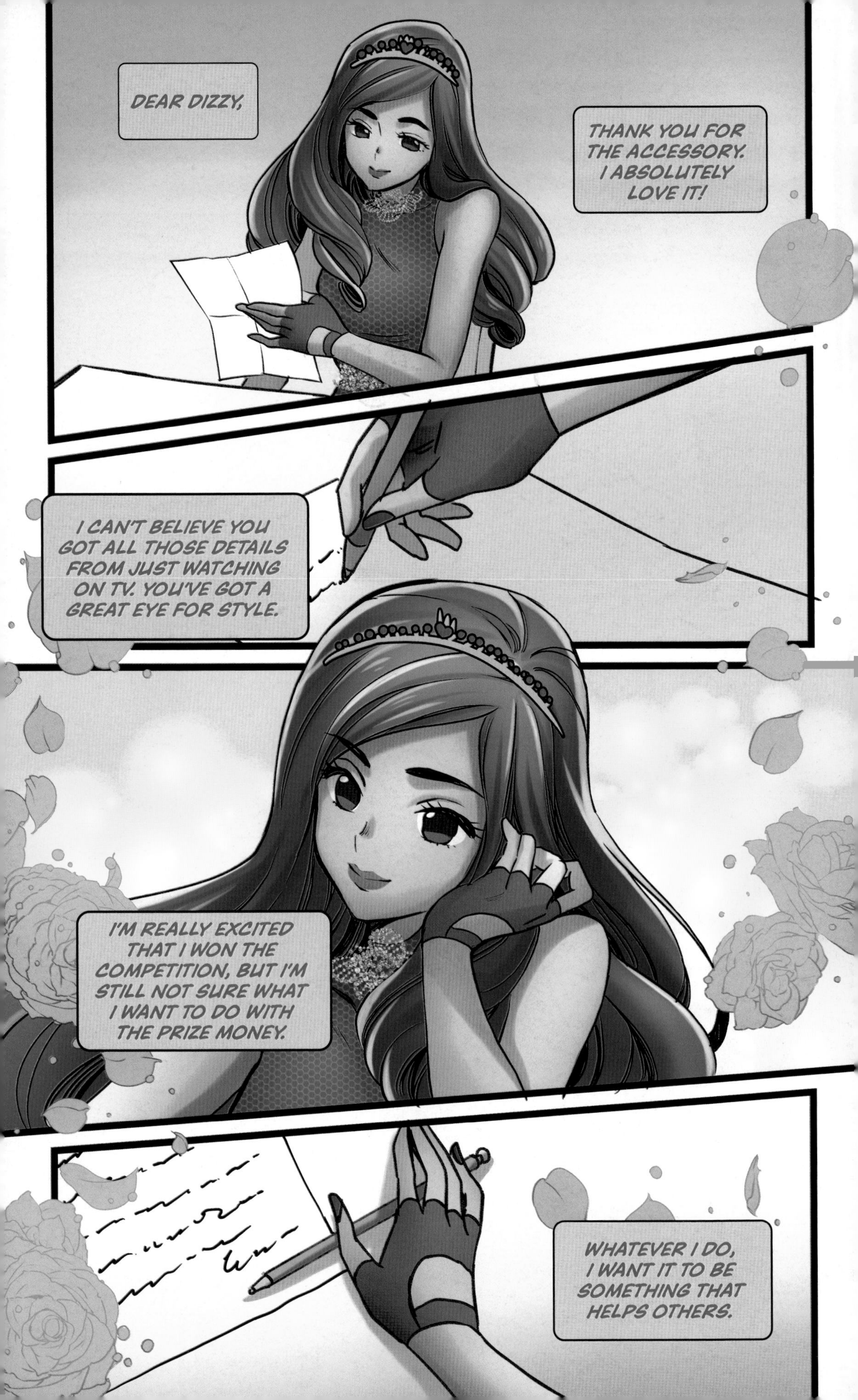
DEAR DIZZY,
THANK YOU FOR THE ACCESSORY. I ABSOLUTELY LOVE IT!
I CAN'T BELIEVE YOU GOT ALL THOSE DETAILS FROM JUST WATCHING ON TV. YOU'VE GOT A GREAT EYE FOR STYLE.
I'M REALLY EXCITED THAT I WON THE COMPETITION, BUT I'M STILL NOT SURE WHAT I WANT TO DO WITH THE PRIZE MONEY.
WHATEVER I DO, I WANT IT TO BE SOMETHING THAT HELPS OTHERS.

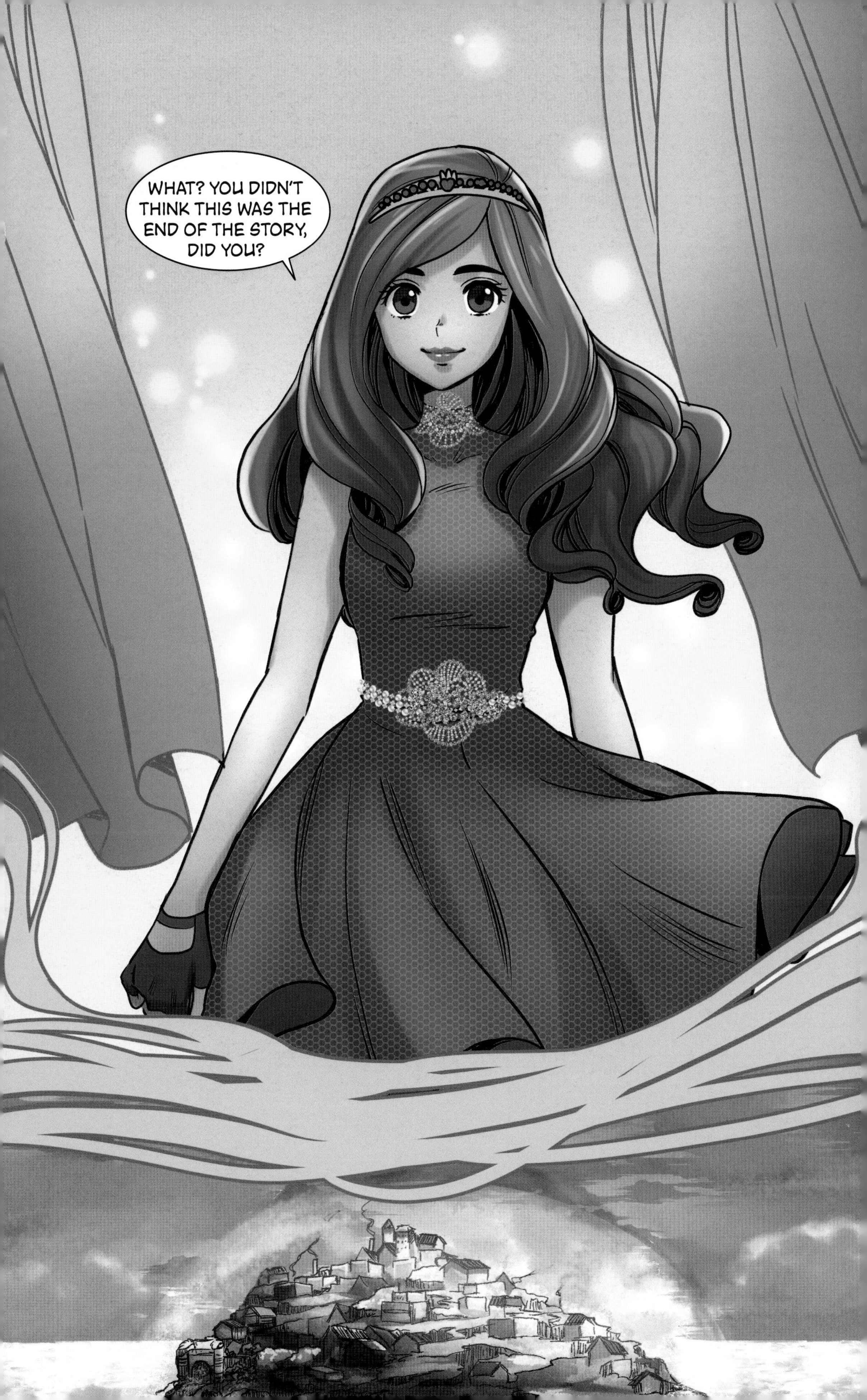
WHAT? YOU DIDN'T THINK THIS WAS THE END OF THE STORY, DID YOU?

DESCENDANTS

Dizzy's NEW FORTUNE

THE NEWEST DESCENDANTS MANGA WITH BRAND-NEW VILLAIN KIDS!

The original Villain Kids have worked hard to prove they deserve to stay in Auradon, and now it's time some of their friends from the Isle of the Lost get that chance too! When Dizzy receives a special invitation from King Ben to join the other VKs at Auradon Prep, at first she's thrilled! But doubt soon creeps in, and she begins to question whether she can truly fit in outside the scrappy world of the Isle.

TOKYO POP

Disney MANGA 漫画

DISNEY CHANNEL

Full color manga trilogy based on the hit Disney Channel original movie

DESCENDANTS

THE ROTTEN TO THE CORE TRILOGY
THE COMPLETE COLLECTION

Adapted By Jason Muell

Art By Natsuki Minami

NEW

Experience this spectacular movie in manga form!

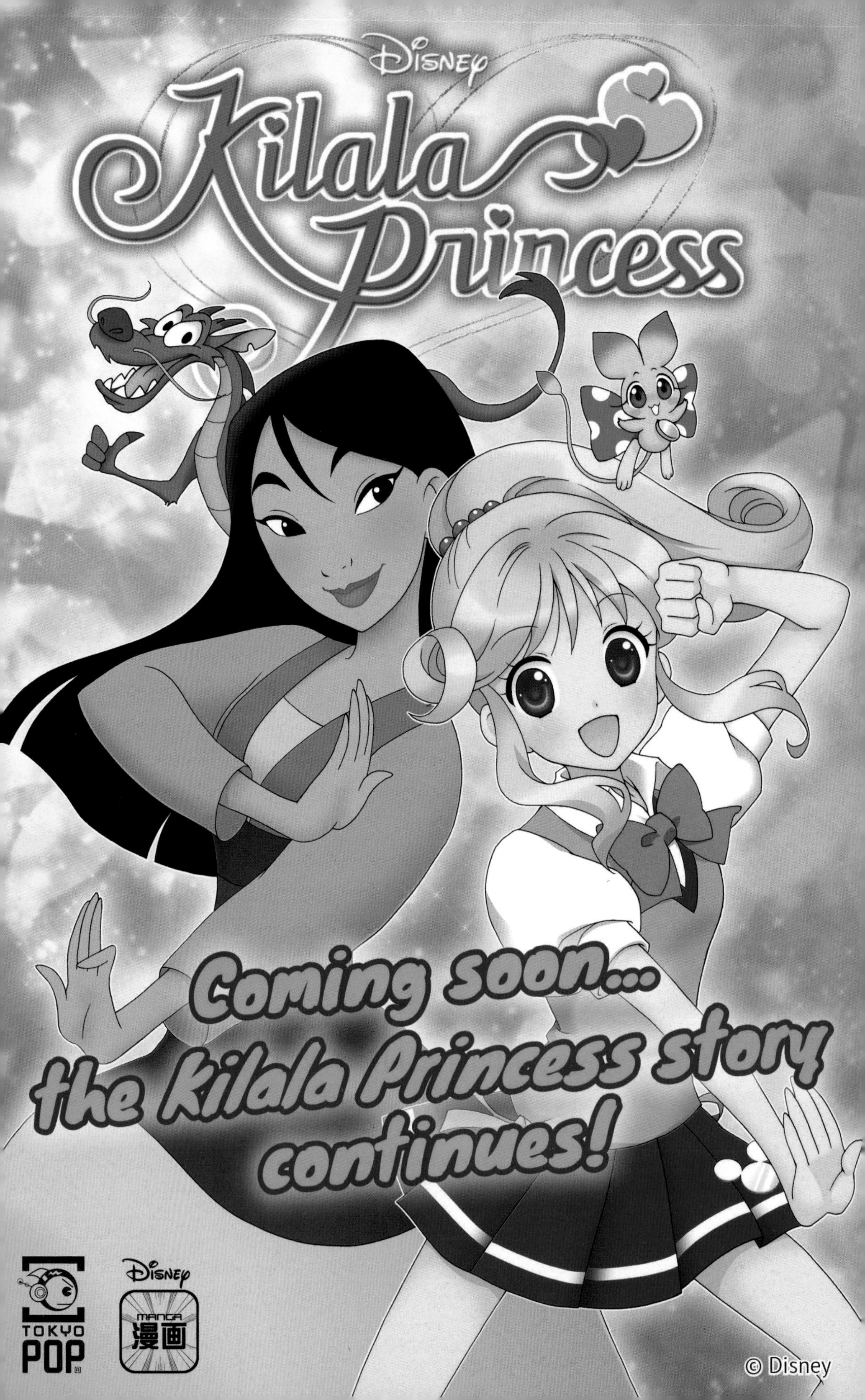
Disney
Kilala Princess
Coming soon... the Kilala Princess story continues!
TOKYO POP
Disney
MANGA
漫画
© Disney

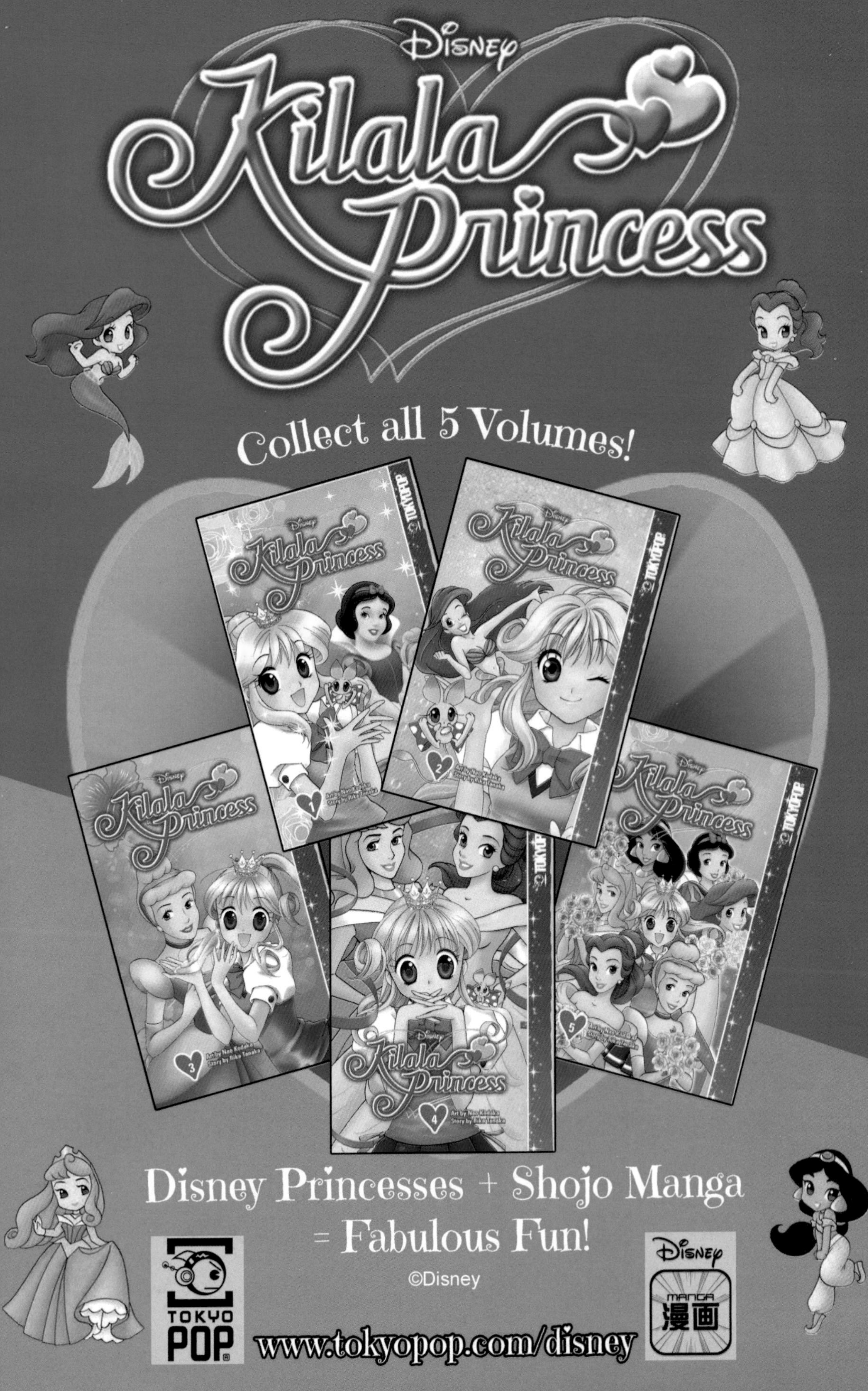
Disney
Kilala Princess
Collect all 5 Volumes!
Disney Princesses + Shojo Manga
= Fabulous Fun!
©Disney
TOKYO POP
www.tokyopop.com/disney
Disney
MANGA 漫画

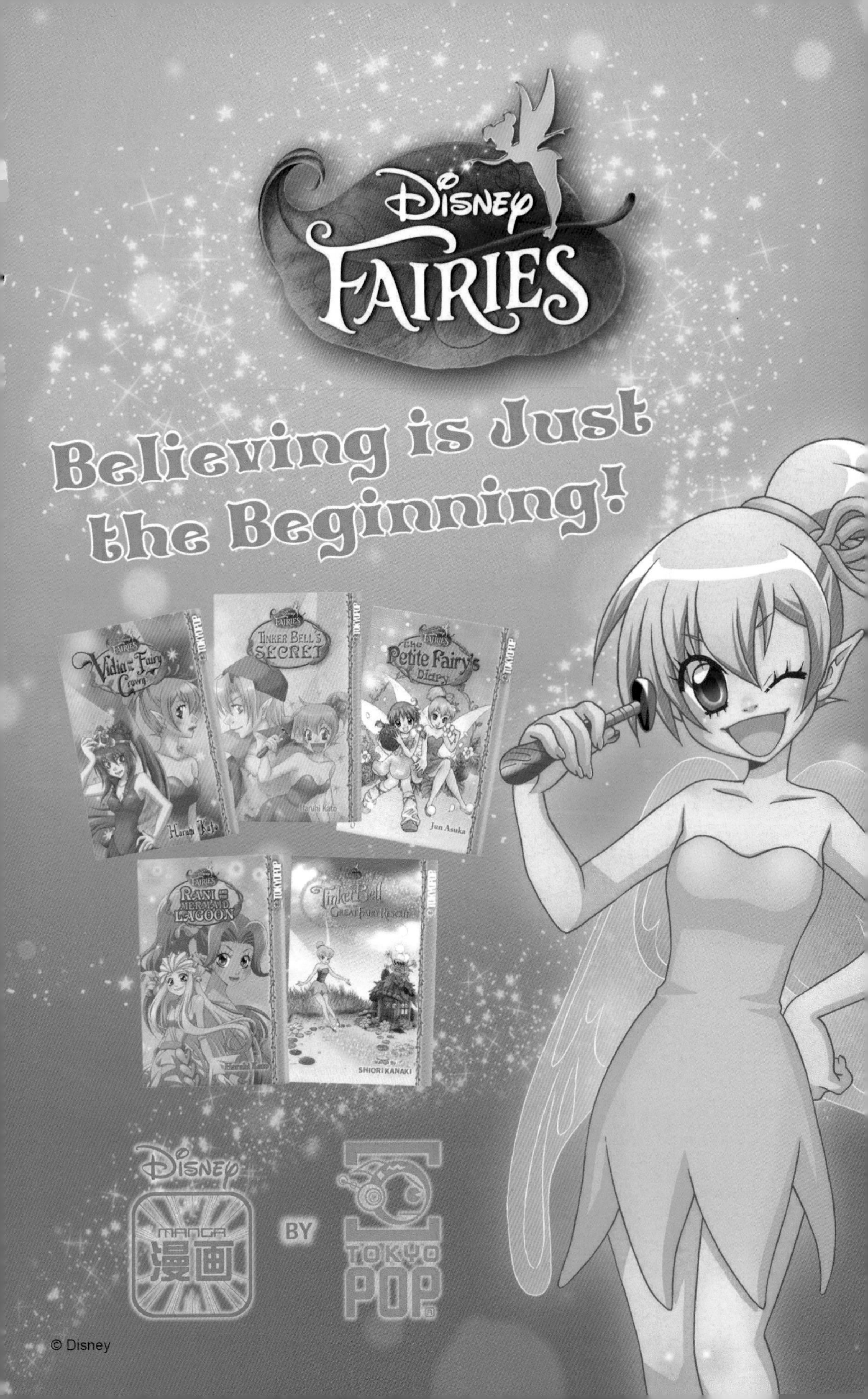
Disney Fairies
Believing is Just the Beginning!
Vidia Fairy Crown
Harumi Kato
Tinker Bell's Secret
Haruhi Kato
The Petite Fairy's Diary
Jun Asuka
Rani Mermaid Lagoon
Tinker Bell Great Fairy Rescue
Shiori Kanaki
Disney Manga 漫画 BY Tokyopop
© Disney

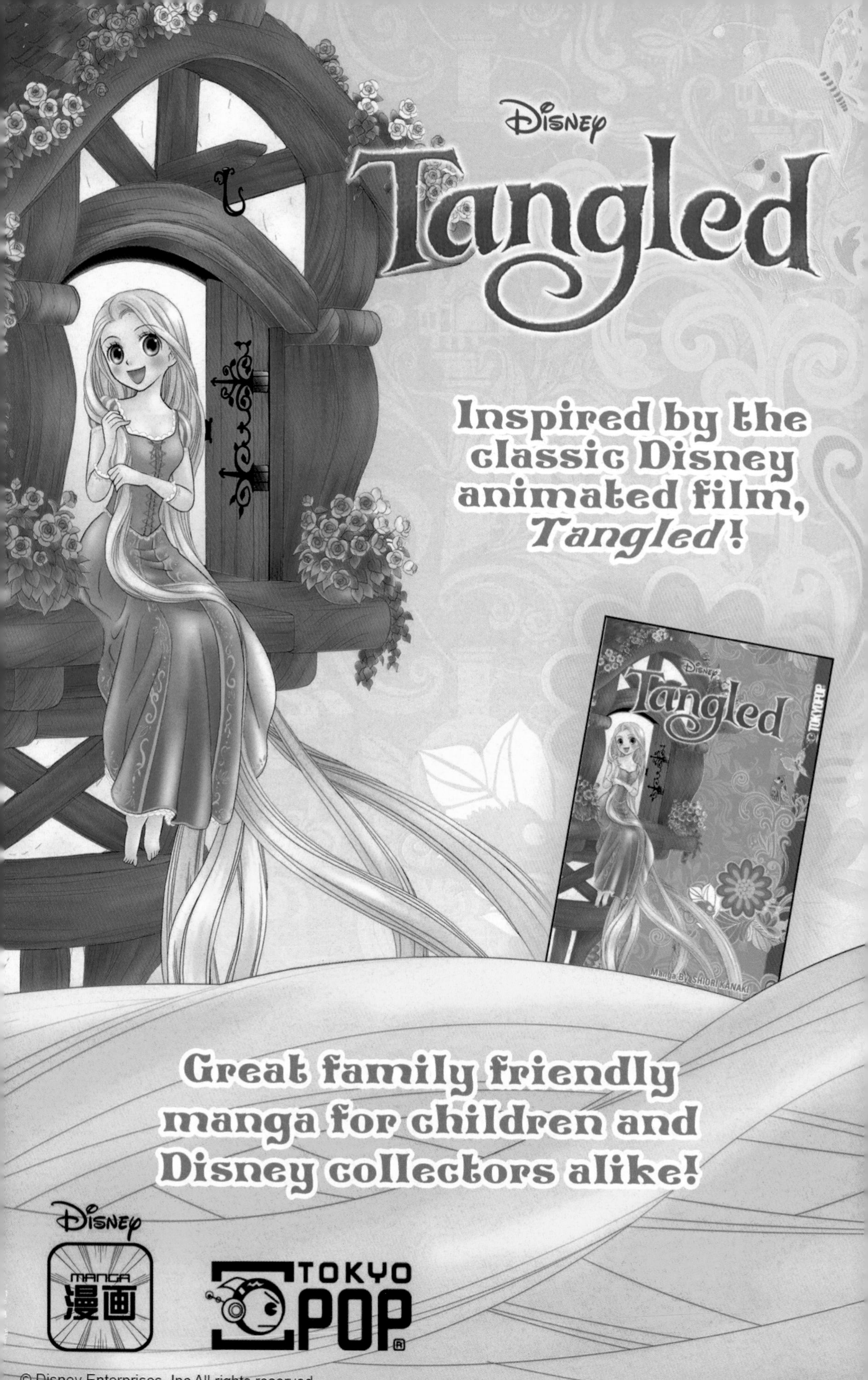
Disney
Tangled
Inspired by the classic Disney animated film, *Tangled*!
Disney
Tangled
TOKYOPOP
Manga By SHIORI KANAKI
Great family friendly manga for children and Disney collectors alike!
Disney
MANGA
漫画
TOKYO POP

Disney Descendants: Evie's Wicked Runway Book 2

Story by : Jason Muell

Art by : Natsuki Minami

Inspired by the hit Disney Channel original movies *Descendants* and *Descendants 2*!

Directed by : Kenny Ortega

Executive Produced by : Kenny Ortega and Wendy Japhet

Produced by : Tracey Jeffrey

Written by : Josann McGibbon & Sara Parriott

Publishing Associate - Janae Young

Marketing Associate - Kae Winters

Technology and Digital Media Assistant - Phillip Hong

Copy Editor - Marybeth Connaughton and Sean Doyle

Editor - Janae Young

Graphic Designer - Phillip Hong

Retouching and Lettering - Vibrraant Publishing Studio

Editor-in-Chief & Publisher - Stu Levy

A **TOKYOPOP** Manga

TOKYOPOP and 　 are trademarks or registered trademarks of TOKYOPOP Inc.

TOKYOPOP Inc.
5200 W. Century Blvd. Suite 705
Los Angeles, 90045

E-mail: info@TOKYOPOP.com
Come visit us online at www.TOKYOPOP.com

f www.facebook.com/TOKYOPOP
🐦 www.twitter.com/TOKYOPOP
P www.pinterest.com/TOKYOPOP
📷 www.instagram.com/TOKYOPOP

ISBN: 978-1-4278-6146-7
Second TOKYOPOP Printing: June 2019
10 9 8 7 6 5 4 3 2
Printed in Canada.

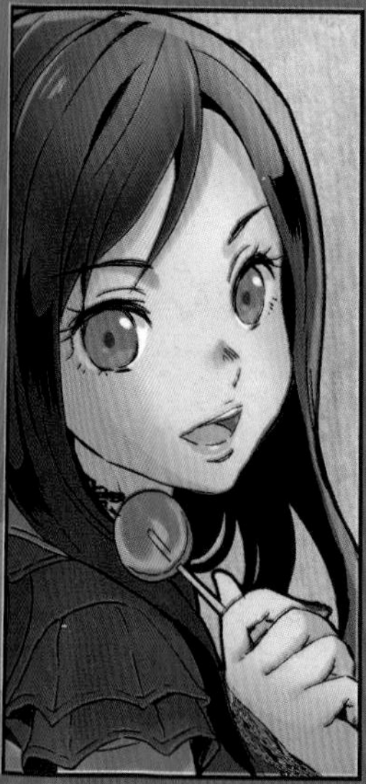
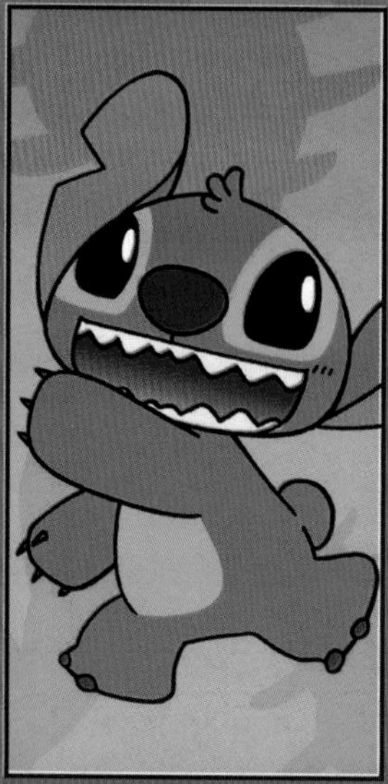
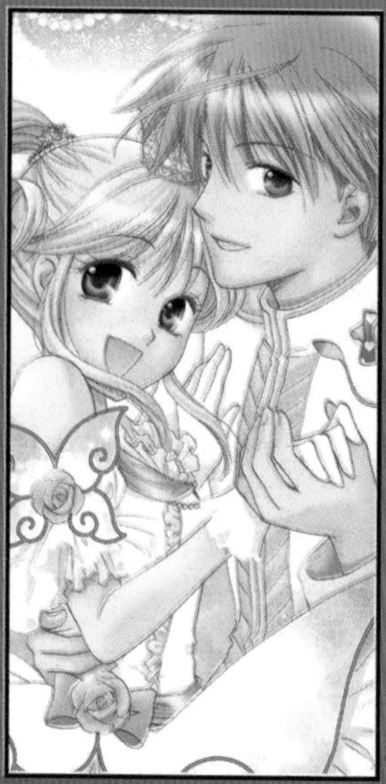
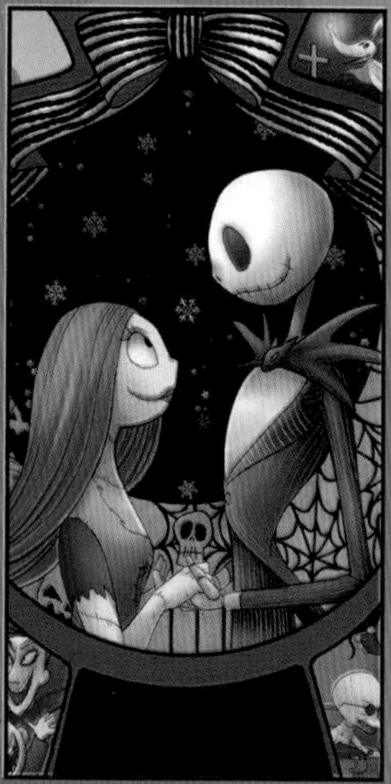
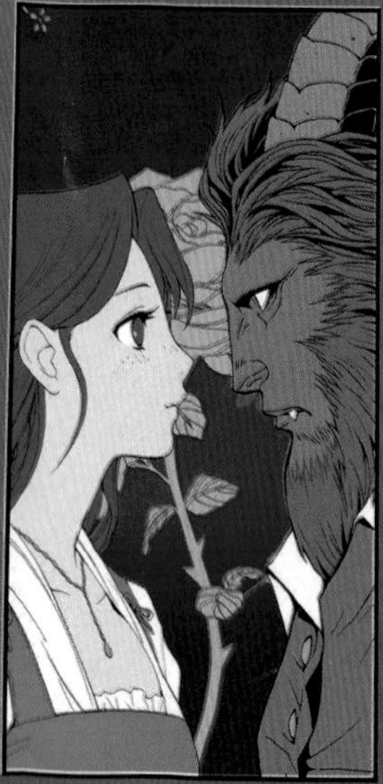
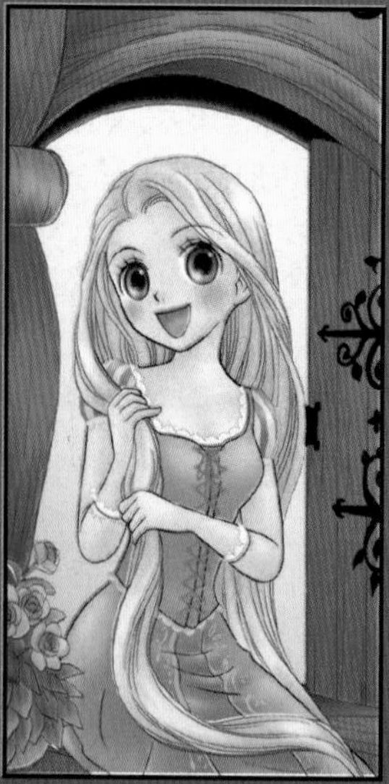
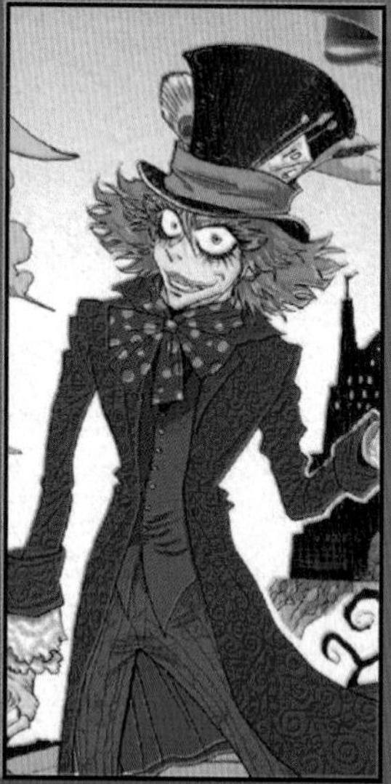
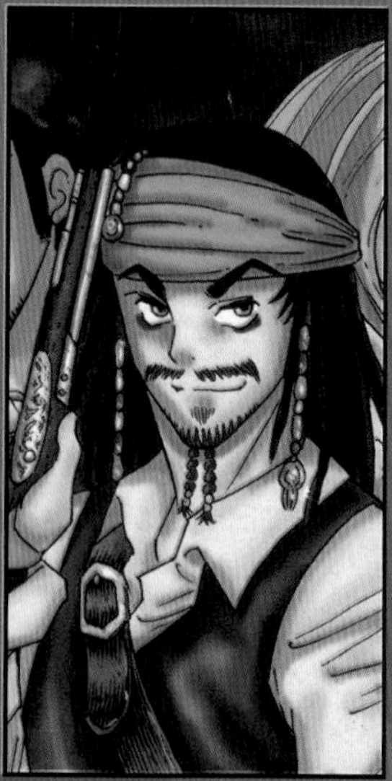
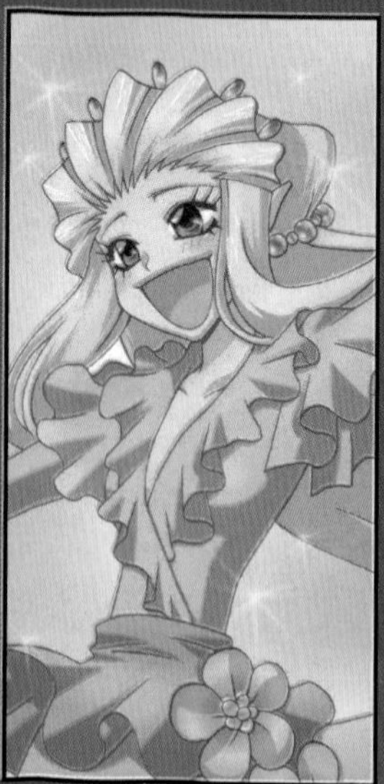
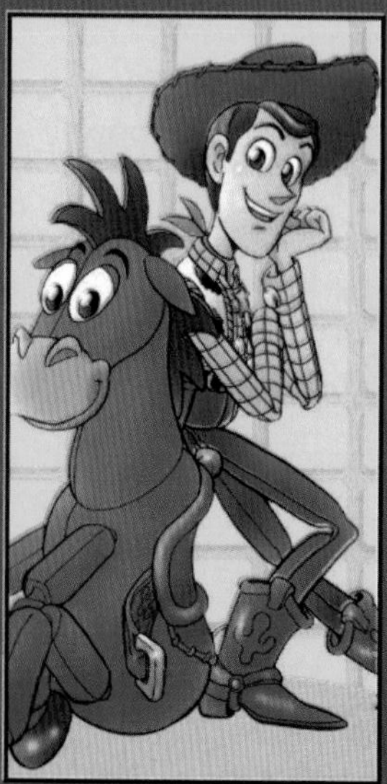
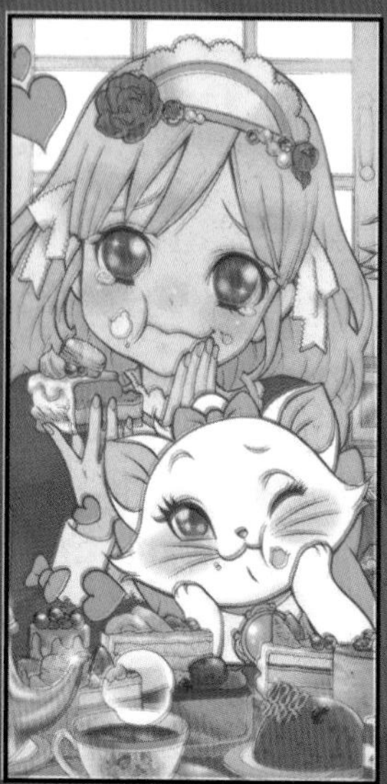
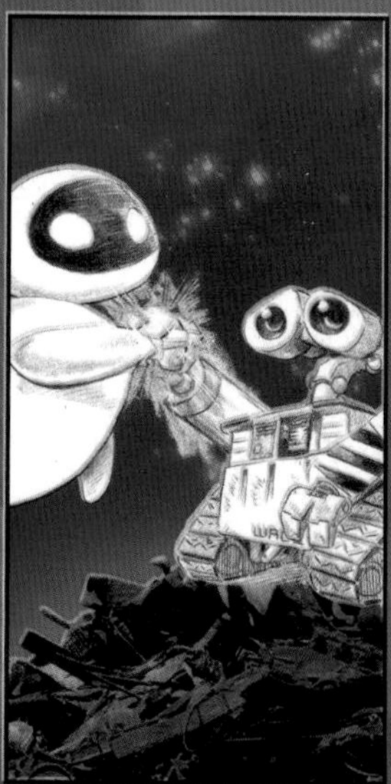

Add These Disney Manga to Your Collection Today!

SHOJO

- [ ] DISNEY BEAUTY AND THE BEAST
- [ ] DISNEY KILALA PRINCESS SERIES

FANTASY

- [ ] DISNEY DESCENDANTS SERIES
- [ ] DISNEY TANGLED
- [ ] DISNEY PRINCESS AND THE FROG
- [ ] DISNEY FAIRIES SERIES
- [ ] DISNEY MARIE: MIRIYA AND MARIE

KAWAII

- [ ] DISNEY MAGICAL DANCE
- [ ] DISNEY STITCH! SERIES

PIXAR

- [ ] DISNEY • PIXAR TOY STORY
- [ ] DISNEY • PIXAR MONSTERS, INC.
- [ ] DISNEY • PIXAR WALL-E
- [ ] DISNEY • PIXAR FINDING NEMO

ADVENTURE

- [ ] DISNEY TIM BURTON'S THE NIGHTMARE BEFORE CHRISTMAS
- [ ] DISNEY ALICE IN WONDERLAND
- [ ] DISNEY PIRATES OF THE CARIBBEAN SERIES

TOKYO POP

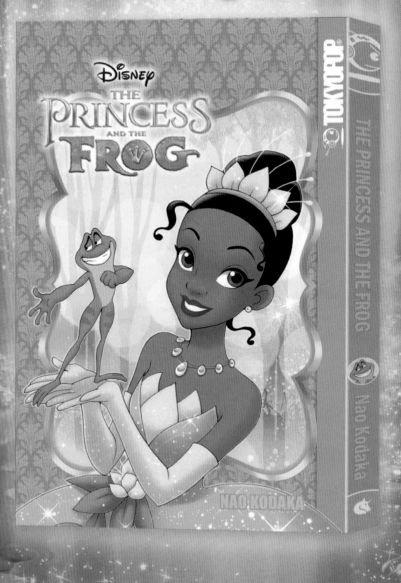